The MADDEST Obsession

THE MADE SERIES

DANIELLE LORI

For my brother Corey.
You always wanted to do something extraordinary, and you did.
You beat us all to Heaven.
I'll love you forever.

Playlist

Jealous—Labrinth

when the party's over—Billie Eilish

White Rabbit—Jefferson Airplane

Piano Man—Billy Joel

Iris—The Goo Goo Dolls

To Build a Home—The Cinematic Orchestra

The Good Side—Troye Sivan

Nevermind—Dennis Lloyd

What It's Like—Everlast

Hi-Lo (Hollow)—Bishop Briggs

bury a friend—Billie Eilish

Sorry—Halsey

Author's Note

The Maddest Obsession spans seven years, from the time Gianna is twenty-one to twenty-eight. Because of this, I've split the book into two parts: the past and the present. Each chapter of Part One will take you to another year of Gianna's life, while Christian's POV is kept within only a few days.

Part Two takes you to the present. It happens to coincide with *The Sweetest Oblivion's (MADE #1)* storyline. Therefore, if you haven't read *The Sweetest Oblivion* and plan to, I highly recommend you do so first.

Danielle xo

PART I

The Past

CHAPTER
One

Christian

New York City
September 2015

"TELL ME ONE FACT ABOUT YOURSELF."

The clock's ticks and tocks filled the space between us. With warm colors and a variety of seating, the room was supposed to be comfortable. Too bad the atmosphere hadn't gotten the memo; the air was thick and cloying, as though every lie told here had been trapped for eternity.

My eyes narrowed as Kyle Sheets' wink from yesterday replayed in my mind. He'd been through the same process—though, different accusation—and had somehow bullshitted his way out of having hentai on his work computer. I was a living, breathing lie, but the idea of being lumped into the same category as that bastard rubbed me the wrong way. He wore sneakers with his suits, for fuck's sake.

Running a thoughtful hand across my jaw, I admitted the truth.

"I have an addictive personality."

Sasha Taylor Ph.D. couldn't stop a spark of surprise from lighting in her eyes, and to hide the human reaction, she dropped her attention to my file resting on her lap. The blonde's pantsuit didn't hold a wrinkle. She'd gone to Yale and was from old money. The thirty-one-year-old was everything I looked for in a woman: intelligent, beautiful, classy.

"Alcohol?" she asked.

I gave my head a shake.

"Drugs?"

Might've been easier.

"Women?"

Woman.

Another shake, but, this time, I smiled.

Her eyes fell to my lips, and she swallowed and glanced away. "We'll come back to this in a moment." She paused. "You do understand why you're here?"

I gave her a blank look.

Her gaze wavered. "Yes, of course you do. Does . . . the incident have to do with your . . . addictive personality?"

I focused my stare on her fire-engine red heels and suddenly hated myself for not having a lesser addiction, like hentai. I'd take that over the other *mess* any day of the week.

It was public, Allister. Go through the motions, that's all I can do.

The words that had fucked me over.

I wasn't a good man, and I worked for even worse. However, I'd learned at too young of an age that the world wasn't made up of black and white. Sometimes, one became so tainted they couldn't get back to the light, and other times, the dark just felt *right*. Even if the latter didn't apply to me, I would never jeopardize what I had built. I'd worked too hard to get here to ever give it up for a woman. Especially one who dressed like Britney Spears' and Kurt Cobain's love child.

"No," I lied.

If I was completely honest, I'd be committed within the hour, or rather, the Bureau would make Sasha Taylor disappear, never to be heard from again.

"Some believe it was over a woman," she supplied tentatively.

I raised a brow. "Are you *some*, Sasha?"

"No."

"Why not?"

"You seem too . . . levelheaded to behave in such a way over a woman."

Cold. She meant cold.

She was right—in the usual case, anyway—but there was nothing usual about the irritating situation that had put me here. I had a close relationship with the cold, in the most literal sense; now, however, I felt the furthest from it. A fire burned in my chest, licking at the edges of what soul I had left.

Sasha shifted in her seat, crossing one leg over the other. "Back to this addictive personality . . . do you often give in to whatever it is that you want?"

Just the idea that I could tasted sweet, doubled the pace of my heart, made me feel hot and edgy. I hated the woman for making my life hell for years, but damn, if I didn't want to touch her, to fuck the memory of every other man out of her mind until she was half as obsessed as I was, until she'd never forget my name again for the rest of her life.

I ran my tongue across my teeth and pushed the feeling down, though the tension in my body didn't release. "Never."

"Why not?"

My gaze held hers. "Because then it will win."

"And you don't like to lose?" Her words ended on a breathless note.

I could almost hear the pitter-patter of her heart as we stared at each other in thick silence.

She pushed a strand of hair behind her ear and looked at her papers, muttering, "No, you don't."

Like the quiet ticks of a bomb soon to detonate, the clock made its presence known. Sasha glanced toward it, and said, "One more question, before our time is up this session. How do you cope with this 'addictive personality'?"

Easy.

"Order."

"You prefer order?" she questioned. "In what circumstances?"

"All of them."

A subtle blush ran up her neck, and she cleared her throat. "And when disorder comes into your life?"

A vision of thick hair—sometimes dark, sometimes blond—smooth olive skin, bare feet, and everything forbidden flashed before my eyes.

The fire in my chest burned hotter, stealing my goddamn breath. Where pain usually hit me like the high of a drug, whenever Gianna Russo—or, sorry, now *Marino*—was involved, it felt like the comedown. Nauseating. It felt fucking bitter.

My response held the slightest clench of my teeth. "I fix it." Standing, I buttoned my jacket and headed to the door.

"But what if it's not fixable?" she pushed, jumping to her feet, my file in a loose grip by her side.

I paused with one hand on the doorknob and glanced at my wrist, at the elastic tie hidden beneath my cuff.

A sardonic feeling pulled in my chest.

"That, Sasha, is when I *obsess*."

CHAPTER Two

Gianna
21 years old
December 2012

I'D FOUND BLISS IN A ROLLED-UP DOLLAR BILL AND WHITE POWDER.

Sometimes, it was euphoric—blood-pumping, heart-racing, top-of-the-world euphoria. Like sex, without the emptiness.

Sometimes, it was a means to an end. One line, and every insecurity, every bruise, faded to memory. One line, and I'd be free.

Other times, it was a cold draft of air and the squeak of a steel door as it slammed shut before me.

The echo resounded off the cell walls and into my ears like pinballs. I swallowed as the deadlock bolted into place.

Stepping forward, I gripped the bars. "Surely I get a phone call?"

The twentysomething Latina officer rested her hands on her gun belt, and, with dark brows lowered, looked me over from my head to my toes. "You're out of luck, princess. If I have to look at that monstrosity of a dress"—she nodded toward my red and gorgeously lacy McQueen—"for another minute, I'll have a headache for the rest of my shift."

I tried to bite my tongue but failed. "Blame it on my dress all you like—we both know the ache will be from that spinster bun on the back of your head, *cogliona*."

Gaze narrowed, she took a step toward me. "What did you just call me?"

"Woah," interrupted another female officer, putting a hand on her partner's shoulder. "Let's go, Martinez."

Twentysomething's glare intensified before she stalked off, her partner following behind.

I turned around to pace but stopped short when I saw I wasn't alone. A redheaded prostitute past her prime sat in the corner, watching me through mascara-caked eyelashes. Her foundation was a few shades darker than her pale skin tone, and her fishnet tights were covered in holes.

"They didn't take your shoes."

I glanced at my red Jimmy Choos.

"They're real nice," she said, picking at her nail polish.

My gaze fell to her bare feet, and I sighed, dropping to sit on the bench adjacent from her.

They hadn't taken my shoes because I wouldn't remain here for long. I was sure I had only minutes until a head honcho in an ill-fitting suit escorted me to somewhere with a couch and coffee—somewhere comfortable, so I would feel more open to gush all the *Cosa Nostra's* secrets.

Disgrace.

Worthless.

Unlovable.

I sawed my bottom lip between my teeth as anxiety brewed in my chest.

"How much did they cost?" my cellmate asked, at the same time a door down the corridor opened and shut. The echo raised the hair on my arms.

I heard him before I saw him.

And instantly knew he was the fed they'd sent for me.

His voice was professional and disinterested, though an elusive timbre intertwined each word: an abrasive edge, like a deep, dark sin one kept locked in the pits of their soul.

His next word—*Gianna*—touched the back of my neck, a brush of steel wings against sensitive skin. I wiped the feeling away with a hand, pulling my hair over one shoulder.

"Probably too much," I finally responded, oddly breathless.

The prostitute nodded like she completely understood.

She was beautiful—behind the makeup, the drug abuse dulling the sheen in her eyes, and the years of servicing New York's finest men, I was sure.

A kindred soul if I ever saw one.

The fed's voice drifted to my ears once more, this time closer as he spoke to Martinez. I couldn't hear what was being said over the commotion in the other cells, but I could tell her voice had softened and her Hispanic roots were coming to the front, her words rolling in a sensual way.

I rolled my eyes. A workplace romance.

Cute.

However, I didn't believe he was taking the bait. I could feel his disinterest against my skin, hear the cold tenor in his voice.

A shiver ghosted through me.

For the love of God, he was only a *fed*. I'd dealt with Made Men since birth.

I leaned back with an indifference I didn't feel and twirled a long strand of dark hair around my finger.

The room grew smaller, the walls closing in like they had too many times before.

I inhaled slowly. Released it.

Turning my head, I looked out of the cell.

Martinez stood in the hall, staring at the fed's back as he came in my direction, a look of pure unrequited adoration in her gaze.

I guessed there was something kindred in us all.

Steel bars trailed his image as he passed each cell, his eyes averted. His stride was effortless. The set of his shoulders, the relaxed carriage of his arms at his sides—the stance oozed confidence and devastation, as though brick and mortar and female hearts could turn to ash at his single command.

His gaze flicked up and caught mine, heavy and emotionless, as if he was looking straight through me.

My heart turned cold in my chest.

Our exchange lasted only a second, but the glance stretched into slow-motion, stealing a breath of air from my lungs. I crossed one leg over the other, baring a generous amount of thigh. Like a warm blanket, a sense of security wrapped around me. As long as they were looking at my body, they'd never see what was behind my eyes.

Nevertheless, the first place he looked as he reached my cell was straight into my eyes. Heartless. Invasive. *Blue.* His gaze burned, as if I was standing in front of an open freezer on a summer day, hot and cold air meeting like tendrils of vapor around me.

As he stood in front of the barred door, with a dangerous presence that touched my skin from several feet away, I was sure he was the one locked up. It simply didn't make sense the other way around.

A dim light in the hall flickered above his head.

His dark hair was shaved short on the sides, faded with an expert hand. Broad shoulders and crisp black lines, his suit molded his toned body. Control. Precision. He exuded it, like the colorful stripes on a venomous snake.

But his face was what grabbed one's attention first. Symmetrical, and flawlessly proportioned, not even his cold expression cut from stone could mar it. The second look showed the type of body women groaned over, and the third revealed intellect in every move he made, as though everyone else was a chess piece, and he was musing over how to play each one of us.

My heart leapt as the cell lock unbolted, and I pulled my attention from him to the concrete wall in front of me.

"Russo."

Nope.

No way.

If I went with him, I'd end up sold into a human trafficking ring and never be heard from again. Fed or not, with those eyes and presence, this man had seen and done things a normal Made Man hadn't envisioned.

I remained silent.

I was going to sit here and wait for the fed in the ill-fitting suit.

His gaze flicked to the prostitute.

"Name's Cherry," she supplied with a smile. "But you can call me anything you'd like."

Some women didn't know what was good for them.

He ran his thumb around his watch, once, twice, three times. "I'll keep that in mind," was his dry response.

My skin flared as I received the full weight of his stare. His eyes coasted down my body, leaving a trail of ice and fire in their wake before they narrowed with disapproval. And just like that, the apprehension from the way he'd looked into my eyes like I was a human being, not a body, drifted away, and he was now only a man.

One who judged me, wanted something from me—

"Stand up."

—told me what to do.

Frustration flickered, lazy and hesitant, in my chest.

I wanted to wait a full three seconds before I complied, but after the first two, I had the sudden and distinct feeling I wouldn't make it to three.

Complying, I got to my feet and stopped in front of the unlocked door. I stood in his shadow, and even that felt cold to the touch.

I hated tall men, how they were always looking down on me, always looming over me like a cloud blocking out the sun. Large men had ruled since the beginning of time, and at that moment, as I grasped steel bars and looked up into blue eyes, I'd never felt a stronger truth.

Impatience stared back at me. "Don't know your name, or just forget it?" His refined and slightly rough voice blazed a path down my spine.

I lifted a shoulder and, as if it made any sense, said, "You're not wearing an ill-fitting suit."

"Can't say the same for you," he drawled.

Oh, he did not.

My eyes narrowed. "This dress is *McQueen*, and it fits perfectly."

His expression told me he couldn't be paid enough to care as he opened the door, sending a cold draft of air to my bare skin.

"Walk," he ordered.

The one-word demand grated on my nerves, but I'd made my bed and now I had to sit on it. My heart drummed in my ears as I stepped out of the cell, beneath his hold on the door, and headed down the corridor.

Catcalls came from all directions.

My skin felt soft to the touch, but twenty-one years had hardened it beneath the surface. Their words, jeers, and whistles bounced off into the abyss, where bruises went to die.

Adrenaline poured into my bloodstream. Harsh lights. Stale oxygen. The squeak of an officer's shoes.

Coming to a fork at the end of the hall, I slowed. I was so distracted with my predicament and this man behind me that when he said, "Right," I went left.

"Your other right." I couldn't miss the annoyed edge in his tone, like I was an airhead not worth his time.

My cheeks went hot with frustration, and words tumbled from my mouth, like they often did. "It would be nice to know where I'm going ahead of time, *stronzo*."

"I didn't realize you needed time to process a simple direction," he responded, and then that deep, dark timbre came to the surface. "Call me an asshole again, Russo, and I promise, you won't like it."

The bite of his words touched my back, and just then, I hated the man a little for knowing Italian.

I stepped into the lobby, the front doors within view. I longed to be on the other side, but in all honesty, I would rather stay here than go anywhere with him.

The expected fed in the ill-fitting suit was supposed to try to gently coax the *Cosa Nostra's* secrets out of me, which, at the worst, would include a too-highly-placed hand on my thigh, but he'd never physically *hurt* a woman. I swallowed, my eyes following the man I'd gotten instead as he walked to the front counter. Large and unyielding. Cold, and most likely unresponsive to any female wiles.

What tactics did he use while interrogating? Waterboarding? *Electrocution?* Was that even a thing?

Apprehension twisted in my stomach.

Badge, after badge, after badge blurred in glints of gold and silver before my eyes, and it was making me feel a little sick.

I walked further into the room and stopped beside the fed.

"Why am I not handcuffed?" I asked, watching two officers escort a shackled prisoner out the front doors.

He tapped a finger on the counter in a rhythm of three—tap, tap, *tap*—and side-eyed me, his stare filling with a trace of dry amusement. "Did you want to be?" His words were laced with deep insinuation and intimacy, and I suddenly knew two things: He was an asshole, and he had handcuffed a woman in bed.

My heart rate quickened from his unexpected response, and, to hide it, I feigned a bored expression. "Thanks for the offer, but I'm married."

"So I can see, with that rock on your finger."

I glanced at my ring mechanically, and, for some silly reason, felt miffed that he held no concern his prisoner wasn't restrained. I could totally be a threat to him and the public.

"I could run, you know," I said, planning to do no such thing.

"Try it."

It was a dare and a warning.

A cold shiver erupted at the base of my spine. "Would you feel good about yourself? Catching a girl half your size?"

"Yes."

There wasn't an ounce of doubt in his reply.

"See, that is the problem with you feds. You love to throw your authority around."

"Weight," he corrected dryly.

"What?"

"The saying is to throw your *weight* around."

I crossed my arms and took in the busy lobby. My eyes narrowed. I swore every woman in the vicinity had slowed their movements to watch him. A middle-aged officer old enough to be his mother stared while she pushed a clipboard toward him from the other side of the counter.

He signed the papers and then handed them back to the non-blinking officer. I bet women did wonders for his ego every day.

A wave of unease pressed down on my chest as someone set my faux-fur coat and purse on the counter.

Electrocution can't be a thing.

"Put your coat on," he ordered.

I paused to grit my teeth because I *already* had one arm in the sleeve.

He grabbed my sequin crossbody handbag from the counter and eyed the faux peacock feathers like they might carry malaria. I'd made the purse myself, and it was beautiful. I snatched it from his grasp, slipped it on, and headed to the front door.

Stopping abruptly, I turned and waltzed back up to the counter, taking my heels off as I went. "Can you make sure my cellmate—goes by Cherry—gets these?"

The officer watched me with a blank expression.

I returned it.

She peeked over the counter, at my bare feet and white-painted toes, and then straightened, her starched uniform rustling. "It's been snowing for the last hour."

I blinked.

"You want to give an opioid-addicted prostitute"—she tilted the shoe to look inside—"Jimmy Choos?"

I brightened. "Yes, please."

She rolled her eyes. "Sure thing."

"Great," I exclaimed. "Thank you!"

Turning around, my gaze met a cold one, which I was sure could frost a lesser woman. He nodded curtly toward the exit.

I sighed. "Okay, Officer, but only because you asked nicely."

"Agent," he corrected.

"Agent what?" I pushed the door open. Snow dusted the parking lot, glittering beneath the four-globe lamp posts. The December air grabbed my bare legs with bitter fingers, the cold fighting to pull me into its embrace.

He observed the scene over my head, eyes narrowing as he looked at my bare feet. "Allister."

"Which car is yours, Agent Allister?"

"Silver Mercedes on the curb."

I braced myself, and said, "Do you think you could unlock it?"

Before he could respond, I was running to his car, the cold biting into my feet and his dry stare burning a hole into my back.

He didn't unlock it.

I hopped from one foot to the other, pulling on the passenger door handle while he walked toward me, not the least bit in a hurry.

"Unlock the door," I said, my breath misting in the air.

"Stop pulling on the handle."

Whoops.

The door unlocked, and I slid into the seat, rubbing my feet on the carpet for warmth.

His car smelled like leather and him. I was sure he wore custom-made cologne to match the suit, but it was worth the money. It was a nice smell, and even made my mind a little hazy until I blinked the feeling away.

He sat in the driver's seat and shut the door, and I ignored the way his presence threatened to swallow me whole.

We left the precinct in silence—a tense yet almost comfortable silence.

Digging in my purse, I found a piece of bubblegum. The crinkle of the wrapper filled the car. His eyes remained on the road, but he gave his head the most subtle shake, conveying just how ridiculous he thought I was.

He was late to the party.

I popped the gum in my mouth and swept a gaze over the car's immaculate interior. Not a single receipt. Beverage. Speck of dust. Either he'd just killed a man and was trying to cover his tracks, or the fed had some OCD tendencies.

I always was a bit too curious.

I crushed the wrapper in my hand and moved to drop it in his cup holder. The gaze he shot me was deadly.

Looked like it was the latter.

I dropped the wrapper in the recesses of my purse.

Crossing my legs, I blew a bubble.

Popped it.

The silence grew so deafening I reached for the radio, but, once again, the look he gave me changed my mind. I sighed and sat back in my seat.

"Tell me how long you've been married."

My eyes narrowed on the windshield in front of me. This man didn't even ask questions—he just told you to tell him what he wanted to know. However, the quiet gave too much room for thought, and I responded, "A year."

"Young age to get married."

I glanced at my cuticles. "Yeah, I suppose."

"You're a native of New York, then."

"I wish," I muttered.

"Don't like home?"

"What I don't like is you trying to small talk to coax things out of me. I don't have anything to say to you, so you might as well take me back to jail."

His arm brushed mine from where it rested on the center console, and I shifted away from the touch, crossing my legs the other way. Was his car small, or was it just me? The heater ran on low, but my skin was burning up. I slipped my coat off and tossed it onto the back seat.

He side-eyed me. "Nervous?"

"Feds don't make me nervous, Allister. They give me a rash."

I ignored the touch of his stare as it swept from the loose curls in my hair, down the red lace over my stomach that revealed a diamond navel piercing, to my bare feet.

"If you dressed a little less like a hooker, the cop who pulled you over might not have searched you."

I pulled the bubblegum off my finger with my teeth and gave him a smile. "If you looked a little less like an anal-retentive asshole, you might get laid every once in a while."

The corner of his lips tipped up. "Glad to hear there's some hope for me."

I rolled my eyes and turned my head to look out the window.

"It must have been a special occasion tonight," he drawled.

"No."

"No? You usually have that much blow on you on just an average day?"

I lifted a shoulder. "I might."

"How do you pay for it?"

"Money."

I blew a bubble.

Popped it.

A muscle in his jaw tightened, and a small amount of satisfaction filled me.

"Is that why you married your husband?" His gaze met mine. "Money?"

Anger stretched in my chest, and I refused to even respond. But, after he voiced his next question, I couldn't keep it in.

"Are you at least a faithful gold-digger?"

Gold-digger?

"Like I ever had a choice in the matter! *Vaffanculo a chi t'è morto!*"

The look he gave me seared, dark and hot.

I pressed my lips together.

Dammit.

He'd barely begun a conversation and he'd already gotten me to admit I didn't exactly have a choice in marrying Antonio.

"Your mom never wash your mouth out with soap?"

I didn't reply. I'd tell him my mamma was the best, and he'd easily deduce my papà would rather lock me in a room for three days than bother with having to listen to me.

"Stupid move, speeding with drugs on you."

I scoffed. I wanted to ignore him but couldn't stop myself from replying. To be ignored felt like a cut in one's chest, and it made me sick to think I'd ever make someone else feel that way. Amusing, as I'd just told this man to go screw his dead ancestors. Italians were creative with their insults.

"It was *three* miles per hour over the speed limit."

His finger tap, tap, tapped on the steering wheel. "Who taught you to drive? Doesn't the *Cosa Nostra* like to keep their women dumb and docile?"

"Obviously not, because my husband taught me."

I wouldn't admit Antonio gave me freer rein than any other man in the *Cosa Nostra* gave their wife. Antonio gave me many things. And maybe that was why it was hard to despise him for what he took away.

"And how is he going to react when you're released to go home?"

"How is your mamma gonna react when you get home past curfew?"

"Answer the question."

I gritted my teeth and tried to ignore the anger brewing inside me by pulling down the sun visor and fixing my hair in the mirror. "Are you asking if my husband hits me? No, he does not." *Hits* was plural, so, technically, it was the truth.

His gaze singed my cheek. "You're a bad liar."

"And you're annoying me, Allister." I slammed the sun visor closed.

The atmosphere grew heavy and claustrophobic, his presence, large body, and smooth movements closing in on me.

"Does he love you?"

He asked it indifferently, as if it shared the same merit as my favorite color. Nonetheless, the question hit me like a blow to the stomach. I stared straight ahead as the back of my throat burned something fierce. He'd found a weakness, and now he was going to poke at it until I bled. Hatred tasted acidic in my mouth.

I would take electrocution over this any day.

I suddenly loathed this man, for getting into my head with his stupid questions and for baring parts of me I didn't let anyone else see.

I blew a bubble.

Popped it.

That was when he'd had enough.

He pulled the deflated bubble straight from my mouth and threw it out the window.

I stared at him, fighting not to lick the unsettling heat of his touch from my lips. "That's littering."

His gaze sparked of indifference.

Agent Allister didn't care about the environment.

No surprise.

He placed his hand back on the wheel, and I suddenly wondered how severe his OCD tendencies were—if he would go home and scrub my spit off his fingers with bleach or not. However, I quickly grew bored of thinking about the fed and turned my head to glance out the window, at the orange glow of passing streetlights and the flurries falling like tiny shadows in the night.

"How many times?"

A vague question, but by his tone, I knew we'd come full-circle and he was talking about my husband hitting me.

"Every night," I said with insinuation. "He makes me scream so loud I wake the neighbors."

"Yeah? You like fucking a man so much older than you?"

Deep irritation flared inside of me. I reached for the radio, turned it on, and coolly responded, "I'm sure he has more stamina than you."

He didn't even deign to reply. I heard only a second of some AM politics talk show before he turned the radio off. What kind of monster chose that over music?

We didn't sit in silence for long before he filled it. "Your stepson is older than you," he commented. "Must be strange."

"Not really."

"I imagine you have more in common with him than his father."

"You imagine wrong," I responded, bored of this conversation and bored of this man. This was the worst punishment. I'd never touch coke again.

"You lived under the same roof as him for a year. You're close to the same age. If you don't have more in common mentally, then surely physically."

I laughed. *Nico and me?* Not in a million years.

Unfortunately, at the time, I hadn't known it would only take one.

"Do you take my file home with you at night, Officer?"

He didn't respond.

An awareness tickled in the back of my mind as the streets grew more and more familiar. A cold sensation settled in my stomach, and as we turned onto *my* street, a heavy and distinct feeling consumed me.

Anger. Deep and *loathing*. He'd let me believe he was the honorable fed when, really, he was nothing but another man in my husband's pocket.

He pulled up to the curb in front of my home and put the car in park.

Resentment poured off me, mixing with the scent of leather and cologne. I was sure he could feel it when he turned his head to look at me. His gaze was as dry as gin, though a light brewed inside as if someone had thrown a lit match in the glass. *Blue.* The look grabbed me by the back of the neck and pulled me underwater.

I inhaled slowly. Released it.

A sudden feeling that I'd met this man before overwhelmed me. Though, the thought soon faded. It would be impossible to forget his face, no matter how much I wanted to forget his presence.

"You pried into my personal life," I growled, grabbing my coat from the back seat.

"You wasted my time, therefore my *right*."

Disbelief filled me. No other man of my husband's would have asked me the questions this one had, and then gone on to call it his *right*.

Venom coated each sweetly-spoken word like candy. "Tell me, Agent Allister, when did you realize you weren't human?"

The subtle glow of amusement lit in his eyes. "The day I was born, sweetheart." It disappeared in a flash. "Unless you'd prefer to go back to jail, get your ass out of my car."

I gritted my teeth but opened the door and stepped out. The frigid breeze tousled my long dark hair against my shoulders. A blanket of snow covered the street, and I welcomed the burn in my bare feet. Turning around, I eyed him with the most disdain I could muster.

"Go to hell, Allister."

"Been there, Russo, and I'm not impressed."

A strong statement, but I believed him.

His eyes were what nightmares were made of, ice and fire, and filled with secrets no one wanted to know. He could only pass as normal because of his too-handsome face—otherwise, he'd be locked up somewhere, the world seeing him for what he really was.

Dirty.

His parting words were short and apathetic. "If you get caught with blow on you again, I won't save you. I'll let you rot in a jail cell."

He wasn't lying.

Next time, he didn't save me.

CHAPTER
Three

Gianna
22 years old
October 2013

BLACKNESS. INKY AND STAGNANT, IT DRIPPED INTO MY SUBCONSCIOUS.

It was often an escape from reality; a comfort in the madness. But this time, it whispered to me—telling me not to wake up now, not to wake up *ever*. Unfortunately, a shrill noise in the distance was louder. My eyes fluttered open, but I closed them again when pain cut through my head like a knife.

Rrring. Rrring.

A groan escaped me, and I rolled over, my hand coming to rest on a bare chest. Something shifted, one puzzle piece clicking into place.

Rrring. Rrring.

Splaying my fingers, I ran my hand across his chest.

Too hot. Too smooth. Not right.

Rrring. Rrr—

"What the fuck do you want?" a male voice grumbled.

Blood, veins, and my heart went ice cold—and, with one fell swoop, my world crashed to the floor around me.

My eyes flew open, the pain in my head ignored for the stronger ache blooming in my chest.

I viewed it in snapshots. My dress on the floor. A slit of light through the blinds. Naked skin. Mine. *His.*

I pulled the sheets closer as a deep sickness churned in my stomach.

He ended the call, tossed his phone on the nightstand, and closed his eyes. After a moment of thick tension permeating the air, he flicked them back open and looked straight at me. We stared at each other as an invasive silence licked at my skin.

"Jesus," was what Nico muttered before he closed his eyes again.

I leaned over the bed and threw up everything in my stomach. Acid singed my throat, and I wiped my mouth with the back of a hand.

Disgrace.

Worthless.

Unlovable.

Whore.

It didn't happen.

Lie, the blackness whispered.

I felt the imprints all over me—hands, teeth, lips—crawling over my skin and into my soul with claws made of heartbreak and metal.

Opening my eyes, I stared at a used condom on the floor.

My ears rang, my lungs closed up, and I couldn't breathe. I gripped the sheets, panic tearing through my chest.

"Gianna . . ."

"I gave him everything," I cried, tears streaming down my cheeks.

"Hell," he muttered before getting to his feet and pulling on a pair of boxer briefs. He went to pick up my dress but tossed it back on the floor when he saw I'd puked on it.

"I was a virgin when I married him. I was faithful."

"I know."

The images from yesterday came back with a vengeance. Our room. My husband. *Her.* Someone I had considered family. I'd always known there were other women . . . but why her? Betrayal cut through my chest, a fresh and burning wound. Tears ran over my lips, tasting salty on my tongue.

"It wasn't enough," I whispered. *I'm never enough.*

"Nothing is enough for my father, Gianna," he said. "You know that."

My throat tightened as I watched Nico grab a shirt from his dresser drawer, because sometimes, I could see Antonio in the way he carried himself.

I was in love with my husband, a man who didn't love me. Maybe I could blame Agent Allister for putting the idea in my head one year ago, but somehow, the pain had led me here. To my husband's son.

The panic attack reared its head, stealing the breath straight from my lungs. "How did this happen?"

"Really? You need me to explain it to you?"

"This isn't a joke, Ace."

"Not laughing, Gianna."

He set the t-shirt on my lap, dropped to his haunches next to my pile of puke, and nodded toward my mouth. "Did my papà do that to you?"

I licked the cut on my bottom lip. "I threw a vase at his head and called him a cheating pig."

Ace made a small noise of amusement. "Of course you did."

Agent Allister was right now. *Hit* had become *hits*, and for some reason, I despised the man, as if he'd set all this in motion. It'd been one year since I'd seen him, but the hatred I felt for him still lay close to the surface.

"You aren't going to tell him," Nico said.

I didn't respond.

"If you tell him, I will make your life a living hell."

A bitter laugh escaped me. My best friend was fucking my husband. How did it get worse than that?

He grabbed my chin and turned it toward him. "We both know you'll take the brunt of his anger, not me."

"It's my decision to make."

He dropped his hand, sighed, and stood up. "Fine, but I warned you. I won't feel sorry for you, either."

I grabbed his t-shirt and slipped it on while he focused on digging through his nightstand drawer.

"Why, Ace?" I whispered.

How could you have let this happen?

I knew why I had. I was a mess. Everything I did was wrong. But

Nico? He always had his head on straight. He maintained control in every move he made.

"I was drunk, Gianna. Really fucking drunk. And, to be completely honest, I still am."

He lit a cigarette, the glow of the cherry red and angry. When he opened the blinds and then the window, and light filled the room, another piece of the puzzle clicked into place. Streaks of red covered his hands and ran up his arms. *Blood.* I didn't know what it was like being a Made Man, but I'd lived around them long enough to know it wasn't easy. That sometimes, the toll of it hit them all at once.

"You look like your papà." The words escaped me, soft, yet also so harsh in the sunlit room. The sins of the night never did sound so good in the day.

He blew out a breath of smoke, his eyes lighting with a flicker of dry humor. *"Jesus."* He shook his head. "Is that what brought you here last night?"

Strobe lights. Dirty bathroom tile. Blow. A drip of sweat down my back. Accepting a white pill from a baggie. Nothing.

"I don't know," I whispered.

"Well, whatever it was, I hope you got something from it, Gianna. Because we're both going to hell." He put his cigarette out on the windowsill and left the room.

I closed my eyes and tried to finish the puzzle, to piece the rest of the night together. But all I encountered was blackness. A blackness that whispered for me to fall asleep and not wake up, *ever.*

A box of chocolates tied with an apologetic red bow sat on our bed when I got home that morning. The same bed my husband had fucked my best friend on from behind.

I climbed into the sheets and ate every one of them.

Days passed, a blur of colors and feelings and a secret eating me alive. It was all upside-down, like viewing the world from a merry-go-round as it spun, head and hair hanging off the steel platform.

They were bad days. Cold. Lonely. *High.*

Antonio had shown his face only once. He came to bed late and fell asleep instantly. I'd stared at the ceiling until the sun streamed through the blinds, the bed dipped, and his presence disappeared as easily as it had come.

Soon after, sleep took me under.

A bright light flicked on, and a draft hit me as the comforter ripped away. I made a noise of protest but choked on it as ice-cold water poured onto my face.

"*Levántate!*"

I sputtered as the water kept coming and jolted to a sitting position. Wiping my eyes, I opened them to see Magdalena standing at the side of the bed with a large mixing bowl in hand.

A shiver rocked my body, and I choked up some water.

"Are you crazy?" I gasped.

She dropped the bowl and ran a hand down her simple white uniform. "*Sí. Pero no tan loca como tú.*"

An ache pulsed behind my eyes. I was soaking wet and agitated, and my words came out harsher than I intended. "You know I don't speak Spanish, Magdalena."

"*Porque eres demasiado tonta.*" *Because you are too dumb.*

I knew that phrase only because she believed it was a great response for everything.

With a groan, I fell back onto the wet sheets. "I don't know who thought it was a good idea to hire you. You're disrespectful, and, quite frankly, a bad maid."

The sixty-year-old turned her nose up. "I am not a maid. I am a housekeeper."

I was sure they were the same things, but I didn't have the fight in me to argue with her.

"Then go housekeep somewhere and leave me alone."

She smoothed a streak of gray hair back into place. Looked at her nails. "You have a party tonight, *querida.*"

"No," I protested. "No party."

"*Sí*—"

"I'm not going to a party, Magdalena," I said, adding, "I don't have anything to wear." *At least, nothing my soul won't bleed through.*

"Nothing respectable, no," she agreed, eyeing me with irises as dark as chocolate. "It's for cancer. *Una cena benéfica.*"

My stomach and heart dipped. "A benefit for cancer?"

"*Sí*. Antonio called and ordered for you to be ready by eight."

Ordered?

Under different circumstances, such as a benefit for sea turtles— my second favorite charity—I would tell him to go fuck himself. But, the truth was, I loathed cancer, and my husband had *a lot* of money.

"Fine, I'll go. But only to write a big check."

I got to my feet and gave the empty chocolate box a kick as I walked past. It disappeared under the bed with the rest of my demons.

"*Bueno.* You have been lazy all week, *señora*. It is not attractive."

Heading into the walk-in closet, I aimlessly pushed clothes on hangers aside. "Thank you, Magdalena," I responded, "but there's no one here I want to attract."

She dug through my underwear drawer. "Because Antonio's sleeping with Sydney?" A lacy thong hung from her finger. "What color do you want, *querida*? Red is good."

The vise around my heart squeezed.

"I see whoever taught you to clean taught you sensitivity as well," I said, adding, "Nude, please."

"I do not clean."

"Exactly," I muttered, walking past her with a loose black top cut off at the midriff and a matching high-waisted skirt I'd made from an old Nirvana t-shirt. With thigh-high boots, it would be perfect.

I set the outfit on the bed and headed to the bathroom.

Magdalena followed after me. "I knew she wasn't a good friend for you from the beginning. Something in her eyes. You can always tell by the eyes. I told you, but you did not listen."

I fought an eyeroll. Magdalena loved Sydney and always told me I should act more like her, that my husband might love me if I did. My housekeeper was a habitual liar, a little crazy, and still the most normal person in the house.

I wished she actually had warned me. Maybe then, it wouldn't hurt so badly.

My throat tightened, and betrayal burned the backs of my eyes.

I grasped the edge of the sink, yellow-painted fingernails stark against the mess strewn across the counter. Dollar bills, the glint of a 9mm, pink blush, a baggie, and a dusting of white powder.

I stared blankly at my reflection in the mirror.

Ashy-blond hair straight from a bottle dripped water down olive skin. I met my reflection's gaze, my soul staring back.

You can always tell by the eyes.

Magdalena turned the shower on. "You stink of depression, *querida*. Wash it away, and then I will do your hair."

I stepped in the shower.

And I washed it away.

Boots clicking on the marble floor, I waded through floating silver trays carrying champagne flutes that glinted beneath romantic lights. A mini orchestra played in the corner of the ballroom, a low, easy beat allowing monotonous conversation to be heard above it.

I was numb in the heart, but trepidation flickered to life in the center. I'd ignored Antonio's order to meet him at the club so we could arrive at the benefit together, and, instead, had come alone.

I didn't want to see him. I didn't want to feel.

And those two always came together.

I had almost reached the donation table when my plan to get in and out before my husband arrived went down the toilet.

"Gianna, you are as beautiful as always."

My eyes shut for a second. I turned around, a coy smile tugging at my lips.

"Aw, you're cute, too, Vincent."

The twenty-nine-year-old and owner of this fine hotel laughed. "*Cute*, what I've always aspired for."

In acquiescence to not getting out of here soon, I grabbed a glass of champagne from a passing tray. "Well, you pull it off magnificently," I replied, my gaze taking in a group of Vincent's acquaintances who congregated behind him.

He ran a hand down his tie, eyes crinkling with amusement. "There's a reason we've just ambushed you, and it wasn't to talk about how cute I am."

My expression pouted in mock confusion. "Trying out new conversation, are you?"

Vincent and his group chuckled. I took a sip of champagne.

Awareness tickled in the back of my mind, and my gaze drifted to the ballroom's double doors. My glass halted at my lips.

Broad shoulders. Black suit. Smooth lines.

Blue.

Something in my chest crackled and sparked, like a firecracker on hot pavement.

Agent Allister stood inside the doorway with a blonde by his side. She held onto his elbow, and he held my gaze.

You can always tell by the eyes.

I envied him at that moment.

His were an ocean beneath ice, where nothing but the darkest creatures could thrive, while mine were a wide open plain.

He saw everything.

Every bruise.

Every scar.

Every *slap* against my face.

I didn't want anyone's pity, but what drove me even crazier was that he was indifferent to it all. I'd forgotten what his voice sounded like but, somehow, I could hear what he would say to me now.

Suck it up, sweetheart. You know nothing of pain.

Contempt pulsed, hot and heavy, in my chest.

It was irrational, I knew, but I blamed the man for putting the idea of sleeping with Nico in my mind.

I blamed him because it was easy.

I blamed him because he was cold enough it wouldn't hurt.

The fed's gaze took in the group of men surrounding me. He looked away, but I saw the brief thought in his eyes before he and his blonde drifted into the crowd. He thought I was a flirt; a tease. He thought I was *unfaithful*.

And now, I couldn't even deny it.

Hatred closed around my lungs and stole my breath.

"I was just telling them about how we first met," Vincent said. "Do you remember?"

I brought my attention back to the group, a hot edge flowing from my chest to my grip on the stem of my glass. Forcing a smile to my lips, I responded, "Of course I do. You bet against my horse and lost, naturally."

"That, I did." He dropped his gaze to the floor, clearing his throat with a smile. "But I'm talking about me getting tossed and then asking you to run away with me to Tahiti. And you saying no because you'd already been there, and Bora Bora was next on your list."

On cue, everyone laughed.

I bit my cheek to hide a smile. "I was trying to save you from embarrassment, but it seems you're a glutton for punishment tonight."

"It seems so," he chuckled. "Morticia is up and running again, and I'm still betting she places this weekend."

"Oh, Vincent," I said with disappointment, "you just love to throw your money away, don't you?"

The crowd grew in size until I couldn't see beyond it, with bets and horse statistics being tossed into the center.

"*Gianna*, are you coming to the Fall Meet this weekend?"

"*Gianna*, are you betting on Blackie?"

"*Gianna*, what about the afterparty?"

It took thirty minutes to extricate myself from the conversation, and by that time, I'd drunk two glasses of champagne and needed to relieve myself. I used the restroom and then headed toward the donation table, hoping to hand in my check and make a clean exit.

When I saw Allister's back where he stood in front of the table speaking with one of the socialites in charge of the event, I stopped in my tracks. Hesitation settled in my stomach, and I took a step in the opposite direction, but, *No way.* I hated the man, though what I loathed even more was that his presence intimidated me.

As if to prove something to myself, I waltzed up to the table and stopped close enough beside him my arm brushed his jacket. He glanced down at me before looking back to the middle-aged woman he spoke with like I was merely a part of the décor.

"Well," the blonde socialite said, a blush warming her cheeks, "my daughter couldn't speak more highly of you, and I'm so glad you could make it. I know how busy a man like you must be. The crime in this city has been growing every year."

"It's been my pleasure entirely, ma'am."

I couldn't hold in a quiet scoff.

Allister's lips tipped up, though he didn't glance my way.

The words he said to me one year ago filled with his voice once again. Refined, slightly rough, with an amused edge like he always knew something the other didn't.

The socialite glanced my way for a second before dismissing me and gazing at the fed, but then, as if she'd just processed what she saw, looked back at me.

She stared without a blink. "I'm sorry . . . can I help you?"

I pulled the check I'd written out of my bra and handed it to her. She held onto a corner gingerly, until she unfolded it and looked at the amount.

"Wow," she breathed. "This is incredibly generous. Thank you so much." She scribbled something on a slip of paper and then handed out a clipboard. "I just need you to complete this short form, please." When I only stared at it, she pressed, "Donor information and a tax receipt." Her voice lowered. "You can claim this on your taxes."

"Oh, I don't pay taxes."

She blinked.

Allister grabbed the clipboard. "She'll fill it out."

"Okay . . . great." She took a step to the side before drifting away.

"Tell me, do you think before you talk? Or do you just let things spew out?"

"Well," I said, frowning, "that time, I didn't think, no. But how am I supposed to know about taxes? Antonio said he doesn't have to pay them."

"Everyone has to pay taxes. It's the *law*."

"Oh, the one you're so good at upholding?"

He shoved the clipboard in my direction. "Fill out the form and shut your mouth before I have to arrest you for tax evasion."

"Seems a little counterproductive, considering you'd have to let me out as soon as my husband finds out."

A muscle in his jaw tightened. "He's your savior, is he?"

I tensed at the dark tone in his voice—a tone that made me feel as if he knew more of my story than he should.

"He's my husband," I replied, as if that said everything, when, really, it said nothing at all.

I grabbed the clipboard. However, he held onto it for a second, his gaze touching my face before he finally let it go. He turned to look out into the ballroom, bringing a tumbler of some clear liquid to his lips. Probably water, knowing what a killjoy he was.

"You look like you got lost on your way to a grunge concert."

"Fortunately, no," I said, filling out the form. "I would be pissed if I missed it."

"What did you do to your hair?"

"What?" My lips formed a pout. "You don't like it? I did it for you. I heard you like blondes."

"You been thinking about me?" he drawled.

"Every day, every hour. You're always there, like a fungus, or an incessant bug swarming around my head."

A corner of his lips tipped up.

Setting the clipboard down, I leaned a hip against the table, rested the pen against my chin, and looked around the ballroom. "By the way, where is your blonde?"

I followed his stare to the woman in question, who was talking to another in the middle of the room. She wore a classy white cocktail dress and a tight chignon. Her posture was perfect and her current smile was tight. I bet she'd never let her hair down.

"She looks . . . fun."

When I caught the corner of his disarming smile, something hot and hesitant flickered to life in my stomach. The feeling immediately brought a bad taste to my mouth.

I pushed off the table. "Okay, well, you have a decent night. I would say great, but I'm doing this new thing and trying not to say what I don't mean."

"Sure you don't want to donate the shoes off your feet before you go?"

Glancing at my thigh-high boots, I clicked my heels together like Dorothy. Unfortunately, it didn't take me home. "I would, but I think your girlfriend's mamma would throw them away."

I looked up to see his gaze trail from my boots to the few inches of naked thigh. It was clinical, assessing, and hardly lascivious. Still, the touch of his stare burned, like an ice cube melting on bare skin beneath a summer sun.

"She's not my girlfriend," he said, taking a large drink of what I was now sure was water.

"I would say poor girl, but . . ." My eyes sparkled with *that new thing I'm trying* as I began to walk past him.

His next words, dripping with something bitter and sweet, stopped me in my tracks.

"Trouble in paradise?"

My grip tightened around the pen I still held.

I swallowed and rubbed my bare ring finger with my thumb.

My marriage was a mockery, and I could never escape it—divorce didn't exist in the *Cosa Nostra*—but I wouldn't be chained by a diamond on my finger, by a symbol of *love*, when there was none. At least, none returned.

I turned to him, expecting to see triumph, but as I met his gaze, my heart stilled before tugging in an unnatural way.

There was something dark and genuine behind his eyes, and I didn't realize until later that he was letting me see it. The steady *drip, drip, drip* of blood. The *clanks* of metal and fire that forged him.

He was up to his neck in blood.

I wondered if, even then, beneath his fake gentleman persona, his black suit and white shirt, he was covered in it.

"What have you sacrificed to stand here today?" The thought escaped me, pushed from my lips by an invisible force. "Your soul?" I stepped closer, inches away, until his presence brushed my bare skin. Running the tip of the pen across his palm by his side, I whispered, "Just how much blood is on these hands?"

He ran his tongue across his teeth, flicking his gaze to the side before bringing it back to me.

Bottomless. *Blue.* My heart beat heavy, because I knew if I stared too long I'd be trapped beneath ice.

"Someday," I breathed, tilting my head, "it's going to catch up with you."

His gaze narrowed in distaste as it fell to the pen I'd bitten between my teeth. It took only a second to connect the dots. *Germs*, most likely.

I licked the end of the pen like a lollipop, tucked it into his front jacket pocket, and gave his chest a pat.

"Have a lousy night, Allister."

Taking a step to leave, I realized how parched his stare had made me. I stepped backward, grabbed the glass from his hand, and downed the contents.

I choked.

Vodka.

The burn in my throat drifted to my chest as I headed toward the exit. Just as I pushed the door open and cool October air enveloped me, I came face-to-face with a familiar set of eyes.

"Going somewhere?"

I tensed and tried to step around him, but my husband's hand found my own and stopped me.

"Let me go," I gritted.

Antonio pulled me closer, wrapping an arm around my waist like we were the most normal couple in the world. As if there wasn't a twenty-five-year age gap between us, as if he'd wooed me instead of having signed a contract for me, and, most importantly, as if he hadn't cheated on me and then tried to apologize with a box of fucking chocolates.

I struggled, but his hold only grew tighter.

"Make a scene, Gianna . . ." he warned.

Antonio was like his son, only wrapped in pain and delivered with a side of righteousness, even as the cross around his neck singed a hole through his skin. After two years of marriage, I didn't believe he could even feel sympathy, and I knew it was how he'd climbed the ladder to be one of the most feared men in the United States.

As for why he was revered—well, when Antonio was warm, he was like the sun. Everyone wanted his attention because, when he gave it, it was absolute, as though you were the only one who had ever mattered. Regardless of the heartache he'd caused me, the walls I'd put up and some I still maintained, I wasn't a match.

Now, I had to figure out how to give up the sun.

"I really don't like waiting around for you."

"I really don't like you fucking my friends."

"Watch your mouth," he chastised, walking us back into the hotel.

Sometimes, it felt like a scream was trapped in my throat, one that had been struggling to get free for the past twenty-two years. It had a voice, a body, fiery red hair, and a heart of steel. I was terrified she would escape, that her echo would burn this world to the ground and leave me standing alone, in smoke and ash. I pushed the feeling down, down, until a light sheen of sweat cooled my skin.

We passed the ballroom doors and, as I glanced inside, my gaze collided with Allister's.

The exchange was a blur of heat, the burn of liquor, a flicker of pitch-black as his eyes dropped to Antonio's grip on my arm. And then it was gone, replaced with gold wallpaper as we walked down a hall toward the terrace.

We stepped outside, and I sucked in a breath. The night was cold and dark, but instead of rubbing my arms for warmth, I let the icy breeze bite into my skin. Maybe I was a masochist, or maybe pain was one of the only things that made me feel alive.

The terrace was empty, save for two guests from the benefit smoking a cigarette.

"Give us a moment, yeah?"

It wasn't a question, no matter how my husband had voiced it.

The men shared a hesitant look but didn't take more than a couple of seconds to drop their cigarettes and head back through the double doors that led into the ballroom. Light fanned across the terrace floor before the doors closed and darkness consumed us once again.

A distant memory swept into the present.

"How could you love such a terrifying man?" my ex-best-friend Sydney had asked me as we sat on my husband's office couch together and he talked on the phone.

I'd only had to think about the question for a moment.

"He listens to me."

I guessed he listened to her, too.

"Care to explain what this is?"

I turned to Antonio to see he held a small, round compact in his hand. My heart beat in the base of my throat. *Here* was one of those walls about to come tumbling down.

"What is it, Gianna?" he bit out.

"Birth control pills."

"Why do you have them?"

"Birth control."

Antonio's eyes blazed with anger, like two flames in the dark. We were devotedly Catholic, and birth control was frowned upon by the Church. But I knew what bothered him even more was that he wanted another child. Another son to rule his empire.

"How long?"

I looked him straight in the eye. "Since the day we were married."

Since the night you stepped on my heart.

The slap across my face was immediate. It whipped my head to the side and knocked the breath from my lungs. The metallic taste of blood filled my mouth.

"The things you make me do, Gianna," he growled. "Do you think I want to hit you?"

My bitter laugh carried on the wind.

The sad part of it all was I only knew from TV this wasn't how it was supposed to be.

He chucked the pills over the railing. "No more, do you hear me?"

I shook my head.

"No. More. Or, I swear, I'll cut you off. No more money, no more secret trips to Chicago—and yes, I know you've been there."

My heart froze to ice and shattered.

"You know your papà forbade you from visiting your mamma." Softness laced through his voice. "I haven't told him, only because I know what it means to you."

She's sick. I couldn't say the words because I knew they wouldn't be steady.

"I have to see her."

"I know." He stepped closer, the smoky scent of his cologne reaching me. "I know everything about you, Gianna. Where you go, what you do, who you speak with." He ran a hand into my hair, and I fought the urge to jerk away because he'd only pull the strands. "You're *mine.* And I look after what's mine."

"If you care about me at all, Antonio, you'll get your filthy hands off me and give me a divorce."

"Do you think I would take just anyone for a wife? I wanted you"—he pressed his lips to my ear—"so I took you, and I'm going to fucking keep you." I tried to pull my head back, but his grip stayed strong. "I allow you free rein, Gianna, but test me, and I will lock you up so fast. Do you understand me?"

"If you think I will even sleep with you now, you are delusional."

"You'll cool off." He ran a thumb across my cheek. "And when you do, you'll realize you want children, too, *cara.*" His grip found my chin, a rough caress. "And don't think I haven't noticed you're not wearing your ring. You'll put it back on when you get home, or you'll wake up tomorrow with it glued to your finger."

The glow of the ballroom highlighted his gray suit as he left through the double doors.

A tremor started in my hands.

The doors closed, and his words came out to swallow me with the shadows.

No more secret trips to Chicago.

No more secret trips to Chicago.

No more secret trips to Chicago.

The tremor moved up my arms, creeping into my vessels and veins. I shook from the inside out. My lungs tightened, and every breath closed them a little more.

Black spots swam in my vision.

I grasped the terrace handrail, the stone like ice beneath my fingers.

In. Out. In. Out.

Light fanned across the terrace, alerting me that someone had stepped outside.

I squeezed my eyes closed, tears escaping my bottom lashes. *Gianna, Gianna, Gianna.* I tensed and waited for it. I waited for the world to recognize how damaged I was on the inside. To crack me open and see everything my papà had from the beginning. A different part of me, one quiet but strong, wanted to shout, to *scream*, to let *her* rule with a steel heart and red hair.

"Do you want to know my favorite?"

My grip tightened on the railing.

In. Out.

"Andromeda." Allister moved closer. "An autumn constellation, forty-four light-years away." His steps were smooth and indifferent, but his voice was dry, as though he found my panic attack positively boring.

His attitude brought a small rush of annoyance in, but it was suddenly swayed as my lungs contracted and wouldn't release. I couldn't keep a strangled gasp from escaping.

"Look up."

It was an order, carrying a harsh edge.

With no fight in me, I complied and tilted my head. Tears blurred my vision. Stars swam together and sparkled like diamonds. I was glad they weren't. Humans would find a way to pluck them from the sky.

"Andromeda is the dim, fuzzy star to the right. Find it."

My eyes searched it out. The stars weren't often easy to see, hidden behind smog and the glow of city lights, but sometimes, on a lucky night like tonight, pollution cleared and they became visible. I found the star and focused on it.

"Do you know her story?" he asked, his voice close behind me.

A cold wind touched my cheeks, and I inhaled slowly.

"Answer me."

"No," I gritted.

"Andromeda was boasted to be one of the most beautiful goddesses." He moved closer, so close his jacket brushed my bare arm. His hands were in his pockets and his gaze was on the sky. "She was sacrificed for her beauty, tied to a rock by the sea."

I imagined *her*, a red-haired goddess with a heart of steel chained to a rock. The question bubbled up from the depths of me.

"Did she survive?"

His gaze fell to me. Down the tear tracks to the blood on my bottom lip. His eyes darkened, his jaw tightened, and he looked away.

"She did."

I found the star again.

Andromeda.

"Ask me what her name means."

It was another rough demand, and I had the urge to refuse. To tell him to stop bossing me around. However, I wanted to know—I suddenly *needed* to. But he was already walking away, toward the exit.

"Wait," I breathed, turning to him. "What does her name mean?"

He opened the door and a sliver of light poured onto the terrace. Black suit. Broad shoulders. Straight lines. His head turned just enough to meet my gaze. *Blue.*

"It means ruler of men."

An icy breeze almost swallowed his words before they reached me, whipping my hair at my cheeks.

And then he was gone.

I grasped the railing and looked to the sky.

My breath came out steady.

The knot in my chest loosened.

The tremor in my veins became the hot *buzz* of an electric line.

And then I did it for everyone who couldn't.

I did it for every bruise.

Every scar.

Every *slap* against my face.

Most of all, I did it because I wanted to.

I screamed.

Days bled into nights.

The next few months slipped away, consumed in a whirlwind of parties, vacations, races, and weekend spa retreats. Drugs and booze were as easily supplied as the silver platter of fresh fruit and croissants that sat on the twelve-seater dining table every morning.

I was young.

Pampered.

Full of ennui.

I imbibed anything that made my heart race. Made me forget. Made me feel alive.

Sometimes, it came in the form of a Colombian-imported powder.

And other times . . . *blue*.

"To live the life of luxury."

That drawl slid into my blood and warmed me from the inside out.

I lounged on a chaise near the pool in a shimmery gold gown, my hair pulled into a messy updo, a dress strap sliding down my shoulder. It was an unseasonably warm March night, and I was taking advantage of it.

I bit into my strawberry as my gaze met Allister's. "Jealous?"

"Closer to apathetic."

The glow of the pool lights cast him in shades of silver, blue, and shadow. Navy suit and tie. Polished Rolex and cufflinks. He stood in front of the terrace doors of my home, a tumbler in hand. His warm gaze took me in, from my hair, to the bowl of strawberries and glass of tequila on the table beside me, to my red velvet stilettos.

"Don't tell me my husband's stories were boring you." Antonio had a way with words, keeping others on the edge of their seats, yet I couldn't force myself to listen to the same tale over, and over again.

"Seems they couldn't hold your interest either. Though, maybe that's just because you knew the part about him fucking his twenty-year-old virgin bride was coming up next."

I flinched. Antonio must be angrier with me than I'd thought.

I hoped he'd made it sound more exciting than it was. There'd been nothing romantic about my first time. It was cold and mechanical, leaving a hollow hole in my chest that I'd tried to fill by gaining my husband's love. What a joke that had been.

"Isn't it in your job description to feign interest in everything he says?"

His gaze flickered with something akin to dry amusement, though he didn't respond. He stepped onto the terrace, tension outlining his shoulders. I couldn't help but think he was weighing his options, and it seemed he would rather tolerate my presence than go back inside.

"Did his crassness offend your tender sensibilities?" I asked.

"Not exactly."

His eyes came my way, filled to the brim with cold, cold fury. It dimmed to something warmer as his gaze slid down my neck and bare shoulder.

I shook off a shiver. "Will you avenge my honor, Officer?"

"Not sure I see a point when you don't have much left."

I pouted. "And just when I was beginning to think you cared."

"Don't hold your breath, sweetheart."

"Strawberry?"

When he looked at the fruit in my hand like it was offensive, I sighed. Then bit off the tip and licked the juice from my lips. His gaze followed the motion, warmer and heavier than the swipe of my tongue.

"Why do you dislike my husband so much?"

"Yes . . . *why?*"

I froze at the sound of Antonio's voice.

Allister looked positively unmoved that my husband had heard me, not even turning around to grace his employer with his attention nor deigning to answer the question. Antonio never cared when I spoke with men, but I wasn't sure how he would react to me being alone with one of his employees.

"What are you two talking about?"

"Mythology," I said in a bored tone. "Greek."

"Ah. My favorite kind."

Allister took a drink, watching the pool. He looked as apathetic as he'd claimed to be earlier, but something else wove through his disinterest. He was *too* apathetic. A shadow of something dark passing by below ice.

"I should have known I'd find you here, being lazy by the pool."

"Yes, well, one can only tolerate the same story five times. Though, I've heard you mixed it up tonight."

Antonio chuckled, reaching my chaise and running a hand around the back of my neck. "Don't be mad, *cara*. It was a tasteful story, I promise." His eyes coasted to Allister, hardening from amusement to jagged steel. "It's not like I told them you bled all over my cock."

I cringed.

The tension was so stifling I could hardly breathe. It settled in the air like late summer humidity, filling my lungs and touching my skin.

I downed my glass of tequila, biting down on it. The liquor burned away the humiliation in my throat. My husband was angry at me for a multitude of reasons, but this—whatever this was—wasn't for my benefit. The two men weren't even looking at each other, but nobody could miss the tightly-leashed venom between them.

"Your friends miss you." Antonio's grasp on my neck tightened enough for me to understand the warning. "Don't be long."

He disappeared inside.

Malevolence danced in the air, refusing to depart. My gaze drifted to Allister. Apathetic, but underlined with something *so* very scary.

A quiet, uncomfortable laugh escaped me. "It would seem my husband doesn't like you either." I swallowed. "Aren't you afraid he'll find some other dirty fed to work with?"

His gaze said he was not afraid in any way.

I'd never seen someone act so unenthusiastic to my husband's face, let alone one of his employees. It seemed Allister wasn't buying what Antonio was selling like everyone else did. It was . . . refreshing, and the first thing I truly liked about the man.

The tension in the air was still so thick I would grow lightheaded if I didn't clear it.

"No date tonight?"

"No."

"What happened to . . ." I briefly flew through the list of blondes he'd paraded around, coming up with the name of the last one. "Portia?"

"Monotony."

"But you were perfect for each other." I sighed, like I was seriously put out. "Both gorgeous, composed, unfeeling . . . What if she was the one and you tossed her aside without giving her a real chance?"

His gaze, so unimpressed with anything coming out of my mouth, touched me. "I didn't know you had such an investment in my relationships."

I got to my feet, pulling the pins out of my hair as I made my way toward him. The long strands tumbled down my back. His body tensed as the click of my heels moved closer, but he didn't look at me until I stood in front of him.

"Have you ever thought that maybe you're the problem?" I took the tumbler from his hand and stole a sip. The vodka in his glass always tasted better than any other.

"I'm guessing you're going to enlighten me?" He took his glass back. He would always turn it to drink from a different spot other than where my lips had touched, but tonight, he drank straight from where my pink lipstick left a mark. It sent a strange rush of heat to my stomach.

I swallowed. "A woman likes some passion and spontaneity in her life. You, Officer, need to loosen up."

"Should I fuck other women in her bed? Spontaneous enough, you think?"

God, he just had to know about Sydney.

I sighed.

I wanted to put a chink in that ice he wore like armor.

Stepping closer, I ran a finger across his jawline, my voice soft. "You have such a handsome face. Does it get you everything you want?"

"Almost."

There was something so significant about that single word it put a hitch in my breath. I let my finger fall from his face with a light scrape of my stiletto-shaped nail.

"One look from you, and women swoon at your feet."

He was growing annoyed with me. "Yet here you stand."

I laughed lightly. "I have no interest in men, even ones as handsome as you."

"Because you're married?"

"Because I'm jaded."

His eyes narrowed. "You're drunk."

My gaze filled with mischief when I slipped my thin dress strap off my shoulder. "And you never are. Don't you ever live on the edge, Officer? Just let yourself have whatever you want?"

The air pulsed like it had a heartbeat as I pushed the shimmery material over my hips, letting my gown fall to my feet.

Chink.

He didn't look away from my face, though the urge was there. Shifting like a breeze heading in the wrong direction.

I stood inches in front of him, in a red bra and panties, with an entire party and my husband just beyond a set of double doors.

His response was simple and exactly what I'd expected from the strait-laced fed, yet it still found the heat to brush my back as I made my way to the pool.

"No."

I looked over my shoulder. "Then how do you ever feel alive?"

A smile touched my lips as I dove into the water. Because his gaze had slid down the curves of my body, and it was the furthest thing from cold I'd ever felt.

CHAPTER
Four

Christian

September 2015

TAP,

> *tap,*
>> *tap.*

Sasha Taylor, Ph.D. watched the motion of my finger on the armrest. Eyes narrowed, lips slightly pursed, it was the expression she wore when deep in thought.

Tap . . . tap . . . tap.

Her gaze met mine, and, as a slow smile tugged on my lips, she swallowed and glanced at the file in her lap to find some resolve. "Tell me about your home life," she finally said, looking up. "Iowa."

I chuckled. "Ah, Sasha, we both know that's not what you want to talk about."

She pulled the charm on her necklace, back and forth, and raised a brow.

"Ask," I said impatiently.

Determination flared in her eyes, and she dropped the necklace. "Fine. Let's talk about your relationship with the number three."

"And here I didn't take you as one to engage in breakroom gossip."

"I don't engage, I merely observe. All means of information are valuable to a case."

"All right." I sat back, rested an elbow on the armrest, and ran a thumb across my bottom lip. "You tell me what you think this relationship is, and I'll tell you true or false."

Hesitation flickered across her expression, but she inhaled a breath and dove right the fuck in. "You only sleep with the same woman three times."

"True."

"Why?"

A whole list of reasons, but there was only one that motivated me to do anything.

"It feels right."

Four times suggested the relationship could go somewhere. Four felt like a sloppy affair, with feelings and questions thrown into the mix. Four annoyed me.

She accepted my answer and continued with her probing. "Some motions, not detrimental to your overall schedule, such as adjusting your clothes, maybe combing your hair, or laps at the gym, you do in some figure of three."

"To an extent."

"What happens when you stop at two?"

I held her gaze.

Tap . . . tap.

She waited on bated breath for the next tap that would never come. "Are you obsessing over the third now?"

"No."

Yes.

"Do you consider yourself OCD?"

"Mildly, self-diagnosed," I answered, looking at the clock. My phone vibrated in my pocket, and impatience burrowed beneath my skin. I had shit to do this evening. I was on suspension at the Bureau, but I'd taken on more work by outside sources, as much as was possible, because if I didn't stay busy I was afraid I'd burn under the heat of my own fucking anger.

I'd climbed my way out of hell, had seen it, tasted it, felt it, and the only thing that got me through had been dreaming about revenge and everything I would have on the other side. I'd planned my future out, from the kind of woman I'd marry to the type of hardwood in my apartment. Nowhere in those dreams had I ever planned for a Gianna Marino.

I should feel reprieved she was married and out of my reach again, but, *fuck* . . . it sometimes felt like an impossible feat to forget her.

"What about contamination symptoms?" she added, averting her gaze like there was something important in my file she'd just now noticed.

"More gossip, Sasha?"

Not surprising. When someone met me, they didn't forget me. Except for one woman, anyway. My face had been a curse when I was a kid, but now, I took advantage of it. To intimidate, to manipulate, to get whatever I wanted. Power. Information. Women. Ironic, that the one thing I now wanted, I couldn't fucking have.

She looked up, flustered with herself. "You don't kiss on the mouth."

"True."

"Why not?"

"It's messy and unnecessary."

Her eyes flickered with confliction. She'd already dug deeper into my psyche than this evaluation should have. Her interest was plain curiosity, the reason anyone decided they wanted to become a psychologist—to crack open a human's mind like an egg, to see what made us tick. What she didn't know was that I didn't tick. I'd made the fucking clock.

"You don't seem to have the same opinion regarding . . . other parts of a woman's anatomy."

I laughed.

I wouldn't have a problem with any part of a certain woman's anatomy. Truthfully, I'd let her spit in my goddamn mouth.

"So, if you're willing to . . ."

"Eat pussy?"

She flushed. "This has gone beyond what it should have," she muttered, fumbling with her pen.

"Are you getting all this down, Sasha?" I adjusted my cuff.

"Why no kissing?" Her uneasy movements had paused, her curiosity unwilling to let it go.

She thought she'd found something, a piece of the puzzle that made me. In truth, she was probably close. If she pulled at this thread hard enough, she might free another.

"Lipstick," I said. "I hate it."

Specifically, red.

A heart-shaped stain on my cheek. The red imprint left on the edge of a dirty glass or a lit cigarette lying on cracked pavement. The twisting of a little black container. I fucking hated all of it.

"So, the reason isn't related to thoughts of contamination?" she pushed.

"No."

It was mostly true. When I was agitated or stressed, my issue with cleanliness magnified, but otherwise, I just liked to be clean. I liked a clean space, clean clothes, and not to put dirty shit, like a used communal pen, in my mouth. Not to wake up with bugs crawling on me. Not to have to wash the dirt off my body in a drinking fountain.

"We're at the end of our meeting, but I have one more question. What is your earliest memory of the number three?"

Knock, knock, knock.

The knocking reverberated in my mind, three heavy thumps I'd still have been able to hear even if I placed my hands over my ears.

"They always knocked three times," I said.

"Who?"

"The men who made me."

CHAPTER
Five

Gianna
23 years old
July 2014

"**H**APPY BIRTHDAY!"

The shout of a hundred different voices hit me as I pushed open the club door. Confetti fell, sparkling beneath dim lighting and tickling my bare skin as it brushed my shoulders. Balloons floated to the ceiling, distorting the view of a photo of me blowing a kiss to the camera that took up the entire far wall. *Birthday* by The Beatles flooded the room.

Valentina ran up on stilettos and wrapped me in a hug. "Happy birthday!"

"Do you think you might have overdone it a little, Val?"

"Is it the photo?" She frowned, releasing me. "Too big, you think?"

Laughing, I kissed her cheek. "It's perfect."

I maneuvered my way into the club, hugging and thanking people for their birthday wishes until my cheeks hurt. My world tilted as someone picked me up by the waist and spun me around. The spinning stopped, and Luca's close gaze came into focus as my feet still dangled a foot off the floor.

"You owe me money, Gianna."

I frowned. "Is this how you wish everyone a happy birthday?"

"Only women that try to wiggle their way out of their debts."

"Oh, please." I brushed a piece of nonexistent lint off his shoulder. "You'll lose the next bet. I'm only saving us time with an exchange, is all."

A dry breath of amusement escaped him, and he set me back on my feet. "I think you're the worst cheat of us all, and you're not even a Russo by blood." He took a seat back at the bar.

"Oh, look," I said, stepping between Luca and Nico, who sat beside him. "I'm so popular to be honored with the great Nicolas Russo's presence at my birthday party."

Nico gave me a half-smile, nursing a glass of whiskey. "Got a meeting tonight."

"Ah," I responded, understanding it would be downstairs in the conference room. "Do you think you could at least pretend to be here for me?"

"You have plenty of people here for you."

I pouted, looking around the crowded club. "True."

We hadn't talked about that night one year ago. Not once, since the morning after. It was like, if we didn't speak of it, it hadn't happened. However, the secret had eaten away a large chunk of my soul. Regret was a hungry beast, and every day, it fed.

Nico and Luca's gazes went to the door. They stood at the same time, and I turned to see a man I didn't recognize—black suit, black hair, the glint of the *Cosa Nostra* in his eyes.

"Who's he?" I asked.

"None of your business," Nico responded. He didn't take his eyes off the Made Man as he cupped the back of my head and pulled me against his chest in a rough, short hug. "Happy birthday," he said, adding, "Try and take it easy tonight, yeah?"

"Sure, Dad."

He pushed me away playfully by the face, and then both Russo men headed toward the man who was none of my business.

Valentina bumped shoulders with me as she ordered a large number of drinks from the bar, and soon after, I was lost in the bottom of a shot glass, bathroom trips, and a heady, uninhibited rush in my blood.

Purple, yellow, blue. The panels beneath my feet blinked back and forth, casting a glow against my bare legs and white dress. Katy Perry's *I Kissed a Girl* blared through the speakers, as the bodies on the dance floor moved together, limbs jiving, hips rolling, lips touching.

Purple. A drop of sweat down my back. *Yellow.* The glide of skin against mine. Running my hands over my neck, I lifted the heavy strands and looked up.

Blue.

My breath slowed, and so did my movements.

I held his gaze as he stood next to Nico at the bar. Allister responded to something Ace had said but kept his eyes on me.

The roll of my hips, the glide of my hands in my hair—they moved to a different rhythm than the beat. Slower. *Sexier.* Like a caress of silk sheets against naked skin. Holding his stare, I lip-synced a line of the song. The words poured from my red-painted mouth, sensual exhales between parted lips.

His eyes darkened.

I'd only been messing with him, but somewhere in the middle of it, my body had grown confused. The blood in my veins heated. My nipples tightened. Sweat glistened like drops of oil on my skin, tickling as it ran between my breasts.

His gaze drifted to my photo on the wall behind me before he met my eyes.

I smiled, lifted a hand, and blew him a sweet kiss.

With shaky legs, I stumbled off the dance floor a half hour later and drifted upstairs to quiet the thumping pulse of music in my head.

I opened a VIP room door and paused with my hand on the knob. A familiar dirty fed stood with his back to me, facing the large window that sparkled with city lights. He had a phone to his ear, and his smooth, deep words reached me. Something about a contract and a bad situation. Sounded intriguing. I entered the room, closed the door, and leaned against it. Allister's back tensed subtly at the quiet *click*, but he otherwise didn't acknowledge my presence.

He'd grown out the top of his fade haircut in the years since I'd met him. It was now long enough to run one's fingers through, to grab a handful of. The thought made me feel warm and strange, and I quickly pushed the feeling away.

He hung up and turned around.

We stared at each other, and a thick, almost suffocating tension filled the air. Two nights on a terrace had been the only other times we were alone. Now, with a closed door, a ceiling, and four walls surrounding us, it felt like there wasn't enough oxygen in the small space for us both.

"Grown bored of your party already?"

There were a number of games we'd played over the last year, at the few functions where we ran into each other. A favorite of mine required us to ignore the other's presence completely, even if an acquaintance chose to introduce us to one another. Another game was that I pretended to be madly in love with him. He hated that one the most, and because annoying Allister would taste sweeter than my birthday cake, it was the one I decided to play.

I slipped my heels off. "Maybe I came up here to be with a man."

Something dark moved through his eyes, but as soon as he leaned back against the glass it disappeared. "Let's hope you're not keeping it in the family this time."

My stomach dropped like lead, and a quiver started in my chest. He *knew*. He knew about me and Nico. I'd seen the fed with Ace a few times over the last year, but I didn't believe they were close enough to share secrets with one another. How much had Nico told him? It felt like I was going to be sick.

I swallowed and tried to keep my voice steady. "You and I aren't related, Officer."

His lips lifted. "Ah, so you came to be with me."

Unease suddenly rose up to choke me, and I couldn't pretend to be normal anymore. Heels forgotten, I turned and grabbed the doorknob, but before I could get the door open all the way, his hand appeared above my head and slammed it shut. The echo sent a tremor through me.

His shoulders blocked out the light. His presence, heavy and palpable, skimmed down my spine. "You started this game," he said, with the rough sound of anger. "Finish it."

I couldn't think with him behind me, cornering me against the door. We'd always stood close—close enough to watch the room and insult each other's looks and intelligence with ease. But this was different. Real, volatile anger poured off him, and it was freaking terrifying.

Plainly, and as bland as stale bread, I said, "The way I feel about you, well, it's put me in a small spot."

"Tight spot," he corrected softly.

I didn't say anything because I was internally shaking. At his closeness, his unexplained anger, the fact I was trapped, and I wasn't getting out unless he chose to let me go. Just the idea he might touch me sent every nerve ending in my back tingling in expectation.

His hand slid off the door and he stepped away.

I inhaled slowly. Released it.

Turning, I watched him walk to the minibar and grab a glass of clear liquid that sat on the wooden top.

"Go entertain your guests, Gianna."

A sliver of irritation ran through me. I hated when he told me what to do. Like he was my lord and master, and I just wasn't aware of it yet.

"That's what I'm trying to do, but I suppose some guests are just assholes."

He braced his hands on the bar and turned a dark gaze to me. He wasn't here for my party but for whatever meeting was happening downstairs. And his expression was making that abundantly clear. But I didn't care for semantics.

"Where is my present?" I asked, padding toward him on bare feet.

"What? The room next door overflowing with presents isn't enough for you?"

"Aw, does that make you mad? That I have friends, and you don't?"

"You need confirmation that everyone adores you, don't you?"

"Yes," I said, straight-faced. "So where is my present?" I tapped the front of his watch, and his eyes narrowed on the movement. "Surely your watch is too much? It's a *Rolex*." When he only gave me a dry stare, I sighed. "Okay, if you insist."

I started to unclasp his watch just to see if he would stop me, to grab my wrist and tell me to quit being annoying like any other man I knew would. He had never touched me. Not once. Not when I'd messed with his tie, taken his glass straight from his hand, or "accidentally" stepped on his foot when he'd told me that at least my blond hair now matched what was inside my head. To be honest, it made me believe he thought I was too lowly to even come into contact with. For a reason I couldn't explain, it bothered me. And it might've been why I touched him even more.

Hands braced on the bar, he only watched me unclasp his watch. My breath grew dense in my lungs. I was simply removing his watch, yet somehow, it felt like I was undoing his belt.

The Rolex slid halfway down my forearm when I put it on, but I still waved it around like I would a new conflict-free diamond ring.

"Thank you," I said brightly. "I love it."

We watched each other, and something thick and heavy flowed through the room. He tipped his glass back and took a large sip. I'd say it was water, but I knew it was vodka. The man could drink, and yet he seemed impervious to getting drunk.

I tilted my head. "Where are you from?"

"Iowa."

A laugh escaped me. "And I'm the Queen of England." I took his watch off, set it on the bar, and spun it with my finger. "Fine. I know what I want for my birthday."

"I'm on the edge of my seat."

"You're not. But that's okay. We can't all have feelings and things."

He put his watch back on, and I grew distracted by the movement. Allister had the kind of hands that made a woman wonder what they would look like against her skin.

"I want a secret," I said, adding, "One of yours, of course."

"And what am I supposed to get out of this?"

"The satisfaction of making me happy." I flashed him a sweet smile.

His gaze dropped to my lips. He looked away, but before he did, I saw a flash of something unmistakably sinful. My heartbeat tripped up on itself.

He braced his hands back on the bar. "Tell me what your husband got you first." His voice was nonchalant, though a tense vibe emanated from him, and it sent a nervous energy through me.

I lifted a shoulder. "I'm sure some piece of jewelry, like he gets me every year. I don't know. I haven't seen him yet today."

"Why not?"

"He's a busy man."

"Too busy for his wife on her birthday?" I recognized his indifferent yet vicious tone and where he was taking this. Frustration chafed beneath my skin.

"Stop," I told him.

"What was Antonio doing today? Or, maybe the right word would be, *who?*"

Anger scratched at my throat and the backs of my eyes. Antonio didn't consume my thoughts anymore. I no longer thought of him with a young, wide-eyed wonder. Love had turned bitter—if it had ever been love, and not infatuation. However, betrayal still stung, and Allister was cutting that wound open to bleed.

I choked on my fury. "I hate you."

"I think about you."

Those four rough words filled the air between us, settling to the floor with a stillness that rocked me to my core. My blood cooled as silence came out to touch me with cold fingers.

I stared, eyes wide.

He watched my expression, bitter amusement passing through his gaze. "There's your fucking secret."

Downing his drink, he dropped it on the bar before heading to the door. He stopped with a hand on the knob and turned to me. "You want to know why I don't touch you?"

I shook my head.

"Because if I did, I wouldn't stop. Not until I'd snuffed out that pretty fire in your eyes." His gaze flashed. "Don't shut yourself in a room with me again, Gianna."

He left, but his warning stayed behind.

My heart tripped over itself as I marched down the stairs and knocked on the heavy door. It swung open to reveal Tara standing on the other side. Her bright smile dropped into a scowl when she saw it was me.

"You know Antonio doesn't like women down here."

She opened a door for a living, yet she believed she was the equivalent of the President's right-hand man. I didn't know why, but every woman who had ever manned this door was a raging bitch.

"You have a second to get out of my way before I have you demoted to taking out the garbage."

Her gaze narrowed to slits. "You wouldn't dare."

"Try me."

Anger rose to her cheeks. However, as though she'd just remembered something important, a spark of mischief lit in her eyes, and she pulled the door open wide.

Something obviously lay in wait for me, but I couldn't find the will to care. I was too frazzled by Allister's earlier words, and furious that Ace had told him what happened between us.

I walked past her and down the short steel staircase.

Cigarette smoke hung in the air, coalescing with dim orange lighting. The card tables sat still, and the booths circling the room unseated. A few men loitered outside the conference room door, and heated conversation filtered to my ears from within. I made my way toward Antonio's office to wait until the meeting adjourned.

As I walked past the conference room, Lorenzo stepped out of the group of men and blocked my path. "What are you doing down here?"

"Trying to eavesdrop on all your secret plans to take over the world."

He slipped his hands in his pockets, a smile pulling on his lips. Lorenzo was the cutest of the Russos, if you were ever going to use that word to describe any of them. Blood splatter and the look of the *Cosa Nostra* usually revoked any sense of *cute* from their description. But, somehow, Lorenzo still retained it. He might be the cutest, but I'd heard he was the kinkiest, too.

"You have a party upstairs," he said. "Why don't you go join it?"

"I have to murder Ace first, then I will."

"Ace is busy."

"I'll wait until he's free."

I needed a second to collect my thoughts anyway. *Not until I'd snuffed out that pretty fire in your eyes.* A cold shiver erupted at the base of my spine. What did that mean, exactly?

Distracted, I tried to step around Lorenzo, but he blocked my path again.

"Go upstairs, Gianna."

Tara's mischievous look came to mind. With a singsong lilt in my voice, I asked, "What's in my husband's office that I'm not supposed to see?"

"Nothing."

"Oh, Lo, I know you can't help it, but has anyone told you, you're transparent?" I rolled my eyes and pushed past him.

John stood beside the office door, one hand clasping the other wrist in front of him. He wasn't Italian, and therefore could never be sworn in as a Made Man, but he'd been a trusted man of my husband's since I'd met him and would probably always be.

"New hairdo?" I asked, glancing at his bald head. It was an ongoing joke between us.

A small smile came to his lips. "Borrowed some of Lorenzo's hair gel."

I could feel Lo's eyeroll behind me.

"Ah, well, I like it." I winked.

I grabbed the doorknob, but John's voice stopped me before I could open it.

"Gianna."

I looked at him to see a somber expression staring back. At this point, I knew what lay beyond the door, but I was so tired of running from it for the last year. My thoughts reflected in my eyes, and he tipped his chin in understanding.

I opened the door and strolled inside.

She sat on the couch, one leg crossed over the other, a textbook open on her lap. When she looked up and saw me, she dropped her pen and stared.

"Hello, Sydney."

She swallowed. "Gianna."

"Don't mind me," I said, sitting on the couch beside her and grabbing the TV remote. "I'm waiting for Ace. I just need to kill him, and then I'll be on my way."

She nodded like she completely understood.

I flicked through the channels, settling on my favorite soap opera, and pulled my legs up beside me.

Sydney's discomfort wafted from her like a heavy perfume. She shifted in her blue scrubs, and I realized she must have come straight from the hospital. She worked as a phlebotomist to put herself through nursing school. I was surprised she still insisted on working—I knew Antonio wouldn't hesitate to pay her way.

"Gianna . . ." She hesitated, thick emotion laced through her voice. "I don't know what to say to tell you how sorry I am for everything."

Betrayal twisted my heart in a brutal grip.

It was the same thing she'd said in a hundred emails, voicemails, messages, and a couple of personal visits I'd quickly ended. Say something too many times and it becomes meaningless.

"If I could go back and change how things happened—"

"No, no, no," I muttered, shaking my head at the TV. "Don't sleep with Chad. He screwed around with Ciara behind your back last week!"

Sydney's attention went to the TV before frustration heated her cheeks. "I know you, Gianna, and I know you aren't so indifferent, not to me."

Bitterness stung my throat. "You do know me. You know more about me than I have ever shared with anyone else. And that is why I can't forgive you, Sydney."

I'd taken a few college courses when I married and moved to New York. "It will help you get a feel for the city," Antonio said. I was in awe of his generosity, the freedom he'd granted me, which I had never experienced before. That was where I met Sydney. I remembered the hours we spent squished together on her dorm room bunk bed, staring at the ceiling and talking about life.

It was the first meaningful friendship I'd ever had. And when it ended, it wasn't the first time my heart had been ripped out. My chest had felt hollow since I was five years old, and sometimes, where emotions should be, there was only numbness. Some called it depression. I called it life.

"You know what he's like," she said softly.

I did know. I knew so well I actually felt sorry for her, but it did nothing to remove the image of him and her together. Or the knowledge they'd been seeing each other for a year now, without any regard to how it would make me feel.

"I didn't mean for anything to happen. I felt sick about the whole thing—"

"This topic is positively boring," I sighed. "I know, let's talk about how my husband is in bed."

She made a noise of frustration. "Stop doing this. Stop pretending you don't care."

"You want some honest emotion from me? Fine." The words poured from my lips without any sentiment. "I hate you. I hate you for what you did. I hate you for still doing it. And I hate you for acting as though I'm in the wrong here. You're dead to me, Sydney. Is that enough emotion for you?"

You're dead to me.

You're dead to me.

You're dead to me.

It resounded in the room on an undying loop, like the skipping of a scratched record.

Her face lost all color, and her voice was so quiet it sounded nearly inaudible. "I'm so sorry for what I did to you."

"So am I," I whispered, resigned.

Silence reached out to consume us both. It masqueraded as a calm, peaceful entity, but it couldn't conceal a volatile edge. We sat in that uncomfortable, deceitful silence. It was her punishment. It was just my existence. She worked on her homework with a shaky hand, and I watched my show while trying not to regret the words I'd said. But I did. They already haunted me, and she wasn't even dead yet.

Fifteen minutes later, Antonio burst into the room with Ace on his heels. They were arguing about something, but as soon as they noticed our presence, they both stopped to stare. I guessed a wife and a mistress sitting side-by-side was a perplexing sight. I aimed to make it more confusing.

I smiled. "Aren't you going to wish your wife a happy birthday?"

"Jesus," Ace muttered. "We don't have time for this right now."

I shot him a narrowed gaze. "You know what *I* don't have time for? You!"

It was an immature response I didn't think through, as I did have some free time, considering I had no job and not a single responsibility, and that thought was clearly conveyed in Ace's dry expression.

Father and son stood beside one another. Together, they could double as a brick wall. An unyielding force of nature. Or something someone might pray to.

My husband's gaze coasted from me to Sydney and, in a twisted, disgusting way, I thought he liked seeing us together.

I hadn't touched him since last October, since I'd told him I wouldn't. But he was getting more persuasive as the days went on, and I was beginning to ache for human contact. For hands and lips on my skin; to lose myself in a sheen of sweat and lust. The desire grew stronger every day, and I knew he was only biding his time until it became unbearable. Antonio might smack me around sometimes, but he had never tried to rape me. My guess was that was a sin he'd be too ashamed to confess. Or, more likely, he thought my resistance was a game I was close to losing, and he was going to feel immense satisfaction when he won.

Thankfully, the way he watched Sydney and me was making me a bit nauseous. I got to my feet and straightened my dress.

"Is there a reason you're not celebrating with the people upstairs who came here for you?" Antonio asked.

"Yes, actually, there is. To shoot Ace. Since I'm not currently armed, I'll let you do the honors."

He rolled his eyes and headed to his desk. "Appease my wife, son. It is her birthday."

I turned to Nico, triumph sparkling in my eyes like a sibling who had just won a battle. But that was a slightly awkward comparison, considering we'd had sex.

Nico shook his head, and then walked to the door and opened it. "You have a second to say what you need to. And you're not fucking shooting me."

"We'll see," I muttered, passing him as I walked out the door.

My bare feet touched the cool concrete in the hall just as the first *pop* cut through the air. A draft hit my face, a *ring* sounding in my ears. John slumped to the floor with a solid *thunk*.

I stared at the splatter of red that slid down the wall in front of me.

My breath escaped me in one rush as someone slammed me to the wall, covering me with their body.

Pop.

Pop.

"Fuck," Nico growled, smacking the wall beside my head. He whirled around, pressing his back to my front. The sound of three close gunshots cut through the air. They rang in my ears and vibrated in my bones.

Something wet and warm soaked through my dress. I touched the spot and brought my fingers up to my face. Red coated my hand like paint.

So much blood.

"Ace," I breathed. "Oh, my god, Ace." My hand shook.

Someone grabbed my wrist and shoved me into my husband's office.

"Do not leave this room under any circumstance," Antonio said. The darkness in his soul had leaked into his eyes, filling them with black. He slammed the door, and I fell back a step, finding balance.

"Oh my god, Gianna!" Sydney hurried over to me. "Where are you hurt?" She ran her hands over my arms and midsection while I stared blankly at the door. When she didn't find a scratch, she breathed, "Whose blood?"

"Ace's."

"Oh, my god."

A *pop* sounded from outside the door, one after the other, and then it went quiet. So quiet my heartbeat pulsed in my ears.

She eyed the door.

"No, Sydney," I warned.

Turmoil flickered through her gaze. "I can help."

"No." Urgency filled my voice. "You heard Antonio."

Tears filled her eyes, one escaping her bottom lashes. "I have a bad feeling, Gianna . . ."

"You love him."

"Yes," she cried. "I don't want to live without him."

She took a step toward the door, but I grabbed her wrist. I wouldn't let her sacrifice herself for love. I couldn't. Love wasn't worth it. Love hurt. I tightened my grip when she tried to knock my hand away. But then the lights went out, and darkness descended on us, with reaching, searching, cold fingertips.

A strangled sound of protest escaped my lips, and I was eight years old again. *Don't you ever shut up, girl? Disgrace. Worthless. Unlovable. Whore.*

My lungs tightened, constricting.

Her wrist slipped from my grasp and disappeared into the darkness.

You're dead to me.

"No," I cried, as I dropped to my knees and fought to breathe.

Sydney got her wish.

She didn't have to live without him.

On my twenty-third birthday, I became a widow of one.

CHAPTER Six

Gianna
24 years old
August 2015

"**C**AN YOU FEEL IT? THE BEAT IN YOUR CHEST?"

I gave my head a shake, long curls sticking to my tear-streaked cheeks.

"Here." Mamma grabbed my hand and pressed it to my chest, over my light pink church dress. "What about now?"

Something pulsed beneath my palm, small but fast, like the flutter of a frightened bird's wings. I nodded.

"It's music," she whispered, like she was telling a big secret.

My eyes filled with awe, but soon, fear crept into the corners of my mind. "But Papà hates music."

"Some men, Gianna . . . can't feel their own music, let alone other's."

Sadness pulled on my chest.

Mamma's gaze grew wet, like mine. "Dance to this"—she pressed her hand to my heart—"whenever and however you want."

"Whenever I want?"

"Yes, stellina." She pressed a kiss to my forehead and my five-year-old heart warmed. "Whenever you want."

"I'm scared of the dark." The whisper invaded the memory, my low, toneless voice sweeping in.

You're dead to me.

You're dead to me.

You're dead to me.

The words came out with the blackness to swallow me whole.

I woke with a start, the sheets stuck to my sweaty skin. Catching my breath, I stared at the ceiling of my apartment. The dream swept me back to the night of my twenty-third birthday.

I sat at the back of an ambulance, the doors open on either side of me. It was hot and humid, though my blood ran cold.

A sheet covered the body, but it couldn't conceal the long blond hair hanging off the stretcher as they loaded Sydney into the back of an ambulance.

Someone stood in front of me, and I brought a blank stare to his. I'd been sitting on Antonio's cold office floor in the dark when he'd found me. Allister hadn't said a word as he picked me up, letting me cry silently on his shoulder while he carried me outside. Before he disappeared back inside, he'd taken off his suit jacket and rested it on my shoulders. It smelled like a man's. Deep, and rough, and masculine. I tried to drown myself in the scent instead of the numbness.

"Do you want to go home?" he asked.

Home?

It had always been Antonio's house more than it had ever been mine. After the Sydney fiasco, I stayed at one of his apartments when I could, just to escape his attentions when he was home. I wondered if Sydney had known Antonio was never faithful to her, that he'd tried to seduce me while claiming to love her. She'd died for him, for *love*. The word left a sour aftertaste in my mouth.

The idea of going home suddenly sounded abhorrent.

I shook my head.

"Where?"

"Ace's," I whispered.

A muscle in his jaw tightened, and something bitter passed through his eyes. "Ace won't be there for a while."

An ambulance had taken him to the hospital despite his protests. He'd been losing a lot of blood from the two bullet wounds he'd received, one in the side and one in the arm. He'd taken those bullets for me, and I was going to nurse him back to health, whether he liked it or not.

"I know," I said.

Allister ran his tongue across his teeth as though agitated, but he moved to speak with one of the dozens of agents nearby.

I followed him to his car. I realized it was the first time I'd ever seen him without a suit jacket. His white long-sleeve shirt molded his broad shoulders and arms. I'd never noticed just how built the man was until now. Maybe I was losing my mind, but I studied his form the entire walk to the car as I trailed behind him, barefoot.

He drove me to Nico's home in the Bronx in silence and then followed me to the back door. I knew the code to Ace's alarm system—not because he trusted me with it, but because I'd secretly watched him type it in once.

Allister stepped inside behind me and shut the door.

"You don't have to stay," I told him. "I'm fine."

"You're in shock," was his response.

He looked around the place, his shoulders tense. He didn't want to leave me here. I thought he even hated the idea. The question was, *why?*

"Why are you here?" I asked, draping his jacket over an island chair. "Feeling sorry for me?"

"No." The word was hard, and the glint in his eye conveyed that he did not feel sorry in any way.

God, he was heartless.

"I'm fine," I insisted.

"Don't lie to me again, Gianna."

I was too numb to be annoyed by his lord-and-master tone. In fact, it felt like I was hanging by a thread high in the sky, though I was too indifferent to care if it snapped.

"Are you hungry?" he asked.

"No."

I headed up the stairs, dropping my blood-stained dress at the top, and took a shower. When I went downstairs twenty minutes later, with wet hair and dressed in only one of Ace's white t-shirts, Allister was still there, leaning against the counter and talking on the phone. His consuming gaze found me, drifting down my body with a mixture of warmth and agitation.

A tremor started beneath my skin, buzzing stronger like an approaching bee that would surely sting.

"Come here," he said after he hung up.

When I reached him, he handed me a white pill and a glass of water.

"Take it."

I didn't even ask what it was; I took it with a sip of water and went to set my glass on the counter.

"All of it, Gianna."

My eyes narrowed at the edges, but I drank the rest as I was told.

"There's more in the cupboard for the next few days." His voice caught a harsh note. "Don't do anything stupid."

He thought I would try to OD on them. I'd experienced far worse than tonight and had never even contemplated suicide. I didn't care enough to try and convince him, though.

As I walked past, he caught me by my t-shirt. I looked up at him. I didn't know why he was here, why he was helping me. Nonetheless, I was suddenly grateful. I didn't want to be alone.

The touch of his eyes ran over my face like a caress. I wasn't sure what he was looking for, but his closeness, the heat from his body, it was penetrating the numbness and warming me from the inside out. My gaze softened, lips parted, as flames licked at my skin.

His grip tightened on my shirt, and I stumbled a step closer. He was too close, and I had to place a hand on his stomach to catch myself from falling flush against him. His abs tightened beneath my palm, but his expression remained unmoved.

"Regardless of what you might believe, Gianna, I'm a grown man. Dress appropriately in front of me next time."

His words broke me from the warm spell I'd been under. He wanted me to respond, to say something so he knew I hadn't fallen off the deep end—the sharp sound of his voice had practically demanded it. It was fake concern, I was sure.

Pushing away from him, I headed to the living room. I lay down and flipped the TV on to a soap opera rerun. I watched it mindlessly while listening to his deep timbre in the background as he talked on the phone.

I fell asleep at some point. And dreamed of a light touch on my face and two rough words in my ear.

After taking a trip down memory lane, I lay in bed until noon. The silence that filled my apartment was so loud it hurt my ears. I liked my freedom, but I hated living alone. I hated being alone. It reminded me of my papà. Of the slam of a door and the lights going out.

Vincent pressed a kiss to my cheek. "You're the most gorgeous thing I've ever seen," he whispered in my ear.

I laughed, trying hard to keep an uncomfortable edge from escaping. "You obviously haven't seen a sunset in the Caribbean."

"I have, and trust me, it doesn't compare. Shall I escort you in?"

I nodded.

Vincent placed a hand at the small of my back and guided me into the club.

It was the grand reopening, after the shooting last year. There hadn't been much damage, and only six casualties—Antonio, his brother, Sydney, John, and two Zanettis. However, Nico had focused his time on revenge and not on opening his club to the public until now.

Vincent's hand gripped low on my hip, in a possessive hold. I didn't realize he'd be here tonight, but it seemed wherever I was lately, so was he. I didn't want to have to turn him down, though I knew it was going to have to happen soon. He was kind-hearted, gentle, and handsome—exactly my type—but I wasn't the woman for him. I wasn't the woman for any man.

I didn't need love in my life.

But I did miss sex.

So desperately that his warm breath in my ear sent a spark between my legs. It'd been six months since I'd pressed my mouth to another's, felt the heaviness of a man's body covering mine, lost myself in touch and feeling. The last time had been with a male stripper I'd met at a cantina in Cancún. It'd only taken the brush of his thumb at the hollow behind my ear until I gave in. It didn't make me feel good emotionally, but physically, it was everything I needed. Hot and sweaty and desperate. I needed human touch like I needed air, and now, I was riding on a thin amount of oxygen.

Vincent led me to a group of our friends at a round booth in a private corner. We joined them with hellos and kisses on the cheeks.

I paused at the man leaning against the booth. "I'm sorry, I don't think I've had the pleasure."

Sharp features and blue eyes met mine. "I'd say the pleasure is all mine."

How charming.

The stranger was a few inches taller than me, wearing a charcoal designer suit and tie. He looked like a gentleman, talked like a gentleman . . . but there was something about him I couldn't put my finger on. Vincent's possessive squeeze on my hip annoyed me.

"I'm going to fetch a drink." I pulled away from Vincent's grasp before he could protest and offer to get me one himself. He would. I thought he might bring me back the moon if I asked for it. He knew who my ex-husband was, the life I was raised in, but, like a true gentleman, he'd never brought it up. If he thought he could survive in my world, he was mistaken. It would chew him up and spit him out before he could even say hello.

I stopped at the bar, realizing Charming had followed me.

"What's your name?"

I tilted my head, meeting his gaze in the glass behind the bar. "Wouldn't you like to know?"

"I would."

"Why?"

"Because I'd like to know the name of the woman I'm fucking tonight."

The corners of my lips tipped up. I loved straightforward people, however . . . something about Charming rubbed me the wrong way.

"Awfully confident," I mused, grabbing my drink from the bartender.

My gaze was pulled to the side by some invisible force. I should have known it was him. It was always him. Allister was headed to a table where two other men in black suits stood together, talking. But, as though he'd felt my presence just as I had his, he glanced over and caught my gaze.

I realized what was wrong with Charming. His blue eyes were dull and cloudy.

Not piercing and deep enough to drown in.

Lovely. I'd let the disgustingly handsome fed ruin an entire eye color for me.

Allister's attention moved to the man beside me. His gaze narrowed and flickered with loathing before he looked away.

My heart rate slowed at his strange reaction, but I quickly pushed the feeling down. I didn't like to think about the fed. Every time I did, an edginess came over me, leaving a hollow and uncertain sensation in my chest.

I'd seen him a few times since he'd taken me to Ace's last year. Our relationship had picked up on the same note it'd always been on. However, it was as if he had never taken care of me that night. He was different, radiating a tension that touched my skin each time I stood by him. His responses were dryer, his tone harsher, and he'd often walk off and leave me standing alone, like my mere presence agitated him. It annoyed me.

"So . . . you gonna tell me your name?"

"Guess," I finally said to Charming, turning my attention to him.

"Hmm." His gaze lit with the challenge. "It's elegant and beautiful, just like you."

I rolled my eyes at his flattery, but I made him guess for another ten minutes until I finished my drink and needed to use the restroom.

Just as I was about to pass the men's room, the door opened, and I came face-to-face with Allister. Oddly, my heart stalled, stealing some oxygen from my lungs.

"Hello, Officer."

He didn't say a word as his gaze bit through my skin.

"*Okay* then," I said. "You have a lovely night."

I tried to pass him, but he stepped in front of me, blocking my path. It'd been a long time since we'd played any game, and anticipation buzzed in my veins.

"What are you doing with Knox?" His voice was low and smooth, and I could feel it in my toes.

I frowned. "Who's Knox?"

"The man you've been flirting with for the last fifteen minutes," he snapped.

"Well, you've just answered your own question, haven't you, Officer? Flirting."

My smile faltered as he took a sudden step forward, forcing my back to hit the wall. A breath of air escaped me. His arms came up on either side of me, caging me in. He was so close my entire body hummed beneath the surface.

"I'm sure the Bureau doesn't approve of this kind of behavior," I breathed.

He was distracted, his gaze beside my head, where a lock of my hair brushed his hand. He pulled it through his fingers, and the small amount of pressure on my scalp tightened between my legs.

The air sparked in the small space between us, and it made me so uncertain I opened my mouth again. "Or maybe harassing women is on the daily agenda—"

"Shut up."

I glared at him.

My hair slipped through his fingers, and his gaze focused on my face. Something dark and lazy played in his eyes.

"You're going to tell Knox it was not nice to meet him and then go join your group of friends."

I laughed, realizing which game this was. It was the one where he pretended to be my keeper, and it was the most annoying one we'd ever played. "Tempting as that demand is, I'm going to have to pass."

The intensity in his eyes was like staring directly into the sun, and I couldn't take it anymore. I dropped my gaze to his tie. It was perfect, like always, and while I would usually adjust it anyway, I didn't reach for it now. His presence radiated tension, and it sent a nervous tremor through me.

"You don't know a single thing about him, Gianna."

"You don't need to know anything about someone to sleep with them." I wasn't even planning on having sex with the man with dull eyes, but Allister goaded the words straight from my mouth.

A small growl sounded low in his throat, and I stared at him, frozen. Someone was taking this game a little too seriously.

His palm slid from the wall, and his voice was calm and final. "You're not going home with him."

I stared at his hand running the length of his tie and knew my libido was completely out of control at the moment, because I imagined his hand on me—in my hair, on my throat, covering my mouth. Heat pulsed between my legs.

"I'll leave with him if I want," I finally managed.

"Try it."

"You don't get to tell me what to do."

"I just did."

This was exactly why I hated this game. A small noise of frustration escaped me, and I ducked underneath his arm and headed toward the ladies' room.

"You heard me, Gianna."

I'd heard him, all right.

Didn't mean I'd listen.

I had always tried not to do things out of spite, because every time, it only led me down a rabbit hole of regret. However, the moments after Allister's stupid game pushed me straight into the underworld's own version of Wonderland.

I washed my hands after using the restroom, and then halted at the end of the hall.

A bad taste filled my mouth.

The lighting was dim, but, as though they were the most perfect couple in the room, strobe lights danced across their forms.

A brunette had a hand on Allister's chest as she stood on her tip-toes to say something in his ear. It wasn't an odd scene—women were always all over him—but it was rare when he acknowledged them, unless they were one of his socialite dates. The sight that sent an odd sensation tightening in my stomach was his hand coming up to rest on her hip, in the most natural way, like he'd done it before.

He was *touching* her.

Why wouldn't he? She was classy, composed, everything I was not. He wouldn't touch me, not if he were hanging off a cliff and I was the only one who could pull him up.

I couldn't keep it in—spite grabbed me in its electric embrace and wouldn't let go.

Allister wasn't going to win this game.

In the end, however, he won. He won everything.

I strode up to Charming, grabbed his tie, and gave him a tug toward the door. He smirked and followed me.

I turned my head in Allister's direction. The brunette was still whispering something into his ear and his hand was still on her hip. But his gaze was on me. I swallowed as his eyes drifted to Charming, a lazy flicker passing through the blue before disappearing into vicious depths. *Heartless.* The look was full of the promise of retaliation. And then he dismissed me, giving all his attention to the brunette, as though I couldn't be stupid enough not to listen to him.

Anger flared in my chest. I wasn't going to let him scare me into losing. What could he possibly do, anyway? He was just a lackey of my family's, and he wouldn't even touch me.

"I'm not sleeping with you," I told Charming. "I'm merely using you to make my ex-boyfriend jealous." The truth would have been a little hard to explain.

"Whatever, baby."

His slimy response grated on my nerves. Now, I could see this man's charm was dropped in a vat of oil.

My apartment was only a couple blocks from the club, and I continued my trek, hoping Charming would just drift away.

Unfortunately, he followed like a lost puppy.

I stopped in front of the lobby doors. "Well, it was lovely to meet you. Thanks for all your help."

I turned to open the door, but he grabbed my wrist.

"Wait a minute. I think you owe me a drink, at least." He grinned. "Or maybe a line or two. I'd like to know what kind of stuff the Russos are shipping out."

A line of blow was like a glass of champagne in my world. Unless we were at a family dinner—then you didn't even know what the stuff was. But I couldn't stop an eyeroll. He'd have known what my name was if he was familiar with my family.

But I did upend his night, and he was obviously more interested in getting his hands on my family's drugs than me, so I opened the door and let him in.

"Gianna," greeted the concierge. The seventyish Irishman had called me Ms. Russo until I'd nipped that in the bud.

"Hello, Niall," I responded. "This is Charming." I patted the man's chest beside me.

Niall sized him up. "Charming," he murmured, but I couldn't tell if he was greeting him or mocking him. I loved Niall.

"He's not very deferential, is he?" Charming asked, an edge of disgust in his voice.

Charming was a total loser.

"He's Irish," I responded, like that explained everything.

I let us into my apartment, leaving the door open a few inches so he wouldn't get any ideas about staying. Heading to my room, I grabbed a baggie off my dresser. When I returned to the living room, it was to find him touching my things. "Here," I said, tossing the 8-ball to him. "For all your trouble."

He practically rubbed his hands together. "Let's find out if it's as good as I hear."

"It is."

I groaned internally when he dumped some powder on the marble counter.

Under the bright lights in the kitchen, it was clear his suit was worn, his shoes scuffed. He didn't have any money and was hard-up for blow. Ugh, why had I let this idiot into my apartment?

His eyes were bright when he lifted his head.

"Told you," I said, slipping my heels off. "Now, take it and go. A rerun of my show is on in five."

"Where's the rest?"

"You get what you get, and you don't throw a fit."

His eyes narrowed, but I wasn't too worried. If he touched me, he'd be found skinned alive in an alleyway by six a.m. tomorrow. And he knew it.

"Fine." He tried to scoop every last fleck of powder off the counter, and I grimaced at the unattractive show.

My gaze caught on someone walking down the hall through the crack of the door. Black suit. Broad shoulders. Straight lines. My heart cooled before icing over. His gaze was lowered as his hands twisted a silencer onto the barrel of a gun.

My throat tightened, and panic bit at my veins.

He looked up. His eyes were cold enough to give me frostbite.

"No," I breathed.

But it was too late.

He pushed the door open, and his lazy, heartless gaze found Charming. A muffled *pop* hit my ears. Blood splattered across the counter and cupboards. White powder dusted into the air as Charming hit the floor, cloudy blue eyes wide open, a bullet hole in his forehead.

Bile rose in my throat, and I hunched over, covering my mouth.

I looked at the door to see a stare of dark indifference as Allister twisted the silencer off and put it in his pocket.

His apathy filled me with an anger so deep I saw red.

"*Figlio di puttana!*" I spat. *You son of a bitch.*

As he turned to the door, cold panic flared in my chest.

"Wait," I pleaded. "Please don't leave me with this! Allister!"

He didn't even look back.

"Ace . . . he's dead." My hand shook around the burner phone I was supposed to use for issues like this. "*Really* dead."

"Who?"

"Charming," I mumbled, eyeing the body on the floor. I wasn't making any sense, but the blood was about to soak into my area rug.

"Where are you?"

"My apartment."

"*Jesus*," he muttered. "What the fuck did you do?"

I paced the living room. "I didn't do anything! Allister shot him and then just left!"

A long pause. "For fuck's sake."

"There's blood all over my kitchen," I whined. I heard Nico talking to someone, and while he did, the blood reached my vintage area rug. "I'm going to kill him," I admitted calmly.

"You're going to tell him thank you, and then shut your damn mouth."

"I'd rather throw myself from my balcony."

"If you fuck my relationship with Allister, Gianna . . ."

I frowned. "What do you mean? I thought he was just one of your men?"

He laughed. "He's his own man. It took my father a long time to convince him to work with us, and if you've fucked it up I'm gonna strangle the shit out of you."

Oh. No wonder Allister always looked at me like I was simple-minded when I'd talk to him like he was the help. I swallowed. "I'm one measly girl. What could I have done to ruin your relations with the dirty fed?"

He grunted. "You're only 'measly' when it's convenient to you. Do not go *anywhere*. Do you understand me?"

"But his eyes are open—"

"Nowhere, Gianna."

"Fine."

I hung up and tossed the phone on the couch.

Twenty minutes later, Lorenzo and Luca entered the apartment. Lorenzo whistled, giving Charming's leg a kick. "He's dead, all right."

I grimaced. "Could you not kick a dead man?"

Luca dropped to his haunches beside the body. "Gianna, do I want to know why this douchebag was in your apartment?"

I was trying to win a game . . . and lost so hard.

"No," I sighed.

Lorenzo rubbed some blow from the kitchen island onto his gums. "I know this guy," he said. "Knox, I think. Real slimy dude, been visited by our enforcers a couple times for gambling debt. Still owes some money."

"I don't think you're going to get it from him now," I muttered, heading into my room. I took a shower and then blow-dried my hair and pulled it up. I dressed in Daisy Dukes and an off-the-shoulder top that showed a few inches of my midriff. When I came back out, the body was gone but blood still coated every surface of my kitchen. Anger grabbed me by the throat and squeezed.

Lorenzo and Luca walked through the front door, laughing at some joke.

"Where does Allister live?" I asked, not able to control the venom in my voice.

Luca snorted. "What do you think you're going to do to him?"

Lorenzo shook his head. "He's not someone you fuck with, Gianna."

"Where. Does. He. Live?"

Luca shrugged. "Sometimes, little girls need to learn a lesson or two." I gritted my teeth at his response but forgot the vendetta as soon as he rattled off the name of an apartment building.

"Call a couple men in. I ain't cleaning up this shit." Luca's voice trailed off as I slammed the front door behind me.

Rage vibrated in my veins the entire drive to Allister's place.

The high-rise was nicer than any special agent could afford. It touched the sky, all sleek lines and dark glass.

Since Allister wasn't expecting me, I had to charm the woman at the front desk with every ounce of sweetness in me. I might have convinced her I was Allister's long-distance girlfriend and that I suspected he was cheating on me. A tear made its way down my cheek.

Shaniqua sighed in sympathy. "Oh, honey, you go on up there. And if you don't beat his ass, I will."

Allister's apartment was one of three on the forty-third floor.

My hand shook with anger as I pounded on the door. After the first three knocks came up empty, I raised my hand again, but the door opened before I could make contact.

Without looking at him, I marched past him and into his apartment. I wasn't sure what I was going to do, but I'd rather not do it in front of the security camera in the hall.

I didn't take in a single detail of the space because all I could see was red soaking into my vintage rug. I tensed as the door shut with a small *click*, and then turned to see him leaning against it. His arms were crossed, white dress shirt pulled tight across his biceps. A single light above the kitchen island lit the space, and a shadow caressed the side of his face. Darkness loved him—I knew without a doubt they were on good terms.

I couldn't help but think this was a man all other men aspired to be. He was the perfect prototype, and everyone else had just gotten the small details wrong.

As he watched me with a dark, half-lidded stare, I became abundantly aware that I stood in his domain. With his large form blocking the door. With the oxygen in the apartment burning up like fuel.

His eyes dropped, almost unwillingly, to coast the length of my bare legs, from the frayed hem of my shorts to my sparkly-painted toes. His attention came back up and, like the glide of a drop of sweat down my back, it brushed the diamond piercing in my navel, over my breasts and my throat, before reaching my eyes.

My heart raced with an edgy beat. I didn't understand it—not him, or my reaction to him—and that made my blood flow with pure anger and frustration.

I strode toward him, and just as my palm was about to make contact with his face, he caught my wrist, spun me around, and slammed my back against the door. It rattled under the contact, and a breath of air escaped me.

Anger heated my cheeks, and I tried to fight him off, to twist out of his hold, but, calmly, he held my wrists in a vise grip against my chest and I couldn't escape. The struggle was fruitless, and eventually I went still, my heavy breaths filling the room. And because I could do nothing else, I growled, "I hate you."

Animosity felt heavy in the air, though I could almost hear the strike of a match as something else sparked to life.

"I warned you, Gianna . . ." It was soft and gentle but underlined with the slightest clench of his teeth. I knew he meant the warning he'd given me about being alone with him.

"You don't scare me," I breathed.

He pressed my wrists against the door on either side of me and slowly slid them above my head. I panted, a languid sensation pulling on my muscles. His grip was like fire, though his presence was intimidating and cold to the touch. A shiver rolled through me as his lips pressed against my ear.

"You never were very smart."

His hands were like shackles holding my wrists above my head as he looked at me—from my eyes, to my lips, to my breasts that moved with each inhale and exhale. I became hyperaware of every breath. The slow, melodic puffs of air. Confusion battled with the warmth making a path beneath the waistband of my shorts.

His gaze met mine. *Blue.* Cool silk sheets beneath a darkening sky. Although, there was something else. A flicker of something bright and full of life. Like the reflection in a neurotic person's eyes. It was madness. It was *obsession.*

A tremble rocked me as he pressed his face into my neck. Inhaled. And then made a low sound of satisfaction in the back of his throat. The deep, rough noise thrummed between my legs, and instinctively, I tilted my head to bare more of my neck. My ponytail skimmed across my bare shoulder as it fell to the other side.

His grip on my wrists tightened, and my eyes grew half-lidded from the pressure.

So, this was what it felt like to be touched by him . . .

Addictive.

He held my wrists with one hand as the other slid down to my throat. Stepping closer, he pressed his front to mine. Until we were flush with one another. Until my breasts burned under the heat of his chest. Sparks lit beneath my skin, sizzling every time he shifted enough to brush my nipples.

His heart, it was beating so hard. And it wasn't from exertion. I wasn't fighting him. I didn't know what this was, but I didn't have a single thought in me to analyze it. I'd never felt more alive.

He stepped away from me so suddenly my entire body screamed in protest. A draft hit my skin, but it couldn't cool the fire in my blood. It was so quiet I could hear the thrum of my heart and the ticking of a distant clock.

His eyes were darker than I'd ever seen them, as though the black of his pupil was bleeding into the blue. He blinked like he was trying to clear his head.

It hit me in a rush.

This man was hot for me—the proof had been pressed against me a moment ago—but now I knew he hated it. He ran his tongue across his teeth, turned, and moved away from me, tension radiating from every inch of him.

I wasn't like any of the women I'd seen him with. He preferred classy, composed, and docile. I was the opposite. He wanted me, and he hated it.

I was his own little game.

If he touched me, he'd lose.

I suddenly knew, this was a game I wanted to play with everything in me.

He moved into the kitchen. With white cabinets and gun-metal countertops, the area was cool and sophisticated, just like its owner. He grabbed a bottle of vodka from a cupboard and, in my humble opinion, poured a little too much into his glass.

The anger from earlier had drifted away under the heat of his hands on me, and while I wanted it back, I wanted to play with him more.

I pushed off the front door. "Why, yes. I'd love one, thank you."

His shoulders tensed the slightest bit before easing into indifference. "I don't remember offering."

"I know," I said, slipping my sandals off and making myself comfortable. "Which was rude, by the way, but I'm gracious enough to forgive you."

He turned to lean against the counter. "I'm relieved to hear it. Now, get out."

I strode toward him, and his gaze watched every step I made. It sent the fire in my blood sparking with electricity.

I ran my finger along the smooth marble counter as I walked around it. "Where are you from, Officer?"

"Iowa."

I pulled myself onto the kitchen island to face him, and a small smile touched my lips. "Not this again. Iowa has never seen your pretty face."

He stared. Drew his teeth across his bottom lip. Took a sip.

I leaned back on my hands. "Such a secretive man," I mused. "Don't you know, sharing is caring?"

"If that's your new motto, then you'll tell me if you've let that prick Vincent touch you."

My smile faltered at the animosity in his voice.

What would he do if I said yes? With the reminder of the blood that surely still dripped down my kitchen cupboards, I was going to let that curiosity go.

"Sure," I said. "I'll tell you, and then you can tell me how many women you've screwed. It'll be like show and tell"—I feigned a pout—"without the showing, sadly."

He wasn't amused in the slightest.

I tried to imagine him with other women, what it would look like. I couldn't picture him making out on a couch. That was my favorite: kissing, rubbing, grinding. Getting so worked up there was no return.

My next words were soft and sensual. I wished I could say it was all for the game, but even the thought of pressing my mouth to this man's sent a shiver through me.

"Do you kiss, Officer?"

Unsurprisingly, he didn't respond. He only watched me with a dry, half-lidded stare that conveyed I wasn't worthy of a single word from him.

My heart pattered to an awkward beat.

I never had preferred large men . . . but, God, I wanted a taste of this one.

His eyes narrowed as I slid from the island and walked toward him. Stepping close enough to feel his heat, I grabbed his glass and took a sip.

I suddenly wanted to know how this man fucked—if his OCD tendencies came to the bedroom, or if it made him even dirtier.

I stepped on each of his shoes and then rose to my tiptoes. With a shot of vodka on my tongue, my lips hovered close to his. Close enough to kiss. Close enough to bite and lick. My breasts brushed his chest and heat shot straight to my core. When his lips parted, I let the liquor trickle from my mouth to his. Pure lust erupted inside me so violently I grew dizzy. I ran my hands up his abs, curled my fingers into his chest, as if I could claw my way through his shirt. He was so hard and warm, and smelled so good I could get lost in him.

Sliding a hand up his neck and grabbing a fistful of hair, I pushed the rest of the liquid into his mouth with my tongue.

Hot. Wet. Exhilarating. My stomach swooped and dived, stealing my breath. I knew without a doubt that sharing a sip of vodka with this dirty fed was the most thrilling thing I had ever done.

Butterflies on fire fluttered through my veins as his tongue slid across mine. With a rough sound from deep in his chest, he sucked the alcohol from it. And then he bit my lip hard enough I yelped and fell back a step.

My lips tingled.

My heart pounded in my ears.

I couldn't catch my breath.

"You're playing with fire, sweetheart." His voice was black velvet set out to freeze.

I secretly loved it when he called me sweetheart. It was rare, but every time he did, there was this rough lilt to it I couldn't place. And it always rolled down my spine in the same way: electric.

His gaze was so cold it gave me chills, and in some careless, terrifying manner I'd never seen from the strait-laced fed, he dropped his tumbler to the floor. It shattered across the tile, sending a tremor through me.

I eyed the shards of glass and muttered, "That's going to be a mess to clean up."

"You couldn't survive me, Gianna." It was just a statement of fact. "Nothing fragile ever does."

Staring at a piece of glass that was so close to my feet it reflected my sparkly nail polish, the broken tumbler took on another meaning.

It was *me*, after this man was done with me.

The panic attack he'd witnessed two years ago was suddenly loud between us. And, unfortunately, it wouldn't be the last he'd ever see.

My mind was spinning, and I blurted the first thing that came to mind. "You killed Charming."

He didn't blink at the nickname. "He's not the first."

"And won't be the last?" I mused. "What about me, Officer? Would you kill me?"

I held my breath as he stepped forward, lightly grasping my throat.

"It would make my life a lot easier," he drawled, caressing my fluttering pulse with a thumb before pressing down on it slightly. His hand on me, rough, and covered in the blood of all his enemies—and most likely innocents—shouldn't affect me the way it did. But I was burning up, and I needed more. So much more.

Nonetheless, he stepped away from me.

I turned to follow him with my eyes as he walked around the island. "I know you probably already feel awful about it, but you missed my birthday this year."

"Awful," he agreed, his voice dry.

"See, I knew it. But that's okay, because you can make it up to me now."

"Ah." A small smile pulled on a corner of his lips. "You want your present."

Of the physical sort, yes. I wanted my clothes off. I wanted to drop to my knees and make this man feel good. I wanted his hands on me, his head between my legs. And if I survived all of that, I wanted him inside me. I knew it would be the best sex I'd ever had.

My eyes must have conveyed my thoughts, because his gaze darkened. "I'm not one of your admirers. I'm not going to hold my dick and pine over you, just waiting for the day you might choose me. If I fuck you, Gianna, nobody else ever will."

My stomach dropped, and I almost choked on my next breath.

"If you don't get your ass out of my apartment while you still can"—his voice drifted to a dark rasp—"there's no going back from this."

A shiver rolled down my spine.

He would tie himself to a relationship with me just because we'd had sex? *Why?* I was sure he didn't apply the same stipulations to his other women, or surely, they'd all agree animatedly. Maybe he was just trying to scare me, but regardless, I wasn't going to underestimate him this time, not now that I knew he was his own man and that he could easily hold my future in his palm if he wanted to.

I didn't want another man controlling my life, especially one who hated that he was even attracted to me.

A piece of glass cut into my foot, and I winced but quietly made my way to the door. "This has been riveting, but, honestly, it's a little intense for a first date. I'm going to have to be more particular about who I swipe right on from now on."

His narrowed gaze fell to my feet. "You're bleeding."

I laughed with an angry edge. "Don't get me started on blood, Allister. You're buying me a new rug."

"Stop."

I ignored him. "By the way, I had to convince Shaniqua I was your girlfriend and that I thought you were a cheating bastard. Hope that's okay."

Before I realized he was so close, he grabbed me by the waist from behind and picked me up. It felt like I was a Pollyanna doll being tugged around. "Put me down, Allister. I don't sleep with feds."

"If I decided I wanted you, *sleep* is not the word I would use."

He set me on the bathroom counter, and for some reason, a rush of nerves shot through me.

"Why don't you want me?" I asked. "Is it because your good looks would pale beside mine?"

His eyes were lazy and unamused as he reached behind me and opened a cabinet. His arm singed as it brushed mine. His body heat overwhelmed me. And his deep, masculine scent made my head dizzy. My limbs felt heavy and light all at once, my skin buzzing like a live wire.

Out of breath, I watched him set a bottle of peroxide, a cotton ball, and a Band-Aid next to me.

He lifted my foot and began to gently clean the cut himself. I swallowed, stunned quiet. I couldn't remember the last time anyone had ever done something like this for me. Not since Mamma. How could a man be so cold, and yet so warm all at once?

My heart tripped over its next beat.

I ached. For human contact. For, unexpectedly, *him.*

I had always been impulsive, never thinking things through. I lived for the moment, for the high and the feeling, and right now, I would do anything to have this man's hands on me.

With a shaky pulse, I slipped my shirt off and dropped it next to his feet. He went so still even the air quieted, but he took his time putting the Band-Aid on before he let himself look up. Bottomless. *Mesmerizing.* And hotter than fire. I unclipped my bra while he watched, letting it drop to the floor.

My breasts felt tight and heavy, and the satisfaction from him just looking at my body was nearly overwhelming. My voice came out on a breath.

"You never answered my question, Officer."

Do you kiss? The silent words floated in the air between us.

He stepped between my legs, and his eyes on my breasts were so hot it sent a flush up my neck. He circled a thumb over the button of my shorts, and my nipples tightened.

"Who am I kissing?"

My heart was racing so fast I couldn't catch my breath.

He popped the button through the hole.

"One of your women," I breathed.

I leaned back on my hands to lift my hips as he pulled my shorts and thong down my legs. He threw them to the side and focused his gaze between my spread thighs. His eyes darkened, and he ran a hand across his mouth.

I couldn't say I was a very modest woman, but I'd never thought I'd be naked, spread-eagled for this man I hated on his bathroom counter. A shiver rolled through me, and he ran a finger down the goosebumps on my arm.

"What do you think?" he said.

He didn't kiss. And for some reason, I didn't know if I should feel pleased or disappointed. What I did know was that I wanted to press my lips to this man's for hours, until I didn't know where I ended and he began.

His thumb traced my well-maintained landing strip. My stomach tightened. My blood was on fire. He'd never looked at me this way, with such a soft, consuming desire in his eyes, like he'd never seen a woman before. Like I was *everything.*

It terrified me.

I gasped as he pulled my head back by my hair, pressed his lips to my neck, and made a wild, rough sound of anger, like he'd just been forced to surrender a hard-fought fight. "Play with fire, sweetheart," he rasped, "you're gonna get burned."

He lifted me off the counter, and I wrapped my legs around his waist. Walking me down the hall, he held me tightly, as if I was precious, or as if he couldn't figure out how to hurt me first.

He dropped me on the bed. My breasts bounced from the impact, and his heavy gaze caressed me there. Slipping a hand up my stomach, he cupped one, squeezed. Rubbed a thumb across my nipple.

I exhaled, pleasure blazing a path to my core.

"Should have known you would be this perfect," he murmured.

My heart warmed but the feeling was interrupted as he flipped me onto my stomach. His hands caressed my ass, each grabbing a handful.

"Wait . . ." I breathed. "Are we going back to the chalkboard? Before you said all that weird stuff?" A shiver shot up my spine as he nipped my ass cheek.

"Drawing board," he corrected, before kissing and lightly sucking on my inner thigh.

"Yeah, that—" I moaned, digging my fingers into the sheets as the wet heat of his tongue swept between my legs. "Oh, God . . ."

He groaned low in his throat, and then he flipped me onto my back, his body covering mine, his hard-on settling between my legs. Placing a hand on either side of me, he leaned in and nipped my breast before sucking the nipple deep. Heat erupted inside of me, liquefying in my veins. I grabbed his biceps, only able to get my hands around a quarter of them. Antonio was tall and strong, but he wasn't this thick. A wave of nervousness rushed in. I preferred normal-sized men because they were more on my level; I didn't fear they could crush my windpipe with a single squeeze.

Maybe I was getting over my head.

But then he switched breasts, pinching one nipple and sucking the other.

Oh, well.

"Take off your shirt," I begged.

I wanted to feel him—the muscle beneath his skin, the heat of his body, the heavy beat of his heart against mine.

I stilled in anticipation when he lifted his head because I thought he was going to kiss me, but he only pressed his mouth to my ear. "I'll let you know when I start taking orders from little Italian girls." It was a harsh and arrogant statement, but his voice was so full of lust it only drove me crazier. I rolled my hips, rubbing myself up and down his erection as he kissed a hot, wet line down my neck.

I moaned, scraping my nails down his arms, trying to crawl into his skin.

He dropped back between my legs, not hesitating before dipping his head and licking me from entrance to clit. The growl of satisfaction that escaped him vibrated against me, and I already fought the imminent orgasm. He ran a rough hand down my leg, pulling my thigh over his shoulder. It was almost tender, the soft sweep of his palm against my skin, and a beat skipped in my chest.

I ran my fingers through his hair, but he shook my hand off, so I grabbed two fistfuls of the comforter instead, while spewing unintelligible English and Italian as he pushed his tongue inside me. *In and out. In and out.* My eyes rolled back in my head, my spine arching off the bed. A drop of sweat ran between my breasts. He worked me like he'd been there before, knowing just how much to give before pulling back.

In a mindless state, I ran a hand into his hair again, grabbing a handful and moving my hips at the same time, trying to keep his attention where I needed it. He let me control the movement for only a second. He nipped at my clit and I yelped, trying to jump back and out of his hold. Pain pulsed in that spot.

His narrowed gaze found mine. "You take what I give you."

I glared, barely biting back the retort on my tongue.

"Go ahead and say it," he warned.

I did say it, because one, he'd goaded it from me, and two, I was a glutton for punishment.

"You're an asshole."

I was expecting it, but I still had to hold in a gasp when he smacked me between the legs. Dark satisfaction crawled up from where I'd hidden her deep inside, fiery-red hair and all.

"Anything else?"

Defiance ignited inside me, but I bit my tongue and shook my head.

"Good," he murmured, his gaze lazy, before sucking at my clit.

It still throbbed with pain, but the wet heat of his mouth was electrifying, setting my entire body on fire. The pressure built and built as he continued to draw out my release for as long as he could. I cried out, squirming against his immovable hold.

I wanted to run my hands all over him, but I knew, if I touched his precious hair he'd stop. So, I rested a hand over his on my thigh, locking my fingers with his, and in pure, mindless lust, tugged at my hair with the other.

Sparks burned hotter, and then, suddenly, the pressure exploded. I came so hard my ears rang, pulling all sounds underwater. I closed my eyes and struggled to catch my breath. A languid sensation pulled on my muscles, and I'd never felt such peace come over me. He said something, but I couldn't hear a word of it.

My eyes fluttered open to see his on me. His breathing was uneven, and his gaze was filled with something soft and dark that I wasn't sure I wanted to understand.

He was much different than a man I would choose in a crowd, but maybe that was why I found him so appealing. He terrified me a little bit, and I always did like to live on the edge.

Crawling to my knees, I knelt in front of him, rested my hands on his chest, and pressed my lips to his neck. The small taste made me feel dizzy. I kissed him from his ear down to his collar, and he inhaled a heavy breath. I tried to undo his tie, but he stopped me by grabbing my wrist. He held onto it as I went lower, running my face down his stomach, kissing his abs through his shirt. His hand settled in my hair, running through my locks.

The ringing of a phone cut through the air. He stilled, and I knew—call it intuition—that if he got up, this was over. I wasn't ready. *Rrring, rrring, rrring.* With my eyes on him, I licked his erection through his pants. He let out a rough noise of frustration. When I reached for his belt buckle, he grabbed my wrist again.

I moaned in protest as he pulled away from me and walked to his jacket, which hung on the back of a chair in front of a large floor-to-ceiling window. I lay on my stomach and watched him answer the call.

"Allister."

His eyes didn't stray from me as he spoke on the phone.

I thought I could hear a man on the other line, and it didn't sound like he was speaking any language I understood.

"When did you last see him?" Allister was quiet for a while before a spark of frustration lit in his eyes. "I'll be there tomorrow." He hung up.

Silence swept into the room.

This was over.

Disappointment . . . and something heavier flooded me.

But then he dropped to his haunches in front of me, ran a hand across my cheek, and kissed me. Shock and warmth erupted in my chest. I moaned, wrapped my arms around his shoulders, and climbed onto him until I sat on his thighs. He tasted so good, so addictive. And I savored every lick and dip, every press of our lips. He kissed me without any reservation, like he had a right to, like I was *his*.

The kiss became different than any I'd ever experienced. More gentle . . . more momentous, and I didn't like that. I reached for his belt, but he stopped me with a vise grip on my wrist.

"Allister," I begged.

"I just had my tongue inside you," he said, annoyed. "You can start calling me by my first name."

I opened my mouth. Closed it.

His eyes darkened as he took in my expression. "You forgot my name."

When I didn't deny it, he shook his head and then dropped me on my ass on the bed. *Oh, God, what was it?* I'd been tipsy when I'd asked him a while ago, and it hadn't helped that I only ever referred to him as Allister or Officer.

"I have to go away for a while," he said, slipping his suit jacket on. "You can stay here tonight, or I'll take you home."

"What's your name?" I asked.

"Do your goddamn homework before getting in someone's bed, Gianna."

I narrowed my eyes. "You know the name of every woman you sleep with?"

"Yes."

I sighed, suddenly feeling very naked. And tired. I didn't want to go to my apartment, not tonight. Magdalena only came by a few times a week, and it was lonely there.

"I'd like to stay here," I murmured.

He stopped in front of me. "We'll talk about this when I get back."

"This?"

"Us."

Oh. A myriad of confusing feelings rushed me at once, so I decided to avoid all of them.

"Do you have a decent cereal selection?"

He ran a thumb across my cheek. "You won't forget me." It was an order, but a tiny amount of vulnerability showed through. It warmed my chest. My hair was a mess, the hair tie slipping halfway down my ponytail. He pulled it from the messy locks and then put it in his pocket.

"How could someone ever forget your face?" I said.

For some reason, he thought that was funny. A smile touched the corner of his lips, and it was so sexy I stood up and kissed him. He made a noise of disapproval in the back of his throat, but he let me have that kiss. Soft, wet, and sweet.

He slipped a business card into my hand. "Call this number if you need anything."

"Sure thing, Officer."

He smacked me lightly on the ass and walked out of the room.

I later did my homework. His name was Christian.

But it didn't matter.

It would be three more years before I'd ever see him again.

I walked down 7th Avenue, struggling to balance my phone, latte, yoga mat, and purse.

"I mean, what kind of guy goes down on a girl and then doesn't even call her back so she can reciprocate?" Those were the first words out of Valentina's mouth after I'd had to juggle my things to get my phone to my ear.

"Why did I tell you about this again?" I asked.

"Because I'm an expert of men, and you wanted me to dissect your pretty fed's brain."

True. "And?"

"I can't believe I'm saying this, but, honey, I don't think he's into you."

I mulled that around. I couldn't say her words felt right—he *kissed* me—but why else wouldn't he have even called after two weeks? A vulnerability had followed me around since that night. He'd seen me naked, had made me come apart under his hands. I'd *begged* him for more. And I'd gotten nothing from him. He hadn't even taken off his stupid tie. Maybe it was all part of his game. Or maybe he was already bored of me. Frustration heated my cheeks.

"He only had Raisin Bran," I muttered.

"What?"

"Nothing." I took a sip of my latte, then said, "He gave me his number."

"Really? Why haven't you called him?"

"Because I don't want to call him. I just want to know why he hasn't called me." *Perfectly logical.*

Valentina laughed. "Listen, your fed is a total hottie—God knows, I wouldn't tell him no if he'd like to go downtown—but he's dirty. And I mean, *really* dirty."

"Trust me, I already know. He killed Prince Charming."

"What? Oh, never mind. I don't want to know. Ricardo told me nobody knows where the fed's from, that he sort of just popped up in the underworld one day with connections from *La Eme* to the *Bratva*."

I dodged a cyclist at the last second. "Yeah, yeah, yeah, he's this super-important guy with super-important connections . . ." I muttered, rolling my eyes.

"Apparently, he's good with computers, like some kind of genius or something. Like Einstein, just without a conscience. Guess that's why the Bureau picked him up. You can't trust anyone who works for the government, Gianna. He'd probably knock up another woman with twins the second you two became steady."

"Your imagination is extraordinary."

"Thanks."

A beep told me I had another call, and when I saw it was from Chicago a zip of anticipation shot through me.

"I have to go, Valentina. I'll chat with you later."

"Toodles."

I answered the other call. "Hello?"

"Gianna."

The sorrow in her voice cooled my veins.

I stopped in the middle of the sidewalk, my pulse fluttering in my throat. "Tara . . . how is she?"

A long pause, and I knew.

I knew my mamma was dead.

"No . . ." I stood still, but the ground moved, threatening to crumble and swallow me whole. My throat felt thick, and my words were nearly inaudible. "I'm supposed to see her tomorrow." The plane ticket to Chicago suddenly weighed twenty pounds in my purse.

"Gianna . . . I'm so sorry, but she's gone. She was strong for so long . . ."

My latte slipped from my fingers, splattering on the pavement. The sun warmed my skin, but inside, I was nothing but ice. My ears rang, and the bustle of this New York City street was shrouded by the hands of grief.

"I'll come see her tomorrow," I said mindlessly.

"She loved you so very much." Tears and a smile touched the nurse's voice. "You were everything to her."

Pink church dress. Her smile. A hand on my heart. "Dance to this . . . whenever and however you want."

Pain, raw and angry, escaped from its cage deep inside and grabbed me by the throat.

"Why?" I sobbed. Why her? Why was this world so unfair? So bitter? Why did love hurt worse than pain?

"The fact she survived such an aggressive cancer for so long was a miracle, Gianna. You were blessed with more time with her."

The only blessing was Tara. She was the only reason I could see my mamma in the hospice center she'd resided in for the last two years. My papà forbade me from visiting—from breathing, if he could.

Tears burned the backs of my eyes, my heart, my soul. "Thank you, Tara, for everything you did for her . . . for me."

"Yes, well, I couldn't live with myself if I kept a mother from her daughter."

As I stared blankly ahead of me, the world felt so big, so heavy, its weight too painful to bear.

Someone bumped into my shoulder, knocking my phone from my hand.

It cracked on the sidewalk.

I didn't remember how I made it home. But sometime later, I stood on my terrace as rain spilled from the sky. Cold. Lonely. *High.* I cried, sobs that rocked my shoulders. I cried twenty-four years' worth of pain. I cried until my stomach ached and I could cry no more.

It was the last thing I remembered as I woke on a hard jail cell floor.

One count of drug possession and driving under the influence.

Numbness had spread through my veins and settled in my heart. I sat with my arms around my knees, staring ahead. I somehow knew Allister wouldn't come, but I didn't want him to. I didn't want anyone to save me. Maybe this was where I needed to be. Nonetheless, I was escorted out of the precinct thirty minutes later and straight to Ace's club.

He glanced at me, shook his head, and looked back at the papers on his desk. "Do you understand the shit it takes to get you out of jail? I have enough on my plate without having to look out for you."

I understood the significance of what he'd said, but still, I felt nothing. Someone's suit jacket rested on my shoulders. It was heavy, and for a second, I thought it was guilt.

"I'd fucking leave you there if I didn't think you'd crack like an egg the first time someone interrogates you. You need a damn therapist, Gianna," he bit out, running a hand through his hair. "The shit you went through . . . Your papà makes me fucking sick. I wanted to end him when I was ten years old."

Our fathers had been family friends. I'd known Nico since I was five, and he six. Maybe it was the perfect romantic story—Nico had seen most of my twisted little pieces. But I could never love Nico. He hadn't saved me.

"I know what you're going to say, but I have to ask it: Would you like to go home to Chicago?"

I shook my head.

"Then your single life is over." His gaze met mine. "Pick one of my men, Gianna, or I will do it for you."

One week later, I became Mrs. Richard Marino.

CHAPTER
Seven

Christian

September 2015

"**H**AVE YOU EVER WANTED SOMETHING, SASHA, SOMETHING YOU COULDN'T shake, no matter how fucking hard you tried?" Her soft, vanilla scent, the impression her hands leave on me for days, her ridiculous clothes, her husky laugh that lights up my body. "Then you get a taste of it . . ." And it gives you fucking chills. "And you forget why you didn't want it in the first place?"

Sasha opened her mouth, closed it. "You want something you can't have." The words poured from her lips in thought and disbelief, like she didn't believe I couldn't have whatever I wanted.

Her and me both.

I rolled the agitation off my shoulders. "I wanted something I *could* have."

"Interesting use of past tense. Maybe you don't want it because you've always known you could never obtain it."

I let out a sardonic breath, hating that Sasha was fucking right.

I'd always set Gianna on an unreachable shelf, and not even because she was newly married to Antonio and oblivious to me when I first met her, but because there was something genuine and astute about her. She'd see me for what I was really was. Dirty. Stained. She'd see everything I'd tried to obliterate about my childhood. And I fought hard to escape my past. I refused to be dragged back.

I should be relieved she was out of reach once again, but, with the recent memory of her lying on my bed, finally staring up at me with sweet, submissive eyes, I didn't feel any form of respite. It felt like something had been fucking stolen from me.

"So, you got a taste for *it* . . . and I'm assuming you realized it was unobtainable once again while in the computer lab last week?"

I ran a thumb across my jaw.

My business overseas had taken longer than I thought, but one month shouldn't be long enough to come home and find Gianna fucking *married*. Hearing the news, nonchalantly, from Ace on the phone had felt like a blow to the stomach. It stole my fucking breath, turned my blood to fire. I'd lost it. I'd destroyed every goddamn computer in that room.

I'd known, if I touched Gianna, it would be over for me. I'd known she would feel too good to ever go back. But, *Jesus*, I wasn't a saint. She was half-naked, her tits in my face, and I'd dreamed about them for so long I had to know what they tasted like. They tasted like they belonged to me; like they were *mine.*

And now, after that realization, she was another man's. I could eliminate that problem within the hour. My hands sometimes shook with the fucking urge. But she wasn't in this like I was. She hadn't called me when she was in trouble. I bet I hadn't even crossed her mind. She'd been under my skin for years, I knew more about her than I ever should, and I wasn't even on her radar.

I suddenly wished I was in Moscow at that moment—to kill my fucking brother. Or better yet, never leave Gianna naked in my bed to go save his ass from the Chechens who'd managed to keep him hostage for the last month. But I knew I could never turn my back on Ronan. He was the only one who understood what made me. He should—he had the same bitch of a mother.

Sasha watched me and cocked her head. "The men you spoke of during our last session, are they still a part of your life?"

"No."

"Why not?"

Because I killed them.

"Your grandparents still in your life, Sasha?"

"No, they're dead."

I let her words fill the silence.

She swallowed. "I hear you've put a request in to transfer to Seattle. That's quite the move."

I could only hope an entire country would be enough.

"In fact, I received an email this morning from our director, who has already approved the transfer on the understanding that I've cleared you, of course."

How passive aggressive.

The Bureau needed me more than I'd ever needed it. Not many could stomach their kill lists and preferred forms of interrogating—not to mention, cleaning up after some sadistic politicians. I could have any job in any outfit I wanted, but the FBI had the structure and front I'd always needed. And to think I could have lost it because of a fucking woman . . .

"I think we both know you are cleared for work. To be honest, I'm not sure why they made you go through this charade."

"Are you disappointed?"

She tucked a strand of hair behind her ear, something light and breathless in her eyes. "No. I've wanted to get into your head for a long time."

My laugh held a dark note. "You're lucky I let you out."

Getting to my feet, I straightened my cuffs and began to leave.

"They have a word for what you've described, Christian."

I paused, my hand on the doorknob.

"Obsession."

A corner of my lips lifted as I stepped out of the room and shut the door behind me.

PART II

The Present

CHAPTER
Eight

Gianna
Present Day

"I JUST—WELL, WHAT I'M TRYING TO SAY IS, WILL YOU MARRY ME?"

I blinked at the man on one knee beside me. Board shorts, no shirt. Holding a massive diamond ring in a black velvet box. If I put it on and fell overboard, I would sink straight to the ocean floor.

Lying on a lounge chair, the yacht gently rocking in the waves, I shielded my eyes from the sun. "Vincent, I thought it was illegal to be married to two men at once? Are you telling me I've been living a lie all this time?"

Vincent sighed. "Everyone knows your marriage is a sham. There's no relationship between you and Richard. You don't even wear a ring."

The diamond he held sparkled in the sun, blinding me. I sat up and wondered why things like this always happened to me. "Even if I could marry you, Vincent . . . I wouldn't because I'd drive you crazy within a week."

"*Crazy,*" Valentina agreed from the chaise beside me, and sipped her mojito through a straw.

"I'm terribly messy," I continued. "Even my housekeeper is messy. That's how messy my life is."

"Gianna, I don't care about any of that. It's just . . . I'm in love with you."

Valentina choked. Then coughed and smacked her chest.

Ironic, how, in our life, a man proposing marriage was less bizarre than an admission of love.

I fingered the gold body chain crisscrossing my bare midsection as my gaze swept the yacht. Everyone's eyes were glued to us. Sympathy filled my chest. Love sucked. I wouldn't wish it on anyone. Well, except Hitler. And definitely Lord Voldemort.

I stood. "Come get a drink with me, will you, Vincent?"

He sighed, lifted his head to the sky. He knew I was going to turn him down gently, but eventually, he closed the ring box with a sad little click and got to his sandaled feet. I padded below deck and headed toward the small bar with every intention of making a really strong drink.

"Why do you love me?" I asked, pouring Patrón into a glass.

He rubbed the back of his neck. "You're . . . so . . . gorgeous, Gianna. Whenever I see another woman, I can't stop myself from comparing her to you."

Was that all it took to love someone?

I reached for the orange juice, but at the last minute, changed course and instead added more tequila to the glass.

"I want to take care of you, Gianna . . . to get to know you better than anyone else."

Now, that was kind of sweet.

Nevertheless, this man would run for the hills the moment he became aware of my daddy issues. Vincent loved the me he saw: the bubbly, fresh, and social me. He wouldn't know what to do with the mess underneath, the one I tried to hide one panic attack at a time.

"Vincent, you know I can't marry you." I turned around, and that's when he kissed me. My full glass of tequila sloshed over the rim and onto my hand. He grabbed my face between his warm, soft hands and pressed his lips against mine. Gently. Passively. Like if he wasn't careful, I'd break.

Bite me. Pull my hair. Push my back against the wall.

Still, the press of his lips was soft and sweet and uninspiring. A sigh of disappointment played in my mind. He pulled back, breaths heavy, like he'd had an entirely different experience than me.

That was the first kiss I'd had since an unmentionable dirty fed. And while a part of me was dying for more, from anyone who could sate the need inside me, the other couldn't be more impassioned.

"That was . . . wow," he breathed.

I tossed back the rest of the liquor. It burned away the taste of his cherry ChapStick.

"Wow, right?" he questioned.

"What?" I mumbled. "Oh, yes . . . wow."

He grabbed my sticky, tequila-doused hand. "Give us a chance, Gianna. I'll take you places—show you the world. There is nothing I wouldn't give you."

I could imagine most women would be over the moon to be in my position right now. But me? It only made me angry. Heat pricked beneath my skin.

"You don't get it, Vincent, do you? I can't just divorce my husband and run away with you." I ripped my hand away and realized I had said that in rapid-fire Italian. Heaviness settled on my shoulders. I took a deep breath and tried again in English. "A divorce isn't possible for me, Vincent."

He swallowed, rubbed his brow in thought. "Okay. We don't need the title then. Just . . . be with me."

God, I wished I was less of a Tin Man. I wished all the possible love I could give hadn't been stolen from me the first twenty-odd years of my life. I wished I was normal. Because here stood this perfect man professing his love for me, and my heart didn't even twitch.

"My life isn't as liberating as you must imagine, Vincent. I can't cuckold my husband. I couldn't promise your safety if it was found out." I sighed sadly. "Mine either, honestly." I was pretty sure Ace was on his final straw with me.

Vincent looked disgusted. "Your own family would hurt you?"

A light laugh escaped me, and I was surprised it wasn't bitter. I guessed I had a better grasp on my demons than I thought. "Maybe not physically, but they could make things very unpleasant for me." *Like sending me home to Chicago . . .*

He ran a hand into my hair, lightly grasping the back of my head. The physical contact had become so foreign over the years goosebumps rose on my skin.

"We can keep us a secret."

"This isn't Romeo and Juliet," I said quietly, pulling his hand from my hair. "But if you push this, Vincent, we might end up like them."

I stepped around him and headed back to the deck.

My mamma's words filled my head with a sense of melancholy and the smell of her floral perfume.

One day, you're going to be a little heartbreaker.

What a terrible fate.

I wrestled my apartment door open, dropping my purse in the process, and then flicked on the light. The bulb in the living room popped and then faded, bathing the room in darkness.

"Oh, no, no, no," I muttered, as my eyes drifted to the light switch in the kitchen. It sat only ten feet away, yet the distance began to stretch until it felt like a mile. My heart tripped over every beat, and I wiped my clammy hands on my swimsuit cover. *You can do it,* I assured myself. *The dark is only an absence of light. It can't hurt you.*

I stepped forward and then froze in cold fear as the darkness morphed into a house of mirrors, reflecting every nightmare I'd ever lived through. My lungs tightened, and I took a step back.

I slid down the wall beside the door in the hall and tried to stop the shake in my hands. Pulling my phone from my purse, I called Lorenzo. It went straight to voicemail. I cursed, choosing the next contact on the list.

"What?" Luca answered.

I swallowed. "My light bulb burnt out."

He was quiet for a moment. "I thought you were over that shit."

"No, I was just high."

"So save me the trouble and do a line."

"My therapist says drugs don't fix problems, they only prolong them." Now, I only used blow when the loneliness seemed darker than the guilt of a high.

"He did, did he? Just how much are you sharing with him, Gianna?"

"Just all the sordid details of your life."

He grunted. "Must keep him entertained."

"Or nauseous," I retorted.

He made a noise of amusement and then hung up.

I pulled my legs to my chest, rested my head against the wall, and once again waited for a man to save me from a problem another created.

Luca stepped off the elevator twenty minutes later, large form, crisp gray suit, and all. I didn't look at him as I stated matter-of-factly, "There are two-thousand-twenty-two bricks in that wall."

He was amused. "If I wasn't wondering that exact thing myself, I'd say you live a sad life, Gianna."

"Ha ha."

While he changed the bulb, I flipped on every light in the apartment for simple peace of mind. "You want a beer?" I asked.

"No."

I got one for myself and plopped onto the couch. As I went to take the first drink, the beer was ripped from my hands. I sighed.

"Really?"

Luca took a pull on the bottle and sat beside me. He was a large man and didn't care how much space he took up. Rather than feeling like a sardine in a can, I stretched out my legs, resting them across his.

"We need to have a chat." He rested an arm across my thighs, his eyes coasting around the living room.

"About?"

"Well, first off, your marriage—or lack thereof—with Richard, and your ever-growing relationship with Vincent Monroe."

I sighed, knowing I was in trouble. "I would love to discuss that with you, but, *gosh*, I'm hungry. Are you hungry?" I tried to jump to my feet, but he grabbed one of my thighs, making me choose to fall back to the couch rather than awkwardly to the floor.

"People are talking, Gianna."

I stole my beer back. "Why do you care if people talk?"

"Ace is getting married, and we need to keep up appearances with the Abellis."

"Oh yeah. Poor Adriana." I pouted my lips and took a sip.

"You will attend the luncheon this Sunday with Richard."

"Yes, sir." I rolled my eyes.

"And this thing with Vincent needs to cool down. Fast." His gaze went hard. "Or I will cool it down for you."

"I promise you, there's no fire where Vincent is concerned." A part of me wished there was—to be swept up in an intense affair, one in which we'd both rather die than be without each other. A part of me ached for it, while the other didn't believe in fairy tales.

"Where there's Gianna, there's fire," Luca muttered, pushing my legs off him and getting to his feet.

"Thank you, Luca."

He made a noise of acknowledgment and shut the door behind him.

Like most nights, I headed to the kitchen. The recipe was my mamma's. All of them were. Some of them I'd forgotten or hadn't gotten a chance to ever ask about, and I often fantasized of going to Chicago in a blaze of glory just to retrieve her old cookbooks. My imagination was a sad place.

The smell of carbonara filled the apartment as I sat at the table with my plate.

The quiet ticking of the clock dulled my mind. A siren blared somewhere below on a busy street. The air conditioner kicked on.

I spun some pasta onto my fork and took a bite.

Unfortunately, loneliness still thrived in the light.

CHAPTER
Nine

Gianna

THE ELEVATOR MUSIC PLAYING SOFTLY IN THE BACKGROUND MIGHT AS WELL have been screamo as I walked down an aisle of my local CVS. I sighed, rubbing my temple. Gunfire always gave me an awful migraine.

It was safe to say the luncheon today went over as smoothly as the Titanic. Or maybe that was being a bit dramatic—there'd only been one casualty, after all. Nonetheless, I could see a forbidden love story in the near future, between Ace and the very wrong sister. I had my money on him breaking the contract with Adriana, so he could have Elena—*literally*. I'd placed my bet with Luca and Lorenzo on the ride home.

I grabbed a bottle of ibuprofen off the shelf and dropped it into my basket. I was perusing the nail polishes when the havoc began.

"Everybody, down, now!" Two men wearing black ski masks stormed the store, slamming the door against the wall. "I said, down!" The taller one fired a shot into the ceiling.

"Oh, for goodness' sake," I muttered.

One of their gazes landed on me. My eyes went wide, and I dropped to the floor.

Someone cried. A baby wailed. Another prayed the Hail Mary.

The masked men—who were very inconsiderate to others, I might add—prowled toward the prescription counter. "Give us what we want, and we won't hurt anyone."

I struggled with opening the painkiller bottle. I tugged too hard, the lid came off, and pills scattered across the floor. A blonde woman clutching her purse from across the aisle watched me in disbelief. I fought an eyeroll. Like she'd never had a migraine at the wrong time. I popped two tablets in my mouth.

"Don't lie to us! You have more!"

"W-we don't have more, sir."

I grabbed a bottle of nail polish from my basket and gave it a shake. The woman's incredulous gaze burned into my skin as I painted the red polish onto my thumbnail. I wrinkled my nose. Too Christmassy.

The men's voices grew frenzied as sirens blared in the distance. Some shuffling ensued, the door dinged, and then they were gone.

I got to my feet, brushed the dirt off my olive-green dress, and headed toward the checkout counter with my half-empty bottle of pills.

"Hello?" I called to the vacant cash register.

I rang the little bell sitting on the counter. Two wide eyes drifted up from behind the register. "Oh, hello." I grinned at the young female cashier. "Can I purchase these, please? Preferably before the police show up and I'm stuck here for God only knows how long."

Unfortunately, that was the moment the entirety of the NYPD stormed the store.

I sighed. Better get some rash cream while I was here.

I was sitting at the back of an ambulance flipping through a pamphlet they'd slapped into my hand for a trauma support group, when the feds arrived. I didn't look up from my brochure as one approached me. If I had to go through the whole question spiel again, I was quitting life.

"Ames Clinical Center," a deep voice read from the leaflet. "Why do I feel like you'd be right at home there?"

My heart hitched, stopping my breath. The sun was heavy and hot, but it wasn't why my skin suddenly ignited from the inside. He had my full attention, but I didn't look at him yet. Simply because I didn't think I could handle the shock of hearing him and seeing him at the same time.

I flipped a page. "I'm not sure, Officer. Have you been there before?" I drew my gaze up to him, my eyes light with the knowledge of his OCD, his blood-stained hands, and trigger-happy finger.

Broad shoulders.

Straight lines.

Blue.

"They haven't tamed you yet, I see." The drawl wrapped around my throat, making it pulse with a maddening tempo.

The sight of him was a punch of fire to the stomach. Some kind of visceral, animal reaction to the mere attractiveness of the man. The memory of the last night I'd seen him rushed back, of his hands on me, and warmth hummed between my legs. He'd been the last man to touch me, and my body hadn't forgotten. In truth, I'd thought about him too much late at night—the rough glide of his palm against my cheek, the press of his lips against mine, the heat of his body. He was easily my favorite fantasy, while I was sure he'd been working his way through every blonde socialite wherever he'd been for the last three years.

Frustration ripped through me. And then an even worse feeling bloomed in my chest—a thorny stem minus the rose; a feeling I'd pushed down every time I thought of him: rejection.

"I'm untamable."

"We both know that's not true."

I stared at him. He wanted to bring up *that* night . . . now? As far as I was concerned, it had never happened. The thought of it in daylight made me feel vulnerable and exposed.

Setting the pamphlet aside, I crossed my legs, leaned back on my hands. "Let me guess, you took a three-year stint from the Bureau to pursue your dream of modeling men's underwear."

He twisted the watch on his wrist, once, twice, three times. Slipping his hands in his pockets, his stare caressed my skin so heavily

I could hardly breathe. He looked pensive, but there was something beneath it . . . like the budding spark of a fire.

I quelled a strange uprising of nerves.

"No?" I probed. "You blackmailed some unfortunate girl to marry you, bought a house in the suburbs, and had two kids."

That was an obvious negative. The next guess escaped me before he could respond.

"You visited Antarctica and realized it was home." I was so pleased with myself for that one, and it showed.

"You done?"

I pursed my lips. "Yes."

"Good. Sheets over there will be heading this way to question you about your relationship with Ace any minute. You can come with me, or deal with him for the next few hours."

I glanced at the special agent in question. He was an attractive man, but my attention couldn't seem to focus on anything other than the fact he wore Asics with his navy suit.

"The lesser of two evils, is it?" I murmured, slipping to the ground and standing in front of him. "Lead the way, Officer."

"Not a very good judge of character," he said, a dark edge in his voice.

I shivered. "Yes, well, we all have our faults."

"Some more than others."

Annoyance flickered through me. I brought my gaze up to his, pity pulling on my lips. "You are so right. A lot of men struggle with impotence. It's nothing to be ashamed about." I patted his chest and began to walk toward his car while ignoring the burning sensation in my hand.

"Still thinking about why I didn't fuck you, huh?"

I paused, closed my eyes as anger tore through me. "The only thing I think about you is how refreshing New York is with you not in it." I continued making my way to his car.

"How you've survived this long with such a terrible sense of direction, I'll never understand."

I stopped, sighed, and then spun around to follow him down the sidewalk. "Don't you know? I have a man hold my hand wherever I go."

"I know—Vincent Monroe. One could debate your use of *man*, however."

I rolled my eyes. "You know nothing about him."

"I know he's only waiting for the day your husband dies to put a ring on your finger."

"The only thing you know is whatever Ace or Luca have told you. That's hearsay in my book, and frankly, none of your business."

Allister had been back for five minutes and already believed he had my story all figured out. I hated how he made my life seem so transparent . . . so *trivial*.

I struggled to keep up with his long strides while simultaneously dodging every New York City pothole in my thigh-high boots. I ended up walking a step behind him, fully immersed in his shadow. How apt it seemed regarding our relationship.

"You changed your hair," he said softly.

I absently touched the dark locks that were my natural color. He always noticed when I did something with my hair. I hated that it made me feel special.

"Yes. I tried to get over you with a makeover. Three years is just too long to wait for a phone call."

"Ah, I wondered how you were faring."

"I won't dye it back for you either. Being blonde is exhausting. I had way too much fun."

"So I've heard."

I tensed. I had a feeling he was talking about the last time I'd been arrested shortly after he'd disappeared three years ago. There was nothing I could say to explain myself, and then I remembered I didn't have to care about what he thought of me.

"You seem to have heard a lot about me," I mused.

"I'm informed about all the disasters in the New York City area."

"Good to know I'm up there with hurricanes and terrorist attacks." I stepped over a banana peel. "So, what unfortunate circumstance brought you back from . . .?"

"Seattle."

"Seattle, then?"

"Business."

"A man of few answers," I murmured.

"Few *words*," he corrected.

His eyes found mine as we reached his car, and just the look sent my heart flipping in my chest. It had been a long time since I'd seen him. But a prickling feeling on the back of my neck made me believe this wasn't the first time he'd seen me in three years. Though, if he'd been in New York—anywhere in my vicinity—I couldn't have missed him. Not with this web of electricity between us that always strummed when he was near. What concerned me was, on the other end of a web often lay a spider in wait to devour its prey.

I swallowed and slid into my seat.

A tense air filled the space, shortening my breath. A feeling that he was going to touch me . . . or hurt me. I trusted the man about as far as I could throw him—a negative number of inches—and a nervous energy coursed through my veins.

Should've tried my luck with Asics.

"So . . . how long are you going to be in town?" I asked.

"Why? Counting the days?"

"You know me so well, Officer. We should play The Newlywed Game." I began to apply some lip gloss just because I needed to do something with my hands.

"You'd think they'd have a requirement for contestants to at least know each other's names," he said dryly.

"You always were a stickler for the rules, weren't you, *Christian?*"

The look he gave me reminded of the heat in his eyes as I'd sat spread-eagled on his bathroom counter. I glanced away and tried to calm my racing heart.

He took me home. He never asked for my address, and I wasn't surprised. Allister seemed to know everything he shouldn't.

"No ring?" he drawled, glancing at my bare finger. "And here I was, sure this marriage would be the one to last." He was mocking me.

I wouldn't be married now if he hadn't disappeared while I was still naked in his bed. I knew it deep inside. Things would've been different if he had stayed. But he didn't. He didn't care enough. And over the years, I'd begun to resent him for it. He didn't want me—he'd made that abundantly clear—yet he had to torment me about my relationship, as nonexistent and embarrassing as it was.

My husband Richard was three times my age. He was the oldest available man I'd had the choice to marry, so, naturally, he was the one I'd picked. Too old to hit me, and, as harsh as it sounded, closer to biting the dust than any of the others.

"I have an idea—why don't you save us both the trouble and not pretend to care?"

"Someone has to. Can't say I'm surprised, though, that your husband turns out to be one of Ace's richest men. Must make the marriage bed easier to stomach."

A bitter laugh escaped me, and I turned my head to look out the window.

"Go to hell, Allister."

CHAPTER
Ten

Gianna

"**H**E INSINUATED I WAS A MONEY-HUNGRY WHORE," I TOLD VAL, PULLING a cucumber slice off my eye and taking a bite of it. "Does this cucumber thing even do anything?"'

"Yes, but only if you can manage not to eat it," Val said dryly, blindly reaching for a bowl of fresh slices beside her lounge chair and handing it to me. "And, seriously, what an asshole! As if you wanted to marry an old geezer."

"I know." I sighed and shoved a cucumber slice in my mouth.

"Can you imagine if you'd picked another of Ace's men? You'd be waddling around pregnant with your third child already." She shivered. Val had so far escaped the same fate with her husband Ricardo only because she was dealing with infertility. Or, so she claimed, anyway.

"Maybe I should have . . . chosen another." The words escaped me, disturbing me as much as Valentina. I was married by name only, but I'd still been held in tight chains while being denied a family of my own. Sometimes, I thought I was beginning to desire more in life.

"What?" She sounded incredulous. "You don't mean that."

"No, of course not," I said quickly. *Right . . . ?* "I'm just tired, is all. Magdalena woke me up early vacuuming while spewing complaints about all the dust."

Valentina laughed. "Magdalena, vacuuming?"

"Apparently, she has a date tonight, and she can't make dinner for him at her apartment because her lazy daughter is home. Her words, not mine."

"Lord, is it weird I want to be a fly on the wall for that date?"

"No," I chuckled.

"If you're letting her use your place, where are you going to stay?"

"I'll probably just sleep at the penthouse after the party tonight." I used to live there the last year Antonio and I were married, when I was avoiding him at all costs. It was Ace's now, but it was still a second home to me.

Val groaned. "Honestly, I'm tired of all these get-togethers with the Abellis. It's not like us women need to get used to their presence for the wedding. I say, let's put all our men and theirs in one room and see what happens."

I laughed. "Exactly. Us women are most likely the only thing keeping the peace."

"True," she sighed. "Women are goddesses."

Legs crisscrossed on the lounge chair, I brought my gaze to the cloudless sky. *Andromeda.*

"So . . . how's he looking these days?"

I ate another cucumber with a crunch. "Who?"

"Christian, of course."

The vision of him standing in front of me a week and a half ago, his hands in his pockets and his lazy gaze on me, floated through my mind. An annoying warmth spread through my body.

"Good," I grumbled.

She laughed. "That good, huh?"

Crunch.

"Gosh, maybe you two should just have sex and call it a day."

A frown pulled on my lips. "I'd rather sleep with Richard."

"Uh-huh, sure."

"I have too much pride to ever let Allister touch me again. There's no better way to tell a woman you're not interested than leaving her naked in your bed for *three years.*"

"Touché."

"Besides, I'm not interested anyway."

Valentina made a *hmm* noise.

I glanced at her. "What?"

"Nothing."

"Oh, for goodness' sake, just spit it out."

"If you don't want anything to do with him, then what do you think of me trying my hand?"

I laughed in disbelief. "With Christian?"

She nodded.

Oh, my god, she was serious. My amusement dropped with my stomach. "Why on Earth would you want to do that?"

"Please. Have you seen him?"

"Of course, but weren't we just talking about what an asshole he is?"

"What do they say . . . the bigger the asshole, the better he is in bed?"

"I don't think they say that, though."

A sly look flickered in her eyes. "If this is upsetting you—"

"It's one-hundred percent not upsetting me, but I thought you were seeing Eddie?"

She waved a hand. "He's stepping out on me, just like my husband. It's time to move on."

I chewed my cheek. "If Ricardo finds out you're seeing other men—"

"Save it. I know, and I'm always careful. So . . . be honest, would it bother you? Because I don't have to—"

"I told you, I don't want anything to do with him, and I meant it."

Gosh, it was hot. The sun seemed to burn hotter and heavier in the last few seconds. I pulled my hair off my neck.

"Okay, if you're sure."

"I'm sure."

I must have had too many margaritas because they were beginning to feel like a lump of lead in my stomach.

My cell phone rang, interrupting my thoughts. I was so distracted I didn't think to check the caller ID before getting to my feet and answering it near the pool.

"Hello?" I dipped my toes in the cool water.

"Gianna."

The hair on the back of my neck rose, and my breath turned to ice.

Disgrace to this family.

Worthless daughter.

Unlovable girl.

Nothing but a *whore*.

The rattle of a slammed door. And then darkness. A darkness so alive sometimes it touched me. Spoke to me. Hurt *me.* "Shh, it's okay. Don't worry, your papà knows I'm here."

You can't scream with a hand over your mouth.

That's where fiery-haired goddesses are made all over the world.

A piece of cotton floated through the air, twisting in the breeze, before landing in the pool.

"Did you hear anything I just said?" my papà snapped.

Hatred filled me with a searing burn. I took a deep breath to steady my voice. "I'm sorry, I'm pretty busy right now. What did you want?"

"Your cousin Silvia's wedding is next month. You'll be there if I have to come get you myself, do you understand?"

Panic twisted in my chest. "I'll have to check with my husband to see if we can make it."

"Cut the bullshit, Gianna. Richard already has one foot in the grave. You are coming to the wedding. I'll have Gina send you the details." He hung up.

It'd been eight years since I'd seen my father. Since he'd bothered to reach out to me. And while a family reunion should always be hopeful, I could, with a sense of dread, only wonder what he wanted from me now. I had a bad feeling it was about my husband's declining health and my soon-to-be independence.

I took a deep breath, fearing I was going to be sick right here in Valentina's pool.

"I swear, if the neighbors don't do something about those damn cottonwood seeds, I'm going to cut the tree down myself," Val grumbled, and got to her feet. "I'm going to take a quick break. Do you need another drink?"

A break was her way of saying she was due another line.

I turned around. "I'll join you."

Interest crossed her face. "I thought it gave you a migraine."

That excuse had just been an uncomplicated way of turning it down without having to explain my therapist discouraged drugs.

I wanted to get better—to put my panic attacks behind me, instead of only masking them with a high. But as that phone call filled my mind and pushed me to the edge of a breakdown, all I wanted was to not fear the past in the dark, if only for a moment.

"I guess it's as they say," I whispered, "the bee has a sting and honey, too."

We all searched for strength in life.

Unfortunately, mine just happened to lie at the end of a line of powder.

At the end of the day, I would rather puke in one of my favorite Prada boots than watch Valentina "try her hand" with Allister. Like he needed any more attention—he had an embarrassing number of women throwing themselves at him already. What annoyed me even more, though, was that he'd always been charming and respectful to each one of them, while he regarded me as if I was a liberal helping of chopped liver.

This all seemed to brew in my head like a pot of burnt coffee the entire evening I spent with Valentina. So, naturally, when Christian Allister showed up to the get-together at Ace's penthouse, looking like an asshole and every woman's wet dream, I'd shut the door in his face. I told you, blow made me brave. But, sadly, not stronger; Christian had easily kept the door open. And that was when he'd noticed I might be as baked as Celia Abelli's bruschetta.

It wasn't like I was proud of the relapse—especially because I'd been worrying about how I would break this to Dr. Rosamund on Monday—but I certainly didn't care for Allister's opinion on the matter. I guessed I should've known he'd give it anyway. He grabbed my chin, looked into my eyes, and then shoved my face away in disgust.

And now, here I was, stewing in the anger and spite he easily brought out in me.

I adjusted one of my pigtail buns in the bathroom mirror, reciting every Italian curse word I knew in my mind. Took a deep breath.

He was out there, being as polite as ever. Where he pulled that charm from, I'd never know. Valentina hadn't wasted any time, drifting to his side and laughing at everything he said. For God's sake, the man wasn't even funny.

"Gianna," Valentina called out. "Come here! Christian was just telling me the most amusing story."

I frowned, not pausing in my trek to the minibar. "Who?"

She faltered, looking to Christian, who stood beside her and who seemed to show no confusion toward my slight. And then she pouted. "Christian, tell her to stop being rude."

His cold eyes were on me as he responded to her. "Of course. Who are you talking about?"

Since he'd arrived, we'd been playing one of my favorite games: pretending the other didn't exist. Though, in truth, I'd prefer if he wasn't here at all. His presence created this edgy sensation beneath my skin, like I was just waiting for the other shoe to drop.

"What's going on between you and Allister?" Luca asked, invading my space near the minibar.

"Apathy," I responded, sipping my Tequila Sunrise.

"He touched your face."

"It's called a lack of boundaries, Luca. Something most men in New York are familiar with." I glanced pointedly at the two inches of space between us. The irony didn't escape me that a lack of boundaries had always fit me where Christian was concerned better than it ever had him. What an annoying realization.

"I don't like it. You are not his to touch."

"Aw, it's so sweet of you to protect my honor, Luca."

He grabbed my wrist before I could walk away. "I'm not protecting yours, I'm protecting Richard's. He's a capo and is due the respect of one."

"Bummer." I pouted, wrenching my wrist back. "Thought I might be seeing a sliver of a soul in you."

Luca left without a parting word, like usual, and then I got caught up in conversation, moving around the room like a social butterfly with an anxiety problem.

My gaze drifted to a sparkle on the floor-to-ceiling window. Christian stood near the pool with Ms. Perfect Elena Abelli, both of their eyes on the nighttime sky. Was he telling her what Andromeda's name meant? A wave of something unpleasant passed through me. I stared at the line of his shoulders, at the smooth cut of hair at his neckline. It was so perfect a physical part of me wanted to run my hand through it to mess it up. The mentally sound part of me wanted to shove him out the door.

I realized then why he'd always been able to get under my skin.

He made me feel like I was a little girl again—hungry for attention and affection.

And I hated him for it.

Ace leaned against the wall staring at the two perfect people on the terrace with an intensity not befitting a soon-to-be brother-in-law by any means. His and Elena's relationship was a volatile situation not a blind man could miss, let alone Christian Allister, Seer of All Things He Shouldn't. Was he interested in Elena Abelli, or was he being his strategic and cold self with an endgame? At this point, it didn't matter, because it seemed Ace's marriage agreement with Adriana was about to be blown out of the water.

"Shit," I muttered.

"That pot sure is smellin' sweet," Nico's uncle Jimmy said as he walked past.

I, as well as Jimmy, might have had quite a bit of money on the gamble that Ace wouldn't go through with the marriage to Adriana, but I still wasn't looking forward to the trouble it would cause.

The next fifteen minutes happened, and that bet was practically in the bag. It seemed Ace had had enough of Elena and Christian's chat, and so, naturally, he pushed her into the pool, leaving everyone staring and speechless.

I gave Elena the change of clothes I'd brought with me because, honestly, I felt bad for her. I wouldn't want to be on the other end of Ace's affections. He was softer in a way than his papà had ever been—I admired Ace's late mamma Caterina for that—but he was still the same pushy, confident man who always got what he wanted. I worried he would bulldoze right over sweet Elena Abelli.

The incident had killed the mood, and the party dispersed soon after.

"Thank you for coming. Sorry about the—" My smile faltered. "Um, situation."

Salvatore Abelli gave me a disapproving look before he and the rest of his family left. Well, at least there hadn't been bloodshed. That seemed to be a recurring theme at these parties with the Abellis.

Nico headed to the door.

"Goodbye, Ace!" I called. "So glad we could finally have a peaceful, uneventful night with the Abellis, aren't you?"

The expression he gave me said he wasn't impressed with my joke.

After saying my farewells to the last of the guests, I shut the door, leaned against it, and took in the mess of glasses and dishes left behind.

"*Dio mio,*" I muttered, and then cursed myself. That was going to be ten Hail Mary's at my next confession.

I sighed, but before I could let it all out, my body tensed. I thought Christian had left earlier, escaping the party as soon as the drama he'd created commenced. Although, as I drifted toward the low timbre of his voice, I knew I'd been mistaken. My heart rate dipped and dived like it'd had one too many Tequila Sunrises.

His gaze was averted as he leaned against the glass railing on the terrace, talking on the phone. Each word was rough, quiet, and not understandable, as though he was speaking a foreign language.

When he looked up and noticed my presence, a flicker passed through his eyes, and he suddenly spoke clear and concise English.

A man of many secrets.

He ended the call, and we stared at each other in silence. Our expressions were apathetic, yet electricity played in the air, hindering the ease to breathe.

"I guess I should say, nice party," he drawled.

"I guess. But it just doesn't have the same effect, considering you *ruined* it and all."

"Ah, so Ace loses his cool and I take the blame?"

I shook my head. "You knew exactly what you were doing."

"Maybe."

"My question is, why? I thought you and Ace got coffee, shared secrets, and went shopping together?"

He shrugged a shoulder. "Fair play."

This was about *payback*? "For what? Wait, don't tell me—he stole one of your women."

The slightest muscle tightened in his jaw, and I faltered.

"Oh, my god, he *did*."

He pushed off the railing and rolled his shoulders.

Who was this woman he wanted so badly? *Elena Abelli?*

A bad taste filled my mouth. Must be from that brownie I'd washed down with booze earlier.

"Well, for what it's worth, I would've put my money on you," I told him.

"Why?" His eyes trapped me where I stood.

I licked my lips. "Well, number one, you're too pretty for your own good. And number two, you hide your dark side well—Ace doesn't even try to."

He nodded slowly, like that made sense.

I lifted a shoulder. "If you want a couple pointers, however, you could probably work on being less of an asshole sometimes. Though I'm beginning to think that's only for my benefit."

My messy life must annoy him immensely.

"I'll keep that in mind." He slipped his hands in his pockets and took a step toward me. With eyes narrowed, his voice was rough and demanding. "Why did you shut the door on me earlier?"

My pulse fluttered, and I took a step back. "Your face triggers me."

Another step. "Why the drugs?"

Another one back. "Why the fifty questions?"

"Answer me."

I gritted my teeth. "Make me."

A shadow crossed his face as he walked toward me slowly, but I still saw the spark of anger in his eyes. "Do you want to know what I learned over the years?"

I shook my head.

"Interrogation. It takes about twenty minutes to break someone—to make a grown man cry for his mother. I could have you screaming in two."

My blood ran hot and cold. "Where does one learn to do something like that?"

"Hell." He said it without pause and so matter-of-fact it sent a chill down my spine. "You'll tell me why you fucked around with blow today, and you'll tell me now."

He was the last person I would willingly share my past with. He already thought of me as a mess; I could only imagine how he'd regard me if he knew all my dirty little secrets.

"You disappear for three years and then come back and demand things from me? You made your interest clear a long time ago, Allister. I'll never answer to you—get used to it already."

Cold eyes pierced me with an arrow through the chest. "What part of 'call me if you need anything' did you not fucking understand?"

My pulse beat unevenly. A part of me couldn't believe we were actually going back to that night.

"Please. When a woman doesn't hear from a man in two weeks, she gets the picture crystal clear." Another response ricocheted off the walls in my head: *You weren't there. You weren't there for me, just like everybody else.*

Resentment wrapped around my throat.

"Or maybe it was just easier for you to accept a new husband with enough money to keep your self-indulgence supported for the rest of your life."

I laughed and then choked on it in fury. "I despise you."

"The feeling is mutual."

He headed toward the door, and I turned to watch him go.

"Tell me, Officer, were you this cold to your mother?"

He stopped in his tracks.

The temperature in the room took a dive, and goosebumps rose on my arms. But I couldn't seem to stop myself. I wanted to hurt him; to make him feel something for once in his life. "I feel sorry for the woman—to birth such a heartless son as you."

He turned around. If expressions could kill, I'd be dead. "Shut your goddamn mouth."

I laughed coldly. "What are you going to do? Make me scream? Is that what you did to your mam—"

The air escaped me in a rush as he grabbed me by the throat and pressed my back against the wall.

"You know nothing of my past," he growled.

His words were different, rougher, than they should have been. It took me a moment to understand the significance while I was trying to catch my breath. And when I did, I stared at him, panting.

The bastard was Russian.

CHAPTER
Eleven

Christian

I COULDN'T SAY I HADN'T KNOWN. JESUS, IT WAS WHY I'D ALWAYS TRIED TO keep my distance from her. I'd known she would trip me up. Though, as much as I wished I could blame my fuck-up on the fact trouble followed Gianna wherever she went, I knew that had nothing to do with it. When she was close, all I could focus on was that she smelled like temptation. Like something I wanted to worship and degrade at the same time.

She'd just had to prod that one spot—that *one* weakness of mine—to make me lose my grasp on control. She'd been right about my mother. I could only imagine the look on her pretty face if she knew I'd been the one to put the bitch out of her depraved fucking misery.

I hadn't given myself up in over ten years. Ten years down the drain because of one goddamn woman. I might as well have spouted Shakespeare to her from below her window.

The next time she spoke back to me, I just needed to fill her mouth with something more productive. The image of her, on her knees, looking up at me with soft brown eyes, played in my mind. It sent a rush of heat to my groin. Made my blood rush in my ears.

With a clench of my teeth, I pushed the fantasy away.

Not yours.

A mixture of fury, regret, and relief burned in my chest.

I could change everything so fast. Make her a single woman. Make her want me. Make her *mine*. The plan began to weave itself in my mind, and when I felt a tremble in the hand still wrapped around her throat, I shut it down fast.

Her pulse beat quickly, expressing her fear—but her eyes, they were filled with defiance. *Triumph.*

"Iowa, huh?"

Bitter amusement filled me. She was put on this earth to aggravate me, to humble me. I didn't know a single damn man who wished to be humbled.

I tightened my grip. "I'm only going to say this once, sweetheart—don't fuck with me. I promise you, next time, I'm not going to be so nice."

I would have killed anyone else who'd provoked me like she had. But somehow, the idea of her lifeless body made my stomach tighten in denial. I often wished she was a problem I could just make disappear—though, oddly enough, her death had always been a hard no for me.

She looked bored. "Say something in Russian."

This was a moment I would love to fill her mouth with something more productive.

I let her go rougher than I should have, and then hated myself for feeling a twinge of regret. Couldn't kill her. Couldn't even hurt her. What the hell would I even do with her? My dick immediately took over, flashing images through my mind of her naked on my bed, ass up, head-down, as she clutched the sheets and begged me for more.

Obviously, I had some ideas.

But something deeper was involved—some foreign, visceral need I couldn't explain and didn't even understand. A hunger that roared in my chest and bled into my veins. If I went there with her, finally had her in the ways I'd dreamed of for years, nothing would be the same. My plans of a normal, comfortable life would be shot to hell. The idea of giving it all up was a physical abhorrence.

"Is that where you went to . . . that night? Russia?" she asked me as I reached the door.

That night. She said it like she was disturbed by just the memory, while, even though I hated it, *that night* had fueled my obsession for her for years. I'd dreamed of it, fantasized of her, and fought a physical battle with myself not to go back to New York just to see her in the flesh.

Contempt spread like frostbite in my chest. I turned to look at her, ignored the soft curves of her body as she leaned against the wall where I'd put her. "Fortunately for Russia, their women seem to have a little more self-respect than to drop their clothes for a man they hate. Guess I needed a change of scenery."

Anger flashed in her eyes.

As soon as I stepped into the hall, a *thunk* hit the door before I could pull it closed.

I gritted my teeth.

She'd thrown her goddamn shoe at me.

"If I didn't already know you're a fucked-up bastard and like pain, I'd be making your face a lot less pretty right now."

Funny that we were both thinking about each other's faces. Just the sight of his pissed me off.

I pulled the door open to let Nico enter.

He walked in, sizing up my new apartment. I'd sold the last just so I wouldn't have any excuse to come back to New York. Fuck how well that worked out.

"You know what?" Ace lifted a shoulder and turned to me. "What the hell."

His fist collided with my jaw.

It felt like a fucking sledgehammer, and finally cleared my head of a certain dark-haired woman since she'd thrown her shoe at me earlier. A welcome reprieve.

I walked toward the kitchen to get a drink.

"What? Not going to hit me back? Too grandiose, or something?"

I let out a sardonic breath. "Or something."

I'd had enough fighting to last a cage-fighter two lifetimes. Fought to eat. Fought not to be touched. Fought to stay alive. The streets of Moscow hadn't been a school trip, and I'd only ended up there because my mother's house had been anyone's worst nightmare.

"You want to tell me what your problem is with me?"

I laughed. "I don't give a single fuck about you."

"Cut the shit. You've had a hard-on for pissing me off from day one."

"Sometimes an opportunity presents itself and I take it. It has nothing to do with you or my cock." *Unless it involves Gianna Marino, anyway.*

I'd always convinced myself I disliked Nico because he was impulsive and reckless. But I knew that was just an excuse for the real reason: he'd fucked her. If I couldn't fuck her, nobody could fuck her. It was that simple. The idea of anyone touching her was a nauseating pill I refused to swallow.

I'd never seen Ace interested in any particular woman besides Elena Abelli. The opportunity for my small vendetta practically landed in my lap earlier. Maybe it was a little immature, considering he'd slept with Gianna only once years ago. But . . . I held grudges. Fucking sue me.

"Elena is mine, Allister."

I raised a brow. "Does she know?"

"She will tomorrow."

"Ah." I leaned against the counter, sipped my drink. "So, that's why you're here."

He rubbed his jaw. "We're having lunch at Francesco's tomorrow to go over wedding plans."

"And what?" I said, amused. "Gonna see if they can do a quick switcharoo for the other sister . . . *or something?*"

His eyes narrowed. "Or something."

"What do you need?" I got straight to business.

"An intermediary."

"Don't think you can handle the Abellis yourself?"

"I know I can. But I would rather not start a war with my future wife's family."

I nodded. "I imagine that would kill the honeymoon. Fine, I'll send someone—"

"I don't want someone, I want you to do it. If her fuck-up brother or cousin gets hurt in the process—"

Jesus, he was hard-up for this girl. I wished I couldn't relate.

"The women should be at this luncheon tomorrow," I told him. A woman's presence always seemed to dull a man's bloodlust.

"They'll be there."

"What time is it?"

"Noon."

"I can be there at twelve-thirty. I have a prior engagement."

"Fine. I'll stall them." He checked his phone. "Are you staying in New York?"

"No. I'm on sabbatical." I'd missed the sight and smells of home. Fuck, who was I kidding? I knew why I was here, and it had everything to do with a grown woman with sparkly-painted toenails.

"Well, if you get a chance, I want you to keep an eye on Gianna and a Vincent Monroe."

Tension rolled through me at just the sound of their names together.

Ace watched me. "Have you heard of him?"

Dry amusement filled me. I knew Monroe's address, social security number, and that he preferred his bowl of cereal in the morning with a side of softcore on HBO.

I nodded. "Some multi-million-dollar hotelier."

"There've been some rumors they're involved, and I owe it to my oldest capo to keep it under control."

"You think I have time to surveil the women in your family?"

If he only knew. I'd only made it one month after the move to Seattle until the pressure in my chest became too much and I couldn't take it any longer. I needed to see her—it wasn't even an option anymore. So, I looked her up just to see if she was still alive. She was a walking hazard to herself and others; I had to make sure. Things might have gotten slightly out of control—checking on her becoming my daily routine—but I wouldn't apologize for it. The sight of her calmed the rush in my ears, the beat of my heart, and I'd finally been able to focus on my work again.

He moved toward the door. "You have more men at your disposal than I do. Get someone to do it."

Over my dead body would I assign some limp-dicked analyst to watch Gianna twenty-four-seven.

"And if she is getting serious with him?" *I'll kill him.*

His eyes narrowed. "If she keeps fucking everything up, she'll make this family look weak. She knows the consequences. If they're involved, he's dead and she'll be dealt with."

"You won't fucking touch her." The threat escaped me, so calm and deadly it stilled the air. Two goddamn slipups in one day. I could have laughed, but I didn't find it even slightly amusing that Ace now knew I had a weakness—he now had something to hold over my head. My entire reputation rode on me being untouchable, and this was going to fuck it all up.

He watched my face, let out an amused breath. "Well, fuck me running." And then walked out the door.

CHAPTER
Twelve

Gianna

A TEAR RAN DOWN MY CHEEK. "IT'S SO BEAUTIFUL."

Valentina chuckled and handed me a tissue. "You only think so because you've won the bet."

"Shh." Nadia Abelli, the bride's grandmother, glared at us from the other side of the aisle.

Val rolled her eyes. "Someone's the party police."

Elena looked so beautiful in her wedding dress it hurt my eyes. And Ace was as sharp as ever, pink tie and all.

I *had* won the bet.

But I was only so happy because the bride and groom seemed so happy.

They looked at each other like they were . . . in love. My chest hurt, and my smile fell. I wished love was visible, like the sparkles on Elena's gown. Or the shimmer of the sun on skin. Then it couldn't be hidden or faked.

I wondered what love felt like.

I wondered if it even existed.

Another tear dripped down my cheek, and I wiped it away.

As the usher directed each pew to leave, my gaze landed on Elena's cousin Dominic walking down the aisle. "Oh, excuse me, Val. I have some business to attend to."

"A little young for you, you think?"

"Shut up, he's twenty. Plenty legal." I winked at her.

She laughed and pulled her long legs to the side and out of the way.

I caught up to the handsome young man and grasped his arm. His gaze slid my way as we continued walking down the aisle.

"I'm here to apologize that you had to take care of me the other night at Elena's little party." My papà's phone call had been haunting me day and night, and I might have gone slightly overboard with the alcohol at her bachelorette. "So, I have a proposal—whenever you go on a bender, I'll be your DD, take you home, take off your shoes, cover you up, and leave a glass of water and a couple painkillers beside your bed."

A corner of his lips lifted. "As much as I would love to accept that very specific and generous offer, I didn't take you home."

I faltered, pausing in the middle of the entrance hall. "But . . . who did?"

He only gave me a reassuring smile and walked away.

The last memory I had of that party was Dominic escorting me to his car. Tequila and self-loathing had churned in my stomach, and I longed to be home before unconsciousness swallowed me whole. I hadn't made it, the night slotted into one of the many I'd never remember.

I stared out the glass doors of the church, and suddenly, my heart slowed as something came back to me.

There'd been strong arms, a warm chest.

And two rough words in my ear.

"I've never seen such a beautiful bride," I exclaimed.

Elena blushed, placing a hand on her cheek. "The compliments today are going to go straight to my head."

"Good. You're too humble as it is. So"—I linked my arm through hers—"how has the married life been so far?" They'd eloped a short while ago. Apparently, Ace couldn't even wait one more week.

"It's been . . ." Her eyes sparkled. "Wonderful. He's been really good to me, Gianna."

"Of course, he has. His mamma raised him better than that, even if he'd like to deny it."

"I wish I could have met her," she said softly.

"She had her . . . issues." An addiction to coke I couldn't judge her for; she'd been in Antonio's orbit, after all. "But she tried hard to be a good person and mother. She gave me a Willow Tree—you know, those porcelain angels—every year for my birthday." My smile fell. "If she only knew I would eventually marry her husband . . ."

Shame was a sinkhole I never knew when I'd fall in.

"Oh, Gianna . . . it's not like you had a choice. I'm sure she would have understood."

"No, I went into that marriage willingly"—anything to get far away from Chicago—"with an open mind and heart. Let's just say, I realized it wouldn't be what I had fantasized it to be the night of my wedding." I laughed lightly. "Anyway, one of those Willow Trees is yours. Come get one whenever you like."

"Thank you, Gianna. I would love that." Her gaze found Nico's across the room. He was talking to his uncle Jimmy. If I stepped between that look, I was sure my dress would catch fire.

If love were visible, it couldn't be far from the soft heat in their eyes.

"Gosh." I fanned my face. "It's getting so sweet in here I feel like I'm in the middle of a Hallmark moment."

She laughed, pulled her gaze away. "Sure, minus the tension and guns."

We both looked around the ballroom of the hotel hosting the reception. The Abellis stayed on one side of the room, while the Russos congregated on the other. The most enthusiastic pair was Luca, who leaned against the wall, chewing on a toothpick and staring at the other *famiglia*, while Nadia Abelli, the party police, flipped through a Vogue magazine. Even the kids watched each other like the others weren't vaccinated.

"Lively bunch, aren't they?" I said.

"Honestly, I'm just glad they're being cordial. For a while, I was sure Papà and Nico would end up killing each other before the wedding."

"*Ohmygod!*" The shriek came from behind us.

Elena closed her eyes before pasting on a smile and turning around to greet Jenny, her brother's cheating girlfriend and one of Ace's ex-flings.

"Oh no, I've just remembered I'm parched," I dead-panned.

"Of course you have," Elena muttered through her smile.

I drifted toward the beverage table, *not* the bar. If I couldn't even remember who had taken me home the other night, I needed to stay clear of alcohol. As for my growing suspicion that it had been a certain Russian, and considering the way he'd taken care of me . . . well, I didn't even want to think about it. Especially since less than two weeks ago, he'd insinuated I was easy, a boring lay, and had low self-esteem in one hit.

My gaze unwillingly searched him out for mere self-protection. Everyone knows where their enemy is in the room. He was either schmoozing some socialite in a dark corner or he wasn't here.

"Gianna! I thought that was you."

I turned to see Samantha Delacorte, AKA the Most Superficial Woman in New York City, beelining straight to me.

I forced a smile. "Samantha, how nice to see you."

She air-hugged me, leaving a cloud of sensual perfume I could hardly see through when she pulled back.

"I'm not wedding-crashing, I swear," she said. "I saw you from the lobby and wanted to say hello. Honestly, Gianna, it's been too long. Are you . . ." She looked me up and down, grimacing at my blue halter tutu dress. "All right?"

I copied the sickly-sweet tone of her voice. "*Honestly*, I've been so busy—charities, weddings, tickets to the race tomorrow—I must have forgotten to keep in touch. I am so sorry."

"Oh no . . ." she started.

I blinked.

"I sure hope Vincent didn't forget to invite you to our trip tomorrow. The end-of-the-summer Bahama trip on his yacht?" She put a hand on my arm, fake pity shining in her eyes. "I'm sure it was just a mistake. I'll talk to him—"

"No worries, Samantha," I said blandly, sizing up the room. "I've found I'm allergic to the sea."

"Bummer." She pouted.

My gaze stopped on the bar, and I stared longingly.

"Well, Vincent, a few others, and I are up in the penthouse suite watching the game. Go, Yanks! You should stop by after this . . . eventful little party. I'm sure Vincent wants to see you, no matter what he says." The sympathy in her eyes barely concealed her satisfaction.

To be honest, I was a little stung Vincent hadn't reached out to me at all. But I knew it was for the best—there could never be anything between us like he wanted. I did miss his friendship, however.

"I'm not going to be able to make it." I pouted. "I made plans with my cat weeks ago."

"Shame. Well, don't be afraid to stay in touch. We all go through periods of depression, you know."

She air-kissed me on the cheeks and then drifted away.

I sighed.

Took a sip of the punch only the kids were drinking.

Tapped my heel on the floor.

This no-alcohol-and-drugs vow was working out just fine—

Val stopped nearby and shook a pack of cigarettes at me with a raised brow.

"*Oh, thank God.*"

I set my punch on a random table and followed her out the door.

"You wanna know the gossip I just heard in the ladies' room?" she asked as we sat on a bench outside the hotel doors and lit a cigarette.

"No."

"It has to do with Christian."

I might hate him, but I still wanted to unravel him like a cat with a ball of yarn.

"Continue."

She chuckled. "You know Jacie Newport—blonde, tall, disgustingly perfect—a member on the ACA charity board?"

I nodded.

"Well, I bumped into her in the bathroom—literally, mind you. She used to see Christian years ago, I remembered, and so I thought it would be the perfect opportunity to find out just how he operates."

I crossed my legs and leaned back. "Please, tell me you're not still interested in him."

"A woman would have to be dead not to be interested, Gianna."

"Just call me Elvira," I muttered.

"Pretty sure she wasn't undead, but I get your point."

I wanted to tell her Allister was Russian. Italians didn't have a great affiliation with Russians here in New York. The *Cosa Nostra* and *Bratva* didn't clash often, but when they did, it was a time us women sat around wondering if our husbands would come home. If I told her, maybe it would turn her off. Though, for some reason, I kept it to myself. I didn't want her to know his secret. It was mine.

"Anyway, turns out the fed doesn't stick around with the same woman for long."

I scoffed. "That's all the gossip you got? I could have told you that."

"Well, surely, you didn't know he's only with the same woman a very specific *three* times."

I frowned. "Like, three dates?"

"More like, three times between the sheets." She smirked. When I still looked confused, she added, "Three romps in the sack? Three rolls in the hay?" I blinked. "Playing hide the pickle? Doing the horizontal hustle—?"

"Are you saying he only sleeps with the same woman *three* times?"

"I'm truly impressed with how quickly you put that together," she said dryly.

My mind whirled.

Tap, tap, tap.

The rhythmic tapping of his finger, the adjusting of his cuffs, the turning of his watch, it all played in my head on a reel.

God, the man was more disturbed than I had thought.

"What if they never get to sex? Does foreplay count as one of the times?" The vision of his head between my legs and my fingers inter-locked with his flashed through my mind.

She chuckled. "I don't know. Trying to figure out if you have two or three turns left?"

"Please. You're the one who wants him, not me."

"Mmhmm."

I ignored the sarcasm in her voice.

Silence settled between us for a moment as we both took a pull on our cigarettes.

"Speak of the devil," she muttered.

My gaze followed hers down the sidewalk to see Allister walking toward us. His eyes were already on me, filled with a magnetism that made everything beyond broad shoulders and straight lines disappear.

"And who *is* he with?" Interest laced through her voice.

I finally noticed he had a companion. The stranger was dressed like a model in a magazine, in a charcoal suit and skinny red tie, but his eyes shone with the darkness only a member of the underworld could exude. He was handsome, but that was inconsequential compared to the intrigue that screamed with each step he took.

While walking past us, Allister pulled the cigarette from my lips and tossed it to the sidewalk before entering the hotel doors.

I sighed.

Valentina laughed.

The night of Elena's bachelorette party fluttered through my mind. I got to my feet. "I need to gather some intel."

She blew out a breath of smoke between red-painted lips. "You do that. And while you're at it, find out the handsome stranger's name."

I caught up to Allister and sidled beside him as he and his compan-ion walked to the ballroom. "Who's your friend?"

Allister didn't even look my way. "None of your business."

"Name's Sebastian." The stranger winked at me, and I could feel it straight in my toes.

"Sebastian what?"

Christian's shoulders tensed.

"Perez."

I placed the light accent behind his voice. "Ah, a Colombian. Well, it's very nice to meet you, Sebastian." I held out my hand, but before Sebastian could shake it, Christian grabbed my wrist and pulled it to his side. "I'm—"

"Married," Christian finished, and then shot the Colombian a look I couldn't decipher.

A small smile pulled on Sebastian's lips. "I'll just go offer my condolences to the bride. It was my pleasure, Gianna."

How he knew my name, I didn't know, but the fact he did made my chest squeal with girlish delight.

Wait, *condolences*?

Oh, whatever.

"You too, Sebastian." I tried to raise my hand to give a flirty wave, but realized Christian still had a tight grip on my wrist.

I brought my unimpressed gaze to him.

His eyes were narrowed on me.

"Who peed in your Raisin Bran this morning?"

He dropped my wrist, smoothed his tie, and eyed the room like he was on security detail. "I find your presence bothersome. Go put yourself somewhere else."

"Fine. I *do* need to find out more about Sebastian." I took a step in that direction, but he grabbed my wrist again. I frowned, looking down at where he held me. "I'm confused. I think this is called mixed signals?"

Something flashed in his eyes like he was going to spill with some other ridiculous command, but then a muscle in his jaw tightened, and he let me go and walked away.

Because he clearly didn't want me to, I followed him.

"I didn't expect you to be one to celebrate love," I said.

"That's not why I'm here."

"Oh? Are you who they hired to supervise the children?"

"More like, the adults."

"Oh, please. We're doing just fine."

"Looks like it," he said, eyeing a room so full of tension a single wrong move could detonate a bomb.

We stopped at the short line to the bar. Waiters flitted from here to there, but it seemed there weren't enough to satisfy everyone's need for alcohol.

My shoulder bumped into Christian's arm while I moved to stand beside him. His body tensed, but apparently he was still choosing to ignore my presence. The small touch lit a fire in me, and I fought the invisible pull to step closer to him. I crossed my arms, putting on my best interrogation pose.

"What were your whereabouts at approximately three a.m. last Friday night?"

His gaze slid to me, sizing up my stance. "Home. Sleeping."

"See . . . I just don't believe you."

"Why's that?" he drawled.

"Lucifer never sleeps."

He appeared almost amused, but I couldn't be sure because he grabbed his drink from the bartender and left me standing there, alone.

I sighed, turning on my heel to follow him. "You're going to give a girl a complex."

"*Another* complex might be exactly what you need."

"Ha ha, very funny. But jokes aside—did you take me home the other night?"

"No."

"Did your good twin take me home?"

He let out a breath of amusement.

He was now walking down a hallway off the ballroom, but I wasn't going to follow him into any dark corridor. No matter if there was a door with *Security* written on it at the end. I stopped, and my frustration with his evasion finally bubbled to the surface and into my voice.

"What did you do to me, Allister?"

He paused, turned to face me. "You think I did something to you?" He laughed darkly. "Felt you up while you were passed out?"

Well, no. *That* hadn't even crossed my mind, but why had he taken me home? He had to have an ulterior motive. "Did you go through my underwear drawer? You know, you can buy used ones for sixty dollars on the internet these days. You didn't have to take me home just to get your fix."

He looked like he wanted to strangle me. "I didn't fucking touch you or your shit. I thought we already went over this?" His eyes flashed. "I've been there before. I wasn't impressed."

That stung as though he had slapped me in the face. The anger sucked the air from my lungs, and my claws came unsheathed in an instant.

I grabbed the glass in his hand with every intention of tossing the contents in his face, though before I could, he ripped the tumbler from my grasp and threw it to the floor. I stared at my failed revenge shattered on the marble but could see nothing but rage. I wanted to hurt him as much as his words had me.

I pushed him, and when he didn't respond, I did it again. Then, I beat on his chest and tried to knee him in the groin.

When he'd had enough, he spun me around, pulled me back against his chest, and pinned my arms with one of his.

"Calm down," he ordered.

"Go fuck yourself." My chest heaved up and down, as I tried to fight my way out of his hold.

His grip tightened, and I sucked in a breath. I leaned against him and dug my nails into his forearm when I realized it was all I could do.

The hair on the back of my neck rose when his angry, mocking words brushed my ear. "Your entire family is just down the hall. What would your husband think if he saw you in such a compromising position?"

Fury was dimming under the heat of his body pressed against mine. The tightness of his arm around me. The scent of his custom cologne. And then there was the undeniable press of his erection against my lower back. The bastard was getting off on putting me in my place. Though, regardless of the circumstances, just the idea that he was hard sent a heavy weight between my legs. I softened against him, not able to get enough air in my lungs.

"He's at home with a nurse. He has pneumonia."

"Ah, I hear that's a killer for an old man like him." His hold loosened, and his hand, ever so slowly, slid from my waist to my hip. The touch seared through my skin, setting my heartbeat crackling like sparks. "Who's next on your husband list this time?"

He turned me, pulled my front against his, the heat of it becoming an overwhelming distraction. But then I reminded myself of what he said to me. Resting my palms on his stomach, I slid them up his chest as I rose to my tiptoes. He watched me through eyes too obscure to read.

We were so close I could smell his aftershave, count his eyelashes. The barest inch lay between our lips. It was too easy to fill—impossible not to—and I let the distance close, my lips skimming his as I said, "Anyone will do. As long as they screw me with a little more passion than you."

I tried to pull away, but his hand slid up my neck, fisted in my hair, and kept my mouth brushing his. He stepped closer, forcing my back against the wall. "You seem to forget that I haven't fucked you."

Each brush of his lips was a douse of gasoline on fire inside me. A hazy wave inside my mind. A wasteful breath I couldn't inhale. I turned my head to the side so I could find the air to speak. "Everything about that night was forgettable. Why do you think I didn't call you?" Sympathy filled my voice. "Seems I didn't listen." We both knew I was referring to what he'd said to me that night: *You won't forget me.*

My heart beat in my ears, and I hated myself for feeling a pang of regret.

His eyes were dark and terrifying; a reflection of skies lit up with smoke and fire. His lips pressed against my ear, words rough and threatening. "Run home to your husband before I make him a widower."

CHAPTER
Thirteen

Gianna

JUMPED TO MY FEET. "GO, BLACKIE, GO!"

The grandstand rattled and roared as the horses closed on the finish line. Ears pulled back, hooves pounding into dirt, muscles sleek with sweat. Adrenaline saturated the air, like the heavy humidity the dark clouds had brought in a moment ago. The end of August was upon us, but the heat didn't want to let go.

My look was inspired by *Clueless* star Cher Horowitz's closet—the small white dress her daddy had refused to let her leave the house in without a coverup. I had some issues with daddies, so here I was, in a small white dress—even sans sheer cardigan—as the clouds grew heavy with rain.

It fell from the sky the moment the horses crossed the finish line. I sat, watched the jockeys lead their horses off the track. Watched the dirt turn to mud.

A hand rested on my shoulder, a gaudy sapphire ring attached to the third finger. "I'm sure you'll have better luck next time, dear."

"I knew he wasn't going to win."

Patricia, a seventy-year-old widow, grabbed her purse. "What did I tell you about betting with your heart? It doesn't win you a dime." She patted my arm. "Well, I'm sure you'll learn someday. Now, if you'll excuse me, I have to go collect my winnings."

A little girl with big blue eyes stared from a seat in front of me, while her parents conversed with another couple. She had to hold her fountain soda with two hands it was so large. "Why would you bet on him if you knew he wouldn't win?"

"Wouldn't you want someone to believe in you, even if you knew you couldn't do it?"

She nodded. "Uh huh." She slurped her soda, looking me over. "You're gonna look silly when you get rained on."

I sighed and stood. Tugged my dress down my thighs and braced myself for New York's unpredictable weather.

I had just reached the overhang outside when I stopped, seeing a familiar face.

"Gianna." Vincent's smile was small. "I didn't know if I'd find you here."

"Of course I came. It's Blackie's last hurrah. I had to wish him well in his retirement." I bit my lip as the soft drip of rain sounded between us. "I thought you had a trip to depart on today?"

"The weather put it off until tomorrow." He looked embarrassed, his gaze dropping to the pavement. "I was going to invite you—"

"You don't have to explain, Vincent. I get it." I shouldn't have been upset—I couldn't have gone even if I wanted to—but I still felt the sting of rejection.

I walked out from under the overhang and toward the sidewalk to catch a cab. The rain was a welcome relief from the heat, falling to my skin in fat drops.

"Gianna, wait."

I turned around.

He ran a hand through his hair and sighed. "I don't like feeling like a coward."

I blinked. "Why would you feel like a coward?"

He opened his mouth, closed it.

An unsettling feeling expanded in my stomach. "Why would you feel like a coward, Vincent?"

"I haven't invited you to anything lately because I didn't want to get you into trouble, but . . . I'd be a liar if I said it didn't have to do with self-preservation as well."

"What are you talking about?"

"I realize now . . ." He grew distracted as his gaze ran down my body, down the dress that was probably transparent by now. "Here." He slipped his suit jacket off and rested it on my shoulders—as always, an exemplary gentleman. "I've known you're a little out of my league when it comes to your family, but now, I get why you're so cautious of them."

Embarrassment warmed my cheeks. Someone had visited him. Had threatened him, most likely.

"Who was it?"

He rubbed the back of his neck, understanding what I was asking him. "I didn't ask for his name. He was a bigger guy, intimidating."

Luca.

I gritted my teeth to calm myself.

"He had a badge on him, made me feel like a criminal just for liking you, if I'm being honest."

Wait, *what?*

My breath stilled, and I asked my next question very slowly. "Did you say he had a badge?"

"Yeah, FBI, if you can believe it or not."

My laugh was dark. "Oh, I can believe it."

That son of a bitch. I was going to kill him. Murder him in cold blood. Toss his body to the sharks.

Was my life an amusement to him? A game, just like all the others we played? Frustration bubbled up my throat.

"I want you to know I wasn't ignoring you, Gianna. I just think it's better if we . . . part ways."

Great. I'd been exiled from an entire group of friends. Vincent was the ringleader—without him, one simply didn't get an invite. On the other hand, I could say I'd never been more turned off in my life. How easily he'd conceded to one measly threat.

"I agree, Vincent."

"You agree," he said, like he was confused.

Did he think I would beg him to keep me in the loop? I'd been a Russo for the last eight years of my life. We wouldn't beg with a gun to our heads.

"I have to go now. Thanks for the jacket."

I turned around and raised my hand to hail a cab.

Rain poured from the sky, weighing down my hair. Soaking my clothes. But doing little to cool my ire.

"Where to?" the cabbie asked.

I rattled off the address to Ace's club.

My hands shook with resentment and something pent-up I couldn't even explain. All I knew was that I couldn't keep playing games with this man. I was going to wave the white flag to our rivalry, because in the end, I'd never win.

I stepped out of the cab in front of the club. It was only two o'clock and currently closed, but I'd been informed of a meeting happening here this afternoon, only because Elena had told me why they'd put off their honeymoon until tomorrow.

Angelica stood in front of the basement door looking at her nails. Her gaze came up, and she pursed her lips. "You can't be here."

"Well, I am. Move."

Her eyes fell down my body. "You know, some of us girls actually use a mirror when getting dressed in the morning."

"Some of you also drop to your knees for a twenty-dollar bill," I retorted, as I pushed past her and opened the door.

Being careful not to get my strappy white heels stuck in the steel staircase, I didn't notice the large meeting currently taking place in the middle of the room until I stepped off the last stair.

I looked up and froze.

Twenty male pairs of eyes pinned me to the spot. All of them filled with the darkness of the *Cosa Nostra*.

I swallowed.

Meetings were always in the conference room.

Why weren't they in the conference room?

Nico sat at the front of the room next to his uncle and Luca. Jimmy looked like he was trying to hold back a low chuckle, but the other two, not so much. Ace's expression said he would strangle me if I was in reach.

Black suits, testosterone, and a thick tension eating away at any oxygen filled the area. Nothing but Abellis seemed to be sitting or leaning against the card tables on one side of the room, including their don, Salvatore, while Russos sat on the other. And smack dab in the middle of them sat a special agent who used his badge to threaten law-abiding citizens for catching feelings for the wrong woman.

His eyes were on me, simmering with an anger that told me I was in deep shit if he caught me alone after this. I was suddenly more worried about his reaction than having to face Ace.

Christian's fury cooled and burned my skin as his gaze skimmed down my body.

And then I remembered my dress. My very white, very wet dress.

My cheeks grew warm, but I refused to show my embarrassment by pulling Vincent's jacket closed.

The words were filled with arrogance and amusement. "A hundred bucks says I could make her that wet."

It was a stupid bet and an even stupider joke, but the fact it came from an Abelli mouth only amplified the tension. Something shifted in the air. The slight lift of a murderer's lips after a kill. A starving dog catching the scent of blood.

"Watch your goddamn mouth," Luca snapped. "That's the wife of a capo you're talking about."

The Abelli who sat toward the middle of the room, his ankle resting on his knee, scoffed. "A capo on his deathbed. She's practically fair game now."

I shifted on my heels, waiting for the smallest cue to get the hell out of here.

"Touch one of our women against her will and see how fairly we'll treat you," Ricardo growled.

"*Against her will?*" The Abelli laughed. "I could have her begging for my cock in no time."

Hardly.

Salvatore Abelli appeared almost amused at the exchange, and Ace only sat there, leaning back in his chair, not in any hurry to stop the words from being hurtled back and forth. His eyes expressed how ridiculous he thought this was, but he seemed resigned to let it play out. And I knew why: I was the perfect experiment to see how the families would react to the other's taunts.

"Keep laughing," said someone else. "Everyone knows you have to pay for any of the pussy you get."

A few laughs broke out.

The Abelli's face reddened. "I'd get more than that. I'll tell you how her ass feels, Rus—"

Without a look in the Abelli's direction, Allister pulled a pistol from his jacket.

Pop.

The gunshot reverberated off the walls and rang in my ears. Everything but my heart went still. I stared, watched the Abelli slump from his chair to the floor.

It was so quiet I could hear each drop of water falling from my dress to the concrete floor. *Drip . . . drip . . . drip.*

A chill passed through me as Christian put the pistol away without a flicker of emotion.

Tony Abelli wiped blood splatter from his face. Luca shook his head. Ace looked at his watch.

"What the fuck, Allister?" growled Salvatore.

The fed's response was as dry as his eyes were cold. "He was annoying me."

Strained silence reigned for a moment, and then Jimmy's booming laughter filled the room, parting the tension like the Red Sea.

My God, this was madness.

I stepped back when everyone's gazes suddenly came to me. "Um . . . I'm just gonna . . . yeah." I took the stairs two at a time and disappeared out the door.

I practically ran through the club, my racing heart pushing me outside and back into the rain. It fell on my overheated skin like a cool caress.

The sky was dark and the streets were quiet. Not seeing a single cab, I crossed my arms and headed down the sidewalk to the next block over.

The club door slammed shut behind me. I halted where I stood, feeling his presence before he'd even said a word.

His cold and brutal slaying still played in my mind, sending a shiver of alarm down my spine. Christian Allister didn't think twice about taking someone's life. I suddenly feared the day he'd decide mine was too great of an inconvenience.

I turned around, thinking that here, on the street, was the best place to face him rather than anywhere else.

The rain blurred the broad span of his shoulders, the blue hue of his suit, the handsome lines of his face, but the anger in his eyes shone through like a flash of lightning in the distance.

The longer he stared at me, the further the tension stretched, wrapping around my lungs and tightening. His gaze descended over my dress. The look burned, from my breasts, to the wet material sticking to my midsection, to my smooth, bare thighs. It was as real as a rough hand sliding down my body; as tangible as the cool drops of rain on my skin.

He broke the silence. "I'll take you home."

It could have been a generous offer, but the displeased edge in his voice, as if he'd rather be doing anything else, ruined it.

Shaking my head, I opened my mouth to refuse—

"I'm not asking you, Gianna."

I bit my tongue. If I argued with him, I had no doubt he'd carry me kicking and screaming to his car. And I didn't have the energy to fight him anymore.

We walked side-by-side into the parking garage. My skin lit like a beacon to each move he made. My pulse played in tune with his steps. My breath faltered with every minuscule touch of his arm against mine. The tension that lay between us grew tauter with every second that passed. Pulling and pulling, until it threatened to snap.

"What are you wearing?" He said it calmly and slowly, but the anger was laced too finely to be masked.

"Dolce and Gabbana."

"The jacket?"

I sawed my bottom lip.

"Let me guess, it's from the Vincent Monroe Collection."

I didn't deny it.

He shook his head, letting out a sardonic breath between his teeth.

Uncertainty slid down my back. He was mad at me for interrupting his stupid meeting no doubt, yet I couldn't seem to hold onto any frustration in return. Not with this pressure in my chest that seemed to expand from a single look from him.

He twisted his watch on his wrist, once, twice, *three* times. "As much as everyone enjoyed that little show back there—A-plus on the entrance, by the way—I'm still trying to figure out if you're an attention-seeker, or just an idiot."

I flinched, knowing it hadn't been my finest moment.

"My guess is the former. Trying to reel in a crowd for your next husband audition?"

Anger finally lit in my stomach, but I quelled it before it could escape. He was trying to goad me. He wanted me to respond, and I wouldn't give him that satisfaction. This rivalry with him didn't make me feel good. It often left a regretful and restless feeling in my chest for days after our exchanges. It couldn't be healthy. I was dropping Christian Allister, just like blow.

"There isn't a man on this earth I would ever marry again."

"But somehow Richard Marino passed muster?" His words were a vicious bite against my skin. "Call me crazy, but I don't believe you."

"Believe whatever you want, Allister. I don't care what you think about me."

"Just everyone else, huh?"

I couldn't tell if he was mocking me, or if he was angry I didn't hold his opinion in high regard. I tried to gauge his expression, but it was just as cold as a Siberian winter.

"You'll marry again, Gianna, because that's what good Italian girls do."

"I'll run before I'm ever forced to marry again." The unwavering words shocked me as they hit the air because every one of them was true. I had never admitted it to myself out loud, even as I'd begun to collect a sizeable nest egg to start over wherever I wanted.

"Ah, sweetheart . . ." He let out a bitter noise as we reached his car. "We both know you weren't reluctant to wed Antonio."

I faltered. I hadn't yet met Christian at that point in my life, so how did he know what opinion I'd held about my marriage? My heart beat, fast and unsure. Did he know why I hadn't been reluctant? Did he know more about my childhood than I would ever tell him? A cold sweat drifted through me. He was so much smarter, so much more perceptive than me, and I despised him for it. I would never beat him.

"I'm done playing games with you."

He opened the passenger door for me like the quintessential gentleman, his words amused and cynical. "Is that what you think we do? Play games?"

"I don't care what you call it. I'm done! With this." I gestured between us. "With you."

Like the set of the sun, his eyes filled with darkness. A merciless darkness that wrapped around my soul and pulled.

The force of the *snap* made me fall back a step.

He slammed the car door. Stalked toward me.

"You'll *never* be done with me."

He grasped me by the throat, pushed me back against the car, and swallowed my next breath in his mouth.

CHAPTER
Fourteen

Gianna

AN EXPLOSION OF FIRE BURST INSIDE ME, SPREADING FROM MY STOMACH TO the tips of my fingers. My blood sizzled. My body tingled. I couldn't breathe.

The press of his lips against mine hit me with such intensity my first response was to push him away. I brought my palms up to his chest to shove him as hard as I could, but when he nipped at my bottom lip and then licked it, soothing the sharp sting with his tongue, *want* filled my veins with boiling water. A moan traveled up my throat. My fingers curled, and I scraped my nails down his stomach, stopping at his belt buckle.

He hissed against my lips and then slid his tongue inside my mouth. I felt that wet glide between my legs. Just the knowledge that his hands were on me sent a tremble through me, but the feel of them—the palm sliding over my hip to the curve of my ass; the gentle yet unyielding grasp on my throat—incinerated any of the resistance left in me. I swayed toward him, my body melting against his.

His lips left mine after I'd only had a single taste of him, and protest flooded my veins. I suddenly wondered how many women he'd kissed in Seattle, but the thought was only fleeting as he moved a hand into my wet hair, grabbing a fistful and tilting my head. He nipped a line down my neck, pulling the skin between my teeth and lightly sucking. My heartbeat dropped like a weight between my legs.

The heat of his body, the force of his presence, the anger in his movements—it stole my breath. With my palms resting on his stomach, I could only pant like some kind of pliant doll while he nipped and sucked at my throat, my collarbone, the tops of my breasts.

His fingers glided up the outsides of my legs, drawing my dress upward until a glimpse of my white thong showed at the junction of my thighs. He dropped his gaze, and the warmth of it seared through the material, brushing my clit as strongly as if he'd touched me there. Heat tugged in my lower stomach. I rolled my hips, closing the small distance between us, trying to find some relief from the ache inside.

A car alarm sounded from somewhere on the street, but the noise barely registered as his eyes followed his hands over my body. He wasn't kissing me anymore. Just touching me, in the soft sound of our breaths and the patter of rain.

He was rough yet meticulous in his movements, as if he was infatuated with every curve and dip but hated himself for it. He slid a palm lower to grab a handful of my ass, and then he placed a slap on my cheek, caressing the sting with a rough palm.

A low moan traveled up my throat, and I lightly bit down on his chest to keep it in. My insides liquefied, my limbs light as air, while I let this man touch my body without even kissing me in return. There was something so filthy about it, so far from romantic—it was making me hotter than I'd ever been.

He rubbed the string between my cheeks, up and down, pausing just before reaching the wet material between my thighs. I couldn't breathe as every nerve in my body waited in anticipation for how low he would go. Desperation was eating away at me, burning and clawing at my insides. I couldn't take it any longer.

"Christian . . ."

His eyes were dark enough to emanate one of my nightmares. They fell to my mouth. He braced his hands on the car on either side of me and leaned in. I was so sure he was going to kiss me, I shook with the anticipation of it, but instead of meeting my lips, he placed a single kiss on my neck.

"If you ran, Gianna . . ." The words were malicious yet somehow as soft and desperate as sex in a war-torn field. He pressed his lips to my ear. "I would find you."

I broke out in shivers.

And drag me back? was what I wanted to ask, but I couldn't find the voice.

At this point, I didn't care what he said. I wanted him so badly I trembled. I could attribute it to the fact it had been too long since I'd had sex or even been touched for that matter, but I knew that wasn't the only reason. No matter how much I hated him, this man had always done something for me.

Cupping his erection, I slid my hand up and down his length, from base to tip.

He drew in a rough breath between his teeth, dropping his gaze to watch me rub him off through his pants.

I'd never thought another man's hard-on was so hot in my life. Just the weight of it filling my palm sent a hazy wave of lust through my blood.

While he was distracted watching the movement of my hand, I rose to my toes and kissed him. A rumble resounded in his chest, half-groan, half-growl, as my tongue met his only once—a hot, wet sweep—and then I pulled away before he could.

I came back breathless. And a bit delirious.

The urge hit me so strongly my mouth watered. I didn't care that it was two o'clock in the afternoon on a Sunday, or that we stood in a public parking garage. I wanted him in my mouth, even if it was all I could get. I worked on his belt buckle with every intention of dropping to my knees right here.

He made a tortured noise and muttered some thick Russian word. Before I could lower myself, he spun me around and pushed my front against the trunk of his car. I gasped but swallowed it as the heat of his body met my back.

He pulled my hair to one side and pressed his face into my neck. A shudder erupted beneath my skin, warm from his soft touch and cold from the volatile energy emanating from him.

"I thought you were done with me, Gianna."

Oh.

I was. *I am,* I wanted to say, but the press of his lips against the hollow of my ear stole my breath and voice. All I could do was shake my head because I couldn't bear to let this end, not yet.

"Say it."

I shook my head again, but my mouth betrayed me. "I'm not."

"You're not, what?" he murmured, tracing the edge of my ear with his tongue.

Goosebumps ran down my arms.

"I'm not done with you," I breathed. I'd always known it wouldn't be that easy.

A growl of satisfaction against the nape of my neck, and then a little nip.

"Back seat."

I listened to the command without a single thought, but before I could get far, a snag caught my sleeve and ripped the jacket off me in one smooth move. I turned my head just in time to see it landing in a puddle on the ground.

His gaze was on me, dry and caustic, but it quickly filled with heat when his attention dropped down my body. My dress was still pulled up indecently, baring the smooth curves of my ass. My skin tingled, and heat bloomed inside me. Letting this man see my naked body was more thrilling than it should have ever been. He was so formal and uptight, anything remotely sexual felt so much dirtier with him.

As soon as he pulled the door closed, shutting us in the back seat of his car, I straddled his hips. He let out a rough breath, watching me lazily, as I ran my hands up his chest, over his neck, into his thick hair, and then down his biceps.

His suit jacket was only in the way, and he let me push it off his shoulders and toss it to the floor. The white dress shirt fit him like a second skin, highlighting his strength, his utter *masculinity*, and I was infatuated with every inch of him. He tensed as I ran my nails down his arms, wanting to sink my teeth into them.

Grabbing my hips, he pulled me closer to sit me on his erection. The hardness lined up with the damp material of my panties, and a wave of lust blurred my vision. I couldn't stop myself from rocking against him. Riding him just like I did my pillow while secretly pretending it was him late at night.

My eyes, half-lidded and hazy, met his.

He traced my lips with a thumb, pulling the bottom one down before releasing it.

I leaned in to kiss him but he held me back.

His voice was dark. "No more Vincent Monroe, Gianna."

"You threatened him."

"Hardly."

I should be angry—angry that he approached Vincent, angry that he thought he held some authority in my life, but at the time, I could only think about how he'd taken me home when I was drunk, took off my shoes, and left a glass of water on my nightstand.

"There is no Vincent Monroe," I breathed.

When he released me, I didn't hesitate to press my mouth to his. This time, he kissed me, lazy and sweet, before pulling back with a long, deep lick that wasn't much of a kiss at all.

Fisting the string of my thong, he ripped the material at my hip, leaving a sharp sting behind. My panties fell down one thigh, baring me to his eyes completely.

He ran a thumb down my landing strip, voice hoarse. "I've wondered if this was still here."

A smile touched my lips. "You've been thinking about me, huh?" I'd only been teasing him by repeating something he'd once said to me and certainly didn't expect his response.

"Only when I need to come."

My smile fell, and my breathing shallowed.

I met his eyes to see he was owning what he'd said completely, and something about the admission was so incredibly hot, it brought a rush of honesty from me.

"Ditto," I whispered.

A groan resounded in his chest, and then he kissed me. Slipped his tongue into my mouth. Pulled my bottom lip between his teeth. Kissing Christian Allister made me feel more alive than any drug ever could.

I tried to undo the buttons on his shirt, but he grabbed my wrists and stopped me. Something cold settled in my stomach. I worked myself free from his grip, and as if he hadn't already denied me once, I tried again, only to get the same result.

"It's staying on," he said harshly against my lips.

He wouldn't let me touch him, not really. And sitting here with my body on shameless display, it suddenly felt . . . humiliating. I pulled away, tugged my dress down, and reached for the door handle.

"Fuck no," he growled, grabbing my wrist. "You got me this hard, Gianna. You're gonna stick around and fix it."

"Fix it yourself, *stronzo.*"

"You're an attention-seeker, sure, but not a fucking tease."

"And you're a selfish bastard who takes and doesn't give anything in return," I snapped.

"*Selfish?*" He laughed. "I ate your pussy for so long last time I can still taste you three years later."

My eyes narrowed. "You're crude."

"Don't play the innocent virgin with me, Gianna. I haven't seen you blush a single time in my life."

I let out a little growl. "I don't like you at all. Let me out."

Why had I thought this was a good idea? There were so many ups and downs with this man it made my head spin.

We stared at each other in a silent battle of wills.

His jaw ticked. And then he pulled his dress shirt from his pants, grabbed my hand, and slid it over his stomach and up his chest. He was compromising with me, allowing me to touch him without taking off his shirt.

I should have left, gone home and finished myself off while fantasizing about his good twin. But, as my hands traveled over skin hotter than it ever should be, that hazy rush of lust pooled in my lower stomach, pulling at my muscles and stretching me thin.

"How many women did you kiss in Seattle?" The quiet question escaped me as I ran my fingers through the grooves in his abs.

His eyes were steady pools of dark blue.

He didn't answer me, but he didn't have to.

He didn't kiss.

A heady sense of satisfaction filled me. *Then why, oh why, Officer, do you kiss me?*

His gaze grew half-lidded as I pressed my fingers into his skin, scraping my nails down his chest. I shifted on his erection, slowly rocking my hips and grinding against him while we stared into each other's eyes. A fire lit inside me, growing hotter and brighter, until I was so close to release I could taste it.

I gasped as he slid his hand into my hair and yanked my head back, pressing the rough words against my ear. "You'll get off with me inside you, Gianna, no sooner."

A shaky breath escaped me, but it came out like a needy whimper with the angle of my head.

He cursed in Russian, tightened his grip in my hair.

I could only stare at the roof of the car, my chest moving in and out with harsh breaths, as he pushed the straps off my shoulders and tugged my dress down to my waist. Pulled the cups of my bra down to bare my breasts. And then he just looked at me with an intensity that licked at my skin.

When he captured a nipple in his mouth, white light shot behind my eyes. His hand released my hair to squeeze one breast while he licked and sucked the other. He switched to give them equal attention. Slapped the side of one to watch it jiggle. With a rough sound, he nipped at it like he was angry, like he was trying to imprint himself on my skin forever.

My eyes rolled back into my head, my pulse throbbing between my legs. If he didn't stop, I thought I could come just like this.

He played with my breasts until I was so far gone I would do anything to feel him inside me—*anything*. I worked on his belt buckle, pulling him out. He was hot and heavy in my hand, and so hard I couldn't resist pumping him in my fist once. He hissed against my throat, and before I could even get a good look at him, he gripped my hips and pushed me down until I'd sunk halfway onto his length.

He groaned.

I gasped.

It hurt. It really hurt. It'd been too long for me, and the bastard was well-endowed. I panted, my thighs quivering as I tried to adjust.

His grip tightened on my hips, and I rested my hands on top of his to try and stop him from shoving me down all the way. I shook my head, as if I'd done my best but it wasn't going to work out in the end.

"All of it, *malyshka*," he commanded.

The warmth in his voice drifted straight between my legs, soothing the sting and filling my stomach with heat.

One of his hands slipped out from mine to trace my landing strip until he found my clit. He rubbed it in a circular motion, and then his mouth found my breasts again, licking and sucking. I moaned, every touch feeding the hot buzz in my core, until, slowly, I slid down, taking him all the way inside me.

"*Fuck*," he gritted, looking down at where we were connected. He gripped my hips tight enough to bruise, tension radiating from him, every muscle in his body pulled taut. "Fuck, you're so tight, *malyshka*."

The feeling of him inside me was so intense, my body trembled. The backs of my eyes burned, and I pressed my face into his neck.

His heartbeat raced against mine.

He was shaking.

"Fuck me, Gianna." He sounded on the brink of control, like if I didn't start moving then I was going to get fucked, hard. That quickly set me in motion; I didn't think I could handle him unleashed yet.

I moved slowly, rocking my hips in a circular motion, grinding my clit against him, shuddering with the intensity.

"You're so goddamned lucky we're in a car right now." He pressed the threat against my ear, his words heavy with a Russian accent that was beginning to drive me crazy. Evoking such a lack of control from the cold fed was addictive. I wanted so much more.

His hands moved everywhere—down my spine, grabbing fistfuls of my hair to angle my head the way he wanted it, gripping my hips to grind me harder against him. He slapped my ass, nipped my neck and throat, sucked my nipples—the feeling of him inside me, the way he was *everywhere*, the way he was holding back and letting me grind on him, it was all too much.

I came so hard spots flew behind my eyes. The fire inside me burst, spreading a warm, tingling sensation throughout my body.

"I've dreamed of that sound," he rasped, nipping at my earlobe.

Warmth filled me like sunlight. I shouldn't take what he said to heart—he was often rude as hell—but, *God*, when he was sweet, it made me feel on top of the world.

I wanted to please him.

I wanted to make him lose his mind.

Reaching back, I rested my hands on his knees and rode him so he could see everything. His gaze caught fire, trailing from my parted lips, to my bouncing breasts, to where he slid in and out of me. I was so wet it was dripping down my thighs and filling the car with an obscene erotic noise.

He suddenly stilled me. Ran his tongue across his teeth.

"You've adjusted, *malyshka?*"

With half-lidded eyes, I nodded.

"Good."

He gripped my hips, pulled us chest-to-chest and bounced me on his erection. *Hard.* Up and down, not giving me a single break from the assault. My moans and whimpers trembled in my throat with the force. My fingers splayed on the window as I searched for something to hold onto that wasn't so consuming. So devastating. So *him.*

"*Oh, God, oh, God.*"

When I climaxed the second time, he swallowed the noise in his mouth. And, with a punishing last thrust and a shudder, he finished inside me. Then, he softly nipped my neck in a rough sort of appreciation.

Our heavy breaths filled the silence. I was so full of contentment, high on a languid post-coital bliss, as I rested my face in the crook of his neck. Curled my fingers in his hair.

"Say something in Russian."

"*Ty samaya krasivaya zhenshchina kotoruyu ya kogda-libo videl.*"

"What did you say?"

"You're annoying."

"I would hate to be Russian if it takes that many words to say something so simple," I mused. I didn't believe for a second that was what he'd said.

Something thick and wet slid down my thigh. My sex-high liquefied and turned to ice in my stomach. Had I really just had unprotected sex—*so* unprotected, by the way his come was leaking out of me—with *Allister*? I did frantic mental calculations in my head, trying to calculate when I ovulated. Which was, of course, *now*.

He must have felt the tension in me because his hand stopped its caress down my back. "You're not on the pill." It was more of an assumption than a question.

I never had sex—why would I need to be?

Pushing away from him, I pulled a bra strap back onto my shoulder as an icy trickle of panic crawled up my spine. "No."

I could only imagine if I got pregnant while my husband was on his deathbed and couldn't conceive with a helper and a bottle of Viagra.

Nothing but a *whore*.

Whore.

Whore.

My lungs squeezed, tightening and tightening with a band that wouldn't release. Tears burned the backs of my eyes.

Two rough hands grasped my face. "Breathe."

His touch dimmed my papà's voice in my mind. I was suddenly envious of Allister; my nightmares were terrified of him. I shut my eyes, focusing on the breathing techniques my therapist taught me.

"We'll get a *Plan B*." His thumb brushed away the tear running down my cheek.

I nodded, shaky.

He let me go, and as he put himself back together—zipping his pants and fixing his hair that I'd thoroughly mussed—something frigid settled in the air. It felt suspiciously like regret. His warmth disappeared, ice coming back to his eyes and shoulders.

If he didn't know the extent of the baggage I carried around before, he knew now. Mortification felt heavy in my chest. Maybe this had been necessary—to make it easy not to speak to him again.

Simply because I'd be too humiliated to acknowledge this had ever happened.

The panic attack soon ebbed, but it was still so cold between us. Even as he helped me adjust my dress and then used a napkin from the glovebox to wipe the come from my thighs.

CHAPTER
Fifteen

Christian

SHUT THE CAR DOOR HARDER THAN I SHOULD HAVE. RAN A HAND THROUGH my hair to try and get rid of the soft feel of her fingers in it. Rolled my shoulders to push away the obsessive thoughts lighting up my back. *Keep her. Make her want you. Make her* need *you.*

Fuck, I shouldn't have done it.

It was like trying to cure an addict by giving him the best goddamn hit of his life.

A bell dinged above my head as I entered the drugstore. It took longer than it should have to find the right aisle because images of Gianna still consumed my mind. Her soft eyes, lips parted, the flare of her hips, her sweet thighs as she shuddered while trying to take all of me.

My heart rate sped up, heat running to my groin.

I was already hard for her again.

It hadn't been my plan to fuck her, but once I had my hands on her I couldn't stop. You'd think it would have given me some relief, but all it seemed to have done was provide me with more images, noises, and real-estate to obsess over.

My eyes coasted over the emergency contraceptives, and I grabbed one to read the information on the back. My hand was shaking. Fucking ridiculous. You'd think I'd just lost my virginity.

Didn't know if I could have stopped myself from coming in her if I'd wanted to. And hadn't particularly wanted to.

An obsessive part of me—the one thoroughly fixated on Gianna's every move—didn't give a shit about consequences. Knocking her up would make its fucking day. It would finally give me a reason to throw my plans in the trash and make her *mine*.

Sounded good, sure—but that side of me was as rational as Gianna's wardrobe. It had the idea she could be this pretty little fuck toy, one who'd be perfectly comfortable warming my bed all day, spreading her legs for me whenever I wanted, while keeping all her questions to herself.

In reality, she'd touch my shit. Reorganize my things. Fill my apartment with sugary cereal. And most importantly, slowly dig her way into my past. And when she did that, she'd hate me more than she already did. Maybe even be disgusted. I couldn't stomach letting her see me in that light.

Gianna wasn't for me.

As much as I hated it, she belonged with someone without any skeletons in his closet. Someone like Vincent Monroe.

My chest burned, rejecting the thought.

Maybe I'd take her out to eat first and hold on to the morning-after pill for a while, give the slight possibility a greater chance.

I ran a hand across my jaw.

Jesus. No.

In the end, I grabbed the generic brand.

My Cherie Amour played on the staticky radio, practically mocking me with its romantic lyrics as I set the item on the counter. The teenage cashier wearing a bored expression and chewing gum looked from my purchase to me, pausing on my neck, where I knew there were a few marks from Gianna's sharp-ass nails.

The teenager met my eyes.

Popped a bubble.

Beep.

Gianna hadn't said a word to me since we left the parking garage. She couldn't have made it clearer that the idea of being stuck with me horrified her—she'd had a full-blown panic attack, for fuck's sake.

I would have found the will to hold myself back if I knew how she'd react. Watching tears fill her eyes was like a stab and a twist to the chest. I didn't fucking like it.

Gianna wasn't in the passenger seat when I headed outside—she was across the street, handing money to a homeless man who looked like he'd just been released from the state penitentiary.

Panic bled into my veins. All I could think about was if she'd walked up to me when I was a teen living on the streets. I would have taken advantage of it so fast.

"Gianna," I snapped.

She tossed me a look over her shoulder.

"Car. *Now.*"

Her gaze flared with annoyance.

The rain had stopped, but her dress hadn't dried enough to be decent. Thankfully, she'd had enough sense to put my jacket on and button it before getting out of the car, unlike earlier at the club. I was still agitated about that little scene, aggravated she'd so visibly regretted sleeping with me, and frustrated I couldn't take her home and fuck her again and again, until she was so thoroughly out of my system I'd forget *her* goddamn name.

She said some parting word to the man—probably about what an asshole I was—and then drifted back to me.

"He was hungry," she explained when she reached me.

"He's heading toward the liquor store as we speak," I said dryly.

"So, what if he is? Everybody needs something to get them through life."

"Right. Must have forgotten I was talking to Miss Blow International."

She rolled her eyes and disappeared into the passenger seat. When I sat beside her, I said, "You're going to tell me why you used a few weeks ago eventually."

The slightest amount of tension rolled through her, but she tried to mask it by looking at her nails. "Please hold your breath."

My curiosity grew tenfold. It was inevitable now that I'd find out.

She looked at the pill I'd handed to her in reluctance. "The last time I took one of these it screwed up my cycle for two months."

The thought that she'd had to take one before sent a bite of jealousy through me.

"Then don't take it."

She scoffed. "I'm not shipping my child to Russia every summer, Allister."

She wouldn't be sending him or her anywhere. She'd be in my home, in my bed. I'd give her anything she wanted—anything but my past and some silly notion of love. Although, I didn't believe she'd be searching for the latter. She'd been burned enough. I hated any man who'd broken her heart, but in the end, they'd made it easy for me. I couldn't give that to her, and neither would she expect it from me.

"I live in Seattle, Gianna, not Russia."

She raised a brow. "Seattle is home now, is it?"

"Yes."

"You're returning soon, then?" There was relief in her voice, and I goddamn hated it.

"A few weeks."

She nodded. Put the pill on her tongue and swallowed it dry.

She always had something to say, yet she remained silent for the rest of the ride. The tension had always been there between us—sexual, loathing, and otherwise—though now we'd slept together, it seemed I was out of her system and mind.

My chest tightened in frustration.

I reached her apartment and looked over to see she'd fallen asleep. Her head was resting on the window, her breaths slow and even. She'd always been able to sleep at the drop of a hat, and deeply, too. I knew I wouldn't get any shut-eye for at least a week, not with the feeling of her hands on me still searing like burns.

I let out a breath.

Swept my gaze over her face. Long eyelashes, smooth cheekbones, pouty mouth—the top lip that was slightly bigger than the bottom—the tiny scar on her chin. She was so goddamn beautiful I couldn't even stand to look at her some days. Because I didn't know what to do with her—to make her scream my name or to punish her for making me feel this way.

I needed to back off completely. To leave her alone and let her live her life.

Let her have her Vincent Monroe.

Because if I touched her again, the deeper this obsession would spread, and I knew where it would end. I'd find some way to keep her. As strong as she liked to appear, she was delicate, flimsy, *breakable*, and too full of curiosity for her own good. She'd want out, and I'd never let her go.

Yet, the more I told myself I couldn't have her, the more I wanted her.

And I wanted her so badly a cold sweat broke out beneath my skin, a tremble starting in my hands.

"Gianna."

She slowly stirred, rolling her head to look at me with hypnotic, dark eyes. They grew half-lidded as sleep pulled her back under. *Jesus.* Today was one of the days it hurt to look at her. A protective urge welled in my chest. Ironic, because it was me she should be fucking running from.

My grip tightened on the steering wheel. "If you expected to be carried inside, you should have fucked someone a little more gentlemanly."

Her eyes opened and narrowed on me. She started to shrug off my jacket.

"Keep it."

There was no way I was letting her walk up to her apartment without it.

"And you say you aren't a gentleman." She let out a sarcastic breath as she stepped out of the car. "Though, just a tip for the next unlucky woman you screw, I would have preferred a box of chocolates over your shitty *Plan B* pill." She slammed the door behind her.

CHAPTER
Sixteen

Gianna

Having sex with your mortal enemy was exhausting. Weight pulled on my muscles as I walked down the hall toward my apartment. I unlocked the door and kicked off my heels, though just as I reached for the light switch, a cold awareness touched my skin, and I froze.

"Well, well, well . . . you show up at the party in one man's jacket and come home in another's?"

My gaze drifted to Richard II, proud manager of *The Playhouse*, which featured the sleaziest strippers in New York. It was the only reliable place to get a fifty-dollar blowie in town.

He was one stepson I would never have to worry about falling into bed with, and it wasn't because he was twenty years older than me. He was merely off-putting in every way.

"Yes, well, us women can't make ourselves too available, now, can we?"

The curtains were open, filling the room with natural light, yet he'd managed to find the darkest corner, where he leaned against the wall. I imagined he'd skittered there like a roach. The bugs were odious little bottom-feeders, but always easy to squish.

"Did you suck Allister's cock?"

I sighed. "And here comes the vulgarity, right on cue. Can't you mix it up for once, Dick?"

I headed toward the kitchen, tensing as I felt him walk up behind me. He grabbed my arm and spun me around.

He was always finely dressed—today, in a pinstripe dress shirt and black pants—but the smell of cheap cologne, cigarette smoke, and stripper sweat clung to him, just like the greasy hair gel barely holding his combover in place.

His fingers dug into my skin. "I followed you out of the club earlier. How long have you been fucking him?"

Always, *always*, plead the fifth.

"I'm not sure what you're talking about."

"You have a hickey on your neck, you little slut."

Dammit. That asshole . . .

His meaty finger traced the bodice of my dress. "If you wanted to fuck an icicle, I could have helped you out."

"Honestly, Dick, it's the Lord's day. Let's keep the penetration talk to a minimum."

"If you make it up to me, I might forget about all this." His thumb rubbed the hickey on my neck, and my skin crawled.

"Fortunately, I don't sleep with my stepsons anymore." I patted his chest. "Drink?"

"You think I'm going to let him make a fool of my father?" he asked, as I headed to the cupboard.

"What about me? Don't tell me I've grounded myself for a week for nothing?"

He examined a stain on his tie. "Whores will be whores. But Allister crossed a fucking line. I won't let my father die a laughingstock."

Translation: he loved a good whore and couldn't find the will to punish her for being easy. It would be a little counterproductive, considering his career choice and all.

I filled my glass from the faucet. "Well, I doubt Allister will be in for confession anytime soon. Better go make him pay, Dicky."

Hesitation flickered across his face, and amusement rose in me.

"Aww," I cooed. "Does the dirty fed scare you?"

He scoffed.

"I don't blame you. The man is too comfortable around a gun." I leaned against the counter. "I'm assuming you snuck out of that meeting like the little cockroach you are and nobody else saw this afternoon's, ah . . . *tête-à-tête?*"

His eyes narrowed—he didn't like bugs—but he nodded.

"Well, then, there's no need to avenge anyone's honor, is there?"

He rubbed his cheek in thought. "It's the principle, though."

"Principles are stupid. Not to mention, I don't remember you piping up today when that Abelli talked crap about me and your papà."

"Harmless locker-room talk. Nobody jammed their dick in my father's wife." He glared.

"Oh, please. You're assuming—nothing more. I'd bet you didn't stick around long enough to see a thing."

He sniffed, proving that theory correct.

Never thought I could appreciate the fact the dirty fed was a cold-hearted, terrifying bastard until now.

"So, are you going to tell me why you were following me around earlier?" I asked.

"Yeah. You need to get your shit out of this apartment, that's why."

I frowned.

"You probably haven't noticed your husband's dying, being Allister's whore and all. The doctor says he's got a week, tops. So, all this shit?" He made a circle in the air with his forefinger. "Needs to be gone by yesterday."

"Well, Dicky, that isn't very hospitable."

"This place is in my father's name, which will make it mine very shortly. Stay if you want, but I'll expect payment." His beady eyes dropped to my breasts.

"Tempting, but I'll pass. The maintenance here sucks; my washer's been broken for a week."

"Don't expect a dime from his will."

I pursed my lips. "I don't want any of Richard's money. I have plenty of Antonio's left."

He let out a sarcastic noise. "Right. Call me if you change your mind about staying here. I'd give it to you easier than I bet Allister does." He shut the door behind him.

I looked around my apartment, at the shelf crammed with books and knickknacks, the paintings—from a cheap Marilyn Monroe portrait to an authentic Picasso—my Singer sewing machine and bags of fabric and thread, the haphazard stacks of magazines with circled fashion ideas in ballpoint bell, and *way* too many decorative pillows. If I was being conservative, I'd say it was cluttered. If I were Allister, I'd say it was a nightmare.

Regardless of that issue, I hated moving with a passion as fiery as the cover of any of my old bodice rippers.

I banged my head against the cupboard.

I didn't make dinner that night. I ate a bowl of Cap'n Crunch while watching one of my cheesy TV shows in Spanish. Magdalena changed the language a while ago, and I hadn't yet figured out how to change it back.

My washer really was broken, and all my dirty laundry could rival the Leaning Tower of Pisa. I walked past the pile in a dreamy, restless state. My body was exhausted, but my mind kept finding things about this afternoon to obsess over. It'd been so long since I'd slept with anyone, and my skin was still charged with an excited, breathless electricity.

The faucet let out a squeak when I turned it off with my toes. The bathwater was hot—almost too hot—but I needed something strong to soothe the ache. I was sore, and more than just between my legs. The asshole had left little marks all over me, including that stupid hickey on my neck.

Minus the whole he's-a-giant-prick thing, there had been something undeniably perfect about sleeping with him. The rough and greedy way he'd touched me. The sound of his voice in my ear. The feeling of him inside me.

A flush drifted down my body.

I dropped my head against the tub. Turned the faucet on with a *squeak* and let the water run until it threatened to tip over the sides.

What a shame it was that Christian had to be the one to reintroduce me to the world of sex. Because now that I was so close to being a single woman, I didn't think I'd be leaving again anytime soon, and it was going to be near impossible to find someone who touched me as good as he did.

Me: *Tell your husband I have to be out of my place soon, but he doesn't need to worry. I'm taking care of it all!*

I knew Ace would be annoyed if I just upped and moved without telling anyone, and I was already on his shit-list. I'd decided to go through his wife so I didn't have to face him regarding that silly club incident yesterday.

Elena: *He said, "Don't think you're getting out of yesterday by going through my wife."*

Elena: *What did you do?*

Me: *Daddy issues.*

Elena: *We're about to board our plane, but the strangest expression just crossed his face . . .*

Me: *What kind of 'strange'? Joyful? Brooding? Devious?*

Elena: *Definitely leaning toward devious . . .*

Me: *Dammit.*

Elena: *He just said, "I've got a place."*

Me: *Definitely not necessary.*

Me: *In any way.*

Me: *Shape or form.*

Me: *At all.*

Me: *Ever.*

Elena: *He says a few men will be over to help you move . . .*

Me: *Will I get out of this alive?*

Elena: *He just smiled to himself.*
Me: *Pray for me.*

I spent the next week packing my precious possessions into boxes, though, admittedly, grew distracted more than once while blowing the dust off my old books and magazines. I'd often end up on my divan, burying my face in some long-forgotten fashion journal or a novel with enough drama to put Jersey Shore to shame.

On Saturday, my laundry had gotten so out of hand, I decided to bite the bull and head to the laundromat. I was watching my reds whirl around in soap bubbles when my phone dinged.

Valentina: *You know how I have this obsession for anything Aleksandra Popova?*

Me: *Indeed.*

Whatever the Russian fashion model wore one week, Val was wearing the next.

Valentina: *Well, I think it's turned into jealousy.*

She'd attached an article captioned: *Can we talk about what Aleksandra was wearing last night? And we don't mean her Polka Siena evening dress . . .*

Probably a real muskrat shawl with the head still attached. Russians were so rustic two thousand two.

I had zero interest in the model and was in the middle of plucking a piece of lint from my maxi dress as I opened the article. I stilled.

The photo showed the gorgeous blonde at last night's Broadway debut, and on her arm was no one other than a dirty blue-eyed fed.

My chest tightened.

He had a hand on her hip, and she had a hand on his arm—the one I'd run my nails down just last week. They looked comfortable together—*perfect*, really—like two connecting puzzle pieces.

He wasn't looking at the camera but at some point in the distance. He appeared handsome and elusive, like some carnal fantasy you could only dream about but never touch. She wore her usual smolder—slightly pursed lips and cat eyes—and, with skyscraper-long legs and stilettos, she was only a couple of inches shorter than him. They probably had all kinds of crazy positions to try out without such a large height difference.

I rarely lost a bet, and I would put a lot of money down on the fact this woman was the one he would finally marry.

My pulse missed its next beat.

I was sure Aleksandra didn't have mental breakdowns after sex. Something bitter spread through me as the thoughts kept whirling in my head. They probably had romantic conversations in Russian. Probably fed each other sips of vodka.

My heart was beating so hard and erratically it hurt. I put a hand over it, growing seriously concerned about a potential heart murmur.

A woman in a pink sweat suit smacking her gum pulled me back to reality. "You going to sit there all day or what, honey? We all got clothes to wash here."

I sent Valentina a quick text before swapping out my laundry.

Me: *Twenty grand says he marries her.*

Valentina: *Lol . . . you're on.*

CHAPTER
Seventeen

Gianna

"HEY, BE CAREFUL WITH THAT! IT'S AN ANTIQUE!"

After gouging a small hole in the wall while bringing an armchair into my new apartment, two of Ace's men dropped it none-too-gently on the hardwood floor. They then dusted off their hands, like a good deed done, and stepped out to create more damage from the lobby to here.

The apartment was cool and modern, with a beautiful view of the Manhattan cityscape. There seemed to be nothing wrong with it—I'd even gone so far as to check for leaky faucets—and that made me even more suspicious. Ace rarely concerned himself with my affairs. The club incident must have annoyed him enough there was some punishment involved with this place. I was just waiting to find out what it was.

I wore a pair of faded overalls, and a red bandana kept my hair back from my face as I sat on the floor amidst an overwhelming number of boxes. There'd been no rhyme or reason to what I'd unpacked so far, and the place was beginning to look like a hoarder's wet dream.

I scratched a nonexistent itch on my cheek and decided to give up and instead bake something for my two new neighbors.

After running to the store to fill my fridge, I spent the next hour in the kitchen, putting a whole lot of neighborly love into some tiramisu.

The sun was just skimming the tops of the skyscrapers when I stepped out of my apartment and knocked on the door at the end of the hall.

My first neighbor was an older lady wearing a Hawaiian-themed muumuu. She squinted at my smile, as if it was so bright it hurt her eyes. Her gaze drifted to the plate in my hand.

"Cake?"

"No, tira—"

"It's been ages since I've had a piece of cake."

She grabbed the plate from my hand and shut the door in my face.

Well. Not exactly the welcome I'd been looking for, but it could have been worse. Though, everyone knows, when you look on the sunny side of things it begins to rain.

The only other neighbor on this floor lived right across the hall from me. I knocked, smiled brightly, and as the door opened, it slipped off my face like the ice cream on a little kid's cone.

The dirty fed's narrowed gaze fell from mine to the plate I cradled with two hands.

Well played, Ace, well played.

Was Allister supposed to be my babysitter until he returned to Seattle? It seemed I was everyone's joke, but I wasn't going to let this sour my mood. I was almost a single woman, after all.

I lifted the plate, finding my smile again. "Cake?"

He looked at the dessert, then drew his icy gaze back up to mine. "Are you high?"

I pursed my lips. "Unfortunately, no."

His eyes swept the hall over my head, as if he thought I might have brought a mariachi band or something as equally ridiculous along. It was then I realized he didn't know I was his neighbor. Interesting.

His voice was full of impatience. "Why are you here, Gianna?"

I frowned. "Are you saying that, after everything we've shared together, I can't bring you some dessert?"

He ran a hand down his tie, his gaze coasting to the two other apartments in the hall. I could hear the wheels turning in that clever brain of his.

"And here I was," I muttered, "telling everyone who'd listen that you and I are an item."

His eyes settled on my door. He ran his tongue across his teeth in thought.

"I've already made it Facebook official. I won't change it back, Christian. The amount of jealousy coming in has brought me closer to world domination than I've ever been."

I knew the moment he figured it out—the mat in front of the door, saying, *"Welcome, Bitches"*—might have given it away. And it was oh so painfully clear he was *not* happy about being my neighbor. In fact, it looked like he'd sucked on something sour.

"Don't tell me you lounge around in a tie, Officer. Goodness, I don't even wear pants."

The sudden anger radiating from him gave me the strong urge to back away slowly until I was in the safety of my apartment. I was beginning to think this joke wasn't all for my benefit.

He let out a sardonic breath as he processed this. Ran his hand across his jaw. Settled his fiery gaze on me. "Are you knocking on my door just to harass me, or do you want something?"

"I want a decent welcoming for one. The muumuu next door was seriously lacking."

"I'm not eating your cake."

Frustration rose in me. Didn't anyone have respect for dessert around here?

"It's not cake, dammit!"

His stare was drier than the Sahara. "You said it was cake."

"Yeah, well, I say a lot of things. It's tiramisu, for goodness' sake. Give it to one of the women you con into your bed. I promise, she'll fall madly in love with you, and you won't have to be lonely anymore."

"Just fuck her and give her some dessert. Is that all there is to it?"

"Pretty much."

"And to think I've been doing it wrong all these years." He crossed his arms and leaned against the doorframe, musing, "You seem to have a vested interest in the women I'm with."

I laughed. *Twenty grand, to be exact.*

His eyes narrowed as if he'd read my mind.

I batted my eyelashes in innocence. "So, I know this isn't the most ideal living arrangement—I'd prefer you were back in your frigid homeland, working to sit the next Stalin on the throne, or whatever else it is you do—but we'll just have to deal with it like two mature adults."

He was not convinced by his monotone response. "And how do you propose we do that?"

"Easy." I drew an imaginary line down the middle of the hall with my foot. "I get this part of the hallway, and you can have this part. As for the pool and gym, I get to use them during the day. You can have them once the sun sets, right after you get home from corrupting good Christian women."

He nodded thoughtfully. "Anything else?"

"Sometimes, I run out of eggs and sugar. In exchange, I'll make sure to keep condoms on hand in case you have company and misplace yours again." My smile was all teeth.

"You've really thought this out," he drawled.

"I have."

"And you even baked for me."

I bristled. "Well, I didn't know it was you I was baking for, if it's any consolation."

He looked at the dessert in my hands as though he'd never tried sugar before. He nodded toward it. "Chocolate?"

"Arsenic."

"My favorite."

He took the plate from my hand and slammed the door.

I sighed.

My neighbors sucked.

Awareness connected me to the door across the hall like a line of static electricity. He was just over there, probably talking Russian on the phone and lounging around in a dress shirt and tie. My skin buzzed with hypersensitivity whenever I changed my clothes, knowing he was so close. My breath caught whenever I heard the smallest noise from the hall, only to realize it was the air conditioner kicking on or Muumuu's walker dragging across the floor.

I was frustrated with all of it.

This living arrangement wasn't going to work out, but I refused to be the one to concede and check into a hotel until he went back to Seattle.

We'd run into each other in the hall twice this week, and he'd made it clear I was on his mind about as much as world peace. He'd even gone so far as to ignore one of my cheery, "Good morning, neighbor's!" completely.

If he could handle this, then so could I.

I fought with my doorknob and the stupid key that needed the perfect wiggle to turn in the lock, an irritable edge biting beneath my skin at the picture Valentina had sent me earlier. Of course, it had been Aleksandra and Christian. They'd seen each other again last night. I bet he let *her* take off his stupid shirt.

The sound of a door closing made the hair on the back of my neck rise, and, with a racing heart, I finished locking up and turned around with a contrived smile. It didn't survive when I saw Christian was only wearing a pair of running pants and a gray long-sleeve shirt. My mouth went dry. I didn't think I'd seen him without even a tie in all the years I'd known him. And, God, could he *ever* pull the gym-junkie look off.

I swallowed. "Why, Officer, you're practically naked."

I'd been so busy looking at his body, I hadn't noticed his expression until now. And it was furious.

"Your view on an appropriate amount of clothes is obviously skewed." His voice was strained. *"What are you doing?"*

I frowned, looking down at my itty-bitty white bikini. "Is it not obvious?"

"With you, nothing is."

"I can't tell if that was a dumb-brunette joke or if I'm so

unpredictable it excites you." I pursed my lips, muttering, "Probably the former, considering you're as excitable as Jack Frost."

"Gianna . . ." It was a warning. For what, though, I wasn't sure.

I rolled my eyes. "Relax. I'm going down to the pool to swim off the entire bag of Hershey's Kisses I ate last night, not to crash one of your silly meetings."

He was going to say something—something rude or demanding—but before he could, he gave his head a subtle shake, expression strained, as if he was having to bite his tongue to hold whatever it was in.

He tried to leave me there, but we were headed in the same direction, so . . . we ended up walking side-by-side down the hall. He stared ahead, his posture strained. His jaw ground tight. The tension he put off couldn't be healthy. He rolled his shoulders. It didn't seem to help.

He bit out a curse.

His arm wrapped around my waist, he lifted me off the floor, and then he was carrying me back to my apartment like a sack of groceries.

"Hey," I complained, though it was half-hearted because the heat coming through his cotton shirt scalded my skin.

"You aren't wearing this downstairs, Gianna. There are kids around."

"Don't pretend you're concerned about traumatized children." His arm was tight around my waist, his body pressed against my nearly-naked one. My blood was boiling and stealing my breath.

He dropped me to my feet in front of my apartment. Took the keys from my hand and, annoyingly, unlocked the door in a single try.

"Go find a swimsuit that covers your ass."

I put my hands on my hips defiantly. "Those aren't in style anymore."

"We both know you don't follow fashion trends."

"Since when do you regulate what I wear?"

"Since you've clearly lost the competence to do it yourself."

I opened my mouth, but before I could protest again, he cut me off with that lord-and-master tone.

"It's not happening, Gianna."

"Fine," I snapped, but I was only listening because the swimsuit *was* ridiculously risqué, with only a thong for bottoms. Sometimes, I thought I did things just to stir up trouble. Just add it to my list of daddy issues.

Spinning around, I headed to my room, pulling off my bikini top and dropping it in the hallway on the way. His gaze ran down my naked back, cool and electric, like the glide of ice on my skin.

When I returned in a new bathing suit, it was to find him looking around my apartment with distaste. I'd gotten most of the boxes unpacked and put away this week, so I was a little upset I didn't get Christian's approval. Not.

"You've thoroughly ruined the place, haven't you?"

"If you mean I've given it some life, then yes." I adjusted my boob in the neon orange one-piece. "Ready?"

He gestured for me to spin around, and, with a roll of my eyes, I did. The suit wasn't modest either, with slits up the sides, but he seemed to approve—if not a bit reluctantly.

We took the elevator together, and my body played havoc on me, remembering how it'd felt to be touched by him. The dirty things he'd said to me. He was only inches away; it would take nothing to close the space between us. Something electrifying played in my veins. Made me dizzy.

"You look like a traffic cone," he told me.

As we passed a potted tree in the lobby, I pushed him into it. He hadn't been expecting it—he actually took a step to the side. Satisfaction filled me at the giant leaf that had the audacity to smack him in the head.

He shot me an annoyed glance.

I rolled my eyes. "Gosh, you're so stuffy. I bet you've never done anything silly in your life. You really need to loosen—"

He shoved me into a towel cart. It was half-hearted because I was able to catch myself before I hit it.

"Close, but no cigarette," I told him, breathless at the playfulness, before we split off in separate directions.

His eyes lit with amusement. "No *cigar*."

CHAPTER
Eighteen

Christian

"**G**ET RID OF HER," I GROWLED AS SOON AS NICO OPENED THE DOOR.

He leaned an arm against the doorframe and rubbed a hand across his mouth that was fighting off a grin. "Not sure I know what you're talking about."

"Bullshit. I want Gianna out of my building by tomorrow morning. And if you don't think I'm serious, I'll find a way to make it crystal fucking clear, Ace." My voice was cold, but I let it warm around the edges suggestively when I said, "How's your wife?"

His eyes flashed, and he sucked his teeth. "You know, if anyone else said that to me, I'd goddamn kill them. But I'll make a concession on your account, considering I own the little nightmare of a woman you're so desperate to fuck. Understandable you'd be a little *touchy*." His voice was dark and mocking. "Not exactly off to the best start, but maybe, if you play your cards right from here on out, I'll let you have her when Richard passes."

Irritation unfurled in my chest. My hand twitched but I wouldn't let myself react. I hadn't had to throw a punch in years, and I wouldn't start now—over a woman, no less.

"If I wanted her, I'd have her already."

He let out an amused breath. "You know, you and I—we're a lot more alike than you think, Allister."

"Doubtful."

He crossed his arms and leaned against the doorframe. "Gianna is a headache when she's married, but single? She's more trouble than she's worth. I was giving you the courtesy of working something out with me, but if you don't want her . . . there are plenty of men who'd be interested."

"I'm not so easily manipulated," I said, not letting myself take his bait on a hook.

"I'm just being practical, Allister. She's a liability. And this time, I'll make sure her new husband is spry enough to keep her in line."

Spry enough to fuck her, was the first thought that came to mind.

Fire burned in my blood, and I saw red spots at just the idea of some other man touching her, pushing his way between her legs.

"I want her out of my building," I bit out, because I couldn't think about Gianna with another man for another second without doing something crazy—like actually going through with Ace's absurd proposal and forcing her to marry me.

"Why don't you cut your losses and check into a hotel? Or are their sheets not a high enough thread count for you?"

I hated hotels. The housekeeping always reorganized my shit, went through my things, and left behind their phone numbers outlined with a goddamned heart.

I refused to stay in a hotel because I refused to let Gianna know how deeply she was under my skin. I couldn't even look at the woman, let alone be near her, without fighting the urge to do things I probably shouldn't. Like tie her to my bed and make her come, over, and over again, just so I could watch the fire go soft in her eyes.

Nonetheless, I wasn't going to last much longer with Gianna running around in a tiny *thong* bikini. But, thankfully, business should only keep me in New York for a couple more weeks.

I was in the middle of negotiations with Aleksandra Popova's father, a Russian politician, during his stay in the States. But it seemed he was more old-fashioned than I'd thought, and he was pushing his daughter on me like an incentive. It was an arrangement I was seriously considering. Aleksandra was beautiful, traditional, and composed. She wouldn't challenge me, ask me questions about my past, or dig her way into my business. She'd make the quintessential house-wife. It would be a good match, even if I had to think about Gianna when I fucked her.

I adjusted my cufflinks. "Use Gianna to fuck with me again, Ace, and business between us is going to be a lot different. Understood?"

A corner of his lips lifted. "Never thought a woman could come between us, Allister. Say, you wouldn't know anything about my sur-veillance camera in and outside the club being wiped clean last Sunday, would you?"

"Must have been a power outage."

"Must have been," he drawled. "What a shame, though. A whole lot of men would have paid to see Gianna in that get-up of hers." He tsked in feigned disappointment, and anger burned my throat.

I turned to leave, but . . . *fuck it.* "One last thing."

"Yeah?"

When I turned to face him, I punched the smirk right off the fuck-er's face.

Ace wiped at the blood on his bottom lip, his eyes lit with amuse-ment. "I guess this makes us even, Allister."

I stepped into the lobby and, naturally, the one person I fought to avoid was leaning over the front counter, playing cards with the pubescent pool boy.

She wore a short little romper—one of those things she'd have to take all the way off to use the bathroom. So impractical. So her. Her dark hair trailed down her back, the longest strands stopping at a point just before the curve of her ass. It was another obsession of mine. Always wavy and uninhibited, just like her.

She looked over her shoulder as if she could feel my stare.

Fuck, she was pretty. With soft eyes, pouty lips, and a body sex doll companies tried to replicate.

Heat ran to my groin, and I clenched my teeth in annoyance.

Why did the most perfect woman from here to Seattle have to be this one?

She frowned at me, then turned her attention back to the kid as if I wasn't even here. Women stared at me; Gianna glared. It was just a fact of life I'd come to terms with. Sometimes, I wondered, if she smiled at me genuinely, all coy and sweet, like I was someone she actually liked, would it finally be enough to end my infatuation with her? Reverse psychology and all that.

But no, she reserved those smiles for scrawny pool boys.

Pool boys with a death wish.

Who knew what his excuse was—a stray eyelash on her cheek, a hair out of place, her soft skin was distracting—whatever the fuck it was, he was going to touch her.

Over my goddamn body.

As I walked past the front counter, I grabbed his wrist before his hand could make contact with a strand of her hair, shooting him a *touch-her-and-I'll-kill-you* look. He paled. I let him go and continued to the elevator.

"Oh, don't mind him." I could hear Gianna roll her eyes behind my back. "He doesn't have a fun bone in his entire body."

Maybe not, but my idea of fun certainly wasn't watching some teenager who wouldn't even know where to put his dick touch her.

Gianna and I exchanged a look before I stepped onto the elevator. Hers said, *Stay out of my business.* Before I could stop it, mine said, *I've been inside that little body and I'll goddamn say who can touch it.*

Her eyes flashed.

Then, she lifted a finger and flipped me off.

CHAPTER
Nineteen

Gianna

THE APARTMENT GODS HATED ME.

I'd been trying not to concern myself with anything Christian Allister-related since that unfortunate afternoon in the back seat of his car. A part of me was still a little humiliated he'd witnessed my breakdown, but the other part couldn't forget he'd been the best sex of my life.

I was still married.

And I wanted to sleep with the biggest prick I'd ever met *again*.

Christian wasn't going to drag me down to hell with him.

Nevertheless, over the next week, I was put within close proximity to the man more than any other neighbor I'd ever had. I'd even physically run into him once. He'd looked at me like I was a vagrant who'd just asked him for money before leaving me there without even attempting a simple apology.

One might think our frequent run-ins would bring us closer together, and, although he did finally respond to one of my cheery, "Good morning's!" with a dry expression while telling me it was noon, we were still about as close as Cady Heron and Regina George.

Five shopping bags hung from my arm as I adjusted the floppy hat on my head and walked through the lobby, heels clicking on the modern concrete floor. I'd been out with Valentina this afternoon, purchasing a few final items to add to my fall wardrobe. I'd yet to tell her about Christian and the fact I'd had rough, unprotected sex with him in his car, and I wasn't going to. She'd make something of it that wasn't there.

The doors began to close, but at the last minute, a hand shot out and held them open. Christian stepped onto the elevator.

His gaze came up and caressed mine.

I tensed and moved to the side, giving him much more room than he needed. His heavy presence stretched about three feet in diameter, and, these days, I did my best to stay out of it. It was like a vortex of dirty thoughts and racing hearts. Not to mention, he was so sexy and annoying, the closer I got to him, the worse the desire became to sink my teeth into the muscle at the back of his arm.

We both stared at the doors as they closed, my wish heavy in the air that somebody else would step on. Nobody did.

Like I said, the apartment gods hated me.

"I don't bite," he said, sounding annoyed.

"Liar."

His gaze flicked to me, and then a slow smile pulled on the corner of his mouth. It was the kind of smile seen on the bad guy's lips after stealing the girl. Warmth rushed beneath my skin; a prickling, breathless heat traveling all the way to my toes.

"Fine. I don't bite women in elevators."

"Whatever makes you feel good about yourself, Officer."

He wore a long-sleeve shirt and running pants, and the light sheen of sweat on his skin let me know he was just leaving the gym. He went every day—even the Lord's day. It was blasphemy.

Standing slightly behind him, I took advantage of the view. I swore the man was made of nothing but broad shoulders and smooth muscle, the defined lines visible through his shirt. The sliver of a white Calvin Klein band showing above the waistband of his pants was enough to send my thoughts straight to the gutter.

I swallowed. "The sun's still up, buddy."

"I've been expecting you to file your complaint. Thing is, I get more corrupting done at night if I work out during the day. Don't want to disappoint those good Christian women."

The thought that he was sleeping with other women made my

gut twist. Nor could I stop a rush of irritation any time Valentina even mentioned Aleksandra's name. Her face annoyed me, and just the idea she had her French-tipped nails anywhere near Christian made my stomach burn. Gosh, maybe I was getting an ulcer. I reminded myself to make an appointment with my GP.

"I've yet to see you even use the gym, anyway," he noted.

"That's because I only run when something's chasing me." The doors slid open, and I stepped out, hitting him with one of my bags. "Just stay away from the pool, and everything will remain civil. Capiche?"

"Of course," he said dryly. "Wouldn't dare to ruin your day of lounging on a chaise with your pool boy on call."

"Careful, Christian." I pouted. "Keep saying sweet things to me, and I might think you like me."

"Dormiste con ella, tú cerdo!"

Slap.

Chad blocked another incoming slap to his face by grabbing his wife's wrist. *"Fue un accidente, querida!"*

I scoffed.

"Un accidente? Tu polla no se deslizó dentro de ella, idiota!" Chloe slapped him with her free hand.

I jumped at the loud clap of thunder that seemed to rock the apartment building. Setting my needle and thread on the living room floor where I was sitting, I got to my feet and padded to the window. The sky was dark, though the glow of city lights caught on the menacing clouds rolling in.

Chloe and Chad were now ripping off each other's clothes while professing their undying love for each other.

I flipped the channel.

The weatherman's words were dubbed over in Spanish, but I

didn't even need to try and decipher what he was saying because the red cloud on his radar that was swallowing up Manhattan was clear enough.

I stood in front of the TV in an oversized t-shirt and lace boyshorts, with a cool rush of anxiety running through me. I wasn't a fan of storms; they were unpredictable and destructive. They made me feel as small and weak as a little girl.

I hesitantly sat back down and picked up the dress I'd been hemming. Thunder rumbled across the sky, and I pricked my finger on my needle. With annoyance, I dropped my things. Took a deep breath.

It was just a little storm. No big deal.

My heart jumped at the *crack* of lightning right outside my window, and that was when the lights turned off. The lampposts on the street flickered and went dark.

No.

I squeezed my eyes closed, waiting for the generator to kick on. We had to have a backup generator, right? It was the twenty-first century, for goodness' sake.

But the lights weren't turning on.

And the dark was closing in.

In. Out.

In. Out.

The floorboards creaked behind me.

"I'm not going to hurt you, little girl."

My lungs iced over.

There's nobody there. There's nobody there. There's nobody there.

"I just want to play with you."

Fear wrapped around my throat and cut off my breath. A tear escaped my closed eyes, running down my cheek.

"Sing me a song, bella."

I couldn't breathe.

Something touched me. Cold fingers running through my hair, the same way they had from ages eight to twelve.

Terror crawled up my spine.

I flew out my door and banged on the one right across from it. I didn't want him to see me like this, but I also didn't want to die. And I was sure I would if I had to be alone in this darkness any longer.

The door opened.

A candle glowed from somewhere inside, casting his form in shadow. His presence, however, was like a light in the dark.

"I'm going to die," I choked out, not able to drag a deep enough breath into my lungs.

"Never, *malyshka*." It was soft and vehement. "Come here."

It wasn't until I was pressed against his warm body that I realized how badly I was shaking. It was like grabbing onto a life raft before almost drowning in the sea. He made a rough noise and picked me up. I wrapped my legs around his waist and rested my face against his neck, struggling for every breath.

"Slowly, Gianna."

He ran a hand through my hair, down my back, and the simple act was so soothing, soon, I inhaled a steady breath. Relief hit me so strongly it brought on a wave of fresh tears. I didn't know how long it took, but when my breathing evened out and my heart rate slowed, I was straddling Christian on his couch, my arms around his shoulders, my chest pressed to his. The panic attack had sucked the energy from me, left me feeling lethargic.

Thunder rumbled in the distance.

A candle flickered on the coffee table.

"What are you afraid of?"

"Everything," I whispered, trailing my finger across the starched collar of his dress shirt.

"You're not afraid of me." We were so close his cheek brushed my tear-streaked one when he rasped, "And, baby, I'm worse than the dark."

Maybe that was why I felt safe from it now.

He was so warm and solid, and he smelled so irresistible, I couldn't stop myself from dragging my face down his neck and making a soft noise of approval. Maybe I was courting the devil, though no one had ever warned me the devil would feel so good.

Tension rolled through him. His fingers laced through my hair at the small of my back, his voice hoarse. "Tell me who hurt you, Gianna."

I didn't even blink that he knew. Of course, he did. Give the man two sticks and tell him to make a boat with them, and he could.

I couldn't deny him an answer. Not now, without an ounce of fight in me. With my body against his, and his smell everywhere. Not in the dark, with his arms around me and his voice in my ear.

"A family friend," I said.

"Is he still alive?"

"No. He died when I was fourteen. Natural causes, unfortunately—no torture involved." My fingers played with the ends of his hair above his collar.

"Shame," he said softly, but a hint of vehemence showed through. "Tell me what he did to you, *malyshka*."

I swallowed. I'd never told anyone but Sydney and my therapist. Talking about it felt like reliving it, but now, there wasn't a possibility of the memories coming back to haunt me. Not with this man nearby. They wouldn't dare.

"He came to my room when my papà had company. He wanted to play games with me . . . wanted me to sing for him. He touched me. My face, my hair, my . . . everywhere. But only after the lights were off. I don't think he liked to see what he was doing. Guilty conscience, I suppose."

His posture remained unmoved but something dark rumbled beneath the surface. "Did your father know?"

"He told me my papà knew, but . . . I don't know. Papà never let on that he did, though I've always wondered."

"Why?"

I lifted a shoulder. "His favorite name for me growing up was *Whore*, even though I was a virgin until I got married. My mamma had an affair before I was born, and we'll just say, I became the target of his rage. He always claimed I wasn't his. Maybe I'm not." My words were quiet, wistful. "When he found out my fear of the dark, he didn't hesitate to use it against me. And here I am now, the healthiest, most put-together woman you'll ever meet."

He wasn't amused at my sarcasm. "Look at me, Gianna."

I did.

"We have a saying in Russia. *S volkámi zhit', po-vólch'i vyt'.* Say it."

I butchered it. A corner of his lips lifted, but he walked me through it until it sounded somewhat intelligible.

"It means, to live with wolves, you have to howl like a wolf."

Is that what you did? I wanted to ask, but somehow knew it wouldn't be well received.

"You've got to learn how to howl, *malyshka*. To tell your demons to fuck off. We all know you have it in you; you tell me to enough. And unlike your demons"—his voice darkened—"I can actually bite you."

I shivered. "I think you just wanted me to speak your heathen language."

He didn't agree, but the thumb he ran across a tear-track on my cheek said more than words ever could. "Worst Russian I've ever heard."

I feigned a frown. "Bummer. I was hoping not to be mistaken for a tourist when I visit Moscow next summer."

He didn't believe me. "You're not going to Moscow."

"Why not?"

"It doesn't get warm enough to laze around by the pool—at least, not for a little Italian girl."

"Hmm," I replied. "Why do you kiss me?"

His gaze dropped to my lips, his jaw ticking in thought. "I wanted to know what you tasted like."

We both knew he hadn't answered the question. He'd known what I tasted like three years ago, if that had been the only goal.

"What do I taste like?"

His eyes drifted back up to mine. They were so deep and serious they held me captive. His next two words tugged at my heart, even though I didn't know the meaning.

"*Kak moya.*"

The lights flicked back on.

It should have broken the moment, but now, I could see the

intensity in his eyes I hadn't been able to in the dark. A possessive heat sizzling in blue flame.

We stared at each other.

My heart raced. My blood burned.

I didn't know what I was doing, but I couldn't stop.

Leaning in, I brought my mouth to his, pausing close enough to taste his breath. I was shaking in anticipation yet he remained still as I took a sweet pull on his lips. He didn't kiss me back, but heat still pulsed and spread through me like fire, tightening in my breasts before descending to my toes.

He licked his lips, drawing a lazy gaze from my mouth to my eyes, as though he'd found the kiss slightly bothersome to his person. It should have been discouraging, but I was too far in to stop now.

I drew my tongue across his top lip and then nipped at the bottom. A low groan rumbled up his throat. The sound hummed between my legs, making me clutch both of my hands in his hair.

And then I licked his lips like an ice cream cone. It had no finesse, just pure, unadulterated *want*.

He made a noise of anger, grabbed the back of my neck, parted my lips with his, and slipped his tongue inside.

Lust exploded behind my eyes, blurring my vision.

"Is this what you wanted, *malyshka*?" His tone was heated, coated in a rough accent.

God, yes.

I could only nod.

He leaned back into the couch like he was settling in for the kiss. I went with him, fingers gripping the collar of his shirt, mouth pressed to his. The man really didn't kiss—I felt it in the lazy, blasé manner his lips moved against mine. But when he was all in on a kiss, it was the deep kind I had to pull back from to take a breath.

My pulse thrummed between my legs as he tasted my mouth, sucked on my tongue, and nipped me when I kissed him softer and sweeter than he liked. He could have it his way. Kissing had always got me so hot I'd do anything after a while, and just kissing Christian was better than sex with anyone else.

My hips rolled, mocking every thrust and glide of our tongues. I moaned, pressing tighter against him, running my nails down his biceps. I'd never admit it to the man, but I was obsessed with his arms.

My breathing grew ragged as my breasts rubbed against his chest every time I swayed into a kiss. Hot pressure built inside me as I grinded against his erection. The lust inside me was burning out of control, growing more frantic with every press of our lips.

He let out a rough breath and pulled away from me, his voice harsh. *"Enough,* Gianna. You have to stop."

"Why?" I nibbled at his jawline and down his neck. He grabbed my wrist before my hand could reach his belt.

"Because another moment of this, and I'm not going to be able to."

I looked at him, confused. "But I don't want you to."

He made a frustrated noise in his throat. "This wasn't what this was about, Gianna."

I blinked, and then the heat inside me dimmed and went cold. The man's hands weren't even on me—*hadn't* been on me the entire time I'd practically mauled him. It seemed like I was always touching him. *What's wrong with me?* He'd listened to my sob story and I'd reacted like a clingy virgin falling for her first lover. Humiliation settled inside me.

And then I remembered Aleksandra. The man had a girlfriend and I was throwing myself at him. No wonder he wanted me to stop.

I swallowed. "I must have lost my head there, Officer. I'm sure, with that face, things like this happen to you all the time."

His eyes narrowed dangerously.

"No?" My voice was hesitant.

"No," he snapped.

Oh.

I climbed off him, got to my feet, and headed to leave.

"Gianna, wait."

His door lay wide open, and I walked through it into the hall.

"Gianna." The word was harsh and vehement. Christian Allister was not happy. But there was something else in his voice. Something

soft and nauseating. Something that sounded suspiciously like *pity*. The day I stuck around to see that on his face was the day I'd willingly roll around in my own self-loathing.

I slammed my door behind me.

CHAPTER
Twenty

Gianna

MY SECOND HUSBAND'S FUNERAL CAME ON A MID-SEPTEMBER DAY.

Sunlight splayed through the trees onto the cemetery floor, silhouetting each shade of black. Black hearts, black suits, black dresses. Polished shoes and Glocks. The *Cosa Nostra* had come to pay their respects in a sea of black.

A light breeze tousled the mantilla veil around my face. As gruesome as it seemed, this was a day I'd been waiting for since the moment I'd been married. I thought I would feel different. *Free.* But now that it was here, I felt nothing. Numbness had spread through my body, filling every vessel and vein.

Elena squeezed my hand before drifting with Ace and the rest of the crowd toward the line of shiny cars.

"You ready to go?" Lorenzo asked.

"I'll find another ride home. I have something I need to do."

"All right. But stay out of trouble."

Slipping my hands into my dress pockets, I headed through the cemetery. The headstone was small and simple. It was the first time I'd ever visited it. The first time I'd had the will.

Sydney Brown, it read. *Beloved Daughter and Friend.*

I stared at the word *friend* for the longest time, searching for the right words.

"I'm sorry," I whispered. "I'm sorry you ever met me, that I ever introduced you to this world. To Antonio." My voice cracked, and I wiped a stray tear from my cheek. "I'm so sorry."

I'd forgiven her a long time ago, but the guilt I felt for dragging her into my twisted life was still a heavy weight in my chest.

My gaze caught on movement to my side.

The procession had left but Christian remained. He stood by his car, hands in his pockets and his gaze on me. It was thoughtful and warm enough to touch my skin like a ray of sun.

It'd been only sheer luck I hadn't seen him since the night I went to his apartment. I'd bared my deepest, darkest secret with him, naively believed it meant something, and been turned down, hard. The cutting ache of rejection still burned whenever I thought of him. And, to my bemusement, that happened to be more frequently every day.

He watched me as I walked over to him.

"Did someone blackmail you to take me home?" I asked.

"Can't I do something nice for someone?"

"For me?" I raised a brow, forcing amusement. *"Please."*

His jaw ticked. He shook his head, his gaze dropping to the ground. When it came back up to me, it was so heavy and humorless it pinned me to my spot.

"I had every intention of coming back for you three years ago, Gianna."

My small smile fell. Shock rocked me at my center. He could sometimes be so blunt when least expected, it stole my breath.

"I was in Moscow those two weeks. But if I had known, I would've stopped it. Your marriage." He looked around the cemetery, at the tent where my husband's casket lay. "All of this."

My lungs felt tight. "It wasn't your responsibility to save me."

His gaze was steady. "Nonetheless, I would have."

"Savior complex?" I joked to lighten the mood.

"No." It was a harsh word.

My throat burned, making my voice bitter. "Why are you telling me this?" *Why are you making me feel this way?*

"You hate me for that night."

"I don't—" I cut myself off. Because there *was* a part of me that resented him for acting like he'd cared and then disappearing, leaving me tied to another unwanted marriage. It wasn't rational—none of it had been his fault—but, still, the feeling was there.

We stared at each other as that awareness settled between us.

"I still don't understand why you're telling me this," I told him. "It's not like it matters anymore." *Right?*

He shook his head, letting out a disdainful noise through his teeth.

My heart beat hard against my ribcage.

His eyes lifted to mine, and they were filled with fire: violence, confliction, and a flash of possession. "Ask me why I kiss you."

I couldn't think. Couldn't breathe.

I shook my head.

Because I was suddenly terrified of the answer.

With his handsome, aristocratic face, he looked like a pissed-off prince who was darkly amused to be denied what he wanted. "I thought you were braver than this, Gianna."

I wasn't. *I'm not.*

"Remember that the next time you offer me your body, *malyshka*," he bit out. "Because next time, I'll *take* it. Regardless if there are still tears on your face. Fuck, I won't care if you cry the whole way through it."

I swallowed.

He'd once insinuated I was breakable, like a flimsy piece of glass. And that truth was suddenly loud in my ears. I needed to keep my distance from this man; nothing good could come from this chemistry between us. It was explosive and addictive but forged in hate and mistrust. He had always won, and I knew, if I explored this attraction further, he would be the victor in the end.

My silence was my forfeit.

He shook his head. "Get in the car, Gianna."

He took me home, and we didn't say another word to each other on the way.

"I think it's too small," I groaned.

"What do you expect, eating all that junk lately?" Magdalena chastised, yanking on the laces of my dress. "There are chocolate stains on all of your clothes."

"I can't help it if I eat my feelings."

"If you aren't careful, *querida*, you'll look like a busted can of biscuits by Christmas."

"Everyone should put on a little weight for the winter," I countered, turning to look at myself in the mirror. My dress was a slim-fitting sheath style, with a lace bustier and a corset that tied up at the back. It was beautiful, but maybe not that practical.

I placed a hand on my stomach. "I can't really breathe that well."

"Don't be dramatic. Now, let me put the finishing touches on your hair. Then, you need to leave. Roberto is coming over."

I was going to complain about this being *my* apartment but couldn't get all the air in to do so. Consequently, when I could speak, what came out was, "Hide the chocolate, Magdalena."

It was Ace's club's fiftieth anniversary, and the place was easily overcapacity. But that was probably the lesser of the illegal activities taking place tonight.

"*Really*, Val?" I sighed. "My husband's funeral was two days ago."

"Oh, come on. You have to jump back into the saddle sometime! Let's be honest, how long has it been since you've been laid?"

I ignored that question and eyed the blind date she'd brought along. Handsome, dark hair, lean build, a couple of inches taller than me in heels. He was exactly my type—or, at least, what I would have preferred not long ago. Though, now, I couldn't help but feel like everything was wrong with him.

Frustration ran through me. I'd been abstinent for so long it felt like I was a virgin again. And now that I was finally free to do as I wished, I couldn't find any interest in men. Well, besides *one*. Christian had reintroduced me to sex, and it only made sense I was feeling a little attached to him because of it.

"At least give him a try, Gianna. He's been anxious to meet you."

The truth was, I needed touch and sex and affection. I *lived* for it.

And I didn't believe I could stand to be without it anymore. Maybe if I forced some interest in this blind date of mine, it would eventually become genuine.

"Fine. Do introduce us, Val."

"See, I knew this was exactly what you needed." She grabbed my arm, and we walked toward a table where her husband Ricardo and my date were talking. "By the way, loving the dress. Very classy steampunk. Can you breathe?"

"Not at all."

She chuckled as we reached the table.

"Van, this is Gianna. Gianna, this is Van." She shoved me toward him like I was a nervous teenager meeting a boy at a dance. I rolled my eyes but stepped forward and offered my hand.

"It's nice to meet you."

He smiled. "I assure you, the pleasure is all mine."

His smile was beautiful, and his voice was rich and deep. The kind of voice that made you feel like he'd seen you naked just from the way the syllables poured off his lips.

I must have been off the saddle *way* too long.

Because I actually *blushed*.

While he kissed the top of my hand, I passed Val a wide-eyed glance. She winked.

A hot sensation trailed down my spine; I turned my head toward the door. My gaze collided with Christian's and stuck there. My heart slowed, each beat incinerating as fire licked beneath my skin.

He'd always been out-of-this-world handsome, and I'd never reacted to him like most of the other women in the room. But now I knew the way his hands felt on me, the intoxicating way he kissed, the sound of his groan when he came. And I wanted all of it again, even though I knew it would be terrible for my mental—and possibly, physical—health.

He took in the blush still evident on my cheeks. Then, his eyes flicked to the side, to my date, and narrowed.

That was when I noticed the woman beside him. Aleksandra Popova was even more beautiful in person, in a classy red evening dress and gold heels. She would be the perfect pin-up model. I'd even bet, behind closed doors, she'd embody the fifties housewife by serving her husband a glass of cognac on a silver platter, all while cooking a turkey and wearing an apron.

Her hand was on *his arm*.

I looked away, fighting off a sudden bout of heartburn. I frowned. I hadn't even eaten much today while trying to fit into this dress. It seemed my health was always in question whenever Christian was present. That should be enough warning to stay away.

"Sorry to break it to you like this, Val, but it looks like your pockets are going to be much lighter soon."

She glanced toward the door, and when she turned back around, it was with a smirk on her lips. "I'm not worried."

Ricardo arched a brow, probably wondering how much of his money his wife had bet.

"I am warning you, though," Val said, eyeing Aleksandra with worship sparkling in her eyes, "I'm about to fangirl really hard."

I wasn't sure which game this was, but I didn't want any part of it.

While Christian usually regarded me with indifference or even distaste in public since the moment I'd met him, tonight, his stare couldn't feel further from either.

Our gazes had caught more than once from across the club, but his remained even after I looked away. The heat of it burned through my skin like fire. His girlfriend stood by his side for goodness' sake, yet every time he looked at me, he might as well have announced to the room we'd had unprotected, adulterous sex.

I'd been so sure that was something he wouldn't tell a single soul, considering he'd always looked down on me like I was beneath him while parading one of his perfect blondes around. Regardless, I couldn't afford to let anyone know we'd been together—Dick knowing was bad enough—because it would take little to deduce it had happened when I was married. And, dammit, that sin should stay between me and the Lord.

He was playing a game.

And I didn't want to play.

So, I did what anyone would do: I refused to engage him and, instead, feigned complete enrapturement in my date. But it was all a facade. The minute Christian stepped in the room, I couldn't focus on anything besides where he stood. The fact he had a hand on Aleksandra's waist. The way it made my blood heat with something itchy and frustrating.

Valentina was hogging his date's attention, fawning over her in a way that made me slightly nauseous. Had he slept with her? Did he *kiss* her? I looked into my drink with a frown, wondering what cocktail Val had brought me. Someone had been too heavy-handed with the bitters.

I was feeling a little salty when Val dragged me over to meet Aleksandra, so, naturally, in the act of balancing my attitude, my voice ended up an octave too sweet when I told the model she and Christian made a lovely couple.

I saw his gaze narrow out of the corner of my eye.

"Well, thank you," she purred in a feminine Russian accent. "I must confess, you have the loveliest dress in the room."

"I'm flattered you think so, though I'm sure some people would say otherwise." I had the urge to flutter my eyelashes at Christian, but instead, chose to pretend he didn't exist.

I didn't even have to look at him to know he didn't like it. He was twisting his watch on his wrist, once, twice, three times.

"Some people don't know what they're talking about. Your necklace—" She stepped closer to lift it to the light. "Isn't it just . . . *picturesque*, Christian?"

"Indeed," he said dryly.

"Where did you get it?" She blinked at me in a curious way, but there was something sharp like claws behind her eyes.

I tugged it from her grasp with a sugary smile. "Oh, just a little vintage shop in Rome. My first husband bought it for me." I drew my finger down the charm like it was something special to me. In reality, I'd almost put it in my Salvation Army donation last month.

"How *sweet*," she cooed. "First husbands are always so sentimental."

"Oh? Have you had one?" I tilted my head.

Valentina watched the scene with fascination.

"Oh, no. I can just imagine—first lovers, first husbands. It's the same thing, no?"

"I wouldn't know. Unfortunately, mine were both the same."

"Shame." She pouted. "I guess I shall have to let you know." I watched her fingers wrap around Christian's arm.

"That would be incredibly enlightening." I tossed back my drink and crunched an ice cube with more gusto than necessary.

"*Okay*," Val drawled. "Gianna, why don't we freshen up our drinks?"

We said our sickly-sweet goodbyes, and I managed to avoid Christian's gaze, even though I could feel it on me like a rash.

"That was . . . *wow*," Valentina said as we reached the bar.

"She's nice."

Val laughed. "You're so out of touch with reality."

"I need a drink. And this time, hold the bitters," I told her.

"Honey, that's a Moscow Mule. There isn't any bitters."

"Well, something's bitter."

"Yes, something *is*." She eyed me meaningfully and then tossed back a shot that was placed in front of her. I followed suit and enjoyed the burn in my throat. I hadn't planned to drink tonight, but I also hadn't expected to feel inadequate in Aleksandra's leggy, six-foot-tall shadow.

"Let's dance," I announced.

"I thought you'd never ask."

She grabbed my wrist and dragged me to the dance floor. We found a spot in the crowd and moved with the bodies, pressing our backs together and rolling our hips. Maybe it was due to my lack of modesty, or maybe it was for pure attention, but I loved to dance with an audience. And right now, there were a lot of male eyes pointed in our direction. Each one lit a spark inside me, slowing, sensualizing, each roll of my hips, the glide of my hands in my hair.

The fact I wouldn't let myself look at Christian made the touch of his gaze more intense. Each one sent an involuntary shiver down my spine. Set a fire in my blood as a drop of sweat dripped down my back.

Out of breath, we reached the men at our table and fell into our seats.

Van moved in to whisper in my ear, his voice deep and raw, "Do you have any idea how gorgeous you are?"

I leaned away shyly, a stupid blush rising to my cheeks. "Yes."

He laughed at my bold response.

My gaze flicked up and caught on Christian. He leaned against the bar, with Aleksandra and Elena in conversation beside him. He wasn't looking at me. His gaze was directed at Van, and it was dark enough I could feel the coldness on my skin. He took a sip from his glass, his expression filling with something volatile and conflicted before he looked away.

Uncertainty ran through me.

If he ruined another relationship for me, I'd scream.

We talked for an hour until I felt Mother Nature's call. I weaved through the crowd and walked upstairs, past the bouncer Ronny who nodded at me, toward the bathrooms on the VIP floor. They were always less busy than the ones downstairs.

I pushed the door open and almost turned straight back around to brave the bathroom line downstairs, because Aleksandra stood at the sink washing her hands. Her cat-eyed gaze flicked to me, and I couldn't back out now. I used the restroom, and when I exited the stall, she was still at the mirror, applying lipstick.

We stood side-by-side at the sink.

She brushed some powder on her cheeks. "I wouldn't be caught dead in that dress."

The truth always comes out in the bathroom, doesn't it?

I reached into my bra for my lip gloss. "Confidence comes with time. I'm sure you'll get there someday."

She was unfazed. "You *vant* him."

I sighed. We were actually going there.

"I *had* him. I don't care for a repeat."

"You lie."

I applied a liberal coat of lip gloss. "You have nothing to worry about. Christian and I will never be a thing."

"Now, *that* I believe. You are not what he needs."

I felt an odd pang in my chest.

I raised a brow. "You know him so well?"

"He is not so complicated. He likes his privacy and his things the way he likes them. I won't demand more from him, and neither will he from me."

How could she not be curious? I didn't even like him and still wanted to know everything about him. In truth, I was nosy beyond belief. I'd never be happy with a superficial relationship with him— the only thing I was sure he was capable of. We'd never work. But, for some reason, hearing that out in the open made me slightly uneasy.

She snapped her compact closed. "We will marry, and you won't get in the way."

"I don't have any designs on him."

"Good." She headed to leave.

There was something on my mind I hadn't been able to get rid of.

"*Kak moya*," I said, smoothing the gloss on my lips and watching her in the mirror. "What does it mean?"

She stopped at the door, assessing me with a look.

"It means, *like mine*."

CHAPTER
Twenty-One

Gianna

DROPPING MY PURSE ON THE KITCHEN ISLAND, I KICKED OFF MY HEELS AND stretched out my toes, wincing at the ache in my feet. I'd had too much on my mind to stay at the club, and while Van's attentions weren't unwelcome, I couldn't find much interest after my conversation with Aleksandra.

I was glad to find Magdalena and her date had vacated my apartment, though I could see they'd enjoyed one of my expensive bottles of wine. Finding some left, I poured the remainder in a glass and leaned against the counter, taking a sip.

A heavy knock sounded at the door.

I sighed.

I'd been waiting for a visit from Luca—or, more likely, a *check-in*—now that I was a single woman. He was probably here to remind me about how not to go to jail. It'd been three years since my last felony offense—you would think they'd trust me now.

I finished off my wine and went to open the door.

My heart dropped to my toes.

Christian stood in the hall, his gaze lowered. He'd removed his jacket but otherwise wore his gray tie, pants, and white dress shirt he'd had at the club. When his eyes came up to me, I realized they were clouded with something dark and terrifying.

My pulse leapt.

On mere instinct, I tried to shut the door on him, but he kept it open with a hand. I took a step back as he entered my apartment. He shut the door, his eyes hot enough to set my skin on fire.

"You've been ignoring me."

I shook my head.

He followed me as I walked backward, his tone demanding a response. "Tell me why."

"You like me," I breathed.

"*Like?*" His gaze flashed with something sardonic. "I don't know if I'd call it that."

I swallowed. "You like me . . . like me."

I didn't know how I could have been so stupid for so long—maybe I was in denial—but it was all clear to me now. He might hate himself for it, but Christian Allister was still into me. *Really* into me. Enough to kiss me. Enough to think I tasted like *his*.

My back hit the living room wall.

"Does that scare you?" A whisper of darkness laced through his voice as he stalked toward me.

I couldn't focus—not with how hot my body was and how uncertain this revelation made me.

I nodded.

"Good." He pressed his hands against the wall on either side of me. "It should." The rasp of his voice sent the hair on my arms on end, and I sucked in a breath as his lips skimmed up my neck. "I've always thought about you." He pressed his next words against my ear. "More than your date tonight could ever think about you."

I shivered.

"I've thought about you so much you're *mine* now." It was a growl that lowered into a threat. "You're lucky you didn't let him touch you, Gianna, because I really don't like it when people touch my things."

I swallowed. "Who touches me is none of your business."

"It's *always* been my business."

As twisted and a bit degrading as his words were, something about them was burning me up from the inside. He was so close, and he smelled so good, his body heat warming my skin. My heartbeat dipped between my legs, and I was suddenly looking through a hazy film of desire. I dropped my head against the wall, drawing half-lidded eyes up to his.

"Why do you kiss me?"

My lips parted as he ran a thumb across the seam.

"It shuts you up."

That wasn't what he'd planned to say two days ago at the cemetery, but I was suddenly glad he'd evaded the question. Just his gaze was too much, let alone the things he was admitting to me.

I remained still, my breathing erratic, as his hands slid down my waist, my hips, skimming the outsides of my thighs. The caress was slow, *reverent*, as if he was trying to memorize the curves of my body. Heat bloomed beneath my skin, tightening in my breasts and burning a lower path.

"You have a girlfriend," I breathed.

"She's not my girlfriend."

His possessive gaze watched mine, almost daring me to stop him, as he eased the dress up my thighs, baring the lacy fabric between my legs. My body shivered in anticipation.

He pressed two fingers against my lips.

"Suck."

Oh, God.

Any sense I had left drowned in a pool of lust.

I didn't hesitate to draw his fingers into my mouth. His gaze darkened when I scraped them with teeth as he pulled them back out.

When he dipped his hand beneath the fabric between my thighs and roughly pushed those fingers inside me, a strangled sound escaped me, and I clutched his waist for something to hold onto. The beginning of an orgasm already stoked a fire inside me.

"You blushed for him," he growled. "You really shouldn't have done that, Gianna. You have no idea what you've just unleashed."

I was too far gone to care what he said at this point. A flush warmed my body as I writhed, panted, moaned, under his touch. Each time he slid his fingers in and out of me, it was slower, easier, like the anger was draining out of him. And then he rubbed against a spot that made me see spots.

His lips skimmed against mine.

"Who makes you come, *malyshka*?"

"*You*," I moaned.

A noise of satisfaction rumbled in his chest, and then his fingers were gone. He lifted me by the waist and carried me a few steps. A gasp escaped me when he dropped me in a rough motion on the kitchen island, after sweeping everything off the surface. Glass shattered. Silverware clanged. Papers flew.

He ripped my thong down my legs, and, with shaky hands, I worked on his belt buckle. Reaching beneath his waistband, I took him in my hand. So hot and hard. I was fascinated with him, dying to explore him further. Though, once again, I didn't get the chance. His fingers dug into my inner thighs as he spread my legs, and then he pushed inside me in one deep thrust.

I choked.

He hissed, his eyes on where we were connected.

"Slow. *God, slow,*" I begged, clutching at his arms.

I still wasn't used to his size, but even more so, something about having sex with this man was so intense I thought I would lose myself completely or do something ridiculous like *cry* if I didn't feel I had a semblance of control over it.

He stilled, and then we were both shaking as he eased out and then back inside. Pleasure burned through my veins. I moaned. Ran my fingers up his chest and held onto his shoulders as he fucked me slowly on the edge of the counter.

We both watched his length disappear in and out of me.

"Christian . . . no condom," I breathed. "*Again.*"

"I'll pull out."

"I think that's how my cousin got pregnant with three of her kids."

That should have been enough to scare both of us, but, with heavy breaths, we only continued to watch him fuck me.

"I'm clean," he rasped.

"I'm not worried. I'm sure your body temperature is too cold for any STDs to survive."

His eyes came up to mine and narrowed. "It sounds to me like I've worked you in, *malyshka*." He punctuated that sentence with a violent thrust that tore a gasp from my throat.

He lifted me off the counter, pressed me against the wall, and fucked me deep and hard. Each thrust sent a wave of heat curling and searing through me. We were chest-to-chest, his hand on my throat, my legs wrapped around him. We still had our clothes on, yet every point of contact was so hot, so maddening, I'd never felt closer to anyone.

He kissed me only twice, both short and distracted, but each time, something warm unraveled in my chest, pooling in my extremities like melted butter.

The orgasm hit me hard, shooting stars between my eyes and knocking the breath from my lungs. I tightened a fist in his hair, lightly biting down where his shoulder met his neck.

With a rough noise, he pulled out and came all over my thigh.

It wasn't romantic in the least, but something about seeing him come undone brought out a tender, grateful part of me. With my legs still wrapped around him, I placed a kiss on his neck, soaking up his smell. He rested his hands on the wall on either side of me, his breathing hard, while I kissed his jawline, his cheeks, his lips.

"If I knew I only had to fuck you to see how sweet you could actually be, I'd have done it a lot sooner."

Warmth ran to my face. And I knew he saw the blush when he ran a finger across my cheek.

"*Moya zvezdochka*." He murmured the two rough words against my lips.

I stilled.

Those words . . . I'd heard them before. More than once.

And then the memory dropped into place.

"*You*," I breathed, eyes wide. "*You were at my wedding*."

Gianna

20 years old

"You look beautiful, *stellina*. Stop fretting."

I dropped my hands from the pins in my hair and turned away from my white-clad reflection in the mirror. "I just don't want him to be disappointed."

Mamma snorted. "He wouldn't deserve you in a gunny sack."

I sighed.

She cupped my cheek, her eyes soft. "I did not wish this for you."

"Mamma, stop." I pulled away from her and headed to the window. I didn't want today—my *wedding* day—to be clouded in pity. For better or for worse, this was the life I'd been given, and I was going to make the best of it.

"*Mi dispiace, stellina.* We only have a few more minutes . . . Do we need to have the sex talk?"

I gave her a look.

She chuckled. "I wasn't sure what you've learned from Signora Tiller."

My private tutors were old enough to be WWII survivors and stuffy enough to be virgins themselves.

I swallowed and turned back to gaze out the window with a dark secret pressing in on my chest. I'd been molested for four years of my childhood and my mother never knew. Even at eight years old, I'd known if she found out she'd try to take me and run again. I'd been terrified the next time she tried Papà would actually kill her. Now, at twenty, I couldn't force that secret past my lips knowing how much it would upset her.

"*Ricorda, mia figlia,* you do not have to do anything you're uncomfortable with. You are young—Antonio will understand."

"I'm not afraid of the marriage bed, Mamma. I'm not even nervous about it. I just want him to . . . like me." *Love me.*

"*Oh, stellina . . .*"

My chest tightened. "Please don't ruin this for me, Mamma."

"You are right, I'm sorry. I think it's time to go downstairs. Are you ready?"

I took a deep breath. "I'm ready."

My first wedding was a lavish affair, with white lilies and tulle bows as far as the eye could see. The guests cheered and threw rice at the bride and groom as we left the church.

The day was beautiful.

The mood perfect.

I was gorgeous—everyone had said so.

I was floating on a cloud of optimism. Right up until I'd gotten lost at the reception in my husband's ten-thousand-square-foot home while trying to find the bathroom. Then that optimism shattered like glass at my feet. And all because of a crack in a door that should have been closed.

Her name was Marie Ricci.

Mid-twenties, girl-next-door looks, slightly cheap.

I knew of her only because she'd played the part of a waitress in a B-horror movie I'd had the misfortune of seeing.

Everything about her was ordinary, but it was impossible to overlook her while she kneeled in front of my husband's office chair, his hand in her dark hair.

That was the moment the first whispers of bitterness crept into my jaded soul—watching my brand-new husband get blown by an Italian actress on our wedding day.

I drifted down the hall, my dress suddenly feeling fifty pounds heavier. I thought my husband had poor taste in sexual partners, but at least he had an amazing library. And an impressive collection of scotch. I had never had more than a sip of alcohol in my life—Papà had forbidden it—but I knew the bottle I was currently pulling the cork out of was more expensive than most people's cars. Papà liked his liquor from so high a shelf God must have put it there Himself.

I took a drink straight from the bottle.

Sometime later, I was sitting cross-legged at the piano, playing a nursery rhyme I remembered from the lessons I'd taken as a child. I went to lift the half-empty bottle to my lips, and instead, ended up falling backward off the bench and smacking my head on the floor. Liquor spread across the oriental rug.

"Ow," I murmured, but when I realized I'd drunk so much it didn't hurt at all, I laughed.

"And they say marriage is bliss," a deep voice drawled.

My eyes shot to the sound. The whole room spun at the movement, and I could only see a large, black-suited silhouette in the doorway.

I rolled my eyes and looked away from the stranger to watch the fan spin around and around. "You sound like an . . . impressionist."

That amused him. "I think you mean, *pessimist*."

I continued to lie in a tangle of sequins, bows, and white gossamer.

"Does your husband know what's become of his pretty teenage wife?"

I shot him a glare and then blinked because there were suddenly two of him swaying back and forth. "I'm *twenty*, thank you very much."

"Ah, my mistake."

"And to answer your question—even though it's none of your business—I'm sure he's still too busy getting blown in his office to notice where I am."

"So, she's already jaded," he drawled.

"I hope he reciprocates," I said, slightly slurring my words. "I'm not sure what the protocol is, but I do believe men should reciprocate. Would you reciprocate?"

"Is this the first time you've been drunk?"

"What gave it away?"

He laughed. It was a deep sound, like the first rays of warmth after a long winter. I liked it.

"Well?" I pushed. "Would you?"

"I'd return the favor if I was interested enough. And I'm not always interested enough."

I frowned. "And women are so eager to please you while getting nothing in return? I'm sorry, sir, but you don't look all that special from here."

He chuckled for some reason, amused at what I'd said. "You're drunk, sweetheart."

I murmured something unintelligible because, suddenly, my eyes were closing, unconsciousness pulling me under.

"You going to sleep there?"

"Yes, I think so. It was nice to meet you," I mumbled. "You're not the first man I'd volunteer to give a blowjob to, though."

Another chuckle, but this time it was closer. "I'll let you know when I'm running short on volunteers, just in case you change your mind."

"I won't—" My eyes fluttered when I was suddenly lifted from the floor, but I didn't have the strength to keep them open.

"My dress is heavy," I complained.

"Ah, so, it's the dress, huh?"

That made me smile. "You're rude."

"You're young," he told me.

"I don't feel it."

"You look it."

"What did you say your name was?" I asked.

"I didn't."

I opened my eyes, suddenly curious to see what he looked like up close, but as soon as I did, the world spun so fast I feared I was going to be sick. So, I closed them again and let this stranger carry me down the hall.

"I hope you're not taking me somewhere to take advantage of me," I murmured against his chest. "I'm a virgin, you know. It wouldn't be very much fun for you."

"I don't know about that," he drawled.

When I was set on a bed, I curled up on my side, heaviness pulling on my consciousness.

My voice was a whisper. "I'll make him love me, you'll see."

A thumb skimmed across my cheek. "If anyone can do it, it would be you . . ." His voice was soft and rough. "*Moya zvezdochka.*"

And then it went black.

CHAPTER
Twenty-Two

Gianna

M Y SHOPPING CART SQUEAKED AS I PUSHED IT DOWN THE CEREAL AISLE, absently knocking two boxes of Count Chocula into the basket. That score would have been the highlight of my day a week ago, but now, I couldn't find any excitement in it because my mind was still stuck on my revelation from the night before.

"How could someone ever forget your face?" I'd asked him once.

For some reason, he thought that was funny.

I felt like an idiot. Though it wasn't only that. It seemed he was always going out of his way to do nice things for me. Sure, it felt like he'd walk a mile to make me miserable as well, but ever since I'd stepped foot in New York eight years ago, he'd been picking me up off the floor—*literally.*

I could still hear the words he pressed against my ear after I'd announced he'd been at my wedding.

"I'm glad to see you remember, malyshka, *because there is nothing I have ever forgotten about you."*

And then he'd dropped me to my feet and walked out the door.

I was halfway out of the store when I realized I'd only come for one thing and almost left without it.

With a bag on each arm, I sighed and turned around.

I needed eggs because I was teaching Elena how to make pasta dough today. And while I might have told Christian to expect my pilfering of his refrigerator the day I'd moved into his building, I wasn't ready to face him yet.

My body was still reeling from last night with this breathless, nervous energy he always seemed to bring out in me. I'd told Aleksandra I wasn't interested in him and then hours later sucked his fingers on command. Maybe the model and him weren't exclusive, but they'd seemed comfortable enough around each other for me to believe they'd slept together. That thought alone made me sick to my stomach. And I wasn't ready to analyze why.

"Mommy, Mommy, can I have it? *Puh-lease*, Mommy?"

I paused with an egg carton in hand to look at the tiny dark-haired girl who seemed so eager to have a . . . single banana. The answer must have been yes because the girl smiled real big and hugged the fruit to her chest. I drew my eyes to the mother, who was cooing at the cutest little giggling baby.

Warmth set in, yet a strange pressure ached in my chest.

I stood there for too long, watching the happy trio until they disappeared around the corner.

I swallowed, confused at the feeling that stopped me in my tracks. A feeling that bloomed like hope and, at the same time, wilted like despair.

Somewhere between the ages of twenty and twenty-eight, I'd forgotten what longing felt like.

"*Mamma mia*, Elena! Are you trying to burn the place down?" I put out the small fire on the stove by smacking it with an oven mitt. Grabbing a corner of the incinerated cloth from the gas burner, I turned around with a frown. "Towels don't cook very well, I'm afraid."

She bit her lip. "I'm hopeless, aren't I?"

"I pride myself on being a positive person and would normally have something uplifting to say here, but . . . I think it's time you hire a cook before you kill someone."

I'd gone to the bathroom for two minutes and come out to my

apartment in flames, while Elena stood in front of the TV, oblivious.

She sighed, dropping to the couch in a dramatic fashion. "If I have to have another Isabel in my house, I think I'll scream."

I nodded. "Screaming certainly helps in most situations."

"You're right, though. I just need to hire someone. It's not like I have a passion for cooking—"

"Or safety," I parried.

"Or, apparently, that."

"You know, this is justice. Women who look like Barbie dolls shouldn't know how to cook. You'd simply leave the rest of us in the dust."

"Stop being ridiculous." She flushed. "By the way, why is your TV in Spanish?"

I sighed. "Insolent housekeepers."

"Have you seen my cell phone?" she asked, getting to her feet. "I'm sure Nico has texted me by now, and he hates when I don't text him back. Especially when I'm with you. I think he thinks you're a bad influence."

"Oh, I'm glad you reminded me—I almost forgot to drag out the drugs and alcohol." I winked. "It's kind of amazing how you ignore him, though. He's had women fawning over him for far too long."

"I don't ignore him on purpose—" She stopped to pick something small off the living room floor. "Hmm . . ." An edge of mischief played in her voice. "When did you start wearing cufflinks, Gianna?"

I kept my expression aloof and went to take it from her hand. "I'm trying out a new look."

She laughed. "*Sure.* So . . . when was he over?"

"Who?" I acted innocent, closing the cufflink in my palm. It burned.

"You know who."

My gaze narrowed on her, though, with a sigh, I gave in. "Last night."

"I knew it!" Her eyes sparkled. "I knew there was something between you and Christian."

"If *something* is sex, sure."

"I think I would pay money for those details."

"How much you got on you?" I joked, just as a knock sounded at the door. With a sigh, because I already knew who it was, I went to open it.

Nico stood there, practically glowering at me.

I grinned. "Oh, you made it just in time for the party! I was just about to let the male hooker out of the closet."

He rolled his eyes and walked past me toward his wife, who stood by the couch looking guilty.

"Been calling you for an hour, Elena."

She chewed her cheek. "I might have misplaced my phone."

"Missed you," he rasped against her hair, pulling her close.

Feeling like I was intruding on something, I went to clean up the kitchen.

"What's for dinner?" Nico asked a few moments later, while Elena searched the place for her phone.

"Fried towel served with a side of half-cooked pasta."

"Huh." He rubbed his jaw and sat at the kitchen island, amusement playing in his eyes.

I turned the burner on to finish cooking the pasta and started chopping the tomatoes for the sauce.

"My wife likes you," he said, voice low.

"Not surprising," I said. "I'm a very likeable person."

"She might have been brought up in this life, but she didn't grow up like you and I, Gianna. She's not . . ."

Damaged? Desensitized? Unsympathetic? Was there a word for all of them?

"Cold?"

He nodded, like he couldn't find the right word either. "I'm asking you to remember that when you spend time with her."

"You're *asking* me? Why, Ace, did you hit your head on the overhang on the way in?"

"Sometimes feels like it," I thought I heard him say, as he glanced at Elena with a volatile and vulnerable look in his eyes. I suddenly feared for anyone who dared to touch a hair on her head.

And then that feeling came back—that confusing feeling that had eluded me for eight years. *Longing.* Longing to be the subject of a look that intense. A look full of something so raw and vehement it could make anyone a believer.

That night, after the three of us had watched Channel 7 in Spanish and ate dinner in silence, I lay in bed unable to sleep. I was . . . perturbed. I was *alive.* My skin lit up like the noises and lights at a carnival.

The cards I'd been dealt would never line up just right for love, but if there was anything close to what it would feel like to be the subject of that *look*, I knew where to find it.

A ray of light from the crack in the bathroom door fanned across the room, spotlighting the cufflink I'd set on my vanity.

He only had sex with the same woman three times.

I still had one more time, didn't I?

I got to my feet, grabbed the cufflink, and headed to the front door. I was only wearing an oversized t-shirt and a pair of thigh-high socks, but my destination was just on the other side of the hall.

Instead of knocking, I tried the handle. It was unlocked. I heard his voice, deep and rich and Russian, before I pushed it all the way open.

He leaned against the kitchen counter, his phone to his ear. His gaze lifted to me and narrowed, before dropping, touching the curves of my body and settling on my bare thighs. I inhaled a cold breath while my skin burned hot. I'd never known another man who could throw me off-balance with a single look. I'd resented it for so long—because it was *him* who made me feel this way—but now, due to a temporary bout of insanity, I was sure, I only wanted more of it.

He responded to something on the phone in his heathen language, his eyes following me as I walked toward him and set his cufflink on the kitchen island. And then I stepped closer. Close enough I had to look up to meet his gaze.

"I changed my mind," I whispered.

He raised a brow.

Stretching up on my toes, I skimmed my lips across his ear, and breathed, "I volunteer."

I watched his face as he searched for the meaning behind those two words, from a conversation we'd had eight years ago. The moment I saw dark understanding flicker across his expression, I dropped to my knees at his feet. Heat flared in his gaze.

I rubbed my cheek against his length that already seemed to be hard and thick. He ran a hand across his mouth, rumbling out some rough Russian words. The bastard wasn't even giving me his full attention, but, apparently, my body didn't need it, because anticipation still danced down my spine at the idea of what I would do.

I could feel his gaze on me as I worked on his belt buckle. The gentle clang of it falling open sent a shiver through me. As soon as I had his pants undone, I wrapped my hand around his shaft and licked him from base to tip. He pulled in a strained breath, but he didn't let it out. He didn't make a sound as he watched me with eyes that had grown dark and hazy.

I laved him with my tongue, making breathy noises of approval like it was the only passion I had in life. And it was starting to feel like it. Heat bloomed in my stomach, moving lower, in a wave that made me squeeze my thighs together to ease the ache. His hand tightened on his phone, the tension in him building to a crescendo I was dying to see fall.

"*Da*," he said to whoever he was speaking to, sounding annoyed. "*Ya slyshal vas.*"

I ran my tongue across his crown and then finally slid him deep into my mouth, bringing my half-lidded, lust-filled gaze up to his.

"*Fuck.*" He threw his phone to the side and then grasped my face between two rough hands, caressing my cheek with a thumb like I was something special, something *precious.*

It momentarily stilled me. A raw wave of warmth flickered in my chest. It wasn't until later I realized that was the moment the first wisps of devotion settled in and my downfall began.

"*Voz'mi menya glubzhe,*" he rasped.

He held my face and slowly slid in deeper. My eyes watered, and I couldn't breathe whenever he reached my throat, but I remained still and let him fuck my mouth. Because I wanted him to use me however he wanted. Because I wanted to be everything he needed.

"Where can I come, *malyshka*?" he asked. "Your mouth?"

I blinked up at him in acquiesce.

His groan rumbled from low in his throat, turning into a hoarse sound when he finished in my mouth. I swallowed and licked my lips, my skin growing hot under the heat of his stare. I now understood why women dropped to their knees without expecting anything in return, because, as humbling as the act might seem, nothing felt more empowering than bringing a man like this to the edge of control.

"*Takaya krasivaya*," he breathed, running a thumb across my bottom lip.

I wanted to ask him what it meant but stopped myself before the question could escape. I didn't want to know. I was sure tonight would be the end of us, as soon as I became just another third, and I knew those two words would only strengthen the attachment I seemed to be building for him.

He pulled his briefs over his softening erection and buttoned his pants. A small squeal escaped me when he suddenly lifted me by the backs of the thighs and dropped me on the island. An unexpected rush of nerves hit me. I'd been naked in his apartment once before—it hadn't left me feeling good in the end.

"You didn't finish your phone call," I breathed, as he dragged my panties down my legs.

"Lie back and spread your legs."

"Aren't you going to kiss me first?" I blinked at him.

My heart burned when he actually did it. He grasped the back of my neck and pressed his mouth to mine, our tongues sliding against each other. A deep, empty ache pulsed between my thighs, and I knew of only one thing that would ease it. I moaned, dug my fingers into his hair, and kissed him deeper.

"So greedy," he murmured against my lips.

His hand slid between my legs. When he pushed two fingers inside me, I groaned and dropped my head back.

He moved his lips to my neck and let out a rough sound. "You're soaked." He nipped my throat like he was angry with me for it. Slipping his fingers out of me, he spread my arousal around. Then, he grasped the backs of my thighs, jerked them up to his shoulders, and pressed his face between my legs.

I dropped back to the counter and closed my eyes as pleasure tore through me, filling my blood with an inferno. I shuddered and writhed as he licked and sucked a path *around* my clit, until I was so desperate, I'd sell my firstborn to get what I wanted. I banged my head lightly on the countertop, moaning, letting out frustrated, needy breaths.

He pulled back. "Tell me why you used at that dinner party."

Now, I knew the bastard's endgame.

"God, I hate you," I gasped.

He didn't respond because he was back to torturing me.

"My papà called me," I blurted. "I have to go home to Chicago for my cousin's wedding."

I was a weak, weak woman.

"When?"

"Saturday." I'd avoided thinking about it for as long as I could, but it was here now. I knew if I didn't show my papà would come to drag me there, just as he'd said he would.

All it took for the orgasm to rock me hard was for his mouth to move over my clit and suck. Light shot behind my eyes, heat tightening in my core and releasing. I moaned, burying my fingers in his hair as I rode the rest of the waves.

He pulled back, eyes dark, as he wiped his mouth with the back of his hand.

The action was so primal and hot a fresh wave of lust flared inside me. I suddenly wanted him inside me so badly I couldn't think about anything else. I slid off the counter, ran my hand across his already hard erection, and kissed his chest through his shirt.

A small shudder ran through him. He fisted a hand in my hair and pulled my gaze up to his.

"I'm not going to fuck you tonight. I don't have time."

My expression fell.

For the simple fact of being denied him. But there was something deeper involved as well. If I didn't get this over with him now, I'd never be over him enough to move on, to find another man who interested me.

I'd forgotten an important fact while sifting through my feelings. Christian was so perceptive he might as well be a mind reader. And I was sure he'd read my thoughts on my face.

His eyes narrowed on me before he reached for his suit jacket resting on the back of an island chair. "You been listening to gossip?"

I chewed my lip. "Sometimes, gossip just falls into your lap . . ."

He slipped his jacket on, in a casual yet kind of scary way. "Do you believe it?"

My pulse wavered like a plucked string. I didn't say a word, because I didn't need to for him to know that I did.

He adjusted his cuffs, eyes focused on his task, but something dark was coiling in him like rope.

My stomach turned cold. I went to take a step back but didn't make it. A gasp of fear escaped me when his hand shot out and grabbed me by the throat. I'd been conditioned to expect the worst from men from a young age, and my heart thundered in my chest as I waited for what he would do.

I expected pain.

So much so, shock and warmth rocked me at my center when he pulled me closer by the throat and kissed me. A sweet pull on my lips and then a soft bite of teeth.

He pressed his lips to my ear, running his thumb across the fluttering pulse in my throat. "I'll say when this is over, Gianna."

He released me, and I turned to watch him head toward the door.

"I'm coming with you Saturday."

I couldn't even protest because I was still wide-eyed and shaken from the moment before.

"We'll leave at nine," he told me.

And then he shut the door behind him.

CHAPTER
Twenty-Three

Christian

MY EYES NARROWED. "WHAT ARE YOU WEARING?"

Gianna looked down at her modest gray cocktail dress and short white heels while unsuccessfully trying to fix a tendril of hair that had escaped her French bun. Then, she looked me in the eye and said, "Isn't it obvious? I'm trying to mold myself into a woman you could love."

I didn't know why the sarcasm in her voice annoyed the hell out of me.

"No."

She raised a brow. *"No?"*

"That's what I said, Gianna. Go put on something else."

She glared at me as she tried to push that unruly piece of hair back once more. That was when I noticed the small tremor in her hand. She was nervous. I hadn't liked this outfit from the beginning, but now I fucking hated it.

I smoothed a nonexistent wrinkle from my jacket sleeve. "My time is precious, and you're wasting it. You have five minutes to go change."

She scoffed. "And what would you like to see me in, Your Highness?"

My bed, spread-eagled and naked.

"What you would normally wear to a wedding your father wasn't attending."

She stared me down for a moment, and, when she realized she wasn't going to win, she turned around in a huff. But I didn't miss a hint of a smile on that pretty mouth of hers before she disappeared into her apartment.

She came back out ten minutes later in a sequined red gown that sparkled under the lights like a disco ball. A slit in the dress revealed her smooth tanned leg and six-inch heels. The sight sent a rush of heat to my groin.

She cocked a brow that dared me to say something.

The woman had no idea.

She thought I *liked* her.

I'd gone out of my way and followed her around for goddamn years just to look at her. I'd insulted her just to hear her smoky voice and witty response. And now, after my move to Seattle, it was hard to believe she was here in front of me. That I could reach out and touch her. That she would let me. It didn't matter if she dressed like a 1970s drug lord's wife or a die-hard Ariana Grande fan—nothing could make me forget her. What was worse was now, I had the memory of her looking up at me from her knees. That image had burned itself so deep beneath my skin I'd never get it out.

As much as I wanted to keep her, I knew I shouldn't.

I couldn't give her everything she'd ask of me.

I was going to take her to this wedding, finish my business with Sergei, and then return to Seattle. Nonetheless, every time I thought about leaving, my collar felt too tight, the air too thick to breathe. I didn't know if I could physically do it.

"Did you bedazzle it yourself?" I asked, watching the elevator doors as we descended to the lobby.

She sighed and reached out to shove me or do something else ridiculous, but I grabbed her hand before she could make contact.

She blinked innocent eyes at me. "I was just going to fix your tie clip. It's crooked."

"No, it's not," I said confidently, without even looking.

She tried to pull her hand away, but I held onto it just because I could. Just because she was so fucking soft. I ran my thumb across her palm. She shivered and wrenched it away.

She did her makeup in the mirror on the way to the airstrip, while I pretended my blood didn't thrum in approval at having her in my space, even doing such mundane, non-dick-related things like applying mascara.

A frown pulled on her lips when she took in the private jet. "Please, tell me this plane doesn't belong to the Bureau."

"This plane doesn't belong to the Bureau."

"Liar."

As we boarded the jet, she muttered something about getting a rash.

The blonde flight attendant smiled and greeted Gianna, but it felt like an unnaturally long time for her to meet my gaze and nervously ask if she could hang up my jacket. She disappeared with my jacket in tow, while Gianna rolled her eyes.

"You don't even notice the way women act in front of you, do you?"

"I notice everything you do, *malyshka*."

She stilled and held my heavy stare for a moment before looking away. "Who's paying for this private plane ride? My tax dollars?"

I took a seat on the white-leather couch, watching her move around and touch everything in sight. "You have to make an income to pay taxes."

"I do. I'm an . . . entrepreneur."

"You're a gambler," I corrected dryly.

"Same thing, really."

"Why does your father want your attendance at this wedding?"

She picked up an FBI paperweight to examine it. "For nefarious reasons, I'm sure."

"Elaborate."

She swallowed. "I'm a single woman now."

"Are you?" I didn't know why that question came out like a threat.

She flicked a hesitant gaze to me. "*Yes*. He probably wants to remedy it."

I knew at that moment she'd never marry another goddamn man but me. And she wouldn't marry me. "And if he does?"

"I told you, I won't ever marry again."

She would leave. The life, the city, *me*.

The irrational thought that I wouldn't be able to find her sent an icy rush of panic through me. And I could find fucking anyone.

I'd never let her leave.

I didn't care if I had to handcuff the little fugitive to my headboard.

The vow seared itself through my body, settling itself deep, and calmed the rush of blood in my veins.

She sat on the chair opposite me and flipped open a fashion magazine. "How are you going to explain why you're with me?"

You're mine. And I go where you go.

"No one will question me."

My phone vibrated in my pocket, and I pulled it out.

Aleksandra: *Father wants to have dinner soon.*

Frustration ran through me. Sergei would only talk to me through his daughter. I was surprised he hadn't paraded her naked in front of me and offered to let me fuck her yet, as motivated as he seemed about this alliance. He wanted to dip his hands in the American underworld while still maintaining his traditional Russian values, and, apparently, a tie with me was the way to do it.

The Russian government had upped regulations on border security, and Sergei just happened to have most of that security in his pocket. I didn't give a shit about Russian politics anymore, but unfortunately, the only relative I had left did.

After being released from the overcrowded cells of Butyrka at nineteen, I'd come to the States, while Ronan chose to stay in Moscow as a measly enforcer in the Bratva. Fifteen years later, he owned his own empire. But he still had a more hands-on approach to getting what he wanted, while delegation—and a bit of manipulation—was a better fit to win over Sergei Popov.

I texted Aleksandra back to tell her I was free on Friday and then slid my phone in my pocket. When I drew my attention back to Gianna, it was to see her chewing her lip, her olive complexion a shade paler.

She was scared of her papà.

It sent a rush of anger through me.

The only one she should be nervous of was me.

"*Voy kak volk, malyshka.*" *Howl like a wolf.*

Her soft eyes flicked to me. They burned a small hole in my chest.

"*Voy kak volk,*" she whispered.

She'd said it right.

And I suddenly knew I was going to keep her.

I hadn't set foot in a church in years. And not even because I thought I'd be smote down where I stood, but because they were either too hot, too dusty, or too pretentious. The magnanimous atmosphere practically swallowed you whole when you entered, yet not a single church had ever fed me a scrap of food when I was thirteen, starving, and humbling myself enough to beg.

Gianna's family nearly knocked her over with hugs and a ridiculous number of kisses as soon as we stepped into the church. She was flushed, wearing a genuine smile I never got from her. One of her aunts glanced at me, fanned herself vigorously with her wedding program, and then looked at Gianna and mouthed, "*Madonna.*"

Gianna sighed and glanced at me. "This is . . . ah—"

I remained silent and let her struggle just because I wanted to see what she would say, but, unfortunately, she was interrupted by a cavalier voice behind us.

"Allister."

Gianna tensed.

I slid a hand to her waist and turned toward her father.

"Saul," I said, the name familiar on my lips.

I didn't look at her, but the betrayed gaze I could feel on my face sent an odd tightness to my chest.

"I didn't expect your presence today." Saul's eyes drifted to my hand on Gianna's waist. "And with my daughter, no less."

"You'd think a man your age would have learned to expect the unexpected by now."

Gianna sucked in an uneasy breath.

It was a cheap insult, but I'd learned over the years that cheap got the quickest results.

Saul's expression didn't falter as he held my gaze. But, as his eyes finally drifted to his daughter, his next words came clipped with the slightest clench of his teeth. "I'd like to talk with you at home before the reception, Gianna."

"I'd love to, but . . . I swear, our schedule has been filling so fast I can hardly keep up with it." She blinked at me. "Do you think we'll have time, Christian?"

I wanted to smile. To kiss her for being such a good little wolf. Instead, I only said, "I think we can fit it in."

Uncertainty crossed her expression.

I liked Gianna's father about as much as I'd liked Antonio. Accepting a hit on their heads would have been a vacation for me. But if Gianna didn't deal with him now, he'd keep coming back until he got whatever he wanted.

"I'm glad to see you can spare a few minutes for your papà." A subtle threat flickered in Saul's eyes. "Until then, *cara mia*." The tightly-reined venom in his voice drifted past us as he headed up the aisle to take a seat at his pew.

Gianna was internally shaken but was hiding it well. Her anger? Not so much.

"Gianna—"

She left me standing there.

As much as it pissed me off that she'd jumped so fast to think the worst of me, I let her have her anger, because it was what she needed right now.

The Catholic ceremony was long and a little melodramatic. Gianna hadn't said a word to me since she'd taken a seat on the pew beside me. Not a single joke or insult. I didn't like it.

She stared out the window and stayed silent on the way to her papà's house. When this was over, I was going to force her to talk to me for two hours straight before she got her orgasm.

One of her cousins, who Gianna had called "Guccio," and who couldn't be more than a teenager, answered the door and led us to her father's office.

Guccio avoided my gaze. "He wants to, uh, talk to you alone, Gianna."

"Fine," she sighed.

I grabbed her wrist when she took a step toward the door. "You don't have to go in there alone."

"It'll be fine. I'll try to make it quick so you two will have plenty of time to talk business afterward." Her eyes flashed with resentment.

My jaw tightened, but I let her go.

She shut the door behind her.

Guccio rubbed a fist in his hand, shifting his weight to his other foot. "You can wait in the parlor."

"I'll wait here."

He swallowed. "The parlor would be preferable."

I sent him a look that let him know he was annoying the fuck out of me. He muttered, "*Okay*," and drifted away. Standing by the door, I could hear their muffled voices inside.

"You move fast, Gianna," Saul said. "Didn't your husband just pass a week ago?"

"A week and a half," she corrected.

"Don't get smart with me, girl. Were you trying to make me look like a fool today?"

"I have no idea how I would make you look like a fool."

"That dress . . . showing up with a man like Allister—it makes you look like a goddamn whore."

She let out a bitter noise. "I was a whore to you when I was ten years old wearing my pink church dress. That word is a little worn out, Papà. Can't you think of something a little original?"

"I see your lavish life in New York has spoiled you." Some papers shuffled. "No matter. I'm sure it's nothing that can't be beat out of you. From what I remember, you were always too easy to break. Tell me, are you still afraid of the dark?"

228 | DANIELLE LORI

Silence.

He chuckled. "That's what I thought. We don't need to discuss such . . . matters right now. Do you think Allister will marry you?"

That amused her. "No. I don't."

She sounded so fucking sure it made me want to drag her to the courthouse right now.

"What do you think, Donny?" Saul addressed his right-hand man, who must be in the room.

"I don't think so, boss."

"Then I'm sure he won't care that you're moving back to Chicago," said Saul. "Once you're settled, we'll talk about arranging a marriage for you. It's about time you have children, Gianna. You're almost past your prime."

"As much as I appreciate the genuine concern in your voice—no. No to moving. No to the marriage. And no to fucking a man of your choosing."

Good girl.

A hand slapped on a desk. "You have a duty to this family, dammit!"

"Duty?" She scoffed. "What have you ever done for me? You sure as hell didn't protect your eight-year-old daughter from one of your sick-minded friends!"

Thick silence crept under the door.

I knew at that moment, when he didn't try to play her accusation off, that he hadn't known. And it was the only thing that would save his life.

"I clothed you, I fed you—"

"Basically, the bare minimum of keeping someone alive. We get it, Papà—you were an outstanding father."

"You ungrateful bitch," he spat.

Her voice shook with emotion. "You know, I feel sorry for you. You were obsessed with Mamma, and she hated you. She hated you so much, she risked running from you again, and again, and again—"

I moved at the sound of a chair slamming against the wall and pushed open the door. My voice was unnaturally calm. "Take your hand off her now."

Saul held her by the face, his fingers digging into her cheeks. His jaw tightened but he released her, stepped back, and then brushed off his sleeve.

I didn't look at her—*couldn't* look at her—because if there was a single red mark on her skin I'd snap.

"Get out, Gianna," I said.

She hesitated.

"*Out.*"

As she headed toward the door, Donny looked to Saul to see if he should let her pass. Saul nodded tightly. Donny shut the door and stood beside it.

Saul sat back in his chair and adjusted some papers on his desk, as if he hadn't just been caught assaulting his daughter. "Have a seat, Allister. It's been a while since we've chatted."

I'd never *chatted* with the man in my life. Never worked with him either. I was only an acquaintance of his through Antonio. And I'd only ever agreed to work with Antonio—an Italian, no less—because I was obsessed with his wife.

I remained standing. "I don't know how I can make this any shorter and sweeter for you—Gianna doesn't exist for you anymore."

"You say that as if you have a claim on her, Allister. Remember, *I'm* the one who put her on this goddamn planet."

"Did you? From what I've heard, someone else fucked your wife harder than you."

Red washed his complexion. "You don't want to make an enemy of me."

"I'm afraid it might be too late for that."

Our gazes burned into the other's.

"You want my daughter? Fine, you can have her. Just don't come crying to me when you find her fucking your repairman. I'm afraid she takes after her mother in that regard."

The man was so fucking bitter he stunk of it. But there was something else there—*guilt*. The boss was getting older and his conscience was filling up. He was just too twisted to know how to apologize and, instead, ended up choking out his daughter instead.

"I'll take my chances."

When I passed his underboss, a single *pop* ricocheted off the walls as I pulled out my .45 and shot him in the arm. He hissed in pain and slid down the wall.

Saul's jaw was tight, but he only arched a brow.

"That's because you touched her." I put my gun away and opened the door. "Every time you touch something that belongs to me, I'll fuck up something of yours."

CHAPTER
Twenty-Four

Gianna

THE *POP* THAT CUT THROUGH THE AIR SENT A SHARD OF ICE THROUGH MY heart.

As soon as Christian stepped into the parlor where I'd been pacing, relief sank beneath my skin and stole my breath.

My pulse raced.

My eyes burned.

The anger, the *relief*, the fear of this twisted family reunion—it all exploded. I strode toward him and shoved him. He didn't budge an inch, and that only made me angrier. A tear slipped down my cheek.

"You've been working with my papà!" I accused.

"I have never worked with your father."

A bitter sound escaped me, making it clear I didn't believe him.

His jaw ticked. "I dealt with Antonio only. As you know, they happened to be in the same circle."

What he said made too much sense. I'd jumped to conclusions because I always assumed the worst in men. But that wasn't only it. I *wanted* to believe the worst in him. Because he made me feel like I was spinning out of control, as if that life raft was slipping from my fingers every time he put his hands on me.

I hated these feelings.

Gratefulness. Uncertainty. *Relief.*

Because, eventually, I was going to drown in them.

And he was going to let me.

Anger came back full-force, burning my veins and the backs of my eyes.

"*Liar*," I cried, and then pushed him again. I wanted to hurt him. I wanted to make him feel what I'd felt when that gunshot had cut through the air.

I beat on his chest until he pulled me against him, shackling my wrists in one of his hands behind my back. I struggled but, with the heat of his body warming mine, weariness suddenly pulled on my muscles.

"Breathe," he demanded.

I inhaled deeply.

"Let it out."

I leaned against him, breathing deep, silent tears running down my cheeks. I wanted to hate myself for crying in front of this man *again*, but I couldn't seem to focus on anything but how good, how *right*, it felt to be pressed against him.

"I heard a gunshot," I said, the *relief* evident in my voice.

Four simple words cut out my heart and displayed it for him to see.

It was bleeding, dripping to the floor at his feet.

He nudged my chin, pulling my gaze to his. His face was close, blurred through my wet eyes.

"I thought you hated me, *malyshka*."

"I do," I breathed against his lips. But it was too raw, too desperate, to sound convincing.

Just when I thought he would press his lips fully against mine, he stepped away. I inhaled an uneasy breath, feeling the loss of him like a cold draft beneath my skin.

His voice was distant. "We should go."

"Wait," I said. "My mamma's cookbooks. I need them."

"Make it quick. I don't think anyone will be inviting us to stay for coffee," he said dryly.

I was curious about what had happened in my papà's office after I'd left, especially regarding that *gunshot*, but at the moment, I couldn't find the energy to question him.

Guccio shot to his feet when we found him eating a sandwich at the kitchen island. He watched, wide-eyed, as I searched the cupboards above the microwave where Mamma had kept her books. I knew my papà well enough to know he hadn't gotten rid of her things. He'd loved her in a disturbing, oppressive way.

When I came up empty-handed, I turned to my cousin, who'd only been seven when I last saw him. "My mamma's cookbooks? Where are they?"

He frowned. "He won't be happy with you taking—"

"Where. Are. They?" Christian's tone was impatient.

Guccio swallowed, then blew out a breath. "Guestroom, upstairs." Then, he slumped back in his chair, defeated.

Ten minutes later, we were each carrying a dusty box of cookbooks out to the car that waited at the curb. I stared out the window on the way to the airstrip, the moment in the parlor stretched between us like glue; messy, and hard to remove.

Apparently, after such a long period of celibacy, I couldn't figure out how to balance the act and the *feelings* part. It was a basic sexual attachment, I imagined, kind of like Stockholm syndrome. There was only one real solution to this problem: I needed to stop sleeping with him.

There. Simple. Problem solved.

But I should have known, nothing about Christian Allister was simple.

We weren't expected to fly home so soon, but after my date had casually admitted to shooting one of my relatives, I'd decided it was best if we skipped the reception.

It felt like a heavy weight had been released from my shoulders from standing up to my papà after all these years, and I knew, I would have never had the guts to do it if Christian hadn't been nearby.

He reclined on the couch while I sat in the chair opposite him for take-off. He'd been distant for the last hour, but now, nothing about him felt uninterested.

His gaze licked at my skin like fire as it trailed up my bare thigh exposed through the slit in my dress. I tried to ignore it, but my body still responded. My breathing slowed. My breasts tightened.

As soon as we were in the air, I felt his rough words between my legs.

"Come here."

A flush drifted down my body.

I shook my head.

I was turned on by just the way he was looking at me. There wasn't a chance I'd hold my ground if he was touching me.

"Women don't tell me no, *malyshka*." His voice was dark and lazy at the edges. "They've always done whatever I tell them to do. *Anything I can think up.* Yet none of it has ever been as satisfying as being inside you."

A wave of jealousy flared in my chest, but some other confused parts of my body had grown hotter with every stupid word from his mouth. I wanted to give in already, and we were only five minutes into our flight. There was one thing I knew that would set a boundary and keep it there.

I raised a brow in challenge. "Take off your shirt."

His gaze narrowed at the corners, holding mine. His jaw ticked in thought, and then what he said next made my heart still.

"Come take it off yourself."

Temptation pulled and tugged inside me.

I fought the impulse for a solid three seconds, because who was I kidding?

This battle was over before it had even begun.

Getting to my feet, I closed the distance between us. I stood between his legs, looking down at him, yet it didn't feel like I had the advantage.

"Thank you for coming with me today."

His hands slid up the backs of my thighs, pulling me closer to straddle him. A sigh of approval escaped me at the contact.

Pressing his face into my neck, he said, "You can thank me by letting me fuck you missionary."

Oh, God.

"It's your favorite, isn't it, *malyshka*?" He nipped at the hollow behind my ear, and I moaned. His lips skimmed down my throat. "You probably want me to kiss you while I fuck you."

Yes.

He grabbed my hand and pressed it against his erection. My blood was burning up as he kissed my neck and I rubbed his length through his pants.

"Take off your dress."

I had my dress unzipped and down to my waist before I realized what he'd done. Pulling back, I glared at him. "You distracted me."

He chuckled. And it was such a deep, sexy sound I couldn't even hold on to the anger.

"Fine." He ran a hand across his jaw and put his arms on the back of the couch. "Have at it, Gianna."

Swallowing, I suddenly felt like I was about to begin a much bigger venture than just taking off a man's shirt. I started at the bottom and had no idea I would be unleashing a masterpiece with each button. A slightly crude if not fascinating masterpiece.

His torso was covered in black and white tattoos, from a Madonna and child on his stomach to a dagger weaving through his collarbone from shoulder to shoulder. A cross on one of his pecs, and a rose on the other. A domed church on his side. A lighthouse on his right arm.

It was the manacle on one of his wrists that really brought it home.

He'd been to prison.

A *Russian* prison.

I traced the US dollar bills on his shoulder and wondered if he knew, while getting this tattoo, that he would end up here, thirty-one-thousand feet in the air, on a United States government airplane.

His abs tensed as I ran a hand down them.

"Will you tell me what they mean?" I asked.

"No." The word was hard.

I trailed my fingers over him, knowing these symbols sometimes meant the wearer had done terrible things to earn them, yet somehow, I was still fascinated by every one of them. Maybe because I already knew he was far from a choir boy.

"Tell me what one means."

"No."

I couldn't stop touching him. Not only because he was hands-down the sexiest man I'd ever seen, but because he was the most *fascinating*. A cold-mannered professional on the outside, and a dirty-playing criminal below the surface.

I wrapped my hand around the manacle tattoo on his wrist. "This one. Tell me what this one means and then I'll let you do whatever you want to me."

"*Whatever* is a strong word."

The way he said it, slightly threatening, sent a shiver through me. "I'm aware."

"I'll humor you, but only because we have two hours of this flight left, and I'd prefer to spend it fucking you. Not because I'm *opening up* to you. Understood?"

Asshole.

I sighed. "And here I thought I was getting closer and closer to a proposal."

"It symbolizes a prison sentence of five years."

Five years?

I had so many questions, but I kept them to myself. I knew if I made a big deal about what he shared with me, it would just make him more resolved not to tell me more.

I did a quick math problem in my head. I'd known this man for eight years. It had to have taken him years before that to build a reputation significant enough to hold the position he did now. He was, what, thirty-three? He'd had to have been young when he went to jail. Early teens, maybe?

God, Russia was barbaric.

I trailed a finger down his cheek, horrified to think about what he'd gone through in prison with this face. He read my thoughts again.

He grabbed my wrist in a vise, his voice harsh. "I don't need your pity. I held my own in prison. I was already bigger than most men at fourteen. Not to mention, *colder*, thanks to—" He cut himself off.

Thanks to who?

My attention caught on something. I dropped my gaze to his grip on me, to the elastic band on his wrist.

"What is . . .?" I trailed off when I realized what it was. And only because I'd worn the same wide-banded black hair ties since I could remember. My heart picked up as the memory came back, of him slipping that hair tie into his pocket while I was naked in his bed three years before.

The surprise hit me so hard I went on the offensive.

"That's mine," I accused, like it was something important he'd stolen from me. I reached for it as if to take it back, but he stopped me by grabbing that wrist, too.

"It's mine now."

He'd kept it—*worn* it—for three years? I couldn't figure out if it was slightly disturbing, or . . . *hot.*

"Fine," I sighed, like I didn't care. "You can keep it." Then, I leaned in and kissed him before he could read the conflicting thoughts on my face.

"I wasn't asking for your permission." He nipped at my lip.

The kiss went deeper, with a hot glide of tongue. Heat drifted between my legs, and I was losing my breath, but somehow, I still found the resolve to mess with him. I smiled against his lips, pulling back to say, "It's cute that you wear it."

He smacked my ass hard enough to sting.

"Almost"—I gasped as he sucked on the sensitive spot behind my ear—"*romantic.*"

A darkly amused noise came from him. "I was going to give it to you nice and easy, *malyshka.*" His lips trailed down my neck, voice nothing but a rumble. "Now, I'm going to make you scream."

A shiver trailed down my spine.

He carried me to a bedroom in the back, dropped me on the bed, undid his belt, and stripped down to nothing. He hung his clothes neatly on the back of a chair, while I would have tossed mine into a pile on the floor. I had no idea what I was doing with this man, but, as I watched him with half-lidded eyes, my skin buzzed with anticipation to feel him against me.

I lifted a leg and rested my heel on his bare stomach. He undid the strap around my ankle and set the stiletto on the floor. But, before reaching for the next foot, he kissed my instep. I didn't know if that was an erogenous zone, but my body lit up like it was.

His body came down on mine, and the feel of his skin against mine for the first time sent a low moan up my throat. A shudder rolled through him as he kissed me softly. My dress was still tangled around my hips, and he merely pulled my panties to the side before pushing into me. I gasped, digging my nails into his shoulders and arching my back to take him deeper.

He was so serious and intense when he fucked, as if he was there to do a job he secretly loved. But, every once in a while, something soft and sexy showed through—the rumble of approval against my throat, like he was showing his appreciation of me lying there and taking it. The, "Made for me," he rasped against my neck as he slid into me deep and slow. The press of his lips against mine and the softness of his caresses, even while he fucked me hard enough I could black out.

Somewhere in the middle of it, I'd lost the rest of my clothes and lay flat on my stomach, while he held each of my wrists beside my head and fucked me from behind.

He stilled, breath heavy, as he brushed his lips against the back of my neck. "I want to come inside you, *malyshka*."

My mind groaned in protest while my body screamed, *YES*.

I'd started my period the day after our last encounter and had just gotten over it two days before, so, statistically speaking, it was fairly safe. Though, what we were doing was risky to begin with; I didn't even have the confidence he wasn't sleeping with other women.

But, at the moment, he was hitting a spot so deep, so intense, it was bringing me to a point I'd never gone to before and tears to my eyes. His bodyweight was heavy as he held me down, sending pure pleasure through my blood. And then there was this feeling in my chest, a lightness and a heaviness all at once.

It was too much.

As I tumbled toward the edge of release, I lost all sense of reason within me.

I suddenly wanted him to do it. Needed him to. Would *beg* for it.

"*Come inside me*," I pleaded.

He pressed his face into my neck and growled with satisfaction.

The sound was all I needed to fall right over the edge.

I might have forgotten some feelings over the last few years, but I knew what this one was.

Bliss.

CHAPTER
Twenty-Five

Gianna

I HAD NOW BECOME JUST ANOTHER THIRD.

I knew it.

He knew it.

The freaking stewardess probably knew it.

He sat on the foot of the bed, his elbows on his knees. The presence emanating from him didn't feel like regret, but something very, *very* thoughtful. Deliberative. I imagined this was how plans for world domination were made.

I sighed and stretched out like a cat. "Gosh, I'm starving."

"You have no idea what starving is." The words were soft and pensive, like he wasn't even aware he'd said it.

I was momentarily stunned.

Because now I knew, at some point in this man's life, he'd gone hungry.

I didn't let myself dwell on it or else the questions would explode from me like confetti, and we all knew how he felt about *opening up*.

He was still stuck in his thoughts while I grabbed his dress shirt and slipped it on. I was buttoning it up and walking past him to the door when he grabbed my wrist.

"Where are you going?"

"Going to find some peanuts. Crossing my fingers the Bureau splurged with the hard-working man's money and have some covered in chocolate."

He pulled me closer, until I stood between his legs. "We landed ten minutes ago."

"We did?" I frowned. "How did I miss that?"

Something sexy played in his eyes. "You were too busy calling out for God."

I wished it didn't happen, but I couldn't stop it.

I flushed.

When he ran a thumb across my cheek, warmth crept into my heart and melted.

"Tell me you hate me, *malyshka.*"

The way he said it, so deep and vehement, slowed the blood in my veins. It reminded me of the heavy weight of his body against mine. Of his hands holding me down.

I tried to say it. I really did. However, as much as it confused me, I couldn't physically push those words past my lips. So, instead, I pulled away from him, flustered with myself.

"This is ridiculous."

"You don't hate me," he said, voice low and resigned. "But by the time this is over, you might."

"This?"

"Us."

Déjà vu played down my spine with something warm and electric.

He watched me with an unsettling conviction in his eyes, while my heart chugged to keep up with the feelings warring inside. The last one to crawl out of the shadows of my mind—the one I was most familiar with—won. *Panic.* I'd been stuck in two unwanted marriages for the last eight years of my life. The idea of any kind of commitment embodied a fist that wrapped around my lungs and squeezed. I tried to mask it as best I could, but I knew he saw it all over my face.

His jaw ticked, a shutter coming down over his eyes. "I'm talking about sex, Gianna."

Oh.

"You mean, like, just sex?"

He nodded, flicking his gaze away from me. "Temporary. Until I move back to Seattle."

Oh.

The fist around my lungs released, but his words had left a sting behind.

Though, for some reason, the glint in his gaze before he'd looked away felt . . . untruthful. A gut instinct told me he was lying to me, but I just wasn't sure about what. I knew he was attracted to me, knew he wanted me in a sexual way—maybe he even enjoyed sparring with me—but it was too hard to believe he was interested in me *seriously*. I was messy. He was as strait-laced as they came.

"Aren't you in a relationship with Aleksandra?" I realized it made me sound like a homewrecker, having just begged him to come inside me for goodness' sake, but really, I had so many deeper issues than this.

"No."

"Are you sleeping with her?"

"I have never slept with her."

I was a little unsettled by the tsunami wave of relief that hit me.

He wanted to sleep with me *four* times? I didn't know if I should feel special or terrified. I was leaning toward a mixture of both.

I bit my lip in deliberation.

Wasn't I just telling myself I needed to stop sleeping with him? Why was I even contemplating this? My mind spun in turmoil, but my body had already decided. It was still vibrating in gratification from the two intense orgasms he'd just wrung from me.

"I'll make it so good for you, *malyshka*."

A tortured moan crawled up my throat, but I couldn't get rid of a tingling sense of warning in the back of my head. Why did this feel like a trap?

"I don't know . . ."

"I don't see the problem." His eyes flickered with a challenge. "Unless you think you'll fall for me."

Ugh.

He had me backed into a corner now.

I'd have to admit I was in danger of *falling for him* or let him fuck me for however long he was staying in New York.

What a ruthless bastard.

Though, maybe this was what I needed. I didn't want to give up sex, but I also didn't want to have to search for another man to take Christian's place. A scoff sounded in my mind—like *that* was even possible. I could use him, just like he'd be using me, couldn't I?

I fingered the hem of his shirt. "I'll have some stipulations, of course."

"Of course."

Walking back and forth in front of him, I listed them off.

"I'm not a sex slave. I won't drop to my knees when you snap your fingers, like you expect all your other women to."

He was amused. "That'll be a hard habit for me to break, but I'll work on it."

"I know how witty and exciting you think I am and that you love spending time with me, but I'm a busy woman. You have to respect my space."

His tone was dry. "You read trashy novels by the pool and spend the rest of your time at Barneys."

I ignored him and made the next stipulation sound so serious it made him smile. "You have to kiss me whenever I want."

"Done."

"Condoms, Christian. You have to learn how to put one on."

"Fine."

My eyes narrowed, because he'd given in to that way too easily. "Anything else?"

"I don't know what kind of kink you're into, but there are some hard no's for me." I was obviously a pervert because I couldn't think of many as I ticked them off on my fingers. "Ball-and-gag-like bondage . . . tickling—hard, *hard* no on that one—and, preferably, no backdoor action."

He stood, making me look up to meet his gaze. "Is that it?"

"I think so," I answered hesitantly, not liking the look in his eye.

"Yes to the first two, no to the last." He fisted my shirt and dragged me closer, pressing the next words to my ear. "I'm going to ruin every part of your body for any other man, *malyshka*, and you're going to thank me when I'm done."

I was making a deal with the devil.

And I couldn't even find the grace to save myself.

The morning after we'd returned from Chicago, I was struggling with my lock before heading to yoga. Christian just happened to be leaving his apartment at the same time. Our gazes caught. Time lagged in slow motion, touching my skin like a heat wave and leaving me hot, flustered, and out of breath. This was where I would usually have something witty to say, but, in truth, I felt . . . *shy?*

He'd screwed me against my door last evening after driving me home. It was hot and fast and rough. Then, afterward, he'd just kissed me. He'd kissed me for so long my brain became mush, my legs turned to Jell-O, and my heart began to burn. And then he'd left me breathless and thinking about him for a ridiculous amount of time.

Now, from only a little eye-contact, heat bloomed beneath my skin, and all the extra-special things I could be saying were stuck in my throat.

What's happening to me?

When he left me standing there without a word, like I was the annoying neighbor nobody wanted to run into, I let out a breath, relieved.

I didn't know what I would have said if he hadn't.

There was a feeling in my chest, heavy, and unstable, and consuming.

It felt too close to panic.

I spent the daylight hours of the next five days shaving my legs, watching infomercials, painting my toenails—basically anything to stay busy until nine o'clock. Because that was when he would come. He'd ignore me in the hall during the day, but once the sun set, it was like I was the only woman left on the planet.

Christian had a routine.

And I'd become obsessed with watching it.

He started with his watch, unclasping it and placing it on my dresser. His cufflinks came next. He set them on the side of his Rolex, approximately an inch to the right. My favorite was the tie—with his eyes on me, he worked the knot loose, slipped it off his neck.

Then, he started on his shirt buttons, the sleeves first and then his collar. He left it on and undone while he worked on his belt, which he rolled up neatly. In truth, that was the only foreplay I needed. His shoes were the next to go—lined up beside each other. Then, he stripped, setting his clothes on the back of my divan.

I would have made fun of him just a week before. But now, I only found it so sexy I sat on the edge of my bed just to watch it.

We did this sex thing backward.

It never started with kissing.

But it always ended with it.

As soon as he was undressed, I made my way over to him. He fisted a hand in my hair while I kissed a path from his chest to his stomach to lower, taking him in my mouth.

I was just another volunteer.

But he always reciprocated.

When I'd taken him to the point he let out a hiss or some rough Russian word, his grip in my hair pulled my mouth away from him and me up to my feet, then he walked me backward to my bed.

Anticipation coiled like a hot wire in my stomach when my back hit the sheets. He started off slowly, pulling off the tiny or lacy panties I always put on for him. Then, he'd press his face between my legs, holding my thighs tightly, like this was something he'd always wanted, and he was afraid someone would take it away. He wouldn't stop until I was digging my nails into his arms and shuddering with release.

He wore a condom the first night, but the next, he'd gotten me so hot, so *desperate,* to feel him bare inside I'd begged for, "Just the tip." The tip had become a few more inches, and then we were just fucking.

He liked to take me from behind, sometimes with me on all fours, sometimes kneeling, with my back pressed to his front and his hands on my breasts. I loved it any way, but he was right—my favorite was missionary. With his arms braced on the bed beside me, with his stomach muscles tightening every thrust, and the intensity in his eyes burning into mine.

Trying to be semi-responsible, I didn't beg him to come inside me again. He always pulled out, coming on a new part of my body every time. And then, for a moment, we just breathed, heavy puffs against each other's skin. While still breathless, he kissed me, short and sweet, before pulling me to the bathroom and starting the shower.

He washed the come off my body, and then he washed my hair. I'd never shampooed my hair so much in my life—my hairstylist was going to kill me—but surely, if she'd had this man's hands in her hair just once, she'd understand.

When he was done, he'd kiss me under the spray of the water. Until I was panting and begging for him to fuck me.

But he never did.

I knew he wanted to. He was hard, letting out a tortured rumble when I wrapped my hand around him, but he would only slow the kiss and step away from me.

I loved when he got a phone call, because when he did, he would stay longer. He'd sit on the divan in my room talking in Russian while he watched me comb my hair, rub lotion on my skin, and get dressed in some slinky thing I was dying for him to give in and take back off. The heat of his gaze followed my every movement, leaving my skin sensitive and hyperaware. As soon as he finished his conversation, he'd leave, when I was already impatient for him to return.

I hadn't had a man in my personal space since Antonio, and even then, he'd never washed my hair, gone down on me half as much as this one did, or watched me with a look in his eyes that made me burn.

I could get used to it.

And that scared me.

Thursday morning at yoga, Val was prattling about the new guy she was seeing. The instructor had already threatened to kick us out twice for talking and we were working toward a third. In my defense, I was hardly involved in the conversation because I was stuck in some Christian-induced dreamland.

Last night, as his hands had been working shampoo through my hair, I'd asked him if he had a weird hair fetish. His reply was, "Only for yours."

"Why?" I'd asked breathlessly.

"I love your hair, *malyshka*. It's the first part of you I saw—the back of your head at your wedding. And then you turned around and looked right at me. But you weren't looking at me—you were looking past me, toward your new husband, with this infatuated glow in your eyes. The first woman I wanted to look at me was too busy staring at another man. That was when I started to hate him—and I still do, even though he is dead"—his voice roughened with a slight accent—"because he got that look from you, and I never have."

"So, who's the lucky guy?" Val's voice pulled me back to reality.

"What?"

"Oh, come on. You've had this post-orgasmic look on your face all morning."

"Shh," I whispered when the instructor shot us a glare.

"Fine. Don't tell me." She crossed a leg over the other and stretched her torso. "It's not like I don't share everything with you. Though I guess I did forget to tell you I finally made it all the way with Christian."

My heart stopped. And the look I gave her could kill.

She smirked. "And that answers *that* question."

I'd just gotten played. Though, it made me realize, the mere idea of Val sleeping with Christian disturbed me more than it should have.

"God, you're such a bitch."

She laughed.

"All right, ladies, out! This is a sanctuary, and you've shit all over it this morning."

I walked to the coffee shop on autopilot, and I was so distracted with thoughts of *him*, I ended up telling the barista the wrong order—even though I'd gotten the same drink for *years*. That was when I realized what a mess he was making of my life.

Five days.

It had only taken five days for me to feel like I needed to find a support group for Christian addicts. I'd had my reservations about this *just sex* relationship from the beginning, and I should've trusted my gut. I was losing all sense of control fast, and I needed to cut the cord now before I became just another mindless Christian groupie.

That evening, I paced back and forth, planning out exactly what I would say. Because I knew if I didn't have a strong argument, he'd win, like he always did. But when a knock sounded on my door and I answered it, all the words I'd planned to say flew out of my head like a flutter of butterflies. He must have had my body trained, because just the sight of him sent my skin buzzing in anticipation.

I swallowed.

His eyes narrowed on me in suspicion. "Let me in, *malyshka*."

I did, even though that hadn't been the initial plan. He headed to my bedroom like he did every night, and I inhaled a breath to find some resolve before following him. He was already slipping off his watch when I reached him.

"We should stop having sex," I blurted.

He didn't even look at me while he worked on his cufflinks. "No."

"*No?*"

"That's what I said."

I flushed. "You can't just say *no*, Christian."

"Give me one good reason why we should stop," he said, unbuttoning his shirt, growing closer to revealing that stupid happy trail on his lower stomach.

"Because!" I sputtered. "God, would you stop taking off your clothes?"

"Because is not good enough."

"Fine! I could name off a whole novel-sized list of reasons. My grande Caramel Mocha, for one—"

"I've waited all day to fuck you, Gianna. I haven't been able to think about anything else but you. Are you done talking now?"

The heat in his eyes seeped into my bloodstream and dulled my anger.

I swallowed. "I swear, it's like talking to a concrete wall with you."

He ran a thumb across my cheek. "*Brick* wall."

He was in nothing but a pair of briefs now, his body heat wrapping around mine and stealing my breath.

"Don't tell me no, *malyshka*." His voice was so deep and almost desperate, like he wouldn't know what to do with himself if I denied him.

I wished I could say I held my ground.

But as soon as he kissed me, promising to fuck me missionary against my lips, it was all over.

CHAPTER
Twenty-Six

Gianna

A GROAN ESCAPED ME WHILE I WORKED MY WHITE SKINNY JEANS OVER MY hips. I let out a breath of relief once they were on, only for my mood to deflate like a popped balloon when I realized I couldn't button them.

"No," I moaned.

I struggled to take them off while cursing Val for getting me kicked out of yoga yesterday. I'd obviously needed the exercise. And giving up chocolate just wasn't a realistic option.

It was October now. The leaves fell in drops of orange and red, and summer was losing its sweaty grip on New York.

I took a cab to the club, where I was supposed to be meeting Elena. She was organizing her sister's baby shower, and I'd volunteered to help. Clearly, I'd do anything to get my mind off a dirty blue-eyed fed these days. He was so intense and consuming, I wondered how many of the women he'd been with were still pining over him. The thought brought a rush of jealous heat to my chest, even though I now knew I was *different*.

Last night, after the most intense session of missionary sex I'd ever had, with my head resting on his pounding heart, I'd asked, "How many women have you been with more than three times?"

For a moment, I didn't think he was going to respond.

"Don't ask questions you already know the answer to, *malyshka*."

It was one.

And it was me.

The knowledge wiggled a heavy feeling in my chest. A feeling that felt too close to panic, yet far enough away it eluded me.

Elena sat at a booth with catering and party pamphlets spread across the table, telling her hovering mother, "No, Mamma, she doesn't like pink."

Celia threw her hands up. "She's having a *girl*, Elena!"

"She wants to do green."

"*Green?*"

I chose to let them finish that conversation and poured myself a glass of iced tea from the pitcher on the bar.

"I'll tell you what, tell me your favorite drink. I'll take you home and make the best one you've ever had right now."

I smiled. "I like it, very original. However, might go over smoother if you didn't live with your uncle."

Benito Abelli had offered a new ridiculous pickup line every time he'd seen me since we first met. It was fun, and harmless, and usually brought a smile to my face.

Elena's cousin leaned against the bar beside me. "The basement is all mine, baby. Even has its own entrance."

I laughed. "You really know how to tempt a woman. I'm not really a basement kind of girl, though."

He pushed a strand of hair behind my ear. "And what kind of girl are you?"

"*Flighty.*" The voice held the slightest clench of his teeth.

I tensed.

Because that word came from the man I'd been sleeping with for the last week. The one who washed my hair and reverted to Russian when he fucked. I caught his form in the bar mirror as he passed behind me.

He'd just insulted me.

We'd done it all the time. It'd been *all* we used to do. But now, it felt like . . . *betrayal.* An unsettling feeling roiled in my stomach.

"Ouch," Benito murmured.

"He means, *perfect*," I said. "He's obviously gotten the terms confused. Easy to do when there's so much air in your head."

If looks were tangible, the one he gave me before disappearing down the hall toward the basement entrance would have been a sharp spank to my ass.

I'd seen him naked and heard him come, but with clothes on, in public, our differences were glaringly obvious. Him, the cold, strait-laced professional. Me, the jobless, *flighty* girl who was still trying to get her life together.

I stayed at the club for an hour, trying to help Elena and her mamma find common ground between their disputes, but unfortunately, there wasn't a color between pink and green that would suffice, so that argument remained at a standstill.

As I watched the clock close in on nine that night, anxiety swelled in my chest. I didn't know what to expect from him when he arrived. Would he act like nothing happened today? I had more respect than to allow him to insult me in public and then screw me in private, right? Though, it did create a boundary that reminded me this was *just sex*. And over the last few days, the things he'd said to me had blurred the line.

But, as the clock ticked by, a niggling doubt arose that maybe he'd realized how different we were and decided to end this.

Nine turned to ten, and ten turned to eleven.

He never came.

Val: *Call me crazy, but I'm still confident on my wager.*

The text came attached with an article titled: *Meeting the father . . . do I hear wedding bells in the near future?*

God, I was so sick of her articles I wanted to chuck my phone out the window. I told myself not to read it, but in the end, curiosity got the best of me.

The picture showed a silver-haired gentleman, Christian, and Aleksandra entering the doors of a five-star restaurant.

He hadn't come last night because he'd been with *her.*

My stomach tied into a knot.

My gaze settled on Aleksandra. She was thin as a rail, while I sat here in stretchy pants next to a half-eaten bag of M&M's.

I got to my feet and stomped through my apartment toward my closet. Clothes flew over my shoulder as I tried to find something to wear. I grabbed a loaf of bread on my way out, but, when I opened my apartment door, it was like a nightmare come to life—all gorgeous, blonde-haired, six feet of her.

Christian stood in front of his opened door, while Aleksandra faced him in a flowy pink dress. She had a hand on *his chest.*

Both their gazes came to me.

Hers widened in surprise, then glinted with a challenge. She turned back to him. "Anyway, I just wanted to return your watch and say I had a great time last night."

Christian was, indeed, holding his watch. The one he took off every night and set on my dresser.

He nodded curtly, his eyes still on me.

"Hope we can do it again soon." She purred it while looking at me with a cat-got-the-cream smile. I hated her.

She drifted down the hall, and, feeling slightly nauseous, I turned to lock my door.

"I didn't sleep with her."

Relief settled in my chest.

And that annoyed me.

"Didn't ask," I said.

"I didn't even touch her."

"Don't care."

"The clasp on my watch broke. I left it on the table at dinner."

"Riveting."

I was flustered, my hand was sweaty, and I couldn't get the stupid key to turn in the lock.

"Gianna—"

I spun around with my bag of bread. "You called me *flighty!*"

"You practically let him fuck you up against the bar," he growled.

"Oh, please. He barely touched me." Was I really expecting a cold-blooded killer to be rational? "I don't have to explain myself to you. This isn't a relationship. *Just sex*, remember?"

A retort burned brightly in his eyes, but he shook his head and held it in. "Where are you going?"

"I'm going to feed the pigeons and reflect on my life choices like a true New Yorker." I turned back around, and each second I struggled with this lock, the frustration beneath my skin inflated and inflated, until it felt like I would burst.

"I didn't get home until after three last night. I didn't want to wake you."

"It doesn't matter. I don't want to do this anymore."

"No." His voice was vehement. "This isn't over."

I'd thought *he* had wanted to end this, and now, the deepness and intensity of his voice warmed my heart with relief and elation. But there wasn't enough room for all these overwhelming feelings, and they all exploded like a tripwire.

I faced him, leaving my key stuck in the lock. "Listen, Christian. All of this"—I gestured between us—"is too much drama for me. I swear, I've gained at least five pounds from the stress! And I am *not* giving up chocolate, dammit!"

His jaw tightened as he watched an angry tear run down my cheek. "There won't be any more drama, Gianna. This is exclusive now."

It wasn't lost on me that I'd just told him I was ending this relationship and he'd countered with making it more serious.

I blinked. "Exclusive, *just sex*?"

He shook his head, something sardonic passing through his eyes. "Whatever you want it to be, *malyshka*."

I swallowed. "You're leaving any day now, Christian. Let's just call a spade a spade. This isn't going to last forever."

"I'm moving back to New York."

My heart dropped. *What*? Why?"

His gaze touched mine as he said, "I missed the city."

Oh.

"You called me flighty," I breathed.

"I meant perfect."

I stood there with a bag of bread in my hand, my key stuck half-way in my lock, while this man I used to despise ran a thumb across my cheek.

What an odd sequence of events.

But I had to say, something about it felt undeniably right.

He fed the pigeons with me. Well, he didn't actually pull off a piece of bread and toss it—menial labor, I guessed—but he did sit on the bench beside me. I'd insisted I didn't need an escort to the park, but was cut off by, "Knowing you, you'll get arrested. I'm coming," and that had been the end of that.

I joked about taking a selfie and wondering if he'd even show up in the picture. He told me he showed up just fine while fucking me in front of the bathroom mirror.

I asked him what *moya zvezdochka* meant. He said it meant, *my little star.*

He asked me what the scar on my chin was from. I told him a lack of self-control and the chickenpox.

I asked him if he kissed all his neighbors or just me. He looked me in the eye and said, "You're the only woman I've ever kissed, *malyshka.*"

I stopped asking questions after that.

Because everything inside me had tilted on its axis.

We walked back to the building while I teased him about wearing a designer suit to the park. He got a good jab in about my galaxy leggings, telling me he must have missed hearing about the Star Wars convention coming to town.

He was cool, icy control.

But something burned hot beneath the surface.

Something shrouded by ice for so long.

I wanted to watch it melt. To unravel him until I understood every layer.

I knew it was dangerous.

I even knew I wouldn't win.

But sometimes, even the best gambler doesn't know when to quit.

CHAPTER
Twenty-Seven

Christian

"I'M DONE. SERGEI IS YOUR PROBLEM NOW."

"Why?"

"Because I don't want to fuck his daughter." My gaze coasted over the bed. Wild, dark hair, smooth olive skin, and twisted sheets. Gianna slept on her stomach, both hands beneath her pillow. My chest felt heavy while I looked at her soft expression. I wanted to capture that look in a bottle and take it with me everywhere. Maybe then, I'd feel like I had some control over it.

"The model?" Ronan let out a half laugh. "Only you would consider that a problem. Let me guess, she saw your pretty face and begged her father to make you hers."

I didn't believe that was the case. Aleksandra was cold and calculating. I often got the feeling I was nothing but a step in her overall plan. And sometimes, that plan felt desperate. "I think she believes I'm the lesser of two evils."

"Hate to see who the other man is," he muttered. "If you're turning down models over there, I'd love to take a look at whoever's in your bed."

"She's Italian," I said, like that explained everything.

"Ah, passionate women. Is it serious?"

A sardonic breath escaped me. "She bet twenty grand I'd marry another woman." I'd run into a little birdie named Val who'd whispered that to me yesterday morning on the street. Well, she'd tiptoed around the topic, but I'd put two and fucking two together. Another reason I'd lost my cool when I found Gianna laughing with some Abelli who had his hand in her hair. How could I say every strand was *mine* any clearer than washing it every goddamn night?

"I like her already." He chuckled. "Why does it sound like you want to drag this little Italian down the aisle?"

Because it felt like if I didn't have my possession of her in writing, she'd slip from my fingers again. I was all in, had known this obsession would only escalate once I'd had her body, her attention, and her smiles all to myself. I'd warned her years ago when she'd pressed her lips to mine. I'd let her do it, because I'd thought it would turn me off and then I could finally put this infatuation with her behind me. I hated kissing, especially the sounds of it from the next room—and what it had usually meant for me—since I could remember. But when she'd kissed me, it hadn't disgusted me in the least. Her lips were soft. Her tongue was hot and wet. And her sigh gave me chills. Violent lust had roared through my blood, dulling my vision. That unsettled me, and then pissed me off enough to step away.

"She says she won't marry again."

"Women say stuff they don't mean all the time."

"She means it. She thinks this is exclusive *just sex.*" Those two words annoyed the shit out of me.

"Sounds like you have an ideal situation going on. She's sleeping with you—who gives a fuck if she doesn't want to marry you?"

"She's in the outfit."

"Ah." He sounded amused. "Messy."

Dating women in the *Cosa Nostra* wasn't a thing. This relationship would blow up sooner or later. Marriage was only the real grasp I could have on her. Otherwise, she wasn't really mine. Whether she realized it or not, Gianna would have to make a decision to marry eventually, and I was selfish enough to make her choose me. Because there wasn't an ounce of me that could let her become someone else's.

"I know you've got some sinister plan in the works, so let's hear it."

Fuck. I hated how well he knew me.

Gianna roused and rolled onto her back. Her soft brown eyes fluttered opened and landed on me. I could feel the heat of them in my chest. Every time she looked at me, it only strengthened my decision. I might have fought it for a long time—for both our sakes—but she was mine now. And she had no idea what I would do to keep it that way.

I held her gaze. "Make her fall for me before I fuck it all up. Then, she won't leave."

"Sounds a little Stockholmy to me, but I like it. I'll figure something out with Sergei." A smile touched his voice. "And if I have to take one for the team and fuck his daughter, so be it."

After I hung up, I switched back to English. "Did I wake you?"

"Yes." She sighed and stretched out. "But I like listening to you on the phone."

I guessed I should feel a little guilty I was conspiring against her, but I didn't. I leaned forward on her ridiculous hot pink divan, resting my elbows on my knees.

"Why?"

"You have a sexy voice." She yawned.

A smile pulled on my lips. She was always so honest. It was a trait I hadn't come across often—I couldn't even say *I* utilized it—though, maybe that was why it was so refreshing. Every word she said was a little genuine piece of her. I wanted to collect them all.

A flush warmed her cheeks. "I'm sorry I fell asleep on you."

I'd stripped her naked and gone down on her, only for her to fall asleep seconds after she'd come. Truthfully, I would do it for the rest of my life with the knowledge I wouldn't get anything in return. I'd fantasized about her for so long, and the dream couldn't even touch the reality.

"Can I make it up to you?"

I absently rubbed my hard-on through my briefs, loving that idea, but then she yawned, her eyes growing heavy.

"Make it up to me in the morning."

"What are you doing?" she asked, as I got into bed with her and pulled her back against my chest.

"Sleeping."

"*Here?*" She sounded terrified.

"Yes. Now, be quiet. I'm tired." I'd never done this in my life. Wouldn't be able to sleep a fucking wink.

"Fine."

It took five minutes until she was out like a light.

I ran my hand over her hip, memorizing the curve and velvety feel of her skin. She had two dimples on her lower back I'd always been infatuated with, framed right above the sweetest ass, and it was all pressed up against me. Her hair was in my face and it smelled like vanilla. All of it was sensory overload. Like an injection of dopamine. My heart beat heavily. The blood rushed through my veins so fast my hand felt unsteady.

When you're obsessed with something for so long and finally obtain it? It feels like coming home to God. And nobody gives up their fucking spot in Heaven.

CHAPTER
Twenty-Eight

Gianna

I T WAS *HOT*.

And why did it feel like my blanket weighed fifty pounds?

I tried to roll over but couldn't move.

Fighting through the heavy confusion and unconsciousness, I realized what was holding me down. There was a man in my room. In my *bed*. Panic bled into my veins, and my eyes shot open.

"Go back to sleep, *malyshka*."

My heart began to beat again.

"*Oh, my gosh*," I breathed heavily in relief. "I thought you were a serial killer."

A low chuckle came from him. "Not too far off."

The fifty-pound blanket was only his arm around me, and the heat—that was all him, pressed up against me. No sunlight came in through the window, but the room was still lit. He'd left the bathroom door open and the light on, like I did every night. The thoughtfulness made my heart feel heavy in my chest. But now that I wasn't alone, it seemed embarrassingly bright in here.

I swallowed. "I could probably sleep without the light, if it's keeping you up." Just the thought started a cold sweat beneath my skin.

"It's not."

I didn't know if I believed him, but I forgot about it when I realized he was hard. A rumble sounded in his throat when I shifted and rubbed against him. God, the man was so warm and half-naked, just the press of his body against mine sent my toes curling in pleasure. If I'd known it felt this good spooning with Christian Allister, I would have climbed into his bed years ago, just for this.

I couldn't help but roll my ass back against his erection. He grabbed my hip, and I thought he was going to stop me, but instead, he grinded me harder against him. Heat drifted and tightened between my legs as I rolled my hips, in nothing but the rustle of sheets and the sound of our breaths.

I turned in his arms, and he rolled onto his back as I straddled him. He ran his hands up my thighs, his half-lidded eyes taking in my naked body.

My gaze dropped to his lips. I couldn't believe he'd never kissed another woman but me. The man had volunteers lined up from here to China, for goodness' sake. Though, I had to admit, the fact I'd been the only one—his only experience in that department—was incredibly hot.

Surely, he'd had to put in an effort to keep from kissing the women he'd dated. One would think it'd be easier just to kiss them, and to me, that meant he had a resilient motivation. I knew it wasn't germs. A couple of the times he'd gone down on me, the man had ventured lower, to a hole I'd never let another touch before, and I doubted he'd just gotten lost. But somehow, I knew, if I wasn't careful with my questions, they would blow up in my face.

I ran my hands up his chest. "What do you do for the Bureau?"

"Whatever they want me to do."

"So . . . say they told you to go set fire to the old lady's apartment next door."

"I'd set fire to her apartment."

I swallowed, and the next question came out a little breathless. "Say they told you to kill me."

I met his gaze.

Possessive blue flames.

And something morally ambiguous.

His hand came up to my throat and his thumb brushed across my pulse. Then, he lightly squeezed. "I'd have to decline."

The pressure building in my lungs released with my next breath, and I forced a small smile to my lips. "Because I'm too much fun?"

"Because you're mine."

My smile fell.

The heat of his stare seeped into my chest, weighing it down with warmth. I slid my hands to the sheets on either side of him and pressed my front against his. I was so much smaller than him, and there was a vivid contrast of my olive skin and his lighter tone amongst waves of chocolate hair and black tattoos.

"Tell me why you kiss me," I breathed against his lips.

I thought he might answer me this time.

He didn't.

He rolled me onto my back and made me forget my own name.

"So, do you have a day job . . . or do you just sit around like a super-hero villain in your suit and tie, waiting for them to tell you which old lady's apartment to burn down?" I asked him the next morning, while I still lay in bed and he was buttoning his shirt.

"I have a day job, like *most* adult Americans," he said, amused. "I start back tomorrow."

I pursed my lips. "Was that a dig on me, Officer? I'll have you know, I have a very busy schedule as it is. You're lucky I can even pencil you in."

On his way out of the room, he grabbed my ankle and dragged me down the bed toward him. His voice was rough as he pulled my face up to his. "Move shit around if you have to and pencil me in for tonight." Then, he kissed me, placing a sharp nip on my bottom lip.

When he left, I fell back to the bed with a sigh and a smarting lip.

I tried to stop it, but I couldn't.

A stupid smile overtook my face.

He got home around eight o'clock that night and stopped short in his bedroom doorway. I was lying on his bed on my stomach, with my feet in the air and my ankles crossed. Naked.

It was bold.

And it was scary.

My palms were sweaty, and my heart galloped at an inconsistent pace.

I lifted a coy shoulder. "I wasn't sure if this appointment was casual or black-tie, so I decided to come with a blank canvas."

His gaze coasted the length of my body so heavily it brought goosebumps to my skin. Walking toward me, he stopped in front of me at the foot of the bed and ran a rough palm across my cheek. If I wasn't mistaken, the smallest tremor ran through his hand.

His voice was soft, but the finest threat wove through. "I can find anyone . . . anywhere." A thumb brushed my jawline. "Makes me a desirable person to have around. Antonio showed his interest in a partnership, but I had enough obligations and didn't want to get mixed up with the Italians. I was going to meet with him and decline. But then I saw you."

My heart went still.

"I sought you out, just to see if you were as interesting as you looked." His grip on my face tightened, like he was angry that I had been. "And I agreed to work with your husband. You fascinated me, but I began to hate you, too. Because I couldn't stop thinking about you, and I couldn't have you. And you were so fucking beautiful." His thumb ran down my lips. "Then, you were single, and I'd already made you hate me, too."

I swallowed as his hand slid down my throat.

"It was a relief, *malyshka*, because we were everything wrong for each other. But nothing has ever felt more right than finding you like this in my bed."

I didn't say anything, because the words became wedged in my throat.

"Come shower with me," he said roughly.

He pulled me to my feet, and I padded into the bathroom behind him. In the shower, he pressed me up against the wall, I wrapped my legs around his waist, and then he showed me just how *right* we fit together—in one way, at least.

I woke up in his bed the next morning to an awful grinding noise. Glancing at the clock, six a.m. stared back at me in ungodly red. I groaned and pulled a pillow over my face to mute the annoying sound.

He'd kept me up until after two in the morning, running his hands and mouth all over me until it felt like I'd been turned inside out, bringing that raw and elusive feeling to the forefront.

The line was blurring.

But it was like trying to stop a train with mere willpower at one-hundred miles per hour.

When I'd tried to return to my own bed, his response had been a simple, "No," and then he'd wrapped an arm around me, and I'd forgotten why I wanted to leave in the first place.

Getting to my feet, I opened his dresser drawer and slipped on one of his undershirts. I found him at the kitchen counter, already dressed in a suit and tie, pouring green liquid into a glass from the blender.

Amusement filled his gaze at my moody expression.

I narrowed my eyes further. "Since all your other women must have been too scared to inform you, I will. There's an unwritten rule— nobody starts the blender until the sun rises, and even then, if it's not margaritas, other conditions apply. Like *green*, Christian. Liquids should never be green."

"You have never looked more beautiful than you do right now, *malyshka*."

I flushed, my heart growing ridiculously warm. "I'm trying to be annoyed with you, if you can't tell."

He smiled. "Ah, my mistake."

I swallowed. Shifted. "Do you eat?"

He raised a brow, consuming that glass of green yuck in one drink.

"Like, solids? Or do you blend all the children's souls beforehand?"

He rinsed his glass out and then put it in the dishwasher. How very neat and tidy. It felt like I was messing up his space just by standing in it.

"Yes, I eat."

He grabbed my hips and set me on the island, spreading my legs to stand between them. He slid his hands up the sides of my thighs, and the warmth of them made me shiver.

I bit my lip. "Italian?"

"It happens to be my favorite." He sucked on that sensitive spot behind my ear, and every vein in my body melted into a puddle at his feet.

"What about allergies? Do you have any?" I gasped, as he pressed his hard-on against my clit in a slow roll. "Well, besides affection, warmth, and sunshine?"

His chuckle was low and dark. "Keep it up, and you'll be too sore to make me dinner."

I hated that he could read me well enough to know I was excited to cook for him, while I still knew nothing about him.

"I should warn you, though, I don't usually cook for men. It's just too much of a risk they'll fall in love with me."

"I thought you were a gambler," he drawled.

All I could respond with was a low moan, because his fingers slid inside of me and then he fucked me so hard I could still feel him hours later.

I had therapy at ten and felt guilty every time I had to evade the topic of Christian and this *just sex* relationship. I didn't want anyone to pop this exciting, sex-crazed bubble I was in, least of all Dr. Rosamund. I wanted to enjoy this while it lasted because I knew it wouldn't be forever. *We were everything wrong for each other.* He was going to realize nothing had changed eventually.

I just didn't know at the time it would only take a few days.

I made dinner at my apartment because I was too afraid of leaving even a speck of flour on Christian's sparkling countertops.

I stared at him intently from the other side of his kitchen island while he took the first bite. A half-smile pulled on his lips, but he otherwise ignored me and ate in silence.

My chest grew warm at his expression. "You love it, don't you?"

A playful glint in his eye. "It's all right."

I grinned. "You love it."

I walked around the island. "You're not feeling light-headed when you look at me, are you? Or maybe warmer than usual?" I put the back of my hand to his forehead, as if I was checking for a fever. "What about your heart? Has it started beating?"

He was amused. "Actually, I have been feeling a bit different."

My eyes widened in alarm.

Then, he grabbed my hand and pressed it against his hard-on.

I shook my head with a laugh, shoving him in the chest and turning to walk away, but he caught my wrist and pulled me closer to say in my ear, "It's delicious, *malyshka*. Thank you for making it for me."

His words settled like molten glass in my blood.

I didn't sleep in my bed that night.

Not the next night.

Or the next.

CHAPTER
Twenty-Nine

Gianna

I STOOD IN FRONT OF MY CLOSET, SAWING MY LIP IN NERVOUS DELIBERATION.

Why had I agreed to this?

Because he was annoyingly persuasive, that's why.

The night before, I was sitting cross-legged on his couch watching one of my "trashy" TV shows, while Christian sat at the island and talked on the phone. As soon as he ended the call, he said, "I need you to go somewhere with me tomorrow, *malyshka*."

"Where?" I asked absently. Chad was feeling up Rachel, while his wife was next door in the delivery room having his baby.

"A work dinner."

I faltered. "Like, a Federal Bureau hosted event?"

"Yes."

I let out a half-laugh. "No way."

"I always have a date, Gianna."

I swallowed, hating every word about to leave my mouth. "I'm sure if you put an ad in the paper, you'll have a variety of blondes lined up down the hall."

He set his phone down a little more aggressively than usual. "If I wanted someone else, I wouldn't be asking you."

"How would you even explain why I'm with you? Some of the feds at this party might recognize me."

"No one questions me, Gianna."

"What if they did?"

"I'd tell them to fuck off."

I sighed. "We haven't talked about . . . dates, Christian. Don't complicate this."

"You're the only one complicating it. If you can't handle going to one party with me without expecting a proposal, then just say so."

Ugh.

He knew I wasn't going to say those stupid words.

Later, I pushed his meticulously-placed toothbrush an inch to the left in retaliation.

After an hour-long deliberation, I settled on a Marilyn Monroe-esque black sequin gown. Sophisticated but flashy. I smoothed the dress over my hips, relieved it fit.

I was locking my door when he stepped into the hall behind me. Turning around, I quelled the nerves inside me and raised a brow. "Well, does His Highness approve?"

His heated gaze ran down my body, but something besides lust passed through his eyes. Disapproval? Displeasure? Whatever it was, it sent a burst of annoyance through me. I'd even worn my hair down for him, dammit. I spun around to go back inside and slam the door in his face, but he grabbed my wrist.

"No, *malyshka*, I like it." He ran a thumb across my cheek. "This is just new to me." He paused, a muscle ticking in his jaw. "And I haven't figured out how to deal with it yet."

"With what?"

"You."

I still didn't understand what he meant, but as he brushed a piece of hair behind my ear and told me in a rough voice I was gorgeous against my lips, all my anger escaped with my next breath.

The dinner party took place at the same hotel as Elena's wedding, but instead of well-dressed Italians filling the ballroom, it was crawling with feds.

Christian laughed at my expression.

My frown deepened. "What if someone arrests me while you're in the bathroom?"

"I'd bail you out."

"If you couldn't?"

"I'd be locked up beside you."

I couldn't stop a smile from appearing.

Women stared at Christian like he was the messiah. Married women, single women, old women, young—didn't matter. Thankfully, only a select few—the bravest ones without a lick of intuition in my opinion—actually approached him. He was polite but distant with them, and I suddenly wondered what he'd be like with them in bed once we came to an end. The thought put a bad taste in my mouth.

"Are your parents as good-looking as you?" I asked him after we'd been there fifteen minutes and the third woman had already come up to introduce herself. For heaven's sake, couldn't she see he had a date?

The subtlest tension tightened in his shoulders. I thought he wasn't going to answer me, but a moment later, he said, "My mother was."

Was?

"What about your father?"

"Never met him."

Oh. Wow.

"Siblings?" I questioned.

"A brother. As for his attractiveness, I couldn't tell you." An annoyed edge wove through his voice. "I don't sit around and wonder about how appealing he looks."

Okay.

I'd hit something a little sore. And I knew it wasn't his pretty face. I'd joked with him about it on many occasions, and he'd always brushed it off with a light shoulder. An awkward tension now lay between us, the kind not even a cleared throat could penetrate.

While Christian went to get us drinks, I found our spot at our table. I was already regretting agreeing to come to this party, and things were just about to get worse.

Setting my clutch down, I turned to see where my moody date was in the room, only to come face-to-face with another fed. My gaze slid down his suit that was one size too big, to the Asics on his feet.

"Hi." He grinned. "I'm Kyle Sheets."

Smiling tightly, I shook his hand, and replied, "Gianna," leaving out my last name. I was sure it was associated with too many criminal offenses to count. It was still Marino, and I had no intention of changing it. Russo was the old me, and my maiden name Bianchi didn't feel right anymore either. Even my name was confused.

"I have to say, you look . . ." He tilted his head. "Familiar."

Here we go.

I offered a coy smile. "Guess I have a common face."

"No," he drawled smoothly, his eyes coasting down my body, "I wouldn't say that at all . . . So, who are you with?"

I glanced pointedly at the name card beside my purse that read, *Christian Allister Guest.*

"Ah, I guess I should've known." He looked disappointed, scratching the back of his neck. "Allister didn't tell me he had such a beautiful girlfriend."

I somehow doubted Christian would tell this man anything.

Looking back, I should have just rolled with it—the man was clearly trying to find out if I was taken or available. But I was feeling a little petty. Christian knew my entire life story, while I'd only found out he had a sibling five minutes ago. And he'd seemed reluctant to even share that with me. All the words out of his mouth had contradicted this *just sex* relationship lately, blurring the line into nonexistence, and I needed to take it back a notch.

"Thank you, but that's probably because I'm not his girlfriend."

His eyebrows rose. "No kidding? You're . . . different than the other women he dates. Thought you'd be more serious, I guess."

"Nope." I laughed, like that would be ridiculous. The man didn't even trust me with the basic details about him. "We're not serious."

I knew before I'd finished the last word my date had found the perfect moment to return. The temperature dropped ten degrees.

Asics' gaze flicked to a spot behind me and above my head. "Allister."

There was no response.

Asics cleared his throat. Looked back at me. "Well, maybe I'll see you around, Gianna."

"Maybe." I smiled.

When he'd drifted away, I turned to my date, whose gaze had iced over. He handed me a glass of champagne while taking a sip of his own drink and looking casually into the room.

His voice was calm, but a sharp edge came through. "He has less than a grand to his name. Wouldn't add him to your husband list quite yet."

His words hit me like a blow to the chest, and I sucked in a breath.

"I appreciate the insight, Officer," I said with a saccharine smile. "Here I was, just about to *pencil* him in."

Tension rolled through him, his presence becoming nearly unapproachable.

Well, this was going splendidly.

As the guests at our table trickled in and took their seats, I might as well have not even been sitting beside him for as much as he acknowledged me.

If there was anything that showed how different and incompatible we were, it was him responding to a question about a new development in biocoenosis—whatever the hell that was—while the deepest thought in my head at that moment was which level of toner I wanted my stylist to use on my hair this week.

I sipped my champagne, smiling above it on cue, while growing more and more resentful of this situation with each second that passed. I was stuck in a room full of feds, I was out of my element, and my date wouldn't even look at me.

The walls seemed to be closing in.

My chest felt tight.

I grabbed my clutch and excused myself, feeling the heat of Christian's gaze on my back until I disappeared around the corner. Standing in front of the bathroom mirror, my hand shook slightly as I turned on the faucet. I should have stood my ground and said no to this date from the beginning. Because that bubble I'd been content in for the last couple weeks was close to bursting. I could feel it in my chest, inflating to the seams with each breath.

It was going to pop.

And until now, I hadn't realized how badly it was going to hurt.

Nausea roiled in my stomach, and I breathed slowly. I really hoped I wasn't getting sick. That was the last thing I needed right now.

I turned the corner in the hall, coming to a stop when my eyes landed on our table. A woman sat in my seat, facing Christian. Her name was Portia. I knew that because she'd dated him years ago. She leaned into him, coyly running a finger down the stem of *my* champagne glass. He gave her one of those rare half-smiles, responding to something she'd said. They seemed familiar, *intimate*, and I knew why. He'd fucked her three times.

"Beautiful couple, aren't they?" A woman close to retirement age stopped beside me, wearing a modest red sheath dress and a gold flower brooch. I knew she was the company gossip by one look at her. "Over half the office had a bet going that they'd get engaged, you know." She sighed, murmuring, "Some hussy probably came along and ruined it for everyone. Not sure when men will ever learn—those women might be good for one thing, but they're worthless in the long run." She trailed her fingers over the pearls on her neck. "Anyway, who are you with, dear? I didn't see you come in."

They're worthless in the long run.

Worthless.

Unlovable.

Whore.

Pop.

The pain radiated throughout my chest, wrapping around my lungs and squeezing.

The Christian-induced haze I'd been stuck in cleared. I couldn't be—my gaze landed on Portia—*that*. I couldn't be the classy, composed woman on his arm. And I couldn't be the woman still obviously pining for him after he'd moved on.

This was *just sex*—he'd said it himself.

It was supposed to be easy and uncomplicated. But I'd never known *uncomplicated* to twist one's heart into a knot and pull.

He'd already won.

My only choice was to forfeit before I lost everything.

"Dear? Are you all right?"

I ignored her and headed down the hall toward the exit, clipping shoulders with a guest on the way out. I mumbled an apology but didn't slow my pace because the backs of my eyes burned and threatened to spill over.

"Gianna? My goodness, I thought that was you!" Samantha Delacorte's heels clicked as she caught up to me. "I never thought I'd run into you here," she said, walking at a fast clip beside me. Her voice lowered. "You know, considering your previous offenses . . ."

My chest hurt, my eyes burned, and I had zero energy to spar with her right now, so I remained silent.

"Anyway, I just wanted to catch up with you to share the big news!" She squealed and shoved a massive diamond under my nose. It looked incredibly similar to the one Vincent had offered me only three months ago, just as he'd claimed to *love* me. Sardonic amusement mixed with a dose of bitterness crept through my veins. If I never heard that stupid word *love* again, I'd be a happy woman.

I offered a half-hearted, "Congratulations," as I walked out the front doors and into a light rain.

"Vincent and I are eloping in Barbados this winter." Samantha halted at the edge of the overhang. "I'll send you an invite!"

"Can't wait," I muttered.

I crossed my arms and headed down the sidewalk away from the hotel. The cold rain slid down my skin, bringing goosebumps to the surface. I should have worn a jacket tonight. Why couldn't I do anything right? Self-loathing churned in my stomach.

I didn't get far before someone grabbed my arm from behind, pulled me around a corner, and pressed my back against an alley wall. His hands flattened on the wall on either side of me, trapping me.

Straight lines. Broad shoulders. *Blue*, burning brightly.

But I saw other things now; other memories piled up on themselves in a fight to the surface.

"You won't forget me."

Moya zvezdochka.

They had built into something significant enough each one twisted my heart in a cruel grip.

Attachment?

Infatuation?

It couldn't be love.

His jaw tightened. "You left."

"Of course, I left. I knew this wouldn't work out from the beginning, and tonight just confirmed it."

"This?"

My throat felt tight. "Us."

Tension gripped him tight. Rain collected on his eyelashes. Something torturous flickered through his gaze.

"What are you saying?" The words were accented, and somehow, it tore my chest down the middle.

"You know what I'm saying." I swallowed. "We knew this would come to an end eventually."

His teeth clenched. "*This* might come to an end for you, but it will *never* be over for me."

My lungs hitched, and a distressed breath escaped my lips. It rained harder, pinging off a nearby dumpster and soaking my skin. I hoped it concealed the wetness pooling in my eyes.

Why did he have to make this so hard? Was I the only one who could see we didn't make sense?

"Why am I the only one being practical about this?"

"Because you've never been in this as deeply as me." No emotion behind those words. Just cold hard fact. Though, a flicker of something passed through his eyes, something soft and soul-wrenching. Something I'd seen in my own before. Something *unrequited*.

"When I said this was new to me, I meant I can't fucking think when it comes to you. I shouldn't have said what I said, *malyshka*. The thought of someone touching you, taking you from me . . ." His gaze flashed with darkness. "It makes me feel fucking crazy."

I shivered as icy rain trickled into my dress. The heat from his body touched my skin, as if I stood at the edges of a fire. I wanted to step closer, the fear I'd get burned pushed further and further away.

His thumb brushed my cheek. "I promise, I won't ever say anything like that to you again."

I sighed. "It's more than that, Christian, and you know it."

"We'll figure the rest out. But I'm not letting you go." His jaw clenched, eyes fierce. "I can't."

He meant what he said.

At least, for now.

A part of me knew this couldn't end well.

But the urge to give in, to close the distance between us, to feel him against me, *ached*. It tore at every cell in my body, leaving something desperate behind. The idea of walking away, back to the cold, colorless life I'd lived before him made me feel sick.

A tear escaped, and he brushed it away with a thumb.

"I don't know what biocoenosis is," I said softly.

"You're not missing out."

"I can't have intellectually stimulating conversations with you."

"I was bored out of my mind."

Last-ditch effort to save myself.

"There are plenty of women who could make you happier, Christian."

"You're the only one I want."

Our eyes held each other's, some thick and unknown feeling brewing between us. Consuming, like panic, and heavy, like need.

He leaned in, brushing his lips against mine. "Moya *zvezdochka.*"

"I think I'm getting the flu," I breathed.

Once he realized I'd given in, he made a noise of satisfaction and kissed me deeply, slipping his tongue into my mouth.

I sighed and shivered.

Pulling back, he slipped his jacket off and put it on my shoulders. A memory came back, of the last time he'd done the same thing. The night he'd taken me to Ace's after the shooting five years ago.

I didn't know how I'd gotten here.

Walking down the sidewalk with this dirty fed's jacket on my shoulders and his hand in mine.

But now I wondered just where I'd be if he had never been around.

CHAPTER
Thirty

Gianna

I WAS SOAKING WET AND SHIVERING WHEN WE GOT BACK TO HIS APARTMENT. He tugged me inside to the bathroom, where he undressed me down to the heels on my feet. The air sat heavy with some unnamed emotion between us, and somehow, both of us knew, saying a word would only congest it further.

Love might have been an annoying, elusive word I'd never understand, but I knew right then and there, I *loved* the feel of his hands on me, the complete attention he gave me as he washed my body and hair, as if I was the only woman he'd ever seen. As if I was *perfect*.

He slipped one of his undershirts over my head and then took me to bed, wrapping his arm around my waist. My limbs and eyes felt heavy with sleep, but the night had provoked a desperate need to feel him inside me. I shifted back against his erection, knowing he'd been hard before we even got in the shower.

He let out a tense breath, then grabbed my hip and stopped me.

"Go to sleep, *malyshka.*"

I wanted to know why he obviously wanted me and still denied me, but soon grew too tired to press it. I twisted around and fell asleep with my face in his chest and his hand in my hair.

The next few nights went similarly.

He asked me to stay and make him dinner before he left in the morning. I must have been an internal misogynist because I did. It didn't take long to realize that, even as meticulously clean and organized as it was, I *loved* being in his space and having something to look forward to, like cooking for him.

What I didn't love?

The fact he wouldn't sleep with me.

Before the kissing and heavy petting could get too far, he'd pull away, and then I'd hear, "Go to sleep, *malyshka*. I'm tired."

The man wasn't tired. He slept an average of three hours a night. I'd usually wake up in the middle of the night to find him sitting at the kitchen island on his laptop or going through paperwork. He was so sexy at three in the morning I couldn't resist sitting on his lap and kissing his mouth and neck until he grumbled in frustration and told me to go put my ass back in his bed.

The third night, I even crossed my arms and refused to come to bed with him. He chuckled, picked me up off the couch, and carried me to the bedroom.

I sighed in frustration, moaning, "I feel used," while rolling over onto my side.

Amusement coated his tone. "How so?"

"You eat my dinner and then don't fuck me afterward. It's rude, Christian."

He laughed. That warm, deep laugh that was too sexy to be angry with.

He usually went to the gym and showered before I even awoke. But a couple times, I woke up to use the bathroom and found him shaving at the sink.

"I have to pee," I told him.

"Then pee." He made no move to leave.

I hesitated.

I wasn't modest about my bodily functions, but as I sat on the toilet and peed in front of *Christian Allister*, it felt so taboo it made me squirm. And it might have turned me on a little. His humored gaze slid to me as I finished my business, a stupid flush rising to my cheeks when I realized he could probably read my twisted thoughts on my face.

When I was done, I sat on the sink in front of him, placing my legs on either side of his. I leaned back on my hands, just looking at him and the steady strokes of the razor.

A corner of his lips lifted.

That was when I realized I *loved* to watch him shave.

He was shirtless, only wearing a pair of white briefs. My gaze settled on his tattoos, and I ran a finger across the rose on his chest.

"Tell me what this one means."

His movements stilled for a second before resuming. I wished I could be in his head at that moment. To understand why he was so conflicted about sharing things with me.

"It means I turned eighteen in prison."

I held in my surprise that he'd answered me without a fight and focused on tracing the rose with a finger. "When did you get out?"

"Nineteen."

I was only nine when he'd first gone to prison, and fourteen when he'd been released. I'd never had a picturesque childhood, but I was beginning to believe this man's was deeper and darker than I had ever imagined.

My fingers trailed lower to his ribs, to a tattoo I hadn't noticed before. It was a constellation; I recognized the open-squared shape. I'd found it with a telescope before, all because of a single night on a terrace. *Andromeda*. It looked darker, fresher than the rest of his tattoos.

"When did you get this one?"

Instead of answering me, he kissed me, lightly nipping my bottom lip. Breathless heat burned beneath my skin, because that was the only answer I needed.

"How do you know so much about the stars?" I asked.

"I read. A lot. There wasn't much else to do in prison."

"You remember everything you read, don't you?"

"Mostly."

No wonder he'd mastered English so impeccably—heck, he knew it better than me. It was surreal to think this man had gained a lot of his knowledge from books while locked up in some Russian prison. A part of me was curious about what he'd done to get imprisoned, but I'd never ask him. I'd learned a long time ago to stay out of a man's business. If you didn't know anything, you wouldn't be lying if inter-rogated. Also, there were just some things about the men in this life a woman didn't want to know.

"So, when did you come to the United States?"

"The day after I was released."

I kissed his chest, looked up at him, and said light-heartedly, "I'm sure immigration loved getting your application."

Amusement played in his eyes. "My record was clean, *malyshka*. I have a knack for technology. I could find out where the President is eating breakfast right now, take a picture, and anonymously post it on social media, all from my kitchen."

My eyes widened. "Are you telling me, as long as I'm somewhere near a camera, you could find me and watch me on your computer?"

"Yes."

"You haven't done it, have you?"

"That would be morally questionable."

"Yes, it would," I said pointedly.

A genius and a criminal rolled into one. It made a terrifying combination.

I decided not to question him further on that topic. "Didn't you miss your family when you moved to another country?"

And just like that, I hit a brick wall.

His stomach tensed subtly beneath my hands, and his tone went cold. "I have to finish getting ready for work, *malyshka*."

That was a dismissal if I'd ever heard one. Though, pleased with how far I'd gotten, I hopped down and went back to bed.

That night, I was so far past sexually frustrated, I decided to be a bit craftier. I wore the sexiest underwear I owned, a pair of knitted thigh-high socks, and nothing else. I was in the middle of making dinner when he came home. He stilled, his eyes going dark as they traveled over me.

He sat at the island, pulled off his tie, and narrowed his gaze.

I'd screwed up his routine.

The heat of his eyes followed me everywhere in the kitchen. I made sure to bend over slower and more often than necessary. If there was one battle I was going to win between us, it was this one.

We ate in companionable silence, but I couldn't even taste the food because just the way he looked at me sent every nerve ending tingling beneath my skin. He helped me rinse off the dishes and clean up the kitchen. Then, he held my face and kissed me softly on the lips.

"Thank you for dinner, *malyshka*."

That was when I knew I *loved* his soft side.

I sat on his lap, his hand playing with my hair, while we watched some political debate on CNN. I couldn't even pretend to pay attention to a second of it with his hard-on pressed against my ass. A part of me knew what he was doing by denying me. I didn't like it. Because it made my chest feel tight and heavy. And that unsettled me.

Somewhere between the beginning and the end, my legs had straddled his, my hands were in his hair, and my lips were parting his as I flicked my tongue into his mouth.

He groaned.

The kiss deepened, and I grinded against his erection. I was so turned-on my vision grew hazy, my blood *burned*, and I was sure I was getting his pants wet by rubbing against him.

"God, I *want* you," I breathed into his mouth.

He made a tortured noise in his throat and pulled back. A thumb ran across my cheek, his eyes conflicted. "Say it again."

I rocked my hips against him, desperation coating my words. "I want you so badly."

"Why?" he asked, his voice hoarse.

"Because . . ." I sighed, searching for the reason and then just letting my first thought escape. "Because it's always been you."

I might not have ever realized it before, but as the words left my mouth, I knew I meant every one of them.

Satisfaction, dark and lazy, flared in his eyes. His lips pressed against my ear, his voice sending a shiver down my spine.

"You win, *malyshka*."

I didn't even get to experience the pleasure of my rare victory over him, because with a *rip* of my panties, he pushed inside me so deeply it tore a gasp from my throat. I dug my nails into his shoulders.

"*Fuck*, I missed this," he breathed.

By now, I'd gotten used to the way he fucked—so hard and unforgiving. Slightly selfish yet somehow still attentive. As he carried me to the bedroom, holding me tightly, still deep inside me, he stopped to kiss me for a full minute on the way, and I knew I *loved* it. The sex was fast and rough, but afterward, he made up for it with his head between my legs until I was begging him to stop.

The next evening, while waiting to cross the street, I got a text from an unknown number.

My dinner is late.

Schoolgirl giddiness filled me at the fact he was texting me, even though I'd let him hold me down and screw the lights out of me last night.

Me: *I'm sorry, who is this?*

Christian: *Funny.*

Me: *Todd?*

Christian: *I'm going to spank your ass.*

Me: *Promise?*

Soon after that exchange, I found him sitting on the couch with some papers on the coffee table before him. I ran my hands down his chest, flashing him my new sparkly crimson nails.

"What do you think?"

"I love them, *malyshka*." He grabbed my hand and kissed it.

That was when I decided I *loved* having this man's approval, no matter how confusing his position in my life may be.

The next day, he came home, paused, then picked up the "Russian for Dummies" book sitting on the coffee table. He raised a brow at me.

I returned the look from my spot on the couch. "How else am I going to eavesdrop on all your phone calls, *malysh?*"

It was the male form of the endearment he called me. A half-smile pulled on his lips as he dropped the book back on the table.

I stood and wrapped my arms around his waist, pressing my face against his chest. "I've been waiting for you to get home all day."

He made a noise of contentment. "What are you doing to me?" His voice was serious and slightly accented. I *loved* that timbre so much I rose to my toes and tried to taste it on his lips.

As the next week passed, each day, I fell in love with something else. With his smell—the way it made my eyes half-lidded and my toes curl in satisfaction. With his hands—the way they made everything else go away. With his voice—the way it could be so rough and sweet at the same time.

I had practically moved in. My stuff was everywhere. Three bottles of lotion sat on the coffee table, and he hadn't complained once about how they weren't lined up neat in a row.

He didn't like it, though, when I moved his stuff around. I'd hear a grumpy, "Gianna," and something like, "There's a reason I put my stuff where it is." I was sure it was somewhere between crazy and nutso.

He watched *The Princess Bride* with me.

He didn't like it.

He played chess with me.

I was a sore loser.

We even played our own version of twenty questions. As long as I stayed away from his childhood and his mother, I was in the clear. Though, I'd soon find out the no-go zone was broader than that.

"Would you visit my grave if I died?"

His eyes grew dark. "I'd die before you were ever in a grave, *malyshka*."

I loved his possessive side.

And I *loved* his dark side, too.

CHAPTER
Thirty-One

Gianna

W E HADN'T BEEN ANYWHERE IN PUBLIC SINCE THE LAST FAILURE OF A dinner party. What we had—*whatever we had*—was working well. But of course, Christian Allister always had to go and complicate things.

"Where are you going?" he asked as I got out of bed and stretched.

"Church." I yawned. "It's been, like, a month since I've gone, and every time I have premarital sex with you, I swear, I can feel the fires of hell creeping up my back."

He chuckled and sat up on the side of bed. "I'll come with you."

I froze. *"What?* No. Christian, you can't come with."

"Why not?"

"Because . . ." I sputtered. "People will think we're together."

His eyes hardened. "You sleep in my bed every goddamn night, Gianna."

"You're not even Catholic!"

"I'm whatever you are."

I had no response for that because it was ridiculous.

I didn't think Nico would have a problem with me dating anyone, even though I'd never quite tested that theory out. I was technically under his protection and, therefore, rules, but I liked to think of myself as a free agent more than anything. However, I did know everyone in the Russo family had either seen or heard some squabble between Christian and me, and if we showed up at church together, I would never hear the end of it.

"Everyone thinks we hate each other."

He walked toward me and trailed a thumb across my cheek. "Then let's show them we can get on just fine."

I bit my lip.

"Are you going to deny me my salvation?"

I couldn't stop the smile, and then shook my head and let out a frustrated groan because of it.

We showered together, like always, but the difference was he seemed withdrawn while we got ready, almost *guilty*. And that started a prickle of alarm at the base of my back. I didn't know what he was up to or why he wanted to go to church with me, but I was beginning to think it was for nefarious reasons.

We stepped into the church, side-by-side, with his hand on my waist. If the entire congregation didn't turn to stare at us, at least ninety-five percent of it did. The heat of all their stares lit my skin. And then the whispering began.

Elena's eyes went wide as we passed. And Ace, with an arm resting on the back of the pew, only raised a brow in amusement.

"Should we close out that bet now?" Val leaned in to ask, after we took a seat beside her and Ricardo.

"No," I bit out stubbornly.

She laughed.

Christian's jaw tightened, though he didn't say a word.

During the service, he rested a hand on the bare sliver of skin between my dress and thigh-high boots.

I thought I loved that, too.

Afterward, the ladies stood around to gossip for a while, while the men drifted outside to do the same.

"I'll be outside, *malyshka*," he said in my ear. And then he turned my face and *kissed me on the lips*. It was short and sweet but possessive, letting everyone know Christian Allister was screwing me nine ways to Sunday.

I thought I heard someone gasp.

"*Wow*," Valentina breathed, fanning herself with her Bible and watching his retreating form. "Tell me everything."

My face burned while stuck in a state of disbelief that he'd actually done that. Maybe—just maybe—I could have passed off our presence here together as a generous deed of me showing a bad man the Lord, but that was completely off the table now.

"It was supposed to be *just sex*," I complained.

Val nodded. "A lot of people bring their fuck buddies to church."

"Could you please control your sarcasm today?" I rubbed my temple. "I think I'm getting the flu." It felt like I'd been about to catch it for over a week now. Must be a persistent stomach bug.

"Okay, let's back it up a little. Just whose idea was this *just sex* relationship?"

"*His*! I have no self-respect, so, of course, I agreed. But now, he's taking me to dinner parties, making me sleep in his bed but *not* even having sex with me, and next,"—my voice rose—"he's kissing me at church!"

"Honey," she laughed. "I'm sure you've just been blinded by the incredibly beautiful man he is, but I'm here to tell you, he has never wanted *just sex* from you. All anyone has to do is look at him when you're in the room to know he's obsessed with you."

I frowned. "What do you mean?"

"I mean, he's obviously tricked you into a relationship."

"He, *what*? He wouldn't—" I cut myself off because, yeah, he *would*. "But, why?"

"Who knows why men do things? He probably thought you would turn him down."

I chewed my cheek. "I would have."

I'd panicked when he'd proposed a relationship on the plane, and now, I knew he'd noticed. I hadn't been ready for anything serious at the time. And I still wasn't . . . *right*? Indecision slid down my spine. I didn't want to give up what we had—in fact, the idea of ending it made me feel sick—but I was also uneasy to think about what he wanted from me in the end.

"What should I do?" I whispered.

"Well, he's certainly a man capable of knocking you up." She pursed her lips, looking at my body. "If you aren't already." I rolled my eyes. I'd had my period not long ago. "So, there's that issue. And I'll be honest and say he's so intense he scares me a little. He wouldn't hit you, would he?"

"No." I was suddenly never surer of anything.

"Do you like him?"

It seemed like a silly question compared to what I actually felt when I thought of him. He excited me. He fascinated me. And he seemed to make me feel happier and more alive than I'd ever been. Saying I *liked* him felt like a disservice, but I wasn't sure how else to explain it.

"Very much so."

"What's he like in bed?"

I narrowed my eyes on her.

She laughed. "Fine. We'll talk about those details later. Are you ready for every woman from ages thirteen to ninety-two to be drooling all over your man?"

"As long as they keep their hands to themselves."

"What about him? Can you wrangle fidelity from him?"

The thought of him sleeping with someone else made me feel nauseous. Though, somehow, I didn't believe he would. I'd known him for a long time and had never once pegged him for a cheater.

"I think so."

"So far, I'd say he's not a bad choice. But truthfully, I've only been humoring you. The man has already made his decision, and that's you, honey. Now, you just have to make the best of it."

I chewed my lip on the short drive home, debating what I should say to him. I debated how I felt about his manipulation and if I was even upset about it. I wasn't sure what to feel, and that annoyed me.

As soon as his apartment door closed behind us, I blurted, "What do you want from me, Christian?"

He turned to me, eyes dark. "Everything."

A shiver trailed down my spine. "This was never about sex."

He reached for his belt and unfastened it, sardonic amusement passing through his gaze. "No."

"You played me," I accused.

"Yes."

"Do you feel bad?"

"No."

I watched warily as he slid his belt out of the loops. Unease played down my back.

"What are you doing with your belt?"

An amused half-smile. "Debating if I need to whip you into submission."

"Ha ha." My voice was uncertain. "But really?"

"I'm getting undressed and then taking you to bed."

"I'm not finished talking." I crossed my arms. "You tricked me."

"Do I make you unhappy?"

I swallowed, shifting to another foot. "No."

"Then, shut up and come to bed with me."

My eyes narrowed. "I don't trust you."

"I can fix that."

"Don't trick me again."

"I won't." Something elusive passed through his gaze. "Come on, before I change my mind and decide to put my belt to good use."

There were things to discuss. Important things I should have demanded an answer to—like what this relationship was, and where it could even *go*. But instead, I followed him to his bed, where we spent the next hours saying everything with our bodies and nothing with our mouths.

Our next public appearance was Friday. This time, when I came out in some ridiculously flashy dress, he pressed me against my door and kissed me deeply, like he needed to brand himself into my skin, until I was rubbing my hand against his erection and begging him to fuck me. He let out a frustrated breath and a, "Can't," followed by something about business at the club.

That morning, while still lying in bed, I'd teased him about the domed church on his side, telling him I hadn't known he was religious. Something cold settled in him after that. He'd gotten up and said he was going to the gym. I didn't hear from him again until I got his text telling me to be ready to go at nine.

Christian knew everything about me, whereas he left me with only small morsels of himself. What I hated most about it, though, was I felt like a coward, merely tiptoeing the edges of his past for fear of him pushing me away. It seemed each day I spent with him, the closer I grew to losing my grasp on control, while his grip only grew tighter.

After kissing me senseless, he was distant during the ride to the club. Distant when he collected me from Nico's office, where I'd been watching TV with Elena, and distant on the way home.

I was going to confront him. The words I was going to say were on the tip of my tongue. But then I stepped into his room to get undressed, and everything changed. The door shut with a quiet click behind me. I stilled, the hair on the back of my neck rising. The air pulsed with something heavy and electric that seeped through my chest and jump-started my heart.

The heat of his body brushed my back. His voice was whisper-soft in my ear as he gripped my hair in a fist, gently tugging my head back. "Who does this belong to, *malyshka?*"

My breath came out unsteady, my pulse slightly cold at the tension in his voice. There wasn't a part of me that wanted to deny him at this point.

"You."

A rumble of approval against my neck. His thumb brushed across my mouth. "This?"

"You," I breathed.

His hand seared through my dress as he slid it down my stomach and cupped me between the legs. "And this?"

My skin buzzed with heat and breathlessness. I inhaled. "*You*. It belongs to you."

He didn't bother to take any of our clothes off before his body covered mine on the bed and he pushed deep inside of me. It was rough though constrained, with his mouth on mine, with his foreign words in my ear, with him holding me down as if I might want to escape. It was like he was trying to prove something to me, like this was all I needed.

And for a moment, I almost believed it.

CHAPTER
Thirty-Two

Christian

"**Y**OU DO KNOW I'M NOT A PERSONAL THERAPIST, DON'T YOU?"

"Didn't you take an oath to help others in need?"

Sasha Taylor Ph.D.'s lips quirked. "I don't believe you're exactly *in need*, but I'll admit, I'm too intrigued to turn you away."

I sat back in my chair, resting an ankle on my knee. "I want to know what my diagnosis is."

She didn't have my file; she didn't need it. She'd thought about me enough over the years—had tried to solve me like an unfinished puzzle.

She touched her pen to her chin, tilted her head. "Well, it's been a while since we last spoke, but going off what I've learned about you from our previous meetings, I'd say you're somewhere on the low end of the OCD spectrum. I believe your behaviors to be more habits than compulsions." She paused, leaving her indecision and unsaid words to hang in the air like fumes.

My unwavering gaze insisted she continue.

She swallowed. "I also highly suspect you're affected by an antisocial personality disorder. Including but not limited to manipulation, exploitation, and, possibly, a lack of empathy for others."

I'd always found mental disorders and their diagnoses boring, but I knew enough to know antisocial personality disorder was just another term for *sociopathy*.

A corner of my lips lifted. "Sounds serious. Should I be concerned?"

She fidgeted, averting her gaze and crossing her legs. "I've often wondered how you passed your psychological evaluation in the hiring process."

"I guess diagnoses are a matter of opinion, aren't they?"

"Indeed," she said breathlessly. "I know you didn't come here today for my expertise on your mental status, so what brought you to my door?"

I looked out the window, running a hand across my jaw.

Her thoughtful gaze settled on my face. "Let me guess, you're here because you've finally obtained what you've always wanted, and now you don't know how to control it?"

My eyes met hers. "I can control it just fine."

I'd never told a more ridiculous lie.

"Maybe *it*, sure. But not how you feel about it."

My jaw tightened.

"This 'addictive personality' of yours . . . it's merely a medical condition you've built up in your head to explain why you've always wanted *it*. To help you understand the reason it appeals to you, and therefore, help you control your reaction to it. But in reality, it's a normal human emotion. Maybe stronger for you because you haven't experienced it in a long time, or maybe you've never felt it."

"You're losing me, Sasha."

Her lips lifted. "No, I'm not."

She clicked her pen. Once, twice, *three* times. "My guess is, now that you have it, you're afraid you'll lose it. Maybe you don't feel like you even deserve her, though that's a trivial point because, in the end, you don't care."

I didn't miss the *her* she'd slipped in there.

"I didn't come here for relationship advice."

"No." She smiled sadly. "You came here for me to tell you it gets easier, that it blows over, and you'll find a sense of control again. It doesn't, and you won't. Love only gets worse."

A sardonic breath left me. "I thought you believed it was just an obsession."

"Haven't you heard? Love *is* an obsession. Some would even say . . . *the maddest obsession.*"

CHAPTER
Thirty-Three

Gianna

I T WAS AN INNOCENT QUESTION.

One that exploded in my face like a tripwire.

That was all it took for me to lose my grip completely. Now, I was drowning in the deep, in the *blue*, and it was too late to save myself.

"I made an appointment to get on the pill next week," I told him one night while lying in bed, my heart still racing and my skin sweaty from a previous and vigorous round of sex.

I'd been slacking with getting on birth control because I was sensitive to medication and the options I'd tried when I was younger all came with an annoying side effect. The pill made me gain weight, and now at twenty-eight, with a slower metabolism, I knew *that* was the last thing I needed. Though it seemed I was going to have to take the contraceptive situation into my own hands by Christian's indifferent attitude about it.

"Why?"

I sighed. "Either you have a hundred children from Russia to Seattle, or you're being deliberately abstruse."

He chuckled, correcting softly, "Obtuse, *malyshka*."

The sound of his soft laugh made my body light up with warmth. "Well? Do you have a litter of children you haven't told me about?"

His silence touched my skin, putting my nerve endings on edge.

"I don't have any children," he said eventually.

"How do you know that if you're going around without using condoms?"

"Because I'm not *going around* without using condoms," he said, tension in his voice. "You're the only one I'm sleeping with, Gianna. I thought I'd made that pretty fucking clear."

I should have stopped here. I should have sensed the strain in the air that stretched the oxygen thin. But I couldn't. Because I was tired of being a coward, of toeing the edge of Christian Allister, while I let him touch me, kiss me, screw me, and *own* me.

"Before me, then. I'm sure you haven't always worn condoms. You seem too blasé about not doing so."

He ran a hand across his face. "Drop it, *malyshka*."

Jealousy rose up in me, piercing a hole through my chest and fueling my blood with bitterness. He'd never been that serious with any of the women I'd seen him with, yet he'd been with one—or several?—without wearing a condom. It made what we were doing feel meaningless. Cheap. The most serious relationship I'd ever seen him in was with Portia, and even then, it hadn't lasted much longer than the rest.

"Did you use a condom with Portia?"

"Yes." It was a vehement response. The truth.

Maybe it had been with someone when he was younger. Some teenage Russian hussy. I hated her. Though, I doubted he would've had much time for girls while being locked in a prison for most of his teenage years.

I was growing resentful of the questions piling up on themselves, being answered with, "Drop it, *malyshka*," and complete evasions. The man had even heard the story of how I'd lost my virginity from my own husband's lips. It seemed only fair I should hear the same.

"How did you lose your virginity?"

The temperature dipped into the negatives, my breath freezing in my lungs. The air turned bitter, as caustic as the sting of a bee against my skin.

He sat up on the side of the bed and rested his elbows on his knees. Tension pulled tight in his shoulders, his voice emotionless.

"Get out."

My stomach went cold. "*What?*"

"I said, get out."

My throat tightened with humiliation and betrayal.

I got to my feet, picked up a shirt from the floor, slipped it over my head, and headed to the door. I stopped, every cell in my body rebelling at the idea of leaving.

"If you make me walk out this door, I won't come back, Christian. Not until you have an answer for me."

He didn't look at me.

Neither did he stop me.

I shut my apartment door behind me and leaned against it, the emptiness of the place touching my skin. Regret fed on my resolve, until I wanted to turn around and take back the final words that had left my mouth. I wanted to—*needed* to—go back and fix everything that had gone wrong. Apologize or beg, whatever it took. Thankfully, my pride held steady; I wasn't going to let him turn me into something so pathetic.

I slept in my own bed that night, for the first time in weeks. It was quiet. A little cold. A tear ran down my cheek, and I told myself I hated him for making me feel this way.

But I didn't hate him at all.

That elusive feeling, close to panic yet far enough away, was something else entirely.

And, as my heart ached with every breath, I suddenly knew what it was.

"*Levántate!*"

I sputtered, shooting up to a sitting position as cold water poured onto my face.

"It is four o'clock, *querida! Eres una vaga!*"

She'd just called me a bum, but I couldn't find any energy to complain. I was depressed. And not even because I hadn't seen or spoken to Christian in two days, but because I thought I loved him. And I wasn't sure how to deal with the feeling. Where it was supposed to go when it grew too big for my chest. How I would get rid of it if he'd finally realized we weren't compatible in the end.

He and I were polar opposites. We didn't make much sense.

But, suddenly, nothing felt right without him either.

Magdalena opened the window. "I told you not to get involved with that man, *señorita*. You did not listen."

She hadn't said anything of the sort. Before he and I had started this relationship, she'd gotten one look at him while I'd been kicking her out of my apartment. Her eyes had gone wide, and then she'd told me to marry him. That I'd have the most beautiful babies, and everyone would be jealous. He'd heard every word of it. Though, it must have been a normal thing for him to overhear because his dry expression didn't falter.

"Do you know what the best thing for a broken heart is?"

"What?"

"Fresh air. It cured *mis hermanas* cancer, too."

It was then I realized I hadn't moped like this since Antonio. And that was a dark part of my life I never wanted to return to. I was not going to let Christian turn me into another one of his heartsick castaways. I crawled out of bed, showered, and then got dressed in something more suited for a club than a walk around the city.

On my way out of the lobby doors, my gaze caught with another's. My stomach dipped to my toes. Just the sight of him—every straight line, polished silver watch and cufflinks, *blue*—it felt like a hit of a drug I'd been withdrawing from.

He wasn't so professional beneath his clothes. Not so cold in the bedroom, with his hand around my throat and the heat of his body against mine. And not so heartless, with his *malyshkas* and rough Russian words in my ear.

Something deep and immeasurable flickered through his eyes before he looked away. We passed each other, almost shoulder-to-shoulder. I could even smell a trace of his custom-made cologne.

He didn't stop me.

And neither did I him.

Maybe this was really over.

My stomach twisted into a knot at the thought. My lungs tightened with every breath.

When I'd first met this man, his presence annoyed me. How did I get here, tearing up at the smell of his cologne?

I walked around the city, absently dodging potholes and cyclists, in thigh-high boots. I ate a hot dog from a food truck. Sat on a bench, watched the sunset, and pretended I was in control of my life. When that was so far from the truth.

I'd never felt so lost.

The low lights scattered and reflected the red of my underwear into the clear water as I waded in the pool.

It was late, past midnight. The pool was technically closed, but it hadn't taken much to coax Trevor the pool boy to slip me an extra key.

I went under, holding my breath until my lungs burned, until it was all I could feel. When I came back up, a prickling sense that I wasn't alone touched my back. My head swung to see someone sitting on the edge of a chaise, elbows on his knees.

Eyes of melted ice and polished steel looked back at me.

My heart stilled and then filled with a desperate hum.

"I was fifteen," he said.

Confusion flickered through me, but then I realized what he was telling me. How he'd lost his virginity.

"I'd been in Butyrka for a few months by then. I was in on murder, but trust me, *malyshka*, they fucking deserved it."

I'd seen him kill a man for *annoying* him, but, by the vehemence in his tone, I believed him.

"They could only convict me on one, and I was a minor, so I got off lightly with five years. Ronan was a year younger and only got four. But he dealt with prison better than I ever could." His eyes grew grim. "I fucking hated that place."

I waded to the side of the pool and held onto the ledge, water dripping off my eyelashes.

"The most sun I'd get some days was a few shafts of light through a ventilation window. We'd only get a shower three days a week. And even then, you had to fight for any soap provided."

I suddenly didn't mind how much he washed my hair.

"One of the correctional nurses noticed I'd read all the books on the shelf. She started to bring me new ones every week. Getting attention from a woman there . . . it started shit with the other men. A lot of them were wary of me. They called me *kholodnyye glaza*. Said there was something missing in my eyes."

Now, I knew his worst days were before he'd even gone to prison.

"They usually left me alone, but one day, someone worked up the nerve to rip all the pages out of one of my books. They were the only thing that kept me sane in that place, the only thing with a little bit of order. I saw red. Beat him unconscious. I would have killed him if someone hadn't pulled me off him. I remember looking down at myself, covered in his blood and mine from a cut on my arm." He let out a bitter laugh. "And all for a fucking book.

"That's when I promised myself I was leaving. I was going to build a life for myself, somewhere far from that prison, and somewhere no one would dare touch my shit. I planned out everything from that moment on." His eyes met mine. "Even down to the type of woman I would marry."

I swallowed, knowing I wasn't what he'd envisioned.

"Looking back, I realize the fight started a riot. The place had always been a chaotic mess in my mind that I hadn't even noticed at the time. I picked up the book and pages, preoccupied with figuring out how to tell the nurse what happened and dreading she wouldn't bring me more.

"I don't know her name. I can't even tell you what color hair she had, *malyshka*. That's how little I looked at her."

The fact he'd always noticed when I changed my hair seemed so much more significant now. A heaviness tugged at my chest.

"I returned her book. And she stitched up my arm. Her hand was shaking slightly. I thought she was nervous to be alone with me—there wasn't a guard at the door due to the riot. But I soon learned that wasn't the case when she rested her hand on my dick."

My breathing slowed, my heart wanting to stop him and my brain demanding he continue.

"She leaned in to kiss me, but I turned my head. I thought for sure she wouldn't be interested after that. But it didn't seem to sway her." He ran a hand across his jaw. "I didn't use a condom with her, *malyshka*. And I can't even say she was the only one. A few days later, when one of the guards escorted me to the medical ward, pushed me in the room, and shut the door, she wasn't alone. Another woman was with her—"

"Okay, I've heard enough."

Only this man would be offered a threesome in prison at *fifteen*. I wanted to rip those women's hair out. They must have been significantly older than him.

"I'm clean, Gianna. I'll show you the paperwork if you want to see it. As for children, I don't have any that I know of."

I was slightly overwhelmed with what he'd shared with me, even though I knew he was still holding something back. This wasn't what he'd been hiding from me two days ago. He was merely offering an olive branch. I didn't believe I had it in me to demand more from him right now, not with that slightly desperate look in his eyes, begging me to accept what he was telling me. I knew he hated delving into his past. It was messy, and he liked all his things lined up neat in a row. And he'd gone in deep for me.

I pulled myself out of the pool, water sluicing down my skin as I padded over to stand between his legs. I ran a hand into his hair, and a rough noise sounded low in his throat. He grabbed my hips, pulled me closer, and pressed his face against my stomach.

"Fuck, I missed you, *malyshka*."

Water dripped off my body, soaking his suit. My throat felt tight as warmth and relief coalesced in my chest.

"I apologize for making you leave."

"Don't ever do it again."

"I won't."

He gripped the backs of my thighs, lifting me up to straddle him. It brought our faces close together.

I leaned closer, until our lips were a hair's breadth apart.

"Why do you kiss me?"

I sighed into his mouth when he kissed me with a sweet pull. "Because you're the only woman who's ever tempted me." His lips brushed mine. "Because you love it." The last one was soft, with a possessive bite. "Because every part of you is mine."

CHAPTER
Thirty-Four

Christian

'D MADE A MISCALCULATION.

I couldn't say it happened often, but the mistake was glaringly obvious in the lotions, hair products, and perfumes that were scattered across the bathroom counter. It looked like a beauty salon threw up in here.

I'd thought I could keep her separate, in a box of her own, all neat and tidy like the rest of my things. She'd already occupied my mind, been so deep beneath my skin, but, fuck, now she was everywhere else, too. My kitchen, my bathroom, my *bed*.

Surprisingly, all the shit she left lying around didn't bother me like I'd always thought it would. Occasionally, it made the back of my neck itch—like how she left the toothpaste cap open *every time* she used it—though, I found it more bothersome when she wasn't around. So bothersome I was fucking *apologizing* to her to make her come back. Things had gotten ridiculously out of hand.

I gripped the edge of the sink. I was in this deep, and a cold sweat drifted down my back at the thought of how it would end. It would never be over for me—I'd known that going in—and the only peace I'd found was believing I could make her stay with me whether she liked it or not. But now, a feeling in my chest grew heavy every time I looked at her. I didn't believe I could bear to see her unhappy. And that complicated things.

My gaze met Gianna's in the mirror as she showed up in the doorway. She wore one of my long-sleeve t-shirts, and the collar was slipping off her shoulder.

"You just missed the best part," she pouted.

I let out a dry breath. "I bet."

We really needed to find a happy medium on movies.

She wrapped her arms around my waist from behind, her touch sending a small shudder through my spine.

"Is this what you do when you go to the bathroom? Stare at your handsome face in the mirror?"

I'd needed to get away for a minute. Couldn't think with her near—her smell, her smile, the feel of her hands on me. It made my head fuzzy and my throat tight. It made me feel like someone was on the cusp of reorganizing every damn thing in my apartment.

"I was thinking," I told her.

"About?"

How to keep you pacified without letting you into my past.

How to make sure you always look at me like this and not with disgust.

"You."

"Aw, you come to the bathroom to think about me? Why, Officer, I feel honored." Her hand drifted down my stomach and over my dick. She frowned. "It must not have been that exciting of a scenario."

A corner of my lips lifted. I turned around, cupped her face, and ran a thumb across her cheek. "I'm always thinking about you, *malyshka.*"

Her lips parted, a blush rising to her cheeks. She rose to her tip-toes, and breathed against my lips, "I really like you."

Satisfaction ran hot through my blood, even though I wanted more than that. I wanted everything she had to give and more. I'd take it slowly, I'd make her love me, and maybe then, she wouldn't leave me when she realized I couldn't give her everything of me she wanted.

She blinked. "Aren't you going to say it, too?"

I chuckled. What I felt was so far past that it was laughable. I would have told her right then, but she wasn't ready.

"I really like you, too," I said, then leaned in to nip her bottom lip. She sighed in my mouth.

That was the only scenario I needed.

I picked her up and carried her to bed.

"You fucking Gianna?" Ace gave me a hard look. "I don't like it. Makes men think they can sample our women."

I sat back in his office chair. "Correct me if I'm wrong, but weren't you living with your wife before marriage?"

He ran a thumb across his jaw. "I had that under wraps. You've been parading Gianna around like she's your goddamn mistress."

"Haven't heard that term since eighteen-ninety," I said dryly. "Someday, you Italians are going to have to get with the times."

"Marry her, Allister, and we won't have a problem."

If only it was that easy.

My jaw tightened. "She's not ready."

"Tough shit. If I'd asked my wife to marry me, she would have said no. So, guess what? I didn't fucking ask her."

I couldn't force Gianna to marry me. I wanted—*needed*—to be different than the other men in her life. She *liked* me. I knew I couldn't handle seeing the betrayal in her eyes now, not after she'd told me that and how much better it had felt than hearing she hated me.

"I could just as easily find someone else for her," he baited.

"Go ahead." My voice was dark. "Might save us both some time if you line her prospects up in a row right now."

"Jesus," Nico muttered. "Fine. Then, think of it this way—this relationship of yours makes Gianna look like a throwaway. Good enough to fuck, but not good enough to marry."

I clenched my teeth.

"I'm not saying it." He rocked back in his chair. "Just the way it looks, Allister."

I got to my feet, finished with this conversation.

"Good luck," he said.

"Fuck you."

His chuckle followed me out the door.

CHAPTER
Thirty-Five

Gianna

SOMETHING SMELLED LIKE PANCAKES. IT MADE MY STOMACH CHURN.

I loved pancakes.

I rolled out of bed, brushed my teeth, and combed my hair, then padded out to the kitchen to find Christian at the stove, shirtless, his hair wet. I loved him like this, the casual side of him not many got to see. Like this, he was *mine*.

But when I wrapped my arms around his waist, he tensed. Uncertainty flickered through me. He'd been quiet the past couple of days, and an insecure part of me was obsessing over what it could mean. Things had been well since he'd opened up to me last week, but I hadn't asked him for more, either. It was pathetic, I knew, but I was scared the next question would push him away for good. And to test it felt like toeing the edge of the dark.

"Are you hungry?" he asked when I stepped away from him.

I looked at the plate of pancakes on the counter and wrinkled my nose. "Not right now." Grabbing the orange juice from the fridge, I poured a glass.

The next words out of his mouth caused me to choke as the first refreshing sip slid down my throat. "We should get married."

I coughed, eyes watering. Slowly, I set the glass on the island and wiped some juice off my chin.

"I don't think I heard you right."

He turned to face me, his eyes deep and unfathomable. "I said, we should get married."

My chest flared from hot to cold. *"What?"*

"You heard me, Gianna."

My pulse raced. "We've only been seeing each other for, like . . . a month."

He let out a sarcastic breath. "You've been mine for fucking years."

The conviction in his voice fluttered through my blood, settling in my heart. The shock had thrown me off-balance, and I didn't know how to react. I walked around the island to put some distance between us; to find some space to think.

I turned toward him. "I told you how I feel about marriage."

He shook his head, his eyes flickering with something heavy. "You know those aren't realistic expectations. Maybe for another woman, but not you."

I hated that he was right. That eventually, if I did stay, all it would take was one man to be interested enough in me. It seemed Made Men just couldn't fathom that a woman could remain single and happy.

My blood pulsed in my ears.

My hands were clammy.

"I told you, I would run."

"And I told you, I would find you." His tone was dark. "You know this is where you belong, Gianna."

I'd never been fond of leaving, but I did know I couldn't willingly go back into another marriage to a man I didn't know. I only understood the edges of Christian, not the deep, dark center that made him, and until then, I'd never truly know him. But now that the shock had settled, I realized I didn't hate the idea of marrying him. That sent a prickling sense of anxiety through me; it showed me how deeply I was under his spell. I *loved* him. And I feared what I would forfeit just to be with him.

I swallowed. "Proposals usually come with rings and bended knees. Sometimes, a nice dinner."

"We both know, that would have made you panic."

When did he learn so much about me while I remained in the dark about him? Bitterness bit at my chest. Why couldn't he just open up to me? Was I not good enough? Too *lowly*?

"I wasn't lying when I told you I wouldn't marry again."

"Things change, *malyshka*."

I would have laughed if someone had told me Christian Allister would ask me to marry him just a few weeks ago. I would've never been able to fathom what it felt like to fall for someone, to care about them so much it hurt. Things *had* changed. I used to hate him, but now, I couldn't imagine being happy without him.

"*Why?*" It rushed out of me, my eyes burning with emotion. "Why do you want to marry me?"

His jaw ticked in thought. "Some people might see you . . . differently by being with me unmarried."

My heart dipped and squeezed in disappointment. This was all about appearances? I guessed I should have known.

"I don't care how people see me."

"I do," he growled. "I don't want anyone to think you mean less to me than you do. You might not see it now, but eventually, it'll get to you, Gianna, and you'll resent me for it."

Maybe what he was saying was true. But, in the end, how much could I really mean to a man who refused to share with me the basic facts of himself? Who didn't trust me? Who grew distant and closed off at the simplest questions?

"I can't marry another man I don't know."

His voice was rough, dipped in something sharp. "I've told you more about myself than I've ever told anyone else."

"That's not a good enough reason for me to marry you, Christian."

"Fine." He shook his head, his eyes flashing with darkness. "How about because I love you, Gianna? Because I think I have since the moment I saw you? Because if you weren't in this world anymore, I would find a way to take myself out of it?"

My heart stopped.

Went cold.

And then lit with fire.

We stared at each other, silence and the vehemence of his voice touching my skin with rough fingers.

"You don't mean that," I breathed.

"I meant every goddamn word I said."

The pressure in my chest grew so tight it brought a rush of tears to my eyes. The only other person who had ever told me she loved me was my mother. And now, it felt like a light had popped and burst inside me, filling me with something warm, sticky, and possibly heartbreaking.

Indecision pulled me in two different directions. I wanted to give in so badly I ached. But the part of me who'd felt isolated, alone, *unworthy* in my past marriage stood firm in my decision. If I married him now, gave him all the cards, I'd never win. He would never give me more when he didn't have to. I could see it in his eyes: full of fire but steady with conviction.

"I won't marry another man I don't know," I said quietly.

His teeth clenched.

I gave him a chance to fill the silence between us.

He didn't.

A tear ran down my cheek, and my throat tried to close around the words before they could escape. "I can't be with you and only get half of you anymore."

Something conflicted flared in his eyes.

I turned to leave, but his words stopped me.

"Try and leave me, Gianna." It was a threat, but there was something else—something rough and untamed—behind it. Something close to panic.

My gaze met his. One last parting look, and then I walked out the door.

Once I was in the hall, my pulse jumped at the sound of a glass breaking. I imagined my orange juice pooling on his kitchen floor right next to where my discarded heart lay.

Ten minutes later, I was sitting on my couch, not sure what to do with myself or where to go, when my front door opened.

My eyes shot to his, but he didn't hold my gaze as he shut the door behind him. He *always* held eye-contact. He'd gotten dressed, not even sparing the tie clip and cufflinks.

"You want to know what made me this way? Fine." His voice carried something bitter. "I'll tell you."

He paced further into the room, stopped a few feet in front of me, and then let out a caustic breath, like he couldn't believe he was doing this. Like he already *regretted* it.

My lungs grew tight with uncertainty, then inflated with relief that he was giving in.

"My mother would do anything for a few bucks, Gianna. Anything to get her high. Heroine was her drug of choice, but she was far from particular."

I swallowed, now understanding why he'd been so unpleasant when he'd gotten me out of jail even though we'd met before. The drugs. He'd probably been disgusted with me.

"Somehow, she got mixed up with a pimp in the Bratva. We all knew when she had a client because they would always knock three times and it would shake the entire one-bedroom apartment we lived in. It was a never-ending cycle. Couldn't get any sleep with the sounds of fucking going on in the other room until four in the morning." He twisted his watch on his wrist. Once, twice, *three* times.

"You think I'm good-looking now?" His gaze filled with sarcasm. "You should have seen me as a kid."

My chest went cold as horror bubbled up inside.

"A few of her clients seemed to be more interested in a pretty five-year-old boy than my mother. And she wasn't hesitant to oblige them. You know what I remember as being the most irritating? I had a United States quarter I kept under my pillow. It was the only thing I owned"— his voice turned acidic around the edges—"and they always fucking touched it. Would pick it up, smile, and toss it back down."

The backs of my eyes burned, a few tears escaping. I let them roll down my cheeks while he continued.

"Eventually, my mother remembered she had two sons. The money could really come in then." His eyes flared with contempt. "That was the first man I ever killed, *malyshka*. Stabbed him in the back with a kitchen knife. I was seven by then. A couple of men showed up, disposed of his body, and she never sent anyone to my little brother again."

I didn't know if he expected me to be judgmental or horrified about what he'd done. I felt neither. Some men deserved to die.

A grimace touched his lips. "Nobody cleaned up the blood right. It just sat there for years, this red, lingering stain." He finished it thoughtfully, as if he was picturing that stain right now. "Russians are superstitious, and eventually, they became too fucking scared to touch me. My eyes disturbed them."

I moved to the edge of the couch, taking a shallow breath.

"But this fairy tale isn't over yet. I think I was thirteen when she stumbled home, drunk or high, probably both. She fell on top of me on the couch, mistaking me for one of her clients." A bitter breath escaped him. "She tried to fuck her own son."

Bile turned in my stomach, rising up my throat.

"That was the night she fell asleep on her back on the floor. She started to gag, but instead of rolling her onto her side, Ronan and I stood there and watched her choke on her own vomit."

My face went pale.

I covered my mouth.

He let out a mocking noise at my expression. "Sorry I couldn't give you the white-picket-fence story you've been waiting to hear."

I ran to the bathroom and threw up everything in my stomach.

CHAPTER
Thirty-Six

Gianna

K NEELING OVER THE TOILET, I WIPED MY MOUTH WITH THE BACK OF MY hand.

A kernel of doubt played in a corner of my mind. And then it *popped* like I'd nuked it in the microwave.

I didn't have a weak stomach.

And while his story was gut-wrenching and disturbing on a few different levels, it didn't horrify me to the point I'd lose last night's dinner in the toilet bowl.

I got to my feet, brushed my teeth, and then went to get dressed.

He'd told me all that thinking I wouldn't want to be with him anymore. I knew by the regretful look on his face before he'd even begun. He thought I would see him as a victim, or maybe even less of a man.

And as for his mother, I felt no remorse.

I didn't see him any differently than I had before. Now, I only felt closer to him than ever. And I wanted to be closer, to know more—*everything*—like what had happened to him and his brother afterward. I wanted to tell him I loved him.

I perused the options on the shelf. Pink boxes. Blue boxes. All kinds of gimmicks—smart countdown timer, extra-quick response time, and an early detection option. It was a little overwhelming. I grabbed the one in the brightest box.

My hands shook as I stood in front of the bathroom mirror and ripped it out of the package. I didn't know why. It couldn't be possible.

I'd had my period a week ago. Granted, it seemed lighter than usual—in fact, the last few had been—but still, a period was a period, right?

After following the instructions, I set the test on the sink and sat on the edge of the tub to wait.

I chewed my lip.

Checked for split ends.

Tapped my foot on the floor.

God, this was ridiculous.

I got up, stomped over to the test, and picked it up.

There was a quiver inside me. It started out slow, working its way to my extremities. It trembled in my veins and burned in my eyes. And when it reached my heart, it squeezed it in a vise, leaving a tight, warm sensation behind.

I slid down the bathroom door, staring at two pink lines.

And I bawled like a baby.

I woke up the next morning at his place, realizing I must have fallen asleep while waiting for him to come home. I could sleep through anything—though, as I ran a hand across his side of the bed, I found the sheets still cold.

I took a shower and got ready for the doctor's appointment I'd made last week for birth control. It didn't sound like I would need it anymore, but I was still hesitant to believe I was pregnant. I was concerned about the bleeding and what it could mean. And I worried about not being on prenatal vitamins, the occasional glass of wine I had with supper, and all the rough sex in between. Granted, the latter had probably gotten me into this mess, so maybe that fear was a little irrational.

I made two quick stops before my appointment. One to the bank, and one to Val's. As soon as she opened the door in a silk robe, I slapped twenty grand cash into her hand. Her laugh followed me all the way to the curb.

As I sat in the waiting room, I sent Christian a text asking him to meet me at noon. It showed he'd seen it, but he didn't respond. A robust nurse with a friendly smile called my name. I wiped my sweaty palms on my dress, took a deep breath, and then followed her.

It was called breakthrough bleeding. Considering I was already *eleven* weeks pregnant and everything had looked good on the ultrasound, the doctor wasn't concerned about it. By my calculations, that meant I'd gotten pregnant the very first time Christian and I had sex. I should have expected nothing less from the man.

At noon, I sat on a bench with a grocery sack filled with every kind of prenatal vitamin the pharmacy had and an excitement and fear of the unknown. I was scared about this baby, slightly terrified about not doing things right—I hadn't had the best childhood to gain experience from. But for the first time in my life, it felt like something had gone right.

Now, I just hoped Christian felt the same way.

I pulled off a piece of bread. "Here, birdy, birdy."

"Reflecting on your life choices?"

My heart stilled at the deep sound of his voice, but I didn't look at him yet. The eye-contact would burn with too much emotion, and I wasn't ready for it.

I swallowed. "Trying out a new career of bird-calling."

"Ah. It seems you'd better stick with gambling," he said, as the pigeons all headed in the opposite direction.

"Everyone has to start somewhere."

"Usually, that somewhere is a little higher than an aspiration to hang out in a park and feed fat pigeons."

"You sound like an impressionist."

A smile touched his voice. "I think you mean *pessimist*."

I finally met his gaze. *Blue.* The look grabbed hold and hung on. It wasn't just ice anymore; it was late nights, rough hands, Russian words, and heavy hearts. His suit and hair were immaculate, as always, but something tired lingered behind his eyes.

"You didn't come home last night," I said quietly.

"I stayed at work." His jaw tightened. "Can't sleep across a hall from you."

"I slept in your bed last night."

Conflict and confusion waged in his eyes. "Why?"

I stood and moved toward him. "I don't care about what happened in your past. It doesn't matter to me. And if you think I would see you differently because of what happened to you as a child, or even what you might have done, you don't know me at all."

His gaze coasted above my head, his jaw ticking in thought. "You reacted differently."

"That wasn't about what you told me . . . but because I'm pregnant, Christian."

His gaze dropped to search my face and then it filled with something dark as sin and satisfied. "You're sure?"

"One-hundred percent. I know it might come as a shock and all, considering how careful we were being—"

He cupped my face with a palm, running a thumb across my cheek. "*Moya zvezdochka.*" I felt the intensity of his relief in the way his hand shook slightly, and it made my throat tighten. I suddenly knew this was the only man I wanted to do this with. Happiness pinged off the walls of my chest, leaving me feeling raw.

He wiped a tear from my cheek. "Are you happy?"

I nodded. "*So* happy."

"Good." His voice was coarse.

He ran his arms around my waist and pulled me closer until I could feel his fast heartbeat. He rested his forehead on mine, cocooning me in his heat and heady, familiar scent: sandalwood and money.

"You don't think I'm only here now because I'm pregnant?"

"I don't care why. Just that you're here, with me."

"That sounds like an unhealthy mindset."

A half-smile pulled on his lips. "You have no idea."

I rose to my tiptoes and kissed him. Heat burst in my chest, sinking into my blood. He held my face and kissed me back. Soft and slow yet deep enough it touched my heart.

I breathed against his lips, "Tell me you love me again."

"I love you, *malyshka.*"

"I love you, too, you know?"

He stilled, and then a rough sound rumbled in his chest. He lifted me so my eyes were level with his, brushed his lips across mine, and said in a deep, almost apologetic rasp, "I'm never letting you go now."

I wasn't sure how I'd gotten here. How the next few years would play out, let alone days. Or the problems we might face. But one thing was for sure. As I walked down the street, with a bag of bread and a hoard of vitamins, holding the hand of one of the most morally questionable men in the city . . .

I knew I *loved* him.

Epilogue

Christian

One Year Later

TAP, TAP, *TAP*.

The ticking of the clock and thick curiosity filled the silence as Sasha Taylor eyed the motion of my finger on the armrest.

"I didn't think I'd see you in my office again."

"Why?"

"People go to a therapist—which I'm not, by the way—to seek advice, or to talk about themselves and their problems. You don't like to do either."

My gaze dropped to the US quarter I rolled between my thumb and pointer finger. "Do you believe in fate, Sasha?"

"I do."

"Why?"

She tilted her head. "I'm not a religious person, but I'm also not naive enough to believe everything can be explained without some form of supernatural intervention."

"I always thought if I believed in fate, I couldn't believe in choice." My voice was thoughtful, as I turned the quarter to let a ray of sunlight shimmer across it. The year was 1955, and the silver was dull and cloudy. Twenty-nine years ago, when I'd stolen it from someone's pocket, it held an optimistic shine. That shine had brought me here, to the United States, to my wife and daughter.

Sasha's gaze caressed the coin in my hand and then slid to the ring on my finger. "You've been married how long now?"

"A year."

To be exact, three-hundred-and-eighty-five days. I'd proposed to Gianna again with a ring, a bended knee, and even a nice dinner. She hadn't wanted another wedding, so we'd gotten married at the court-house. I had the date tattooed on my ribs right next to Andromeda.

"And your daughter? Katherine, isn't it?"

A smile touched my lips. "We call her Kat. She's five months now."

To be exact, one-hundred-and-forty-eight days.

"And how has it been, adjusting to a newborn?"

"Kat's colicky—doesn't sleep very well." Just like me. When she woke up multiple times each night, I got up with her, sometimes fed her a bottle Gianna had pumped beforehand, and held her until she fell back to sleep. Gianna had insisted she do it all at first, but I'd quickly ended that. "She looks like my wife." That was the only thing I needed to see to know she was mine.

My chest grew full as I thought of them. I checked on them when they were out. Knew where they were every minute of the day. My fleeting conscience told me it was morally questionable, but we all did sketchy shit just to gain some peace.

"And how is she adjusting to the baby?"

Yesterday, I'd arrived home to find Gianna teaching an atten-tive-eyed Kat how to make carbonara. She was a more caring and de-voted mother than I'd ever witnessed before. She'd read book after book about how to take care of Kat during her pregnancy. Now, she was on to some ridiculously-optimistic-colored novel about how to be the best parent you could be.

There wasn't much I liked to do more than watch them together.

I didn't deserve them.

But in the end, that was a moot point—just as Sasha had once said.

"Does that coin mean something to you?"

I drew my gaze up to her, a flicker of amusement passing through me. Getting to my feet, I set the quarter on the table between us. The clink of silver on hardwood was subtle, but the finality of it rang like a church bell.

Her words stopped me with one hand on the doorknob.

"You said *believed in fate*, as in, you are a believer now." Her voice touched my back with inquisitive fingers. "What made you change your mind?"

The thought of Gianna and Kat never existing without me in the picture wasn't possible. They were a static pair. I'd merely reached into the right pocket at the right time and made them mine.

"I stole someone else's fate, Sasha." I twisted the knob and opened the door. "And I'm not going to give it back."

She raised a brow. "And if someone comes looking for it?"

A smile pulled on the corner of my lips. "Let them come."

And then I shut the door behind me.

Acknowledgments

I wrote this book throughout a few pivotal and difficult times in my life, and I have many people to thank for helping me complete it.

To my husband, who survived on macaroni & cheese for a month while I worked toward my deadline and who has unfailingly supported me in every way.

To my family, whose messages of encouragement came when I needed it most.

To my friend and fellow author T.L. Martin, whose help and critique have become invaluable.

To my editor Bryony. Your insight has made this novel one-hundred times better.

To Sarah at Okay Creations for the beautiful cover, and Stacey Ryan Blake for the formatting.

And to the bloggers/reviewers who have gone above and beyond to spread the word about this book. I am eternally grateful.

Love,
Danielle xo

Connect with Me

Sign up for my newsletter to receive information on upcoming releases and sales.
authordaniellelori.com

Like my author page on Facebook.
www.facebook.com/authordaniellelori

Follow me on Instagram for pictures of my dinner.
www.instagram.com/authordaniellelori

Follow me on Amazon.

And don't forget Twitter.
twitter.com/DanielleLori2

authordaniellelori@gmail.com

Books by
DANIELLE LORI

The MADE Series

The Sweetest Oblivion

The Maddest Obsession

The Alyria Series

A Girl Named Calamity

A Girl in Black and White

A Girl with a Tragic Ever After (Coming Soon)